inked

KAREN CHANCE

MARJORIE M. LIU

YASMINE GALENORN

EILEEN WILKS

BERKLEY BOOKS, NEW YORK

THE BERKLEY PUBLISHING GROUP
Published by the Penguin Group
Penguin Group (USA) Inc.
375 Hudson Street, New York, New York 10014, USA
Penguin Group (Canada), 90 Eglinton Avenue East, Suite 700, Toronto, Ontario M4P 2Y3, Canada
(a division of Pearson Penguin Canada Inc.)
Penguin Books Ltd., 80 Strand, London WC2R 0RL, England
Penguin Group Ireland, 25 St. Stephen's Green, Dublin 2, Ireland (a division of Penguin Books Ltd.)
Penguin Group (Australia), 250 Camberwell Road, Camberwell, Victoria 3124, Australia
(a division of Pearson Australia Group Pty. Ltd.)
Penguin Books India Pvt. Ltd., 11 Community Centre, Panchsheel Park, New Delhi—110 017, India
Penguin Group (NZ), 67 Apollo Drive, Rosedale, North Shore 0632, New Zealand
(a division of Pearson New Zealand Ltd.)
Penguin Books (South Africa) (Pty.) Ltd., 24 Sturdee Avenue, Rosebank, Johannesburg 2196,
South Africa

Penguin Books Ltd., Registered Offices: 80 Strand, London WC2R 0RL, England

This is a work of fiction. Names, characters, places, and incidents either are the product of the authors' imagination or are used fictitiously, and any resemblance to actual persons, living or dead, business establishments, events, or locales is entirely coincidental. The publisher does not have any control over and does not assume any responsibility for author or third-party websites or their content.

INKED

A Berkley Book / published by arrangement with the authors

PRINTING HISTORY
Berkley mass-market edition / January 2010

ISBN: 978-0-425-23197-5

BERKLEY®
Berkley Books are published by The Berkley Publishing Group,
a division of Penguin Group (USA) Inc.,
375 Hudson Street, New York, New York 10014.
BERKLEY® is a registered trademark of Penguin Group (USA) Inc.
The "B" design is a trademark of Penguin Group (USA) Inc.

PRINTED IN THE UNITED STATES OF AMERICA

10 9 8 7 6 5 4 3 2 1

contents

skin deep

KAREN CHANCE

1

"GET it off! Get it off!"

"I'm trying!" Caleb grabbed a numb stick out of a drawer. "It would help if you'd stay still for half a second!"

"You stay still with claws in your ass!" I snarled, as they sank in a little deeper.

"I can't do anything if you're going to continue hopping around like that, Lia," he rumbled.

I glared at him, but it didn't do any good. It probably wouldn't have anyway—Caleb did the strong, silent, imperturbable thing pretty well—but it was especially futile now. Like me, he was a war mage, part of the supernatural community's police force. Unlike me, he was a respected, highly decorated member with years of experience. He was currently stuck with the worst job in the Corps—deactivating, categorizing and storing illegal weapons—only because he'd been wounded. An explosion had seared his retinas, leaving him virtually blind until his eyes healed.

"Are you *sure* you can do this?" I demanded, eyeing the swath of gauze wrapped around his buzz cut.

"Sonar vision," he reminded me, tapping a small ward on his temple. The blue and silver tat showed up nicely against his cocoa skin, its colors flashing as the tiny dolphin smacked his finger with its tail. "I can see almost as well with echolocation as I could before. Now assume the position."

"It's the *almost* I'm worried about," I muttered.

"I can let Jamie do it," he threatened.

"Sure, I'll take a crack at it," the wiry Scotsman punned shamelessly.

Normally, I might have taken him up on it. Despite the ratty Arthur Dent bathrobe he insisted on wearing, Jamie was among the department's foremost authorities on magical wards. But at the moment, he was also among the walking wounded, having been hit by a spell that had left him prone to fits of uncontrollable shakes. It set his hands and red-gray curls dancing on a regular basis, although it hadn't noticeably affected his sense of humor.

"You stay away from me," I told him severely, just as Caleb yanked my jeans down and pushed me over the specimen table.

"If you two want some privacy, I could always take a break," Jamie offered.

"You make sure it doesn't get away in case I miss," Caleb ordered.

"What do you mean, in case you miss?" I demanded, only to have my face shoved down to the cold metal tabletop. Since that was in no way necessary for the operation in hand, I had to assume it was to shut me up. I normally would have had a few things to say about that, but instead I bit my lip on what was actually quite a lot of pain.

"That's better," Caleb said, with the suspicion of a smile in his voice. "Now I just have to—uh-oh."

"Uh-oh?" It was hard to talk with my cheek smashed against stainless steel, but I managed anyway. "What the hell is going on back there?"

"It appears to have . . . er, taken cover, lass," Jamie volunteered. Caleb didn't say anything, but his shoulders were shaking suspiciously.

"Gimme that thing!" I grabbed the numb stick away from him and twisted around. A small snout and a pair of bright yellow eyes peered up at me from the waistband of my panties for a second before disappearing again. "Son of a—ow!"

"They don't like to be out in the open," Jamie reminded me. "I think it's trying to hide in your—"

"I know where it's hiding!" I waddled to the adjacent storeroom, slammed the door and the jeans hit the floor—just as tiny fangs took another bite out of tender flesh. Miniscule they might be, but they hurt like hell. "Goddamn it!"

"If you need any help," Jamie's lilting tenor called, "don't hesitate to ask." I was thinking up a suitable reply when he murmured to Caleb, "Get the camera."

"I've got pictures, too," I reminded them as the damn thing made a dash up my back, its claws leaving tiny pinpricks all along my spine.

"You told me you destroyed those!"

"Military Tactics 101, Jamie. Never give away a strategic advan—Auggh!" I cut off as a wave of heat fried what felt like half my shoulder.

"Lia!" I heard the door open, but I didn't care. I ripped my shirt off one-handed, still waving the numb stick around, and caught myself a glancing blow on the side. My left buttock immediately went dead, my leg collapsed and I fell to the floor.

I lost sight of the little menace for a minute, but spotted a tiny tail headed south when I rolled onto my back. "It's on your leg!" Caleb informed me.

"No shit!" Something red and black and vicious had sprinted back down my torso to perch on my knee, and I could swear it was laughing at me. Caleb lunged for it with another numb stick, but it darted back up my thigh. He was too late to pull up and my right knee collapsed.

"Don't help me!" I panted, as the damn thing reappeared on my stomach, its painted wings fanning out just above my belly button. It was 2D, as all wards are on the skin, merely thin black lines and brightly colored paint. But I swear it felt heavy, warm and all too real.

"Give me your stick," I told Caleb, as the ward eyed me warily, a tiny cloud of painted smoke issuing from its nostrils. "I'm going to trap it between two of them."

"And if you miss? That thing was taken off a dark mage, Lia," he reminded me, suddenly serious. "I'm guessing it can do more damage than we've seen. A lot more."

"Let me worry about that."

"Not to mention that you've been hit with a numb stick twice already. Once more and you'll be out cold."

A few stray sparks tickled my stomach, glowing gold against my skin for a moment, before dissipating and leaving tiny scorch marks in their place. "I'm not going to numb myself," I told him through clenched teeth.

"Uh-huh. And what am I supposed to tell the doc if—"

"Just give me the damn stick!"

The tat didn't wait for Caleb to make up his mind. It suddenly dove for cover again, making it as far as the pink satin rose on the front of my panties before Caleb and I almost simultaneously stunned it. "You all right?" he demanded, as the tat froze against my skin, still wearing a small smirk.

"Ask me that in half an hour, when I can feel my butt," I told him unsteadily, as I gave the thing a careful poke. It didn't move, but it didn't come off, either.

Magical wards appear as tattoos on the body, but in their inert form, they're small gold charms that fall easily away from the skin. Only that wasn't happening here. I poked it again. Nothing.

"Why isn't it coming off?" I demanded, trying not to sound as freaked out as I felt.

One look in the reflective side of the nearest shelf told me I wasn't fooling anybody: my gray eyes were wide and startled, my color was high, and my long brown hair was everywhere.

"I told you it was taken off a dark mage," Caleb said, squatting down to have a closer look. He muttered the standard release spell we used on especially stubborn charms, and nada.

I glared at it, fresh out of ideas. I hadn't worked in what the Corps only half-jokingly called the dungeon for very long, and wasn't an expert on magical wards. I had one myself—a small horned owl that had been a present from my father when I joined the Corps—but it had never gone bat-shit crazy and attacked me. At least, not yet.

Caleb tried again, this time with a spell strong enough to raise goose bumps on my skin. But the tattoo was still a tattoo, its colors glowing warm and jewel-bright against my stomach. "It must be a talisman," he informed me.

"So what? My owl's a talisman."

"Your owl is *part* talisman. It gathers energy from the natural world or pulls it from a built-in reservoir to avoid draining you every time you use it. But there are rare wards that are pure talismans—that don't draw from your own magic at all. It looks like that's what we have here."

"That still doesn't explain how we get it off!" I said, brushing at it uselessly. I could feel the raised outline against my fingertips, but there was nothing to grab hold of. Just skin and ink.

"That could be a problem," Caleb said, helping me to my feet. "Talismans like that are illegal because they're made by draining the magic of a living creature into the tat. It gives them a large reservoir, but sometimes characteristics of the creature are passed on as well. Tats like that have their own minds, in a way."

"So you're saying it'll turn loose when it *wants* to?"

"Or when it runs out of power."

"And that will be when?"

He smiled like a man who didn't have a dangerous magical weapon stuck under his belly button. "No way to know." He picked my jeans up off the floor and tucked the numb stick in the pocket. "I'd keep this, if I were you. The effect wears off after a while."

Great. I grabbed my jeans and assessed the damage. On the plus side, the stinging pain in my backside was no longer noticeable, thanks to the numb stick's deadening qualities. On the negative, the knee that had been hit didn't seem to be working too well, and threatened to give way whenever I put any weight on it.

And then a flash went off, almost blinding me. "Jamie!"

"Now we'll talk about those pictures," he chuckled, clicking the door shut.

I threw my clothes back on and barreled through the door. "You conniving little bastard! Fork over that camera right now or I swear—"

"Mage de Croissets! What precisely is going on here?"

I stopped, jeans unzipped and shirt askew, blinking away afterimages. Shit. The boss *never* came down here. It was practically the only advantage to working in the dungeon. And now it didn't have even that much going for it.

My eyes slowly adjusted to show me the wavy silver hair, high forehead and sour expression I'd feared. Richard Hargrove, better known as Dick to his friends or The Dick to the rest of us, had been brought out of retirement after the war started. He was old-school, demanding things spit-polished and perfect, like his excruciatingly correct posture. It made his too-thin form, which as usual was encased in a dark-colored three-piece suit, look even more skeletal than it was. I didn't like the guy, but I kept wishing he'd eat a sandwich.

"Well?" The barked word surprised me, and these days, that wasn't good. The piece of contraband we'd been working on before the ward went nuts flew off the examining table and through the air—straight at the source of the disturbance.

Hargrove ducked as the five-foot-long metal staff tore through the air just over his head. It went on to shatter a reinforced glass door, obliterate a computer, take a bite out of a wall and lodge like a quivering spear in one of the steel-plated elevator doors. That would have ended it, except that this was a wizard's staff, which apparently still had some juice left in it. It melted a chunk of the door into a sizzling silver mess.

And then it exploded.

The remainder of the glass door protected us from some of the pieces of flying metal, and the shield Hargrove threw up while still on one knee absorbed the rest. I would have helped him, but it was all I could do to rein in the waves of magic thrumming under my skin, begging for a spell, an aim, a *target*. I concentrated on not gasping as the now-familiar vise clenched around my gut. It felt like all of my organs were twisting together, as if they were trying to wring themselves out. I'd have clawed at my flesh to straighten them out, if that hadn't been a completely crazy idea.

As it was, my fingers clenched over the circle of radiating lines just below my third rib. It looked like a stylized sun a little larger than the pad of my thumb, but the ugly silver scar was a blank in my memory. They say you never hear the one that kills you. But you don't hear the one that knocks you cold for three days, either.

Or the one that leaves you a magical cripple.

"Watch it," Caleb murmured as the boss turned toward us, his shield riddled with glass and metal, like a porcupine with fully extended quills.

"Are you under some semblance of control?" Hargrove demanded icily.

I nodded and his shields fell, causing the trapped pieces to drop to the floor with a clatter. Jamie ran to gather up the remains of the staff, while Caleb helped the boss back to his feet. I didn't budge. Hargrove had caught me on his glare like a bug on a pin, his expression somewhere between murderous and mortified. I didn't understand that last part, until I belatedly noticed the man standing off to one side, out of the line of fire. No, not a man, I realized, as the spicy, musky scent of Clan hit me.

"It's good to see you again, Lia."

"Mr. Arnou," I said awkwardly.

"Sebastian, please." He paused, glancing at Hargrove's furious expression. "We are family, after all."

Well, crap.

"YOU might have mentioned that you were related to the werewolf king!" Hargrove whispered viciously, as we trudged up eight flights.

I glanced up the stairs, to where the individual in question was being regaled with some story by Jamie. Despite his recent brush with disaster, Sebastian Arnou appeared unruffled. He reminded me of my mother, who had been so comfortable in human form that it had been almost impossible to believe that she was anything else. Only the occasional scent of something rare and wild gave it away, or a too fluid movement when surprised.

Or watching her morph into a 150-pound wolf, of course.

Not that I'd ever seen Arnou's leader in wolf form, or caught off guard, either. And today was no exception. He was wearing a crisp tan suit that set off his short dark hair and vivid blue eyes. His shoes were Prada, his watch was Piaget and his demeanor was set on pleasant. It was difficult to imagine anyone who looked less like the slavering beast of legend.

"His title is *bardric*," I explained. "The Weres don't actually have a—" I stopped at the blistering look Hargrove sent me. "And he's more of an acquaintance, really."

Hargrove threw a sound shield around us with an impatient gesture; I guess he knew about Were hearing. "He said you were family!"

"It wasn't meant literally. I recently did a favor for his clan and they, um, sort of adopted me. It's an honorary thing."

Hargrove didn't look satisfied. "Then perhaps you can explain why he insisted on seeing you after the incident this morning?"

"What incident?"

"A Were, or what was left of one, was fished out of a ditch along Highway 91 by one of our patrols. They saw several men dragging it out of a drainage tunnel, and when they went to investigate, the men ran off, leaving the corpse behind. Of course we informed the Clan Council. I assumed they would send someone for the body, but imagine my surprise when the Arnou himself showed up to take possession! And demanded to see you and Kempster."

"Jamie?" I'd assumed I was in for it, but I'd wondered why Hargrove had ordered him upstairs, too.

"And he wants the most current map we have of Tartarus. But he won't say why."

I assumed that Sebastian wasn't asking for a map of the Greek underworld, but of its Vegas equivalent. Back in the eighties, an extensive network of drainage tunnels had been put in place beneath the city to help control the runoff from the brief rainy season. Since they were dry much of the year, they'd quickly been settled by bums, druggies and the portion of the supernatural population who couldn't pass for human even with a glamourie.

Over time, bars, brothels, markets and casinos had opened up, forming a mirror image of the world above, only more desperate and a lot more dangerous. Someone in the Corps had named the place after the deep, dark pit reserved for evildoers in Greek mythology and it had stuck, maybe because it was so apt. I couldn't imagine what interest Vegas's shadow city could hold for someone like Sebastian Arnou.

"Jamie used to be a tunnel rat," I said slowly. "If anyone is interested in Tartarus, he'd be the one to ask." The Rats were a group of war mages who once patrolled the tunnels, before the current war in the supernatural community pulled them to other duties.

"But why you?"

"I'm dating his brother," I admitted, because it wasn't exactly a secret. Cyrus had haunted the infirmary while I recovered from my recent brush with the hereafter. And ever since, he'd been showing up for lunch in the cafeteria, despite what it considered food. He'd become so much of a staple that people had almost stopped staring at him as if he planned to eat them instead of the rubbery quiche.

"And is that all?"

I shrugged. "Technically, I *am* part of his clan. Sebastian trusts me. Well, as much as any Were ever trusts a mage . . ."

Hargrove threw an arm across the staircase, halting me in my tracks. "Let us have one thing perfectly clear," he told me, gray eyes flashing. "Were or not, you are Corps. Therefore you answer to me, not to some *bardric* or whatever he is."

"I'm not a Were," I said flatly. "My mother was a member of Clan Lobizon, but my father was human."

"Be that as it may, I won't have someone on my team hiding things from me. The Weres have the right to deal with their own kind as they see fit, but if *anything* about this bears on our activities, I expect to be informed. Is that understood?"

"Yes, sir."

Hargrove shot me a look that said it had damn well better be, but fortunately there wasn't time for more. One didn't keep a king—or the equivalent—waiting. A moment later, we caught up with the others at the top of the stairs and pushed through into the busy main corridor.

The Central Division of the War Mage Corps is part of the North American branch of the Silver Circle—the most powerful magical association on earth. Only it wasn't looking much like it at the moment. The war had trashed our previous digs, causing a precipitate and only half-completed move to new quarters beneath a large warehouse. It was crowded, the air-conditioning didn't work half the time and the place tended to smell of dust, body odor and the ozone tang of magic.

Today, it smelled like dung.

I glanced around, wondering what new problem had cropped up since I'd passed through this morning. Unlike the lower levels, this one was open to the public. As usual, it was crowded with a microcosm of the current war. Mages, apprentices and lab techs hurried along, skirting the long line of arms dealers waiting for permits. Informants slunk past with furtive expressions, hoping their tidbits were worth a payout. Mercenaries loitered against the walls, awaiting interviews for the kind of service the Corps preferred to pay others to do. And someone was selling chickens.

Okay, that was new.

A squat-necked, big-bosomed woman with nut brown skin and a graying braid squatted near the stairwell, surrounded by wicker cages of live chickens. They stared at us accusingly out of bright black eyes, their beaks protruding through slits in the weaving. A glance down the corridor showed a variety of other small food animals, bleating and squealing from cages dotted here and there among duffle bags, backpacks and fifty or so scruffy-looking people.

Hargrove grabbed a passing mage who couldn't get away fast enough. "Lieutenant!"

The lieutenant stopped, looking resigned. His arms were full of baby goat, which was nibbling on his lapel. Like all war mage attire, his coat was spelled to resist damage, although that wasn't working so well in this case. The goat took a nibble, the lapel grew back, further intriguing the goat. Repeat.

"Yes, sir."

"What are all these people doing here?"

"I'm sorry, sir. We had to bring them down. They were picketing out front and drew the attention of the human police—"

"I told Aaronson to get rid of them an hour ago!"

"Yes, sir. But they refused to leave without seeing you," the lieutenant said, before getting jostled aside by a man with black eyes, a weather-beaten face and a hank of greasy hair.

"It's the gangs!" The man held up his arm, displaying a nasty burn. "They burnt us out this morning and we want to know what you're going to do about it!"

"Where did this attack happen?" Hargrove demanded.

"In an encampment over on Decatur."

"I know of no approved housing in that area."

"It's a flophouse, sir. In the drain," Jamie explained.

Hargrove scowled at the injured man. "You were warned months ago that continuing to remain in an unsecured location puts you at risk. The Black Circle—"

"Do we look like we have anything those bastards would want?" the man demanded.

Personally, I thought he had a point. The powerful dark mages who composed our main enemy in the war tended to aim a little higher. But Hargrove wasn't impressed. "They are known to hit civilian targets for the terror value."

"All your secure locations cost too much!"

"We have arranged free safe houses for indigents—"

"Yeah, in the desert! Our homes are here!"

I couldn't imagine anyone considering a murky, dangerous drain to be "home" and apparently, neither could Hargrove. "Be that as it may, you have the option. Should you choose to ignore it, there is little I can do. Other than offer you medical assistance for the wounded—"

"We don't need charity! We need protection!"

"What you need is to moderate your tone!" Hargrove snapped. "And to face realities! I do not have the personnel to protect you if you choose to remain underground. That is why you were specifically instructed to evacuate—"

I stopped listening because a young man was tugging on my sleeve. He had gray eyes, dark hair and coltish limbs poking out of clothes that were at least two sizes too big. He looked like me ten years ago, before I grew into my height. He also looked lost, like maybe he'd misplaced his family in the crush.

"Do you know where I can find . . ." he glanced down at what I belatedly realized was an orientation packet. "Uh, Mage Beckett?"

Christ; the kid was a recruit. I opened my mouth to tell him to go home, to finish growing into his clothes, to finish growing *up*, but Hargrove beat me to it. "How old are you?" he snapped.

The boy's eyes widened in dismay as he belatedly recognized Central's resident terror. "Ei-eighteen, sir."

"You don't look it!" The kid appeared vaguely insulted, but he had the sense not to talk back. "Make sure you have proof of age. You will be asked for it," Hargrove told him, before informing him where to find his drill instructor.

The young man nodded and backed off fast, only to trip over someone's battered suitcase and lurch into a cage holding a piglet. The animal bit his shirtsleeve and held on. The boy panicked with his soon-to-be-boss's eyes on him and slung a spell—which was just one syllable off. It should have given the pig a small electric shock; instead . . .

"Oh, dear," Jamie said, as the pig swelled like a ripe melon, bursting through its woven home with a startled squeal.

I started to mutter the counterspell to shrink it back to size, when Jamie stepped on my toe. Oh, yeah. I fell silent and let him take care of it, then watched the red-faced teenager scurry down the hall toward the gym. It should have been funny—the kind of story you laughed at with your buddies years later. Only I wasn't sure that kid would have a later.

"He doesn'a look eighteen," Jamie murmured.

"He doesn't look *sixteen*," I said, my magic surging. I managed to tamp it down before we had another incident, but the effort made my headache worse. I had to get over this; I *had* to get well. We needed people in the fight who would do more than serve as target practice for the dark.

The lieutenant was left to deal with the angry man and we pressed on, but we'd only gone a few yards when Sebastian stopped by the doors to the medical facility. "Dr. Sedgewick will bring us the results as soon as he's finished,

Mr. Arnou," Hargrove informed him, attempting to mask his impatience with a tight smile.

"I would prefer to see the body for myself."

The smile vanished. "From what I understand, it was in . . . less than pristine condition when brought in."

"Nonetheless."

Hargrove waited, I guess expecting more of an explanation. He didn't get one. "Very well. But I warn you—it isn't pretty."

"Bit of an understatement," Jamie muttered a minute later, which was how long it took us to pass through the crowded waiting area, walk down a hall and enter a small room near the end.

I didn't reply, because I was busy swallowing my breakfast back down where it belonged. Cafeteria food tasted the same coming up as it did going down, I decided, feeling pretty pathetic. But Jamie was also visibly green and even Hargrove had two spots of color high on his cheeks. It looked a little like rouge, next to his pallor. Only Sebastian appeared unruffled.

That surprised me since the body lying on the autopsy table was Were. At least, that's what Sedgewick, the Center's chief medical officer, alleged. I had my doubts. At first glance, it just looked like a heap of raw, red flesh, bled out like butcher's meat ready for carving. But on closer examination it resolved into a tangled mass of limbs, some recognizably human, others not. But it was virtually impossible to tell what it might once have been.

Because every inch of skin had been carefully removed.

"Oh, it's Were all right," Sedgewick said when Hargrove voiced my doubts. The rotund little doctor was more animated than I'd ever seen him, his blue eyes sparking over his dull green scrubs. "And one born to it at that."

"How can you tell?" Hargrove demanded, his lip curling in disgust.

"They have fundamentally different anatomies from humans, even those later infected with the Were strain," Sedgewick said happily. "For example, the subclavius muscle stretching from the first rib to the collarbone." The scalpel he was using as a pointer flashed under the lights as he traced it. "Most of us no longer have one as we don't need it to walk on two legs instead of four. But all born Weres have at least one."

"As do some humans, as you just inti—"

"But that's only one indicator," Sedgewick broke in. He looked hopefully at Sebastian. "I've only done an external exam so far, as I know your people have some sort of problem with autopsies. But if I could remove the brain, you'd have a much clearer view through the cranial—"

"It is our custom that the body be left as untouched as possible after death," Sebastian said evenly.

"Yes. Yes, well, of course," Sedgewick said, his expression making clear that he didn't think much more damage could be done to this body if he tried. "Well, if you *could* see inside the nasal cavity, you'd notice a series of indentations lining the septum. They're powerful chemoreceptors for detecting pheromones. They connect directly to the hypothalamus, the brain's control center for basic drives and emotions—sex, hunger, fear, anger. They allow a Were to track a mate, hunt for food and detect potential dangers—as they once did for our ancestors before we evolved beyond that sort of thing." He rocked back on his heels, looking pleased with himself.

"But why does it—he—look like *that*?" Hargrove demanded

Sedgewick frowned. His masterful display of medical knowledge had obviously not elicited the admiration he'd expected. "He looks like that because someone skinned him alive partway through the change," he said impatiently. "That's what killed him. Well, that and the massive blood loss, of course."

I vaguely heard Jamie make a choked noise and run out of the room. I would have gladly joined him, except I couldn't seem to move. If I hadn't been staring at the evidence, I'd have said that what Sedgewick claimed was impossible. Weres changed in the blink of an eye—even faster, for the old ones. How could anyone—

A cell phone interrupted my thoughts, its jangling tune more than a little embarrassing under the circumstances.

"Sorry," I muttered, reaching for my back pocket. Cyrus had changed my ringtone a few days ago, and his sense of humor was rivaled only by Jamie's. I didn't get calls working so far underground and had forgotten to change it back.

Only it wasn't my phone that was ringing.

"We may never get another body like this," Sedgewick was saying mournfully.

Sebastian looked at the doctor like he thought he might be a little mad. "I sincerely hope not!"

"But I've already learned so much, merely from a topical exam," Sedgewick wheedled, attempting to summon up some rusty charm. "For example, I never knew that the change begins with the extremities. For some reason, I always assumed it started with the trunk of the body and radiated outward. With a chance to do a proper autopsy, I could learn so much—"

"The body will be returned to the family intact," Sebastian told him flatly.

"But Mr. Arnou—"

"Colin, leave it!" Hargrove snapped. "You're supposed to be looking for clues to the man's identity, not satisfying morbid curiosity." He glanced at me. "And answer that thing or shut it off!"

"It's not mine," I said, wondering who else around here had "Werewolves of London" for a ringtone.

"It was found under the body," Sedgewick said grumpily, waving at another phone that lay on a specimen tray. I hadn't noticed it before because it was chrome-bright, like the tray itself.

Like the phone Cyrus had given me on my birthday.

Like the one he always carried.

An electric charge ran up my spine and down into my hands, making them shake. I clutched my phone tightly to keep from dropping it. It was 11:30, I reminded myself sharply. Cyrus was probably on his way here for lunch, ready to bitch about the cafeteria's idea of chicken salad . . .

"And if you want to know who he is—or rather *was*," Sedgewick said, picking up the phone. "Call one of the numbers in here and ask. Or do I have to do everything?"

He hit a button and the phone in my hands leapt. I dropped it and it went skittering across the tiles, spinning to a stop by the plastic container Sedgewick had placed hopefully at the end of the table. I stared at it, feeling my thoughts scatter and break, fracturing as the floor sank dizzyingly beneath me.

My chest felt pinched as I sucked in a lungful of air, but it didn't seem to help. A bone-dead chill settled through me and my knees gave out. "Lia!" someone said, but I barely heard.

The last thing I remember before darkness washed over me was two tinny, cheerful howls merging with the white-rush-roar in my ears.

3

"IT isn't him. Lia, do you hear me? It isn't Cyrus!" Someone was holding me, close enough that I could feel the body heat radiating from him. It was hotter than usual for a human, and some part of me found that oddly reassuring.

"Mr. Arnou," it was Sedgewick's voice, sounding clipped and impatient. "It's merely a faint. She'll come around in a moment."

Sebastian paused to draw a breath. And when he started speaking again, his voice had gone low and smooth and dangerous. "For all your vaunted knowledge of our anatomy, Doctor, it appears there are a few things you do not yet understand about Weres."

"And that would be?" Sedgewick had obviously dropped the charm act, because his voice was almost nasty.

"A Were who has lost a mate can turn feral, knowing nothing, seeing nothing, except revenge. I have witnessed a small female of our kind carve her way through five strong Were guards to reach the one who had taken her mate. And then kill him, before dying herself." His grip tightened enough to hurt. "I do not wish to see it again."

I came around completely with a grunt of pain, to find

myself draped across Sebastian's lap. We were in Sedgewick's tiny office, sitting on his ugly plaid couch. The doc was behind his overflowing desk while Hargrove hovered in the doorway. "But Lia isn't a Were," Sedgewick said testily. "Therefore, whatever questionable—"

"Colin," Hargrove began warningly.

"—methods your people use for revenge don't concern—"

"Colin!" Hargrove's tone snapped like a whip. "With me."

Sedgewick started to protest, but Hargrove somehow got him out the door without a major incident. I didn't see them go because Sebastian had bent over me, his eyes searching mine as if he expected me to go berserk at any moment. I didn't feel berserk; I felt sick. I really hoped I wasn't about to yak all over royalty.

"It isn't him, Lia," Sebastian repeated, low and distinct. "It isn't Cyrus."

"Then who?" I croaked, struggling to sit up.

"Grayshadow," Sebastian said, his face expressionless. "At least, that was his Were name. In the human world he was known as Alan Thompkins."

"But the phone—"

"It's Cyrus's, yes, but the body isn't."

"How could you tell?" I asked thickly.

"Scent." His mouth twisted in a wry half-smile. "Those archaic chemoreceptors. And if you noticed, the body was missing part of the right front paw. Grayshadow was missing three fingers on his right hand, a relic of an old duel."

I swallowed. "I didn't really look that close."

My head was pounding and my throat felt like a desert. I spied a small fridge sitting at the end of the sofa, wedged in between an overstuffed filing cabinet and the wall. Its sole contents turned out to be a six-pack of mineral water and a beer. The beer was warm. I drank it anyway.

"If you already knew who he was, why let Sedgewick examine him?" I asked, after a minute.

"I was hoping he would tell me that the skin was removed after death, and that something else had killed him."

"Yeah, because that would be so much better!"

"Yes. It would."

The strain in his voice surprised me. While Cyrus was considered mad, bad and dangerous to know, Sebastian's reputation matched what I'd seen so far—elegant, composed and levelheaded. Only he wasn't sounding so much like that now.

"Don't you think it's time you told me what's going on?" I demanded.

Sebastian wordlessly pulled a manila folder from under his suit coat and handed it to me. It contained photos, big glossy ones in full color that might have been taken from the exam room down the hall. Only the backgrounds differed. Instead of brushed steel, these bodies lay on red, rocky soil, cracked asphalt and scrub brush. Three bodies, three different places of death, but the same gruesome method.

"Grayshadow was the fourth—that we know of," he said, when I looked up. "The first was a week ago. Forest Walker of Maccon. Then White Sun of Arnou and Night Dancer of Tamaska."

"And Grayshadow belonged to which clan?"

"Arnou."

"So two out of four were Arnou." Sebastian nodded. "But why were they all . . . like that?"

"Our pelts are prized possessions in many circles. If taken at the moment of transformation, they retain much of the magic needed for the Change."

He said it so matter-of-factly, that it took me a second to get it. "Wait. You think someone killed them *for their skins*?" I stared at him in horror.

"So it would seem." His voice was as smooth and untroubled as if that earlier lapse had never happened. But his eyes were clouded when they met mine. "It appears that we have a Hunter."

I looked down at the too-colorful photos. My nausea was back, big-time. "But how? Weres change so quickly—"

"A spell is required to strip the skin from the body before the change can be completed."

"You think a mage did this?"

"They are one of the few predators to which we are vulnerable."

My head was spinning, a combination of numb stick, shock and warm beer. It felt like I was simultaneously getting too much information, and not enough. "Okay," I said slowly, trying to sort out my jumbled thoughts. "Right now, I'm not interested in this Hunter, mage or not. I'm interested in why Cyrus's phone was found under a dead body, and one that had no clothes to hold it. Was it planted to make us think it was Cyrus? Because any Were would immediately know that it wasn't."

Sebastian's jaw tightened. "It was, I think, a message to me."

"What? Some kind of challenge?"

"More likely a warning not to interfere in this creature's affairs."

I frowned. "And you would need a warning because?"

"White Sun was my Second, my right hand. When I learned of his death, I asked Cyrus to check with his contacts in the underworld, to get me a lead on this creature. A name, a location, anything."

"And did he?"

"I didn't want to discuss this over the telephone," he said, not answering me. "And as you know, Cyrus and I cannot meet."

I nodded. Sebastian had recently been elected wartime chief, which was what *bardric* actually meant, of the North American Were clans. In order to get the votes of those leaders who were more impressed by brawn than brains (in other words, most of them), he'd asked Cyrus to challenge him for the right to lead their clan—a dispute that could be resolved only by combat.

As they'd planned, Sebastian won the fight and the election, but losing made Cyrus *vargulf*—an outcast—in Were society. The brothers intended to reveal the truth after the war was over, allowing Cyrus to reclaim his position. In the meantime, he was using his disreputable reputation to spy on the Were underworld for his brother.

"So how were you getting information?" I asked, and immediately knew I'd hit pay dirt. Because Sebastian licked his lips. Full-grown Weres, especially High Clan, don't show nervousness. It's viewed as a weakness and is drilled out of them early. So that little gesture was the equivalent of a human throwing a hissy fit.

"I didn't like the idea of Cyrus chasing this thing alone," Sebastian finally said. "And I knew he could cover more ground if he had help. I therefore sent Grayshadow to act as a go-between—"

"Wait." I stared at the gory photos and, suddenly, my brain didn't seem to be working at all. "That man in there . . . who ended up like that . . . You're telling me he was working with Cyrus?"

"Yes. He was supposed to bring me a report this morning, but he missed the meeting. And shortly thereafter, we received the call from Central."

"Then where is Cyrus?"

Sebastian met my eyes, and I knew the answer before he said it. "I don't know."

"You don't *know*? And we've just been *sitting here* for the past twenty minutes?" I leapt up and started for the door, but Sebastian got there first. I tried to push past, but he wasn't budging. I could have moved him; hell, the way I felt I could have moved the *wall*. But that was likely to bring security running and I didn't have time for that.

"Lia!" Sebastian grabbed me by the upper arms, tightly enough to remind me of just how much brute strength that polished linen was hiding. "Listen to me! The only report from Cyrus I received said his quarry was hiding somewhere in Tartarus. But there are four hundred miles of tunnels. We could search for weeks and never find them!"

"So what are you saying? We just sit here and hope for the best?" Because that so wasn't happening.

"No, we must go after him."

That stopped me. "We? As in . . ."

"You and I."

"But you're *bardric*. You can't put yourself—"

The skin along his jaw stretched white over the bone. "What I cannot do is let my brother die at the hand of a monster!"

"Then send someone else!"

"And who would you suggest? Cyrus is *vargulf*—dead, as far as the clan is concerned! I cannot send a team in after him without admitting the deception. And if I do that, the Council will be within their rights to call for a new election, one which almost certainly would go against me."

"And your position is worth more than Cyrus's *life*?"

Those blue eyes flashed, and for the first time, he looked more like a predator than a diplomat. "My most likely replacement is Whirlwind of Rand. He hates our alliance with the humans. One of his first actions in office would almost certainly be to undo it!"

I stopped struggling for a moment. The Corps was supposed to be a police force, not an army, but lately we'd had to be both. One of the few saving graces had been the Weres, who were as vicious in combat as legend said. They'd saved our asses more than once, however much the Corps might not want to admit it. I honestly didn't know what we'd do without them.

"Grayshadow was my Third," Sebastian told me more quietly. "And the only one, other than White Sun, who knew the truth about Cyrus. Now that they're both dead, I do not know who I can trust, and I cannot risk making a mistake when the repercussions could be disastrous."

I was trying for calm, trying hard, but it wasn't working that great. "But how are we supposed to find him without help? The only witness is dead!" And if I didn't find Cyrus soon, he might be, too. I suddenly couldn't seem to get enough air in the claustrophobic little room.

"You will lead me to him."

"If I knew where he was, don't you think I'd have told you?" There was a weird, teakettle sound. The air around us had gone into motion, sending Sedgewick's piles of clutter flapping against the ceiling like trapped birds.

"Lia!" Sebastian's fingers bit into my arms, bruising hard. "Sedgewick was wrong! Our abilities are not defined by the limitations of anatomy. We are magical beings, and when we make connections, they are magical also. In some cases, mated pairs among our people have been known to share images of what one is seeing, or to experience something of what the other is feeling—"

"For Weres, perhaps. I'm not one!"

That won me a hard glance. "We both know that isn't true."

"My mother was Were; I am human," I repeated, angry that he couldn't seem to understand. "Considering how often I have to say that, maybe I ought to get a tattoo!"

"Tattoos are only skin deep. What you are runs through to the bone."

"What my *mother* was. Lobizon tried to turn me, but they failed. You know that!"

The leaders of my mother's clan had pressured her for years to have me undergo the Change, but she had always hedged, telling them it was my decision. And her rank was high enough that they had been unable to force the issue as long as she lived. But barely two days after she died, they sent a group to attack me, intending to take the choice out of my hands. Sebastian had saved me by adopting me into Arnou, which as the clan of the current *bardric*, outranked Lobizon. As long as I remained under his protection, they couldn't touch me.

Sebastian didn't say anything for a long moment. "How certain are you that we are not being overheard?" he finally asked.

"Pretty sure. The Corps usually spies on *other* people."

"Be certain."

I threw a silence shield around us. "Okay."

Sebastian slanted a sharp look at me. "I could not allow someone into my clan, not even for Cyrus's sake, without knowing the truth. You carry Neuri. Why bother to deny it?"

It hit like a quick punch to the gut, leaving me breathless. No one ever said that word aloud, not even me. It was the elephant in the room, the thing that even my mother had tiptoed around in case uttering it somehow made it more real. I'd been fifteen before I learned the name for the problem that would define my life: Neuri Syndrome.

It occurs sometimes when the mother is Were and the father is not, which is why female Weres rarely marry outside the clan. It's a variation on lycanthropy, but doesn't permit its carriers to change. It also prevents them from ever getting the full-blown disease—and therein lay the problem.

Weres have a low birthrate—the disease often proves deadly to children younger than five or six, killing many in the womb—and therefore periodic "recruitment" is necessary. The clans feared that carriers of Neuri might pass their resistance on to their children, who might disseminate it to their kids and so on. Married to Weres, they would weaken the clan by infecting the bloodlines. Married to humans, they might ensure that, one day, there would be no one left to turn.

Of course, that argument had made a lot more sense in the medieval world when people tended to live in small villages and rarely traveled. The local gene pool had been limited, and contamination from Neuri had been a real threat. With the much larger, more mobile population of the modern world, the danger was miniscule. But I hadn't noticed anyone changing the old kill-on-sight rule.

My mother had fought her clan elders not to give me a choice, as she'd claimed, but because the disease I'd been born with had already made it for me.

"I haven't denied anything," I told Sebastian angrily, when I got my breath back. "I just don't see any reason to broadcast my status as metaphysical leper to every Were I come across. That's a good way to get dead, or have you forgotten?"

"I am not the one who has forgotten something! Carriers of Neuri *are* Were."

"No! We aren't! We're prey, that's why there's so goddamned few of—"

I stopped because something rippled over my skin, something that raised the hair on my arms, on the back of my neck, and sent chills down my spine. Something liquid and dark and compelling. I stared up into eyes that were no longer blue, but brilliant, inhuman chartreuse. I tried to turn away, but hard fingers bit into my arms.

"Not Were, Lia?" he murmured. "Then you don't taste the wind in the back of your throat? Don't see the night light up for you, with every branch, every blade of grass crystal clear and vibrating with life? Don't hear the earth under your feet, whispering to you, revealing its secrets?"

I was running, light as the wind ruffling the tops of the trees. It was almost dark, but I could see every stone, every bit of life scurrying, slithering or darting, quick and startled, out of my path. Every tiny tremor in the earth that bore my weight, every scent on the breeze that flowed around me, carried stories of friends and enemies, of water and food, of mile after mile of fascinating, vivid ground to be explored.

The forest came to life with sleek, dark shadows. They ran close enough that I could feel the heavy, nonhuman heat of them, smell the rich, heady scent of Clan, see the slide of fur over heavily muscled bodies. Their eyes filled with the lambency of living jewels as they howled, sending an unearthly chorus floating out over the valley below us. It tightened my skin, pulled at my heart, set my breath to racing until it tore out of me in a cry of pure delight.

Then Sebastian let me go.

The lights came on and the sounds of the busy medical facility rushed back—gurneys rolling over tile, nurses gossiping, the fridge humming. And the world went flat, like it had lost a vital dimension. The colors were just colors, washed out and lifeless, and although Sebastian's arms were around me, I felt them less than I had the whisper of that scent on the wind. He sat, regarding me with a faint smile, even as part of me grasped for something rare and precious that was no longer there. And mourned its loss.

I'd seen my mother return from night runs, panting and out of breath, her eyes glowing, her cheeks flushed, more alive than she ever was between four walls. And I'd never understood until now. She'd never shown me what she saw, what she experienced. Maybe because she'd known how cruel it would be when I realized I could never reach that place myself.

The part of me that was wolf was trapped by my disease. It lived crippled and caged inside a prison of a body that couldn't flow, couldn't reform, couldn't let loose the magic of its other self. I'd never even seen my wolf, and I never would.

Until today, I'd been at peace with that.

"That foolish doctor," Sebastian was saying. "Pitying us for our 'primitive' anatomy, when we are privy to an entire world he will never know!"

"*You're* privy!" I gasped, so angry I could barely see. "You did that!"

"Yes, but I could not have formed a memory bond with a human. Carriers of Neuri are Weres, Lia," he repeated. "They simply do not change."

"Then they aren't Weres!" He was the head of my clan and I owed him big-time. So I didn't curse him into next week. But it was close. My whole life I'd struggled to be accepted, had battled against the tide of prejudice from both sides. I wasn't human enough for the Corps, wasn't Were enough for the Clan. And always, always, there was Neuri, that damned disease that wouldn't let me truly be either. But at least I hadn't fully understood what I was missing.

For the first time, I realized the truth of the phrase I'd said so many times: I really wasn't Were. And God, how it hurt.

"Many of us have spent much of our lives in human form," Sebastian said—calmly, damn him. "It does not invalidate what we are. It does not make us less Clan."

"But if you choose to stay in human form, no one cares! They don't try to kill you for being what you are!"

"Perhaps not. But I regularly run into difficulty with the leading clans for trying to work with the humans instead of isolating ourselves in our own little world—and thereby limiting our voice and our power. I choose not to let someone else dictate the decisions I make or how I define myself."

"But that's just it. You *choose*," I said, furious that he couldn't see that simple but so important difference. "The Corps hates me for having a Were mother; Lobizon hates me for not changing when that's the one thing I'm physically unable to do! I never had a choice about any of it!"

"And if you had?"

"What?"

"Would you have preferred a different mother?"

"Of course not!"

"A different father then? One who was Clan, so you would never have had to face the uncertainty of Neuri?"

"When Lobizon sent the squad to change me by force," I told him, fighting to keep my voice steady, "my father stood by me against a dozen Weres. Despite the fact that every single one of them was faster, stronger . . ."

I broke off because I was once again back in those dark streets, watching a mass of shadows slink around a wall, expanding in a blink into larger, more graceful, and more deadly shapes. It had been the beginning of the worst night of my life, as they chased us for blocks, almost overpowering us a dozen times. And the whole time, I'd been certain that, just days after losing my mother, I was about to lose my father, too.

"He could have been killed. He almost *was* killed," I finished, quietly furious. "He could have left me—they didn't want him, they'd have let him go—but he stayed anyway. He risked everything for me."

"You seem to admire the man a great deal."

"Of course I do!"

"Then I must admit to being confused. You said you've never had a choice."

"I haven't!"

"Yet it appears that the life you have is the one you would have chosen."

I started to fire back a response, and then stopped as his words sank in. "We cannot change what we are," he said simply. "Only what we do."

"And what do you expect me to do?" I demanded. "Because I don't know how to make this connection you want. I don't even know how to start."

"It isn't a task to be performed or a skill to be learned. It's instinctive."

"Can't you track him?" I was desperate for another answer, any other answer. Cyrus's life could not hang on the tenuous thread of my Were heritage. It just couldn't.

"Not through a city, not without having a very good idea of where to start looking. There are too many conflicting scents."

"But he's your brother!"

Sebastian shook his head. "After the challenge I was forced to sever ties, and for it to look real it had to *be* real. In Were terms, I am no longer Cyrus's brother. The ties between us were cut, metaphysically as well as legally, by the ceremony making him *vargulf.* And an Outcast wolf has no clan until he forms one by taking a mate."

Leaving Cyrus exactly one hope. Me.

"NO." Sedgewick didn't even bother to look apologetic, not that I'd have believed it coming from him.

"I'm fine," I insisted urgently. Hargrove had taken Sebastian off to confer with Jamie, and I didn't have a lot of time. The release form was on Sedgewick's desk, but so far, he'd refused to so much as glance at it. "I was planning to go back on active duty soon any—"

"Oh, were you? How kind of you to enlighten me." He was in rare form even for him. He'd taken Sebastian's refusal to allow him to carve up the so-fascinating corpse hard. And since this was Sedgewick, that meant that the rest of us were going to suffer, too.

"You know what I mean," I said, trying for composed while a thrumming instinct urged *hurry* with every beat of my heart. "After you release me."

"Which I haven't done. And won't, for at least another two weeks."

"Two weeks!"

"You almost died, mage, not even a month ago!" he snapped. "Or did I imagine the puddle of blood in the hallway, and the five hours I spent in surgery patching you up after that son-of-a-bitch shot you?"

"I've been shot before," I reminded him. Although not at point-blank range. I'd uncovered a traitor in the Corps and almost gotten killed taking him down. I was better now, except for my magic, which had yet to completely stabilize. But it would have to do. "And I'm not going to be doing anything strenuous—"

"I know you're not, because you're going to be here."

"Sedgewick!"

"That's doctor to you. And you can whine all you like, but I will not sign a release for anyone whose magic is acting as unpredictably as yours!"

"You said that would even out!"

"And so it will, once you're fully healed." I started to speak, but he cut me off. "Let me put this in very simple terms. Your body had too many assaults on its magic at one time. Now it is stuck on high alert, very similar to a person's immune system revving up to combat a serious infection. With the exception that your magic is attacking anything it perceives as a threat—whether it actually is or not! That makes it erratic and dangerous and therefore *restricted to base*!"

"But—"

"Although if you think you can convince Dick otherwise after almost decapitating him this morning, be my guest," he finished, with the smug expression that was factory standard for assholes.

I left before I was tempted to put Sedgewick in one of his own hospital beds. I slammed out into the corridor, furious but already planning how to get around his prohibition. He might not have a problem saying no to me, but the leader of the Clan Council was another matter. I'd let Sebastian talk to—

Something hit me with enough force to slam my head back against a row of lockers. I saw stars, and my lip split, spraying blood across my chin. I could taste it—hot and metallic-sweet as I grabbed for a weapon, before I belatedly remembered that I wasn't currently authorized to carry one.

I threw myself around the side of the lockers, trying to prepare a rough-and-ready spell that might carve through my assailant's shields without taking out half the corridor along with them. I expected another attack, one more serious than a crack to the jaw, but there was no follow-up. I peered out through the small clear space under the lockers, looking for feet, but there weren't any. That didn't necessarily mean there was no one there. But if someone was hiding behind a cloaking spell, the distinct lack of pummeling was odd.

After a breathless moment, I emerged to see the same white tile, the same pale walls, the same water fountain that no one had ever bothered to hook up. I put a hand to my face, expecting to feel the pain of a split lip if not a broken cheekbone, but only soft skin met my fingers. There was no wound, even though the ache was still there.

It wasn't helped by the shock of icy water that came out of nowhere and hit me square in the face. I coughed, wiped my eyes, and looked up to find that the corridor was gone. In its place was a hot summer day, with the sun glaring down from a vivid blue sky.

It gleamed off the chrome fender of a beat-up motorcycle and the dark brown hair of the guy washing it. The hair tickled his neck because he didn't get it cut as often as he should, like he remembered to shave maybe twice a week. Whiskey brown eyes that were the same shade in either form met mine, sparkling with challenge.

I blinked, but it was definitely Cyrus. He had the stripe of sunburn across his shoulders he got in the spring, after last year's tan wore thin, and he was wearing the ragged cutoffs with the yellow splotches from the time we'd painted his living room. They rode low on his hips, showing off a hard stomach and thighs heavy with muscle. The sight was enough of a distraction that it took me a minute to notice his accessory—a now-empty bucket clutched in one hand.

"Big-time war mage," he taunted, yelling to be heard over the blaring radio. "Is that the best you can do?" I followed his gaze down to the water balloon I gripped in one hand. *"I* bet you can't even hit me," he jeered, dodging

*back and forth along his driveway, deliberately using only
human speed.*

I took a drink of the beer I'd gone into the house to get
and grinned back, making very sure not to watch the garden
hose that was slithering toward him through the grass like
a long green snake. And then it pounced, pumping jets of
icy water all over his bare torso. He cursed and whipped
around, grabbing it in a two-handed grip that only made it
that much easier to spray him full in the face.

"You cheated!" he sputtered, looking outraged, before
putting on a burst of speed that made him only a blue and
tan blur as he tackled me around the shins.

I went down, but hit tile instead of grass, so hard that I slid
all the way across the corridor, bashing my head on the side
of the water fountain. I lay there for a minute, panting, until
an orderly caught sight of me and hurried down the corridor,
looking concerned. I waved him off and staggered back to
my feet, amazed to find that I wasn't dripping wet.

I exited medical and propped myself against an empty
piece of wall down the hall while I waited for my heart rate
to edge back into the safe zone. A couple passing mages
gave me the once-over, but looked away when I scowled
at them. I rested my head against the wall and swallowed,
wondering if I was crazy.

The day I'd just relived had been a few months before I
moved to Vegas, when I was still working for the Corps's
Jersey office. Like most Weres, Cyrus didn't care for city life
and felt claustrophobic in apartments. He'd had a house on a
few acres in Galloway, close enough to Atlantic City to make
his cover as a ne'er-do-well with a gambling habit believable,
but far enough away that he could breathe. I'd driven down
onc Saturday with a six-pack and a birthday cake to celebrate
his turning the big three-oh, and found him feeling playful.

He never did finish washing that bike.

I hadn't thought about that day in months, but it had been
just as clear as if it had happened yesterday. Clearer, because
I couldn't taste yesterday's fettuccini like I had the chlorine
in that water or the smoothness of that beer. I'd never had a
memory that real.

If it was just my memory.

Had Sebastian been right? Was I somehow tuning in to what Cyrus was thinking about? If so, it would quiet the biggest fear I had about this proposed expedition.

Mated was a Were term, and not one that was usually applied to human-Were couplings. My parents had been married for more than four decades, but no Were had considered them mated. I think most of Lobizon had assumed that Mother was going through some kind of phase and would eventually come to her senses. Because human marriages, even long-standing ones, didn't bind two people as closely as a mating.

Or so I'd heard. It wasn't like Mom had bothered to explain exactly what the term meant. With Neuri forcing me to keep my distance from the clan, she'd assumed I would marry a human. So had I, until I met Cyrus. Not that we'd gotten around to talking marriage. In fact, we'd only recently gotten back together after a lengthy split. So mating didn't seem too likely. Not to mention that Cyrus had never so much as uttered the term.

But despite occasional rumors about my mental stability, I didn't go around hallucinating.

I didn't want to feel hopeful, in case I was wrong. But I didn't think I was—that crack to the jaw still hurt like a bitch. And if that was what Cyrus was currently experiencing, then he was already in trouble.

"And I'm telling you, a map won't do you any good!" My thoughts were interrupted by the sound of Jamie's distinctive burr coming down the hall. "Tartarus isn't fixed like the city above. The tunnels are, o' course, but the rest of it . . . floats around, so to speak."

"What rest of it? I thought the tunnels *were* the city," Hargrove was frowning at the map he had in his hand.

"That's a typical newbie mistake," Jamie said kindly. "The tunnels are like the roads above—they get you from place to place. But the markets, the shantytowns, the bars—they're mostly carved out of the surrounding ground. One of these days, I fully expect half the city to implode, they've undermined so much of it."

"Then those caverns should be on the map," Hargrove insisted, trying to hand it to him.

Jamie didn't even bother to glance at it. "If that thing's more than a week old, it's out of date; if it's more than a month, it's useless. There are turf wars going on all the time, and the city shifts with them. You have to have someone who knows the signs to get you anywhere, much less to get you back. You need a guide."

"I thought you—" Sebastian began, but Jamie was already shaking his head.

"I've been out of it too long. Sure, I could figure it out, given time. The main markets are pretty stable, although I doubt your beastie is holed up anywhere so public. But what you need is someone who has been there recently. And that lets out every tunnel rat we have."

They disappeared into medical, probably looking for me. I stared at Sebastian's back until the closing doors hid it from view. Then I took off in the other direction.

If a dark mage was responsible for this, then a mage needed to go after him, not someone who would be just as vulnerable to his spells as Grayshadow had been. I knew Sebastian wanted to help, but he'd said it himself: if he died, the next *bardic* might not be so interested in maintaining ties with the humans. Not if it was going to get some of his people killed.

So I was going alone. Well, more or less.

"NOPE, nothing." The moon-faced mage behind the desk made a brief moue of disappointment to show camaraderie before preparing to blow me off.

"What do you mean, nothing? A bum, a bag lady, a freaking pimp. I don't care!"

"Yeah, I got it the first time," Michaelson told me, scowling. He was already having a rough day, and I wasn't making it better. "Look, I gave you the report, okay? That's all I got. If you want to talk to street people, go to a police station; hell, go to the street! But you won't find 'em here."

"Since when?"

"Since we started needing the lockup for more dangerous types."

"Nsquital demons are not dangerous!" I pointed out, referring to the red-haired creature who had just been escorted in back.

"Ever had one spit at you? Anyway, he was selling weapons to the wrong people, so we picked him up. But he'll probably be out on bail in a couple hours, after he gives up his cache. These days, if it doesn't relate to the war, nobody cares."

He motioned the next person in line forward, without so much as another sympathy pout. I was jostled out of the way, over near a window where a bounty hunter was waiting to turn in a prisoner. The guy in question didn't look dangerous, just an average junkie with waist-length dreads, dirty cargo pants and a long-sleeved black tee. Except for the stench, which was enough to clear the sinuses. I gagged and looked around for another perch, but the place was packed.

"Thanks. I've been wanting to do that since I caught him," the bounty hunter said. I realized he was talking to me, and glanced over. His prisoner's matted mane now littered the floor around his feet, like long fuzzy brown snakes. Uh-oh.

The man clutched his head. "My hair!" he screeched. "What did that bitch do to my hair?"

The bounty hunter raised an eyebrow as the guy's remaining locks sheered off. "You should learn some manners," he chided.

"Witch! I said witch!" the guy told me desperately. Too late, because I couldn't regrow hair. Not even when my magic was working properly.

"Been to Tartarus recently?" I asked him, as he felt around his now-bald head.

"What?" The guy looked at me like I was crazy.

"I picked him up in a bar there this morning," the bounty hunter told me, collecting his payout.

"What's the charge?"

"Possession, suspicion of dealing," he said, on his way out the door.

"Possession of what?" I asked baldy. He ignored me. "What were you dealing?" I demanded, jerking him closer.

"You got no proof! I had nothing on me," he spat, glaring at me. "And anyway, punch shouldn't even be illegal. You'd think it was dangerous or something—"

"It is."

"Punch" was the street name for a mind-altering concoction derived from a distilled wine made by the Fey. It was said to give a wicked high and to enhance latent magical abilities. But like all drugs, it carried risks—addiction, mental instability and, for longtime users, insanity.

"Only if you get greedy," baldy sulked. "You can drink yourself to death, too, you know, and nobody cares."

"Alcohol doesn't give humans the ability to curse each other into oblivion," I pointed out. "A couple brothers did just that last week. Seems they had some mage blood back in the family tree. They got into an argument over some girl after an irresponsible asshole sold them punch, and one of them wished the other would go to hell."

Baldy winced. "Yeah, but you got him back, right?"

"Not yet. We don't know which hell dimension ended up with him."

I tightened my grip on baldy's arm as a harried-looking Apprentice hurried over. As packed as this place was, it would take them most of the day to process and release him, which would seriously mess up my plans. I dug battered credentials out of my back pocket and flashed them.

"I know who you are," the kid said, looking a little freaked.

Sheesh. Kill one department head and they never let you forget it.

"I need to question this one," I told him. The kid nodded, already backing up. "I'll bring him back later," I called, then hustled my new guide out the door before anyone with seniority noticed what was going on.

"I'm not going anywhere until I see my lawyer," the guy told me. "I know my rights! You can't just shave my head!"

"Take it easy. It looks good on you." Well, better than the dreads.

"Didn't you hear me?" he demanded, starting to struggle. "I want a lawyer. I want—"

"You want to shut up before anything else comes off," I said, dragging him into the locker room.

"Mage de Croissets to the CMO's office immediately." The magically enhanced voice was loud enough to make me jump.

Shit.

I parked the guy on a bench and yanked open my locker. A sawed-off shotgun, two handguns, a couple of potion grenades, four throwing knives, a stiletto that fit nicely down my boot, my potion belt secured around my hips, and I felt more like myself. That lasted until I opened the little packet on the top shelf, the one I'd sworn never to use again.

The two foil halves separated and something black and slimy oozed out onto my wrist. "Okay, that's nasty," baldy informed me, as a ward in the shape of a large black leech sank into my skin.

"This from someone with a tongue stud," I said, right before the power drain hit.

It was like a blow to the gut, immediate and brutal. So that's why they had me lie down last time, I thought dimly. I sank to the bench, waiting for the nausea, the dizziness and the all-around ick factor to die down a little.

My fingers ached to rip it off, with the skin if necessary. It's worse at first, I reminded myself as the tat pulsed clammily against my wrist. It was heavy and cold, and made me want to shudder. But it was working. I'd never felt less like using magic in my life.

This class of ward wasn't designed to give added power in combat, or to enhance the senses or to heal. It did just one thing—absorb magical energy—and did it very well. Wards like it were used in surgery to keep a patient's natural protective energies clamped down so surgeons didn't have to worry about being attacked while they worked. In my case, I'd worn one early in the healing process to help regulate my magic.

It had done the job, but had left me feeling weak and listless. I'd finally persuaded Sedgewick to remove it, promising to keep it on hand in case of emergency. I'd never planned to let it anywhere near me again. But if I was going into the field, I had to wear it or risk accidentally attacking someone who didn't have Hargrove's shields. The tat would make powerful spells impossible and even weak ones difficult, rendering me a lot less dangerous—to everyone, including the bad guys. But I couldn't see an alternative.

After a moment, I got up, threw on a leather trench to hide the weapons, and grabbed my guide. "What's going on?" he demanded. "Are you taking me to lockup?"

"Nope. You got a name?"

"Dieter," he said suspiciously.

I didn't bother asking for a last name, since it would probably be fake anyway. "Well, we're going on a field trip, Dieter."

"Where to?"

"It's a surprise."

5

I parked my Hog next to the long concrete runoff channel along Highway 91. I didn't have to ask if this was the place. The old Las Vegas sign, veteran of a million plastic mementos and gaudy key chains, was glittering right across the road. And according to the report I'd wheedled out of Michaelson, the body had been found practically in its shadow.

As usual, a couple tourists were taking turns posing in front of the sign, grinning toothily. It wasn't a great day for it. To the west, the sky shaded dung brown at the horizon, then yellow, then a sick and ominous green. The air felt heavy, like maybe one of Vegas's brief spring showers might not be far off.

"Aw, man! You gotta be shitting me!" My reluctant guide stared into the concrete gully below, looking a little wall-eyed. Then he took off.

I watched him scramble down the road for half a minute, before throwing a lasso spell around his ankles and giving it a yank. I'd been nice, waiting until he veered onto the curb so he'd hit dirt instead of asphalt, and twisting the spell so he'd land on one shoulder instead of full face. But he didn't look appreciative when I walked over and jerked him back up.

I manhandled him down into the channel, our boots splashing through a thin, braided current and a bunch of soggy adult entertainment flyers. Ahead were two large tunnels, maybe ten feet wide by six feet high, a few of the thousands of concrete boxes linked together under the city's urban scrawl. They were pitch dark and not very friendly looking, but I didn't understand the severity of the struggle my prisoner was putting up.

"What's your deal?" I demanded. "I thought you got pulled out of one of these this morning."

"Not this one. And I'm not going in there. You may as well shoot me now! Better that than those damn things eat me!"

"What things?"

"Kappas. This drain's infested with 'em. Everybody knows that."

"Kappas, huh?" I peered into the mouth of the western tunnel, but saw only cobwebs and drooling algae. The place smelled like mildew and old shoes, but I didn't pick up any of the distinctive fishy odor of kappa feces. "Kappas are Japanese," I said. "We don't have too many problems with them in Vegas."

"I don't know where they came from. But a bunch moved in and took over the whole tunnel."

A heavy stream of runoff gurgled under my boots, but hardly enough to satisfy a river imp. "When did these kappas move in?"

"About a week ago."

"Huh." This was where the Hunter had dumped the body, so he wasn't likely to be hanging around. But the kappas were interesting. It was exactly the kind of story someone would circulate who didn't want anyone poking around his hidey-hole. And if he'd been here once, there was a chance he'd left something behind.

The guy's acne-covered chin took on a mulish tilt. "I'm not going in there and you can't make me. I know my rights.

You have to guarantee my safety and you can't! There's too many of 'em. They're like freaking piranhas! I'm—"

"You're *not* going in there."

He stopped midrant. "I'm not?"

"Nope." I really didn't expect any trouble, but you never know. I dragged him back up the embankment and across the road. The tourists had gone, so I lassoed him to the Vegas sign by one ankle. "You're going to wait for me here, safe and sound and ready to interpret anything I bring back."

"What happens if you don't come back?"

"Then you'll be waiting a long time."

I returned to the entrance of the drain and pulled out my flashlight. I shone it around, but there wasn't much to see. A stream of runoff swallowed my ankles before disappearing into darkness. Long skeins of cobwebs fluttered overhead. Mud squelched underfoot, smelling sharply of garbage and man-made chemicals. Oh, yeah. This was going to be fun.

My natural unease was strong enough that it took me a minute to notice the other, subtler urge plucking at my senses. The more I looked down that drain, the more convinced I was that I shouldn't be here, like the very air was wrong, alien, *not for me*. I got the definite impression that this place didn't like me; that it wanted me to leave. Now.

So I went in.

Patrol had noted the presence of a decaying protection ward over the west tunnel entrance. It was the kind that played with a person's senses—in this case fear—and was the standard keep away for the supernatural community. It seemed like overkill to me. Like anyone would *want* to go in there.

The protection ward grew stronger as I moved forward, making me feel like I was battling the tide with every step. I pushed on anyway, trying to ignore the spell screaming that somewhere, just up ahead, something horrible waited. It was terribly real and absolutely convincing, like being a child staring into a dark closet and having complete certainty that evil lurked inside.

It didn't help that, if I was in the right place, it just might.

And then my flashlight blew out.

I shook it a couple times, cursing, which only caused the bottom to come off and the batteries to fall out. Batteries I couldn't find without a light. I bit the bullet and gave my owl tat a metaphysical nudge. I felt the power drain immediately, which wasn't good, but when I opened my eyes the pitch black had transformed into something closer to a dark night—all outlines and shadows. I still couldn't see clearly, but I comforted myself with the fact that neither could anybody else.

I found the batteries, but they didn't help the piece-of-junk flashlight. I finally gave up and went on, deciding I might be better off. No need to announce my presence, assuming anybody was still hanging around. I actually doubted it; patrol had done a brief walk through, and found nothing: no kappas and no clues.

But then, they hadn't had my motivation.

The protection ward finally cut out twenty or so yards up the tunnel, allowing me to breathe. That was a huge relief, but it was the only improvement. The floor had sunk or the water had risen, because it was now shin high. The temperature had also gone up, enough to plaster my hair to my skull and stick my T-shirt to my skin. And I became increasingly aware of an ache running up both legs, like maybe spelunking through the drains of Vegas wasn't on my approved activities list.

I'd gone maybe three hundred yards when I spied flashes of dim light up ahead, spotting the wall like visible Morse code. It turned out to be coming from behind a ward, if you could call such a half-assed attempt by that name. It was spitting and crackling around the edges, lighting up a graffiti-covered junction box. It made me wonder why anyone had bothered.

Usually, going through a warded door into an unknown location makes my skin crawl. Most of them are designed so that the outside resembles the wall or whatever surface they are mimicking, but the inside is transparent. That leaves the person outside blind, while anyone inside has a clear view— and a clear shot. But in this case, the gloom of the drain ensured that all anyone saw was blackness until I stepped through, with shields up and gun drawn.

And realized that the most dangerous thing about the place was the smell. The acrid tang of wet, charred wood hit my nostrils like bad breath. The ward was concealing a cave maybe twenty by twenty-five, which looked like it had recently been doubling as a barbeque pit. The ceiling was black with soot, the remains of a bonfire scarred the floor, and smoke had almost obliterated the graffiti burning across the walls. The only artwork still visible was four savage vertical slash marks, dripping with painted blood. Colorful.

I could see, courtesy of the mass of wires that spilled out of a wall, like the innards of a small animal. It was the back of the vandalized junction box, which was being used to power a couple of bare bulbs. It looked like whoever had been last out the door had forgotten to turn off the lights.

I poked around the ash that covered everything like matte gray snow until my back ached and my hands and pant legs were coated. But all I uncovered was a rotting corduroy couch, a few pieces of singed plywood and an empty whiskey bottle. I threw the last against the wall, just to watch it shatter. The Hunter was long gone, after torching anything that might give a clue as to his identity. This was a waste of time.

I hit the corridor again in a foul mood, which wasn't helped by the sudden appearance of a chorus of crickets. Their chirping filled the drain, echoing weirdly in the small space and sounding like a too-cheerful orchestra had moved in. The noise limited my hearing as effectively as the dark interfered with my sight. It made me progressively more paranoid as I went along; soon I was looking nervously over my shoulder every few seconds.

That was stupid since I couldn't see more than a few feet in any direction. I kept doing it anyway, though, and my imagination was working overtime. In that gloomy pit, every unidentified sound became the scrape of claws on cement, every watermark on the walls, a hulking monster.

Which is why I almost ran into the real monsters coming from the other direction.

There were three of them, still in human form, more or less, although the curtains of greasy, stringy hair and the baggy pants made it kind of hard to tell. But they were Weres, as their reaction on catching sight of me made clear. They didn't change and they didn't go for guns. But those were the only saving graces.

I flung up a shield in time to keep from being skewered by the first guy's knife, which slid off to scrape against concrete. But the impact sent me reeling, and successive jolts jarred through my bones as the men took turns battering my less-than-substantial shield. It was weak because of the leech, because of the power drain from my owl, and because shields don't work that great against Weres anyway. It wasn't going to last.

"I'm Lia de Croissets!" I told them loudly. "Of Arnou!" If it was revenge they were after, fine, but I wasn't the Hunter.

The pummeling didn't change, except maybe to get harder. "I'm Corps!" Nothing.

I reviewed my options and decided they sucked. In such a confined space, a potion grenade would gas me, too, and any spell I could fling at the moment wouldn't have much effect on three adult Weres. Fortunately, the whole silver bullet thing is a myth; lead works just fine—if you manage to connect.

But therein lay the problem. A Were's advantages are speed, recovery time, speed, inhuman strength, and speed—as the four of them were busy demonstrating. I couldn't even see the punches battering my shield, but I could feel every one.

I decided that debate was useless because I was going to be dead in a minute if I didn't do something. I wrestled the shotgun out of its back holster and got a grip on my Luger. The next time they sent me staggering into the far wall, I whipped around, let the shield go and fired.

And figured out why I was the only idiot using a gun.

I'd emptied the Luger in an arc that was hopefully wide enough to hit at least one of them. It did—one screamed and went down, clutching his leg. But the rest of the bullets hit the walls, sparked off the concrete and ricocheted. The tunnel suddenly felt a lot like a shooting gallery, with bullets whizzing and striking everywhere.

Another Were stumbled like he'd tripped, and crashed face-first into the water. The last tried to get up but slid on the scummy surface and went skating across the tunnel to slam into the other wall. It looked almost like a comedy pratfall, until he recovered, pushed off, and leapt at me, changing in a blur of motion.

In wolf form he was more resistant to magic, and although I managed to get a shield up in time, it did little good. Claws raked my arm, hot and sharp, stripping my gun away. It went skittering across the muck, out of reach, and we hit the floor with the Were on top—all three hundred pounds of him.

The impact alone was enough to drive the breath from my lungs, but I also hit my head against the side of the wall, stunning me. I expected to feel hot breath in my face, teeth ripping my flesh, oblivion. But instead he merely lay there, trapping me under a crushing weight I couldn't hope to throw off. I heard the sound of feet limping past—his buddies going hell-bent for leather toward the mouth of the tunnel.

And then nothing.

The mountain of fur and muscle on top of me didn't move, other than to drip something warm and sticky onto my face. After a minute, I realized that one of the ricochets must have hit him as he was leaping for me. What I couldn't figure out was how to get him off.

And it wasn't like I had all day. He'd landed across me, with only my head, shoulders and feet sticking out. Water was running up to my ears, and his weight was slowly forcing me farther underneath. If I didn't get him off, I was going to drown in less than two feet of water.

Pushing and pulling did no good, and neither did attempting to wriggle out from under him. The body was almost completely muscle, with very little give. I had potions that could eat through flesh and bone, but even assuming I could reach one, I couldn't use them without possibly dissolving me, too.

I needed my power, and there was only one way to get

it. My left arm was trapped under the beast, so I used my mouth, muttering the release spell while trying to find an edge to the leech with my tongue. The thing didn't want to let go, still gorging itself on my power. But I finally snagged a slightly raised corner and ripped it away.

It felt exactly like a huge slug wriggling in my mouth—beyond awful—and it immediately began trying to sink into my tongue. I spat it out, disgusted, and raised a shield, hoping it would lift the Were's body a foot or so and give me some wiggle room. But instead, I got maybe half that much before the shield collapsed with a final-sounding pop. And the force of his body falling back down was hard enough to push my head under the filthy, mineral-tasting water.

Whatever air was in my lungs rushed out under the pressure. My chest was tight and the urge to breathe, when I knew I couldn't, was almost overwhelming. I don't care what training you've had, being caught under water seconds away from drowning is one hell of a good reason to panic. So I did, throwing the dumbest possible spell under the circumstances—a fireball.

It shouldn't have worked. That spell requires a lot more energy than shields, not to mention it works best in dry conditions—or at least when not cast under water. So it was a shock to hear a muffled roar and to feel the huge body suddenly fly off me.

I sat up, spitting out filthy runoff, and dragged in several huge breaths. I was so busy exploring the wonder that was oxygen that it took a second for me to realize what had happened. The red tide swirling around me was my first clue, the shattered bone sizzling in the water was the second. The body had literally exploded on top of me, leaving me sitting in what remained of a rib cage, along with blood and other substances I preferred not to think about.

I'd forgotten: just as the tat took a few seconds to start working, it also took a few to release the stored magic back into my system. The shields had been pulling from a dry well, but the fireball had had more than an hour of accumulated force behind it. I was lucky it hadn't taken out the whole freaking drain.

A push got me to my knees, a stagger got me to my feet, and a step took me to the wall. I fell against it, the cool cement heaven against my cheek and palms. I just stayed there for a minute, breathing hard.

But only for a minute. Because those guys hadn't been Clan, they'd been *vargulf*. It was obvious by how they looked, by the untrained way they fought and by the lack of any and all Clan insignia. And I didn't think a bunch of outcasts had shown up to avenge the murder of a High Clan wolf—especially not after attacking a member of the group that had found the body.

So they'd been looking for something.

Something I'd missed.

I shoved off the wall, tripped on a spent shell casing and went down hard on one knee. I staggered up, wishing I had the breath to curse, and retraced my steps. My knee ached and almost gave out on me twice, and my left arm throbbed in time with my heartbeat. I checked myself out in the dim light of the cave.

Gore matted my hair, slicked my coat, and stuck my shirt to my skin. My bum knee felt weak and rubbery, but probably more from the adrenaline afterburn than any real damage. But the arm was another matter. My shields had slowed the attack down, and my coat had provided an extra layer of protection. Yet it was still lacerated badly enough to need stitches.

Great.

I wrapped a handkerchief around the wound and tugged my sleeve back down. The coat had already started to heal the tears in the leather, with short brown filaments stretching across the gaps like threads in well-worn denim. Too bad flesh doesn't heal as fast.

I really hoped I didn't have to beat up anyone else.

The cave was still silent, smelly and frustratingly empty

when I returned. Had those guys really been headed here? Or was there some other hidden space along the miles of drain ahead? I decided to do a check of the immediate area before sifting through the ashes again, and started for the door.

And looked up to see myself lounging at a bar.

Cyrus wasn't looking, but she was hard to miss: with long, messy dark hair, clan-gray eyes and a red-stained mouth that stood out starkly from her pale skin. She was leaning back against the bar on her elbows, her mile-long, leather-clad legs in front of her, crossed at the ankles. Watching him.

It seemed to Cyrus as if the volume of the room suddenly turned down, as if the colors dulled to shadows, except around her. Because even better than those stunning looks was the faint but unmistakable scent of Clan. It wreathed his head like the finest of drugs, cutting easily through the smoke and alcohol and cheap cologne of the bar. It caught him off guard, with no defenses up, and landed like a sledgehammer.

It was hard to believe that it had only been two months since he found himself out on the street: a pack animal with no pack. He'd told Sebastian he could handle it—hell, this whole thing had been his idea. It would be hard, he'd assured his brother, he wasn't kidding himself about that, but the goal was worth it. He'd been so certain he was right, so sure of himself, so cocky.

He almost pitied that man now.

Of course, that man had never had people he'd once called friends turn away in disgust at the sight of him. He'd never had his own family refuse to look him in the eye, their glances jumping over him as if he was an interruption, a glitch in their visual field. An error. He'd never lain awake at night with the gnawing, ever-present, sickening absence of something as vital to him as the air he breathed. That man had been Cyrus of Arnou, High Clan and wolf born, with the whole weight of a prestigious house behind his every word and action.

This man was just Cyrus. And he'd been appalled at what he'd discovered about him.

Just Cyrus avoided places where he was likely to meet Clan, dodging confrontations he knew he couldn't win. Because he fought alone now, while even the feeblest member of the weakest clan had dozens of brothers behind him. Just Cyrus ducked his head and turned away when he saw family coming, before they could do it to him. Just Cyrus desperately wanted to slink back, tail between his legs, begging to be taken in, even knowing what it would cost his brother.

Because Just Cyrus was weak.

The only thing that still allowed him to look at himself in the mirror everyday was the knowledge that wanting and doing were two different things. He might not be the man he'd thought he was, but he wasn't quite that sniveling creature that haunted his nightmares, either. Because he hadn't done it. Not yet.

And now he found himself by the bar, with no memory of how he got there, staring at an obviously High Clan woman like she was the last oasis in the desert. He expected to be ignored, rebuffed, cursed, although there was no way she could immediately know what he was. Lately, it had started to feel like he had his shame permanently tattooed across his forehead.

She swung her legs around and tipped her head sideways to look at him. "Buy you a drink?"

"I thought that was my line," he said, not trying, because this wasn't going anywhere.

"Yeah, but I'm the pushy type. I like to get it out there early."

"You're Clan. It goes with the territory."

"I'm not, actually."

He leaned in despite himself, the heady scent of a fertile female of his people flooding his senses. "Oh, you are," he said, already half drunk with it. "You very definitely are. To whom do you belong?" The usual Clan courtesy slipped out before he could stop it.

"Myself. How about you?"

Her answer didn't make sense, but the question did. It was almost the first thing two strange Weres asked each

other, because the answer would influence everything that
followed: who are you, where do you rank, who are your
people?

Where do you belong?

"I'm vargulf," he said shortly. "I don't belong to
anyone."

It came out sounding harsh, even to him. He waited for
it, the look of disgust, the hastily mumbled excuse, the rapid
retreat. And didn't get it. "Good," *she said, leaned over,*
cupped the back of his head, and kissed him.

And she was right, he thought vaguely, his hands on her
waist, sliding over silk and skin-tight leather. She was the
pushy type, at least until he got on board. Then the prac-
ticed tricks gave way to something soft and startled. It went
through him in a rush, a tidal wave of emotions carrying
him along with it, even as part of him wondered what the
hell he thought he was doing.

"Got someplace to be?" *she asked as she broke it off.*

"I'm all yours," *he told her hoarsely, already sliding off*
the seat.

The bar dissolved into a dank, smoke-blackened room.
I fell back against the wall, eyes stinging hot and watering.
I remembered that night, but it was a little different seen
through Cyrus's eyes.

I'd kept getting saddled by the Corps with any and all
cases involving Weres, supposedly because of my "special
insight." But the fact was that Mom rarely spoke about her
other life, and she'd been so ill those last years that I'd hated
to constantly bother her with my problems. I'd decided I
needed an outside source, someone I could pay for insights
into the Were world. And as luck would have it, a few days
later a patrol logged a report about a brutal beating behind a
bar involving an "unaffiliated Were" and members of a local
clan. I'd gone to check it out.

It had been a night of surprises, starting with how I'd
reacted. Cyrus was handsome enough to turn heads, but I'd
met plenty of attractive men before. And none of them had
made my stomach tighten at one glimpse, had need crawling
over my skin, had my fingers itching with the urge to stroke.

And when we kissed, heat and power, hunger and desire thrust into me in a wave of sensation that had left me reeling. I'd spent the entire evening—at a restaurant, because I didn't dare take him home—quietly freaking out about my sudden lack of self-control.

It had also been a surprise to learn that he was *vargulf*. The report had seemed to suggest it, but most outcast wolves look like the guys I'd met in the drain. They weren't hard-muscled types with thick dark hair and assessing brown eyes. And although the few I'd come across still smelled like Clan, there had always been a faintly sour undertone to it. Cyrus had smelled *good*, rich and male and musky-sweet.

I looked around and wondered what surprise I was supposed to find here.

I decided to start with the couch, because it was the most disgusting thing in the room and I wanted to get it out of the way. I'd already been over it once and had found nothing under the dust and ash except a few hundred cigarette butts shoved between the seats. The fire had eaten away one side, but given up halfway, probably because of the soggy state of the moldy cushions.

The remaining fabric was coming apart and a hole gnawed in one end raised the possibility of rats. I pushed my useless flashlight in there and rattled it around. Nothing ran out, so I formed a shield around my hand and poked it through the hole. And immediately felt something weird.

I pulled out a small velvet pouch that looked pretty new— no mold, no smoke damage, no bite marks—and opened it. Inside were three gold charms, each in the form of a miniscule wolf. All were different, all were beautifully made, and all were powerful. I could feel the hum of their energy even through the shield, a thrumming beat, almost like the pulse of tiny hearts.

Despite working with Caleb and Jamie for two weeks, I wasn't an expert on wards. But I knew quality when I saw it. These had to be worth a small fortune, especially now, with prices inflated due to the war. So what the hell were they doing here? And what, if anything, did they have to do with Cyrus?

I wrapped them in one of my socks, having run out of handkerchiefs, and stuffed them in an inner pocket of my coat. I tagged the body on the way out, to let patrol know it was mine, and picked up the slug ward—now extra slimy—off the floor. I stuck it back on my skin without looking at it.

Calling in had to wait until I made it back to the mouth of the drain, where I was able to get decent reception. Caleb must have still been at lunch, because I actually got through.

"Sedgewick's frothing at the mouth," he told me, without so much as a hello. "The man is *pissed*."

"He's always pissed."

"Yeah. Not like this. You need to get back here."

"I'm working on that. By the way, have any licensed wardsmiths reported a robbery lately? A big one?"

"The Black Circle's hit a few places," he said slowly. "What are we talking about here?"

"Wolves. Powerful. Expensive. Three of them. I don't know what they do yet."

"I thought you were looking for your boyfriend?"

"It's complicated."

"I've noticed that with you. But no, no wolves." And that settled that. Because Caleb would know. He didn't usually work in the Dungeon, but he'd been there for three months since his injury. And he was the kind who paid attention.

"Thanks. Uh, and can you let patrol know that there's a body in that drain off 91?"

"Another one?"

"Yeah. Tell them to bring a baggie."

"Lia . . ." He sighed. "Just be careful, all right?"

"Aren't I always?" I hung up before he could answer that, and went to collect my guide.

He was taking photos for a family, but dropped the camera when he saw me emerge from the wash. I waited until the tourists drove off, then crossed the street. He looked a little pale. In retrospect, I probably should have used the handkerchief on my face before making it into a bandage. Oh, well, too late now.

"What . . . what . . ."

"You were right. Those kappas are a bitch. Any other mysterious new monsters suddenly turn up anywhere?" He shook his head, wide-eyed. "How about wardsmiths? You know any of them?"

He blinked. "Like personally?"

"Like any way."

"There's lots in the tunnels. Everybody's making wards now."

Yeah, like the idiot who had done the protection ward on the cave. But the charlatans getting rich off people's wartime paranoia weren't who I needed. Becoming a master or even a journeyman wardsmith took decades of training. No fly-by-night con man had made those wolves.

"I'm talking about someone good. Someone professional."

"If they were *good*, they wouldn't be in the *drains*."

Normally, I'd have agreed, but I didn't think the guys who attacked me had had the money to buy those wards. And no local, licensed wardsmiths had been robbed. So whoever had made the wolves either wasn't from around here, or wasn't licensed.

"I guess we'll just have to stay here, then," I told him. "And clean out those kappas."

"There's a guy who hangs out at Tilda's Place, over by the Tropicana," Dieter said quickly. "They say he's pretty good."

I smiled. "Let's go find out."

I peered into the dark drain dubiously. "There's a bar down there?"

Dieter nodded. "Tilda's. It's been there forever. The dwarves like to drink at her place, so they cut her a deal on the rent."

"Dwarves?"

He scowled. "Yeah. Nasty little fuckers. They run the market."

I peered into the maybe eight-by-six tunnel again. I spotted cockroaches, spiders and a few creepy orange crawfish. But no people—of any kind. "There's a market down there?"

He shot me a pitying look. "You don't know much, do you?"

"Lately, it doesn't feel like it."

"It's one of the biggest in Tartarus. And they know it, too. You wouldn't believe what they wanted to charge me for a booth. So I tried just walking around, hitting the entrances and stuff, you know? And they *still* wanted to charge me! Like, I wasn't even *sitting down* and—" He stopped abruptly.

"You know, come to think of it, there are probably other wardsmiths if I ask around."

I grabbed him by the back of the shirt as he started off. "Let me guess. The dwarves don't like you, either."

"They might have said something about not coming back."

"For how long?"

"Like, you know. Ever."

"Then we'll do this quick."

The tunnel curved after half a dozen yards, blocking out the rectangle of light behind us. Smothering blackness came crushing in on all sides, and the ward hiding the market had no telltale light leaking through to help me zero in on its location. I could feel it, buzzing somewhere up ahead, but couldn't quite—

A skinny young guy with spiked red hair came barreling out of a wall on a wash of light, pushing an overloaded shopping cart. He skidded to a halt, the cart's wheels making tracks in the muck. "Potion supplies?" he asked, not missing a beat.

"Excuse me?"

"It's one of the main reasons your type comes down here," Dieter said, as the vendor started pawing through his mobile shop. "It's either buy contraband, hire an assassin or find a good time. And you look like you could do your own killing."

"What about the good time?"

The vendor suddenly thrust something into my face— something brown and scaly, with a gaping maw of teeth. I put two bullets in it before I realized it wasn't moving. It landed on the floor a few feet away, spinning slowly on its curved shell.

"If you ask me, you could use one," Dieter said, swallowing. "You're real tense."

"You shot it, you bought it," the vendor added, picking up the still-smoking carcass.

"What the hell is it?"

"Dried armadillo. Keeps evildoers out of your home."

"Too late."

I forked over a ten rather than waste time arguing, which turned out to be a mistake. As soon as the pale concrete wall rolled back, I found myself mobbed by a line of hawkers selling the magical equivalent of snake oil. I barely noticed. Because stretching out behind them was a sight designed to make anyone's jaw drop.

I'd expected something along the lines of the previous drain—gloomy, smelly, depressing, dangerous. I'd expected a bunch of little dirty caves filled with huddled, desperate people. I'd expected a low ceiling, bad air and vermin. I hadn't expected an enchanted forest.

But that's what spread out in front of us in a dazzling expanse. Softly glowing branches shed a delicate white light over a huge cave. They draped the booths that filled the space, crisscrossed above footpaths and climbed up stone support pillars. Some people had even stuffed twigs into colored glass jars, making lanterns that spotted their booths with watery puddles of amethyst and plum, turquoise and jade, ruby and amber.

My brain finally supplied the name—hawthorn. I recalled a few basics—originally from Faerie, burns brightly with the application of a simple spell—but that description left a lot to be desired. The branches threw gently waving shadows on the walls, ceiling and floor, shadows with leaves and berries, neither of which the dried branches had.

"This way!" Dieter was tugging on me, obviously embarrassed to be seen with the gawking tourist.

I followed him through a maze of cardboard and plywood shanties. Inside, medicine women, folk doctors, astrologers, fortune-tellers and cut-rate sorcerers plied their wares. Dogs and children ran underfoot. People laughed and bartered around the shops, or called to each other across the aisles. After the deadly quiet of the drains, it felt like a madhouse.

Dieter skirted the main aisle, heading for a narrow path where animals bleated and squealed from cages on either side. Most were nothing out of the ordinary, but the same couldn't be said for the smell. I stopped, gagging at the most offensive odor I'd ever encountered. "Is there another route?"

"Not unless you want to go by yourself. I'm not supposed to be here, remember?"

My eyes were already starting to water. What the *hell* was that? "And the dwarves don't come this way?"

"*Nobody* comes this way since they moved in the bonnacon."

He nodded at a huge shaggy animal with small curled horns pacing back and forth in a nearby pen. Unlike the other large animals, this one wasn't in a barbed wire cage. Instead, pieces of corrugated aluminum had been nailed haphazardly to the sides of a wooden frame, creating a pen that was almost six feet high. Maybe the height was to help block the smell, but if so, it wasn't working. I'd encountered poison gas that didn't reek like that.

"Do I want to know?"

"You really don't," Dieter said as we edged around.

A large black nose with a ring through it poked over the top of the pen as we passed, and a low, menacing sound issued from behind the metal. "I don't think he likes you," Dieter observed.

I would have made a comment about that making us even, but it would have required taking a breath.

We finally emerged into (relatively) fresh air beside a packed bar. It was outlined with a row of lanterns made out of green and amber beer bottles. They swayed cheerfully on their wires, splashing moving colors on the floor below. Behind the counter, vegetables were being stir-fried in huge, shallow pans, sending clouds of fragrant steam skyward. My stomach reminded me that I'd skipped lunch, but we didn't stop there.

A couple streets over was an even more impressive establishment, in a tent formed out of army blankets. Over the entrance, someone had rigged an old Vegas sign: COCK-TAILS was spelled out in fat, fifties-era orange bulbs. Inside, hot dogs sizzled on a cinderblock grill next to the bar and every folding card table had its own flickering candle. They weren't needed for lighting, but added to the unexpectedly inviting atmosphere.

We didn't stop there, either.

We did stop at the entrance to a small dark cave, sitting all on its own at the end of a side street. Once my eyes adjusted, I understood the reason for the lousy lighting—and why the place made no effort to advertise. The smugglers, assassins, illegal arms dealers and narcotic pushers that made up 90 percent of its clientele probably preferred their privacy. I recognized half a dozen wanted criminals slouched at tables in the shadows. One must have recognized me, too, or maybe just what I was. He raised a glass in a mock salute. He knew I wouldn't take him in—not when he'd be back on the street in an hour.

"Stop looking like that!" Dieter said, sounding a little stressed.

"Like what?"

"Like you want a fight!"

I realized that my hand had automatically gone to my potion belt. I slowly removed it, and the shadowy shapes on either side of the door relaxed slightly. We threaded our way through the crowd to a slab of plywood raised on sawhorses—the bar, I assumed. The tables were packed, but the area around the bar was empty. That probably had something to do with the presence of a large, reeking Awsang behind the counter.

"That's Tilda," Dieter said, appearing unfazed by the smell. I found that I wasn't that bothered myself. I had new standards now, excitingly.

I perched on a stool and summoned up a smile. It was a little hard to tell if Tilda smiled back. She was busy slurping something from a plastic Burger King cup through her hairy proboscis. Since Aswangs are carrion-eaters, I was just as glad I couldn't see what half-rotten delicacy lay inside.

"Beer in a bottle?" I asked hopefully.

The slurping continued. Guess that meant no.

"I'm looking for a friend," I told her, figuring it was worth a shot. I reached for my wallet intending to show her Cyrus's photo, but found that it was gone. And a moment later, so was the stool. I hit the floor and a giggling kobald scurried out from under me, heading for the door as fast as his child-like legs could carry him.

My lasso caught him around one chubby foot before he could make his escape. He tried to shake it off, but I strengthened the spell and started dragging him back, ignoring the stream of profanity I couldn't understand anyway. He wiggled and squirmed and left furrows in the dirt floor with his fingernails, but I wrestled him closer. Until he shape-shifted again, into a column of fire, which the lasso couldn't hold.

He flew out of the door on a wash of sparks, but with no hands he'd been forced to drop my wallet. It hit the floor with a *thud* and a sizzle, so I lassoed it instead, put out the flames and pulled out Cyrus's photo. There was no visible reaction from the barmaid to any of this.

I added a twenty to the picture, and the bill disappeared faster than I could blink. But Tilda only shook her head. "She doesn't know him," Dieter translated unnecessarily.

"He might have been in Were form—"

I was going to describe his markings, but never got the chance. Tilda spat a great wad of brown-tinted yuck on the floor. "She doesn't serve Weres," Dieter interpreted.

"Why not?"

"Since you guys left, the gangs have turned into a major pain in the ass. They're all bad, but the Weres are the worst. Like this morning, a bunch of them burnt out the settlement where I was staying. I lost everything."

"That sucks. So do you see him?"

Dieter put his head down on the bar. "I lose my entire stash, get caught by that fucking bounty hunter and meet you—all in the same day. My life more than sucks. Sucking would be a step up."

"Yeah. So do you see him?" I repeated.

"See who?"

"You said there was a wardsmith here," I reminded him, striving for patience.

Dieter's eyes flitted around the bar, or at least as much of it as he could see without actually sitting up. "Guess he's not here today. He don't come in all the time."

If he'd had any hair left, I'd have pulled it. "Do you know where he is when he's not here?"

Dieter gave a horizontal type of shrug. Then he seemed to find an idea worth getting vertical. "You know, if you bought me a drink, it might—" I slammed a knife down, catching his collar and pinning his head back to the bar. "You could have just said no," he told me irritably.

"Answer the question!"

He rolled his eyes up at Tilda. "That ward guy been in here lately?" She made some odd noises that in no way resembled speech, but Dieter seemed to understand. "She said he's got a shop around the corner, only he likes to drink so he's usually here. But she hasn't seen him today."

"What's the name of the shop?"

"They don't have names. But you'll know it."

"How?"

"Well, a little clue would be that it has 'wards' over the door," he said, pretty sarcastically for a guy with a knife millimeters from his jugular. But then, considering his personality, it probably wasn't all that unusual for him. "Can I get up now?" he whined.

I pulled out the knife and manhandled him out of the bar. Around the corner, we came across a support column that seemed to serve as a sort of community message board. Up close, it was obviously dwarf-made, smooth and organic-looking, like wind-sculpted rock. Only the wind wasn't responsible: the minerals needed to form it had been magicked from the surrounding soil.

We found an ad for "wards and charms" and directions to a shop near the end of the path, in a primo location where three trails merged. It was the usual tent made of army blankets and two-by-fours, but was bigger than most and had a plank with a hand-painted thunderbird above the entrance. It didn't actually say "wards," but around here, a pictogram was probably better anyway. I pushed back the blanket serving as the door and we went in.

The tent appeared to have several rooms, with the outer fixed up as a showroom. A lantern swung overhead, casting golden light over a couple chairs, a tattered Navajo rug, a floor-length mirror and a glass showcase. There didn't appear to be anybody here.

I walked over to the showcase. Two glasses stood on the counter, the light through their contents casting a pink stain over the case. I bent over and sniffed the nearest one—and almost passed out.

"Is this what I think it is?" I held it out to Dieter.

He snatched it and took a long breath. "Whoa. No wonder he stopped buying from me!"

"The wardsmith was a customer?" Dieter suddenly looked shifty. "I won't turn you in," I told him impatiently. "I'm after a killer, not a drug user."

"A killer?" His expression veered into panic.

"No one you need to worry about. Now answer the question!"

"He bought pretty regular," Dieter admitted, his eyes on the bright swirl of ruby liquid. "That's how I knew him."

"But you didn't sell him this?"

"Are you kidding? That's Fey wine!"

"Isn't that your stock in trade?"

He rolled his eyes. "I sell punch, okay?"

"What's the difference?"

He picked up the glass and held it next to the other. "That." The contents of the second glass were pale pink, the color of rosé. The liquid in the one I'd handed him was a deep bloodred.

"Punch is cut." I guessed. A lot, judging by the color.

"Hell, yeah. Full strength, that shit'll make a vamp drunk!"

"What would it do to a human?"

Dieter shrugged. "Depends how long he's been using. You build up a tolerance after a while. But I don't know any human who uses it straight. By the time you get that far in, you're usually gone."

"Gone?"

He made the circle around his temple that was the universal sign for crazy. Great. The guy I needed to question might be passed out somewhere, or worse.

I tipped the contents of the uncut glass onto the dirt floor and scraped my boot across it. Dieter's face fell. "Aw, man! Do you know what that was worth?"

"About ten years, assuming you don't have any priors. You need to find a new line of work."

"Maybe I should start making wards," he said sullenly. "This guy must be doing okay to afford the pure stuff."

I followed his gaze downward, to the case the glass had been sitting on. It was full of small gold wards. Nice ones.

A chill ran up my back.

Dieter slid open the back of the case and picked one up. It was more like a chain than a charm, consisting of six ants linked together in a golden line. "Hey, what do you think this one does?"

"I don't know." I was more concerned about why the case hadn't been spelled shut.

The blanket covering the door into the next room fluttered slightly. I pulled a gun, moved carefully around the case and snatched it open. "Auggh!" Dieter let out a screech, and I almost shot him.

"What the hell is wrong with you?"

"Look!" He stuck out his right hand. The ants had done what they were designed to do and melted into his skin. They were roaming around, checking out the territory, crawling over his fingers and down to his wrist.

"You shouldn't pick up powerful wards without knowing what they do."

"*Now* you tell me?" He started jumping around, shaking his hand uselessly. The ants ignored him. So did I.

A walk-through of the next room yielded nothing of interest, except that a cabinet full of expensive supplies was unlocked and unspelled. Yet there was no sign of a struggle. There was also no third room where the wardsmith might be taking an ill-advised nap. He was simply missing.

I went back into the front and found Dieter half naked. He'd torn his shirt off and was slapping at his chest. The ants had crawled up his arm to his torso, where they were roaming around like dogs on a scent.

I felt around in my pocket for the numb stick, and looked up to find Dieter glaring at me. "Do something! You got me into this, you crazy bitch!"

"That's witch," I said mildly, and left the numb stick where it was.

The glass case contained a few dozen wards, mostly smaller ones that you could buy in any shop. But a few were outstanding, including a large elk, a popular Native American totem for stamina. I shielded my hand and picked it up. A smooth, steady energy throbbed under my fingertips.

I couldn't figure out what a wardsmith this good was doing in Tartarus. Even with a drinking problem, most shops would take him on, or at least buy his work—and for more than he was likely to get here. Wards like this were worth their weight in gold these days, and those that could be used as weapons were even more—

Dieter suddenly thrust a long, pale foot onto the display case. He was down to a pair of faded blue briefs, so the movement gave me more of a view than I liked. "Look! Look what they're doing!"

The ants had congregated around a bruise on his ankle and appeared to be nibbling away at it. Every time one of them took a bite, a tiny piece of the bruise disappeared, replaced with unblemished skin. "Cool."

"They're *eating* me!"

"They're healing you," I told him. "Shut up."

I glanced down at the case, and noticed something strange. All the wards were totems associated with things like healing, stamina or defense. I knelt and checked out the under stock, and it was the same story. Not a single one was for combat, despite the fact that those were the ones bringing in the most money these days.

I stared down at the gleaming menagerie and it stared back, unable to tell me if I was onto something or if I'd started off on a wild-goose chase. I was beginning to think the latter sounded the most likely. All I had for a day's work were some expensive wards and a missing wardsmith, neither of which might have anything to do with Cyrus.

It wasn't unusual for a bunch of outcasts to stockpile weapons. The war had a lot of people paranoid, and *vargulfs* had no clan to back them up if they got into trouble. And a bunch of Weres might prefer those weapons in the form of wolves.

As for the wardsmith, he was probably passed out some-where, courtesy of too much wine. Waiting for him to wake up and stumble back wasn't too appealing when he might not have anything useful to tell me. Barring more clues from Cyrus, my best option was old-fashioned police work. I needed to know where he'd been seen last, who he'd talked to, who had been with him. I could circle back and question the wardsmith later, assuming he ever showed up.

"Get dressed," I told Dieter. "We're out of here."

I checked my phone, having some questions for Jamie or Caleb, but I didn't have any bars. And then I didn't have a phone, either, because one of Dieter's flailing arms ripped it out of my hand. He was dancing around again because the ants were on the move. They'd finished with the ankle, leaving only pale skin and coarse black hair behind, and were crawling up the inside of his leg.

He brushed at them frantically until they disappeared beneath the edge of his boxers. And then he lost it. He tore the shorts off, slapping at his butt and various other things while I went for my phone. And found something a lot more interesting.

Dieter's dance had disturbed the rug, revealing a line in the sand covering the floor. I retrieved my phone, tossed the rug back and found a trapdoor. And a second later, I found the wardsmith.

8

HE'D been folded double and wedged into the small space so tightly that it took me several minutes to get him out. But it was obvious from the start that there was no real rush. A cigarette still dangled from his lips, but there were no lungs left to smoke it with. They'd been torn out along with the rest of his chest.

It had been a Were attack. The claw marks were clearly visible, but I didn't really need them. Few things kill a man so fast that he doesn't even have time to look afraid.

I heard an odd, choking sound, and looked up in time to see Dieter's bare ass heading out the door. I threw a lasso spell after him, but only got it around one leg. He went down, scrabbling for purchase in the dust. A few people stuck their heads out of nearby tents, attracted by the noise, and wasn't that just all I needed.

"Cut it out!" I told him, irritably, but he either didn't hear or didn't care. He turned over onto his back and started kicking his leg, trying to shake the spell off, but only succeeded in tightening it further. "He can't hurt you," I pointed out, reeling him in.

"It's not him I'm worried about!" He leaned back, trying

to use his weight against the spell, but that just resulted in him getting yanked down the street in little hops, one leg stuck out straight in front of him. I gave a final heave and he fell through the door, his nose landing maybe a foot from the corpse. "Auggh!"

"Just tell me what you know," I said, because something had really spooked him. I couldn't believe that this was the first dead body he'd seen—he lived in Tartarus after all.

"That's the Predators' mark!" He pointed a shaking finger at the deep wounds on the man's chest. "They always leave the body carved up like that. It's like their signature or something."

"The Predators?"

"A Were gang. One of the worst!" He took off again and this time, I let him go. Things were starting to get a little dangerous for a bystander, even a not-entirely innocent one.

I bent over the wardsmith again. He had a bent back, a scraggly beard, pouchy cheeks and was wearing an old pair of jeans and a faded sweatshirt. He looked like a street person, but the Thunderbird tat on his arm was a stunner. I'd never seen one like it, and it practically screamed quality. It was also a talisman, or it would have fallen free of the body when he died and his magic failed.

I brought out the three wards I'd found in the sofa and compared them. Each wardsmith has his or her own personal style, sort of a signature on their pieces. An expert could probably have told at a glance whether the same hand had made these. Unfortunately, I wasn't one. But there was something in the rounded, almost abstract quality of the pieces that looked awfully—

The attack came so fast that I never even heard it—at least consciously. But my shields slammed into place right before a blow landed across my chest, jarring through my bones into my teeth. If I hadn't had shields, it would have killed me. As it was, I went skidding on my back through the side of the tent and across the road, before rolling into the open side of a used-clothes shop.

I landed in a pile of sweaters the proprietor was sorting

and bounced back up, fighting with the smothering blanket
I'd taken with me. I tore free just in time to see someone
lunge for me in a blur of motion. And the next thing I knew
I was flying backward through the air with what felt like
half my ribs broken. I struck down with a thud that jarred
my whole body, momentarily knocking my breath out, and
then he was on me.

The guy—young, greasy brown hair, angular face, baggy
pants—was one of the Weres I'd fought in the first drain,
the one who had taken a bullet in the leg. Only the wound didn't
appear to be slowing him down much. He hadn't changed,
which limited his strength, but then, he was doing fine without it. He picked me up by the legs and began bouncing me
back and forth between the floor and the low, rocky ceiling,
trying to pop my shields.

It wasn't exactly a textbook maneuver, but it was doing a
hell of a job anyway. I'd have flung a spell, but the commotion had brought people running out of their booths, clog-
ging the walkway. A Were would shrug off anything safe
enough to use around the vendors, and the ricochet effect in
here meant no guns.

I was trying to get a hand on my potion belt when he slung
me into a column. My shields collapsed, my head struck
rock and everything whited out for a second. I blinked back
to consciousness in time to see a blur of motion streaking
down the corridor, about the same moment I realized that
the wolf wards were gone. Damn it!

I got up and then went back down to one knee, as a stab
of agony ran through my temple and spread over my skull.
My head was spinning, my wrist had almost been wrenched
off and whatever had been done to my chest was making it
hard to breathe. That was okay. I wasn't planning any hero-
ics in a cavern full of civilians. I just wanted to get close
enough to get a tag in place.

By the time I got to my less-than-steady feet, the screaming had reached earsplitting decibels. That seemed a little
odd for a group used to Weres acting badly. And then a
crowd of people almost ran over me, headed for the back of
the cavern. One of them was the Were.

He blew past me like lightning, and close on his heels was a huge, malodorous beast with small curled horns, a large shaggy body and an evil glint in its eye. Someone had let the bonnacon out, and it seemed to have a grudge against Weres, or at least against this one. It let out a bellow worthy of an enraged ox and plowed past me at a full gallop. The fumes in its wake were almost suffocating, but even worse, everywhere the creature went a trail of destruction followed. And not merely because it weighed a couple tons and didn't bother sticking to the paths. But because—

"Oh, my God!"

"Cool, huh?" I glanced over my shoulder and saw Dieter. He'd acquired some jeans and a pair of sandals, courtesy of one of the abandoned shops, I assumed. He also appeared to have found some backbone. Instead of shaking, he was bouncing on his toes, looking pleased with himself.

"It shits *napalm*?"

"I said you didn't want to know."

"I assume you let it out?"

"Yep."

"Why?"

"'Cause this is why everybody pitched in and bought the thing. Bonnacons hate wolves; it's like they're natural enemies or something."

"I meant, why help me?"

"I wasn't. That fucker was one of those who burnt me out this morning."

"He's a Predator? You're sure?"

"Damn right I'm sure! I woke up to see my tent burning over my head and that bastard holding a torch. I lost everything because they decided they didn't need the competition." He grinned as the Were ran past screaming, with his hair on fire. "Let's see how he likes it!"

The Were didn't seem to be liking it. It also distracted him enough that he ran full tilt into the large COCKTAILS sign, which crashed to the floor, sending bulbs bouncing and then shattering against the hard-packed ground. A second later, he changed, leapt over a counter and was gone—impossibly fast for so huge a beast.

"You said you were staying off Decatur, right?" I asked Dieter.

"Yeah."

I smiled. I hadn't managed to tag the Were, but it didn't worry me too much. You don't need a tag when you have an address.

"So, we going back to jail now?" Dieter asked hopefully.

"Naw. They'd just process and release you."

"Yeah, but sometimes they feed us first."

I tucked a fifty in his jeans. "Lunch is on me."

IT took me precious minutes to get out of Tartarus. The old man weighed maybe a hundred and fifty pounds, and no way was I in any shape to carry him out of there. But leaving him behind wasn't an option, either. Not with a ten-thousand-dollar tat on his arm and a hungry Aswang in the vicinity.

I would have normally used magic, but right then I didn't have any to spare. So I rigged up a travois out of plywood and blankets from the shop and dragged him out. Weak sunlight was filtering through angry clouds when I emerged, matching my mood. I leaned against the side of the drain, heedless of the mildew sliming my coat, and dug out my phone. The fact that it took me three tries to grab it probably wasn't a good sign.

"You wouldn't happen to have seen a young man?" Caleb asked, before I got a word out. "Bad skin, lots of piercings, dreads—"

"Doesn't ring a bell."

"Well, I'm sure it'll come up at your court-martial!" Jamie said heatedly. Oh, great. We were on speakerphone.

"I don't think I'm likely to be put on trial for borrowing a junkie for a few hours."

"No, but you might be for disobeying the direct command of a senior officer!"

"Hargrove isn't that much of a—"

"Not him! Sedgewick! The old man told him he'd sent you on an errand, or he'd have you up on charges right now!"

"*Hargrove* is covering for me?" Okay, now I knew I was hallucinating.

"Yeah, and I'd love to know the story behind that one," Caleb put in.

"So would I," I told him. "But it'll keep. Right now, I need some—"

"You need your head examined!" That was Jamie, of course.

"Yeah. Concrete is pretty hard when you get slammed into it by a three-hundred-pound Were."

There was a brief silence. "Is that the body the patrol just brought in?" Caleb demanded.

"I've only tagged two today so far, so—"

"And where's the other one?" Jamie again.

"Tartarus. Some big market over by the Tropicana. I found a wardsmith stuffed into his own drop safe and then got jumped by a Were. He stole some wards, so I'm assuming he's the one who did him, although—"

"What wardsmith? What was his name?"

"Like I said, we never made it as far as introductions. But he was still warm when I arrived; no rigor. So I'm guessing—"

"What did he look like?"

"Would you let me finish a sentence?"

"It's important, Accalia."

Something in his tone cut through the static. Not to mention that he never used my full name. "Older guy, shabby clothes, Thunderbird tat on his left arm—"

"Shit!"

Jamie didn't say anything else, and Caleb took over. "Sounds like you've had a busy day. Why not come in? We can get your story straight before you see Sedgewick."

"Can't, although it would be great if you could reroute a patrol by here to pick up the body."

There was some quiet conversation I couldn't quite hear, and then Caleb came back on the line. "Will do. It'll be about fifteen minutes."

"I'll be here."

I passed the time on the phone with a guy I know in

research. The Predators were composed of outcast wolves, as I'd assumed. There were twenty to thirty of them and they were known for being big dealers of illicit drugs—including the Fey variety. I guess I knew what Dieter had meant about competition. They also had a reputation for brutality.

"I kind of got that from the name," I said, as an ambulance came around the corner. Four guys got out, two medics and . . . crap.

"Nice to see you, too," Caleb said, hiking an eyebrow at me. I guess I might have said that last bit aloud.

"Where is he?" Jamie demanded, splashing through the current. A stretcher was whizzing through the air behind him, trying to keep up. That was definitely not SOP in an open area in broad daylight, any more than was the huge sword he'd slung over his back. But Jamie didn't look like he gave a damn.

I indicated my makeshift travois, which I'd parked inside the drain to keep it out of sight of passersby. Jamie knelt beside it and pulled back the blanket. And said a word he rarely employed in the presence of a lady—or even me.

"You knew him?"

"His name was Toby Wilkinson, and he was a damn fine wardsmith."

The two orderlies reached us and transferred the body to the stretcher. "Why was a talented wardsmith hanging around the drains?" I asked.

"Because he was a stubborn old coot who wouldn't listen to reason, that's why!"

"Could you be a little more—"

"Six years ago, Toby was one of the best weapons-grade wardsmiths in the southwest. Then a group of kidnappers took his daughter and demanded an exorbitant ransom. Toby paid it instead of coming to us, afraid they'd kill his only child if he didn't do precisely as he was told."

"I'm assuming they killed her anyway?"

Jamie nodded. "Didn't want to risk being identified. But it wasn't her death that sent Toby over the edge. It was the fact that they killed her using one of his own wards."

"Jesus."

"What could they possibly have hoped to gain by that?" Caleb asked.

"Nothing. That was the devil of it. We caught them eventually and one of them cracked. Said they'd thought it would be quieter than shooting her or some such. It was pure coincidence that the ward they used to suck the life out of her was one made by her father."

"And afterward?" I asked, pretty sure I already knew.

Jamie shrugged. "Toby went off the rails. He started drinking, lost his practice, disappeared for a few years. The next time I saw him, he'd hung out his shingle in Tartarus. Turns out he'd been studying with some Native American master out in Arizona—healing spells, defensive wards and the like."

"And weapons. I didn't find any in his shop, but I'm pretty sure he was killed over some wolf tats. And I didn't think they were used for defense."

"They're not. But Toby didn't make weapons. He swore he'd never again allow his energy to be used to destroy the innocent."

"Are you sure? Because—"

"He's dead, isn't he?" Jamie snapped. "I warned him when we had to pull out that Tartarus wasn't safe—not with his inventory and with the price of wards these days. I practically begged him to at least make a few weapons for his own use. He flat-out refused."

I frowned. This case was getting murkier, not clearer, as I went along. I needed some answers, and I knew of only one person who might have them.

"What are we waiting for?" Jamie echoed my thoughts. "Let's go!"

"Go where?" I asked, starting to worry.

"Don't tell me you don't know who did this!" He glared at me, hands on hips, red-gray hair flying, face fierce. His whole five-three frame was quivering with emotion.

"I have an idea, yes."

"Or where to find him?"

"Yes to that, too. I was waiting around to ask if you know anything about the drain over on Decatur."

"I know everything about it," Jamie said impatiently.

"Can you draw me a map of the interior?"

"I'll do better than that. I'll show you!" He hopped back into the drain, splashed over to where I'd left my bike and threw a leg over.

"Jamie!" He waved, started the engine despite not having a key and took off in a cloud of dust, leaving Caleb and me staring after him.

"I didn't know he could ride," Caleb said, as Jamie ripped through a median, slung across the path of an oncoming truck, jumped the sidewalk, clipped a streetlight, wobbled, corrected, and tore away in a squeal of my tires.

"He can't."

"Maybe we can get a ride with the ambulance," Caleb offered after a moment.

Well, crap.

9

THE ambulance let us off on a patch of raw desert by Decatur Road. Jamie was nowhere to be seen, but my bike was leaning against a chain-link fence. The fence protected what had been an open air channel and was now a raging river.

A few dust-dry areas still ringed the sides of the channel, but through the middle, the wash seethed. Water with a skim of oil and gas rushed past a corroded stove, lying on a rapidly diminishing sandbar. Trash—beer bottles, cigarette butts, and fast-food wrappers—bobbed in the current, swirling madly toward a tunnel protected by a large grate and a patch of weeds.

I stared at it dubiously. This had seemed simple enough in my head: the gang lost their old hideout this morning, so they burnt out their rivals in the shantytown to make themselves a new one. But the reality wasn't looking so cut and dried. I glanced around, but there didn't appear to be any lookouts. Maybe they thought that with Were hearing they didn't need any.

Or maybe no one was crazy enough to want to hide out in the middle of a river.

"Could we have the wrong address?" I asked hopefully.

"My luck's not that good," Caleb muttered, swinging himself onto the fence. I hauled myself up after him and we dropped to the other side.

Even standing on the bank, I could feel the ground tremble. Angry gray floodwater rushed around my legs and threatened to sweep me off my feet as we angled into the channel and sloshed across to the grate. It was festooned with newspapers and old crime scene tape, which it was attempting to keep out of the maybe four-by-four tunnel opening. Caleb shone his flashlight inside. "See anything?"

"No." Nothing good, anyway. Water churned around a small area just inside, like acid in a stomach. It foamed along grimy walls, mixing with bits of trash that had made it past the grate, before being sucked down the dark gullet of a tunnel. I could feel the current growing, pushing relentlessly against my shins, trying to shove me inside the hungry mouth.

And my doubts grew along with it.

What if all the gang knew about was the death of the old man? Yes, I wanted them brought in for that, but waiting a little while wouldn't do further harm to Wilkinson. The same couldn't be said for Cyrus. And this little trip seemed less and less likely to yield results the longer I thought about it.

With a setup like that, I was surprised Wilkinson hadn't been murdered long ago. And although it hadn't looked like anything had been taken, I didn't know what he'd kept on hand. As for the Were, maybe he'd followed me from the first drain, waiting for the opportunity to reclaim his property. He might not have had anything to do with Wilkinson at all.

Likewise, the fact that that body had been dumped along 91 might have nothing to do with the gang. Maybe the Hunter had placed it there at random. Maybe he'd learned that the gang was using the drain for a hangout and was taunting them. Maybe a lot of things. Because the other alternative was that a bunch of Weres were hiding a Hunter. And why did I have trouble believing that?

I started to pull back, but stopped when the drain flickered out, like a T.V. switching stations. For a moment there was nothing, no rushing water, no dark tunnel. And then I was staring at Cyrus.

He was standing in his living room, clutching a small plastic guitar. "I Love Rock 'n' Roll" was blasting from the T.V. And a woman who looked a lot like me was standing in the kitchen behind him, holding a small casserole dish.

"Okay, rock star. I think it's done," she said, sounding dubious.

"I'm almost through," he told her, fingers flying. He was going to win this with human speed, damn it. If every nine-year-old in the country could do it, how hard could it be?

"You realize that's only level one, right?"

"You mean, sort of like making a soufflé?" She'd been at it all day, with much creative cursing. It still amazed him that a woman who brewed her own potions couldn't cook worth a damn.

"A soufflé is Freebird on expert," she said crossly, as the last few notes faded away.

Your mother doesn't count as a fan, *the screen informed him.*

Damn nine-year-olds.

He joined her in the kitchen to find her staring into a small white container and biting her lip. They watched as the contents slowly melted, like the witch in The Wizard of Oz. *"We could try it,"* he offered manfully.

"Try what? There's nothing left!" She poked at the sad remains with a spoon.

Cyrus threw an arm around her shoulders and kissed her flour-streaked cheek. She was warm and smelled like butter and spices and Lia. He was suddenly starving, but not for food.

"You know what they say about the best way to a man's heart?"

"Yeah."

"They lie."

An hour later, she dropped a daub of sauce from the calzones they'd ordered in, and he leaned over the kitchen table and caught her wrist, putting his mouth over the pulse point. He slowly licked the sauce away, daring her with his eyes. The taste of her pulse under his tongue was enough to escalate the slow rolling pleasure of her company into something more. He wanted. Now.

They'd been dating for months, but he sometimes wondered if she realized it. Lunches and dinners spent talking about her cases had slid into movie nights at his place, laundry dates at hers and weekends spent riding the motorcycles they both loved. Yet she still treated him more like a colleague than anything else.

It was driving him out of what was left of his mind.

She grinned, and it was purely her, the insolent charm that made him respond to her from the very beginning. "All right, rock star. Let's see what you've got." He just sat there for a moment, sure he'd misunderstood. Until she laughed and pulled him up from the table. "You keep looking at me like that, and we won't even make it to the bed."

They did, although he was never quite sure how.

The scene abruptly flipped back to the drain and I staggered, the water almost sucking me through the opening. A hand came down on my shoulder and Caleb said sharply, *"Lia,"* in the tone that meant he'd said it at least three times before.

I grabbed on to him, breathless, queasy and more than a little freaked out. That just didn't get any easier. Especially not when viewed through someone else's eyes.

"What is it?" he demanded. "What happened?"

"Nothing." I got my legs back under me. "It's just . . . I think we might be in the right place, after all."

Caleb looked uncertain, staring past me into the drain like he thought something was about to jump out at us.

And then something did.

"What! Hold!" Jamie threw a shield up, which knocked Caleb's spell awry. It bounced off and crashed into the water on our left, sending a great wash of steam into the air. "Are ye daft, man?"

"Sorry." It looked like I wasn't the only one who was a little jumpy. But Caleb recovered fast. "Why'd you go in without us?" he demanded. "What if you'd had a seizure in there? What if it left your head under water?"

"What if you stop acting like I have one foot in the grave?" Jamie shot back. "And I went in because I needed to check on conditions."

"How are they?"

"Bad. And going to get worse. It's raining in the mountains."

"So? We're here," I pointed out.

"Vegas sits at the bottom of a basin," he said impatiently. "It's surrounded by mountains and a lot of hard desert soil used to four or five inches of rain *a year*. When it gets a couple all at once, like the forecast for today, it can't handle it and all that water comes running down here. That's why the drainage system was created in the first place."

"I think we can handle a few inches!"

"Inches in the mountains translates to feet here. And of all the drains in the system, this is the worst to be caught in during a flood. It runs all the way under the Strip, with no manholes or cross tunnels to catch you. If a wall of water came up behind us, we could be washed for miles."

"We have shields," I reminded him.

"And how long do you think they'll last when we're slamming into concrete like three idiots in a pinball machine?"

"So you're saying we need to do this fast?"

"I'm saying we need to do this later!"

I shook my head violently. "Cyrus is in there. It has to be now!"

I pushed into the drain, which at this point mostly involved just letting go of the outer edge of the inlet. It swept me through the mouth of the tunnel and onto what remained of a sandbar. The noise was deafening, with the small, enclosed space amplifying every sound. Each car rattling overhead sounded like a 747 taking off, and the river around my legs roared like the ocean. But at least I couldn't hear Jamie cursing anymore.

Once I got back to my feet, I discovered that the tunnel itself was fairly spacious. But that was the only good thing. The air was murky and the same shade as the water, but I didn't dare use a flashlight. In the inlet, it could be mistaken for sunlight; farther in, it would immediately announce the presence of an unwanted visitor.

But without light, it was difficult to imagine how I was supposed to find anyone in here. There were no markers, no stuttering wards, no anything. Just a long, dark tunnel and me. *If there was ever a time for metaphysical bread-crumbs,* I thought, just before an image vivid enough to touch slammed into me.

Cyrus ended up on his back, with Lia prowling up his body. She'd left her hair undone and it flowed over her shoulders in a dark wave, tickling his chest after she stripped his shirt off. His hand slid under that shining mass, the strands sliding silken-slick between his fingers, to grasp her nape. He brought her down for a scorching kiss before skimming down her back and over the sweet curves below. She groaned and that combined with the skin to skin contact to bring a growl to his throat.

"Down, boy," she told him, sitting up to straddle his shoulders. Her eyes were a perfect ice gray in the moonlight filtering through his bedroom curtains. Wolf eyes.

The brief glimpse into Cyrus's brain flickered out, leaving me staring into the dense gloom of the drain. That was all right, I told myself as I pushed off from the wall. It looked like I had a guide.

The pressure against my legs doubled as I moved forward into the channel, because the water was compressed into a smaller area. Making things even more interesting were the seams in the concrete where the rectangular drains had been slapped together. They formed dangerous ledges underwater, vying with rocks and bottles and submerged sandbars to see which could trip me first.

"Why would the gang kidnap your boyfriend?" a voice demanded.

I whirled to find Jamie right behind me. All the noise had muffled his footsteps, and I hadn't heard him approach. "I'm not real clear on that yet," I said, lowering my gun. "But Caleb's right. You shouldn't be here."

"And you should?"

"This isn't Corps business. It's personal."

"And what d'ye think it is for me?" Jamie demanded. "I'm not about to let Toby's killer walk free!"

"You're the one who just said we should leave!"

He threw his hands into the air. "Because no one's here! Tartarus dwellers are very conscious of the weather—they have to be. They probably cleared out hours ago—"

"Not this group."

"Are we going to do this or not?" Caleb asked, appearing out of the gloom.

Jamie rounded on him. "I don't even know why you're here!"

Caleb raised an eyebrow. "I see better in the dark than either of you. And you can't take on a whole gang on your own."

"*There is no gang!* If they were here, they'd have to be in the old shantytown. There's no other caves in this drain." Jamie sloshed around a bend and up the tunnel with the surefootedness of someone who knew where he was going. Caleb and I followed as best we could. "There!" He pointed at a decaying ward that was buzzing fitfully, showing glimpses of the room beyond. "And as you can clearly see, there are—"

"A whole lot of Weres in there!"

Caleb threw out a shield as Jamie dove for one side of the entrance. I stayed where I was, scanning the group for Cyrus. He wasn't there, but the guy I'd fought at the market was. He was easy to pick out with all his hair singed off on one side. He met my eyes and a shiver went through the group, a mass change that left us staring at eight full-grown Weres—for about a second. Then they melted into the back wall and were gone.

I ran after them—or tried to. But the ward over this entrance wasn't just for show. I hit what felt like solid rock and bounced back. I watched the ward flicker on and off while Caleb and Jamie were debating whether or not the tunnel could hold up to the blast necessary to take it out. And then I jumped through the next time it failed.

I lost the tail of my coat when the ward flicked back on

again, but no skin. I was across the room in a heartbeat, barely slowing down at the wall. It was an illusion—it had to be—because Weres could do a lot of things, but dissolve into thin air wasn't one of them. I missed the hidden door slightly, and banged my left shoulder on hard stone, but then I was through.

A long tunnel stretched out in front of me, supported by wooden braces every few feet like an old mine shaft. It wasn't lit, and visibility was no better than it had been in the drain. But unlike the tunnels outside, this one was absolutely quiet—no rushing water, no rattling cars, no pounding footsteps. It was as silent as a tomb, and wasn't that a great mental image.

I jumped when Jamie and Caleb came in behind me, even though I'd been expecting it. "Something's wrong," Caleb said, an array of weapons hovering around him like a lethal cloud.

"What gave it away?" Jamie asked testily, throwing up his own shields. He looked pissed, maybe at me for rushing ahead without backup, maybe at himself for overestimating the gang's intelligence. Or possibly the long, silent corridor was creeping him out, too. "The fact that with Were hearing, they should have heard us coming a mile away?"

"Yet instead of ambushing us in the tunnels or attacking when we showed up, they run?" I added, ripping the leech off my wrist. There were no civilians here.

"All of that," Caleb agreed, just as a Were came out of nowhere, slashed at his face and leapt back through the opposite wall.

"Caleb!" I saw him fall, but didn't have time to grab him before the tunnel was suddenly full of Weres.

One lunged for me, and by the time my conscious mind registered it, I was already moving. My elbow slammed back into my assailant's ribs, my body turned into the movement, and I used the momentum to spin my opponent face-first into the nearest wall brace—and was thrown back against the opposite wall hard enough to stagger me. Then the Weres were gone again, like lightning.

"Lia!" It was Jamie's voice.

I looked around, panting. He was on the floor beside Caleb, who was swearing inventively. "How is he?"

"He is feeling like a goddamned punk," Caleb said, struggling to his feet.

I checked him out. It looked like the blow had been hard enough to knock him off his feet, but hadn't gotten through his shields. He was unhurt, except for his pride.

"The gang was using another den until this morning," I told them. "How did they set this up so fast?"

"They didn't," Jamie said, getting to his feet. "We've lost more than one suspect down here through the years and could never figure out why. Looks like the residents of the shantytown carved themselves a back way out."

"A lot of back ways," I amended, wondering which innocent-looking stretch of wall was going to open up next.

"All right. Form up," Caleb ordered, taking point.

"Why do you get to go first?" Jamie groused.

"Because I'm the only one here who can see through illusions," he said, tapping his little dolphin. "Sonar doesn't bounce off them like it does real walls."

We formed up with Jamie in the middle and me bringing up the rear, our shields out and our nerves tight. Or at least, mine were. Caleb was back to his usual, unflappable self. "There's a doorway on either side of us, like a cross tunnel," he told us. "You want to go straight or branch off?"

"How the hell should I know?" Jamie demanded. "There's no way of telling where they are in all this!"

"Lia?"

"Give me a minute." I bit my lip, trying to feel for the bond Sebastian had said was there. I was past doubting him—it was either responsible for the glimpses I'd been getting into Cyrus's brain all day, or else I'd totally lost it. Since Cyrus's life might hang on it, I preferred to believe the former. The only problem was that I still couldn't sense anything.

Come on, Cyrus, I thought desperately. *You've been chatty all day. Don't cut out on me n—*

Her skirt had ridden up to midthigh, and he pushed it higher. She had a few days of stubble on her thighs, enough to feel under his hands as he worked to get the damn dress unbuttoned. He finally tugged it off, leaving her in a scrap of silk thin enough that he could put his mouth on her and still feel her heat. He rubbed his nose against her until she snarled, "Stop teasing."

"You were right," he told her. "You are pushy." Her only answer was to reach back and pop the button on his jeans, pulling his briefs down. She ran a finger over the tip of him, turning his whole body into one exquisite ache. "You win," he gasped, and snapped the flimsy cords on her panties before tossing them aside.

The scene cut out abruptly enough that I staggered and nearly fell. But it had been worth it. Along with the images, I'd received a definite sense that they were coming from somewhere directly ahead. "Go straight," I told Caleb.

"How do you know?"

"I just do. Go!"

A dozen yards ahead, Caleb snapped, "Cross tunnel," seconds before we were jumped from either side. My brain registered the number—too many—and then I wasn't thinking anymore. Just senses, reflexes and training, surer than conscious thought.

Explode a potion grenade, watch sickly green smoke immediately obscure everything. Feel the burn, eyes watering—ignore it—veer to the side as they lunge for my old location. Grab the nearest Were—one in human form. A hard chop to his wrist and bone snaps; he yelps and his hold on his weapon loosens. Twist it out of his hand, shove the Luger to his jaw and pull the trigger twice.

I looked up, searching for another target, but they had vanished like smoke. Caleb was on his feet, breathing a little hard, a glowing whip tight around the neck of a Were in full wolf mode. It was basically the same spell that I used for a lasso, except without the safeguards. As was demonstrated when he pulled away and the head lolled, burnt through to the bone.

"Which way?" Jamie demanded, panting hard, his blade sheened with blood.

His fingers returned to her hips, sweeping up to her back as she moved closer, finding heat and soft, soft skin. Her eyes slid closed, her lips parted as he licked deep into her. She wasn't vocal; the most he received was a soft "oh, yes," but she started to move with him after a few minutes, breathing quick and fierce. He gripped her thighs with both hands and pushed deep, his hips straining helplessly into the air at the sounds she made. She arched against him and came, so hard he felt her throbbing against his tongue.

"Straight!"

We ran.

An arm lashed out of the left-hand wall ahead, and Caleb threw the whip around it, severing it at the elbow. "Cross tunnel!"

Something jumped out at me, all hot stinking breath and yellow eyes, jaws grinning madly as they opened in front of my face. And then disappeared after taking a face full of a potion designed to eat through metal. Something hit like a hammer blow to the small of my back, and I stumbled and went to one knee, but my shields absorbed most of it. At this rate they weren't going to last much longer, and how the hell many of them were there, anyway?

"Which way?" Caleb panted.

She sat back on her heels and gulped a few breaths while his body took him from desperate to something close to crazy. She looked down and laughed, her bare skin gleaming in the low light, taut and smooth except where the sweat beaded and distilled the light. He grabbed for her, his fingers leaving tracks in the sweat on her skin. But she had a hand on his chest, pushing him back down. His wolf growled, taking it as a challenge, but she only grinned and backed down his body, sleek and lithe and fucking slow, and all he could do was lie there while she took her own sweet time.

"Lia!" Caleb was shaking me.

"Straight!"

"There is no straight! There's a cave wall dead ahead!"

"There can't be!" I moved around Caleb, who took up a defensive position at my back. The wall was solid under my hands, with no magical camouflage that I could detect. But I knew what my senses were telling me. "He's here—right here. I can feel it!"

Caleb glanced at me over his shoulder. "There may be a chamber on the other side, but we'll have to go around to get to it. Which way?"

I hit the wall with a fist. "I don't know!"

A Were grabbed Jamie, plucking him off his feet, shields and all, and dragged him through a ward on the left.

"Left it is," Caleb muttered, and dove after him.

1Ø

I started to do the same when an image hit me hard from the other direction.

She sat up over his thighs and worked his jeans the rest of the way down his body. "There's, in the—" he said, and choked off, squeezing his eyes shut as she wrapped her hand around him.

The image cut out as quickly as it had begun, leaving only one thought behind. Cyrus. I needed to get to Cyrus.

I went right.

The side tunnel was smaller, with little room on either side to maneuver. There was no time for subtlety; they already knew we were here. It was only a matter of time before they found me, and moving slowly did not improve the odds. I threw a silence shield over me and pushed ahead, as fast as the narrow opening would allow.

The pale illumination from the main hall cut out after the first curve, leaving me in utter darkness. So I felt my way, trying to go slow enough not to miss anything, while every extra second felt like a betrayal. The shield masked my footsteps and labored breathing, but it also muffled sound coming to me from outside. Not that there appeared to be any.

A silence that was almost physical descended, syrupy and heavy in my ears.

He heard the dresser drawer slide open and the crinkle of a condom wrapper. It got a little easier once she rolled it on him, and then she just climbed on him and slid down in one move, and it went straight from hard to impossible. He heaved up from the bed and she met him halfway, sliding her arms around his neck and licking into his mouth. She could probably taste herself on his tongue, he thought dizzily, as he rolled her over onto her back.

Much later, as he was trying to choose between an imminent heart attack and the unprecedented disgrace of having to ask for a break, she rolled on top of him and whispered in his ear. "You know, you might really be a rock star."

And, okay, maybe he wasn't all that tired.

I tripped on the uneven floor and hit the opposite wall, hard enough to cause my concentration to wobble. The sound shield slipped and I bit my lip on a curse, before carefully reinforcing it. I didn't know why I bothered. I was sweating, my skin hot and stinging where the salt had soaked through the makeshift bandage on my arm and hit the bloody claw marks. And these tunnels didn't reek like the drains, giving me no scent camouflage. A Were would smell me coming a mile away.

The tunnel curved abruptly, bending around to the right again, and dim light stained the walls ahead. It was enough to let me see the dark streak coming at me, flying down the corridor. I fired two blasts from the shotgun and threw myself to the side. A large Were slid to a stop at my feet, half his head missing, a swath of red painting the floor behind him.

I leapt over the body before it stopped moving and, a moment later, the tunnel dead-ended into a small chamber. An electric lamp threw a single pool of light in the otherwise dark room. I had a split second to notice a large shape slumped by a chair, then I was grabbed from behind.

I spun, forcing my attacker into the wall. I pressed up against his back, my forearm locked across his throat, a knife in my hand, coming up—

"Lia!"

I froze for an instant, then my tat managed to focus on my assailant's face. I spun him around and stopped, staring. For a second, I didn't get the whole picture, just pieces here and there. Dark hair stuck up in wild tufts, sweat gleamed at a temple, a bruise decorated a tightly clenched jaw. And there, finally, what I'd hoped to see most—whiskey dark eyes glittering in the low light. Cyrus.

And then I started noticing other things, like the fact that his skin was gray from exhaustion, his lip was split and half his face was a yellowing bruise. But none of that mattered next to the fact that he was unquestionably, miraculously *here* and *alive*. He pulled me to him, slowly, careful not to startle the half-crazed war mage, and then his hands were in my hair and he was kissing me with passionate hunger.

He drew back after a few seconds, and the series of expressions crossing his features—disbelief, incredulity, outrage— was pretty impressive. "What the hell are you doing here?"

I licked my lips, trying to make the transition from making out to making up. "I came to rescue you?"

"Rescue me?"

I glanced around. Cyrus looked pretty beat up, but he was in one piece, which was more than I could say for the Were slumped on the floor behind him. A set of manacles had been ripped out of the wall and the chain wrapped around the creature's neck, hard enough to half sever it from the body.

"Well. It seems awkward now."

"I warned you off—twice! And I know you received the messages!"

"What messages? I haven't heard from you since—"

"The memories!"

"Oh." Those messages. "I thought you were sending me clues how to find you."

Cyrus threw up his hands. "How is sending you Danger/ Ambush an invitation to come closer?"

"You never sent me—"

"The garden hose?"

"What?"

"You ambushed me."

It took me a moment to get it. "Oh, come on! That's hardly the same thing as—"

"At that distance, there was no way to send anything but memories, and the most powerful are the ones we both shared. That's why I sent the soufflé for Disaster. As in, coming in here would be a very bad idea?"

I blinked. "You used my cooking to mean disaster?"

"It was a metaphor."

"And what was the scene at the bar supposed to tell me?"

"What bar?"

"Never mind." It sounded like I'd been picking up on a little more than was intended.

Cyrus bent to relieve the dead guard of his gun and his shirt rode up. He looked as though he'd been stitched together out of spare parts, his belly livid with bruises. I drew in a sharp breath. "You're hurt!"

He shoved the gun in his waistband. "They used me for a punching bag for the last twelve hours, hoping Sebastian would sense it and come looking for me."

"Sebastian?"

"This was a trap for him. Luckily, he was smart enough not to fall for it. What I'd like to know is why you weren't."

I did a little reciprocal glaring, half-pissed, half-scared. You had to do a lot of damage to Weres to outstrip their healing ability, but his body clearly hadn't been able to keep up. I strongly suspected that he was on his feet out of pure stubbornness.

"I came because Sebastian asked me," I told him. "He showed up at Central this morning, after patrol hauled Grayshadow's body out of a ditch—"

"Grayshadow is the one behind this! He was here until a few minutes ago, torturing me. Then you showed up instead and now he's gone to challenge!"

Cyrus strode back the way I'd come. I caught up with him edging around the body of the Were. "I think I'm a little behind on—"

"Yes, you are! Which is why you don't come charging alone into a maze infested with creatures who have nothing left to lose!"

"I thought we'd settled this. It's my job."

"No. Your job is policing the human population. This is Were business. Sebastian had no right—"

"Sebastian had every right! Or am I not part of Arnou?"

Cyrus rounded on me, quietly furious. "You were brought into Arnou *for your protection*! Not so you can take on an entire gang by yourself!"

"And what about you? I wouldn't have been here in the first place if you hadn't decided to take on a Hunter alone!"

"There is no Hunter! And I had no plans to play hero. I was trying to find out who was killing our people. I intended to hand Sebastian any information I discovered and let him deal with it."

"So what went wrong?"

"Everything," Cyrus said bitterly. "Starting with my supposed helper. Grayshadow wants leadership of the clan. He hates the alliance with the humans and he's half insane with ambition. He knows that replacing Sebastian now will not only give him control of Arnou, but will also make him *bardric*."

I shook my head. "There must be some mistake. Grayshadow isn't doing anything these days. We have his body at Central—Sebastian ID'd it for us himself."

"He ID'd the corpse of a *vargulf*, an enemy of the gang Grayshadow hired to help with his scheme. The man was once part of Arnou, so he smelled right, and with that much mutilation, who could tell?"

I sorted through the mass of information he'd just dumped on me, and grabbed the biggest nugget. "You're saying Grayshadow is the Hunter? But he's a Were."

"*There is no Hunter!* Grayshadow used the terror that term holds for us to cover his tracks. If Sebastian had shown up to rescue me, he'd have killed him as he did White Sun and blamed it on the Hunter. Then with both of them dead, he'd waltz into Sebastian's position with no opposition. He's my brother's Third."

"But Sebastian didn't show."

"No, he sent the Corps instead. So Grayshadow has gone with Plan B: to challenge. Sebastian's inability to stop the

Hunter gives him cause. And White Sun was the only warrior Arnou had likely to win against him. No one else will
dare take the challenge, meaning Sebastian will be forced
to fight himself."

"I take it you don't think he can win."

Cyrus paused at the entrance to the main tunnel, breathing heavier than he should have been for the short hike.
"People think that because Sebastian is a diplomat, he's a
pushover. He's not. I've sparred with him enough to know
that. And he's younger and faster than Grayshadow, although
possibly not as strong. If it was a fair fight, it would be an
even contest."

"*If* it was?"

"Grayshadow doesn't want a chance to win," Cyrus told
me grimly. "He wants certainty. And he thinks he's found a
way to get it."

"The wolf wards." A few things started to click into
place.

"You've seen them?"

"I had them in my hand—briefly."

"Well, Grayshadow has them now. He showed them to me
when he returned this afternoon. He wanted to gloat about
the fact that while Sebastian might defeat him, he couldn't
take out five wolves at once."

"Five?"

"Himself and the four wolves he killed. The life force he
stole from them will give him unbelievable strength. No way
can Sebastian stand against that. No single Were could!"

"That's why he was at the wardsmith's," I guessed. "To
pick up the final ward. And once the man had delivered it,
he was of no further use. So he killed him and left one of the
gang behind to wait for me, to retrieve the rest of the weapons once I tracked the guy down."

"I don't know about that. I just know what he plans to do
with them now." Cyrus started for the corridor, but I pulled
him back.

"But why did Grayshadow go to all this trouble? If he
wants to discredit Sebastian, why didn't he just tell everyone
the truth about you? Sebastian said he knew!"

"Because the only way he becomes *bardric* is by inheriting the office," Cyrus said impatiently. "By our laws, the *bardric* is the chief of the leading clan—in this case, Arnou—whoever that may be. But if a new election is called because Sebastian has lost the chiefs' respect—which would almost certainly happen if they found out about me—"

"It would go to Whirlwind of Rand."

"Very likely."

"So instead of discrediting Sebastian, Grayshadow plans to kill him. But that doesn't explain what you think you're going to do."

Cyrus's jaw tightened. "Kill him first."

He changed and slipped out the door so fast, I didn't even see him go. But I heard Jamie curse and the sound of a knife hitting wood. "Jamie, no!" I hit the main tunnel at a run, to find Jamie and Caleb facing off with a huge black and tan wolf.

"It's Cyrus!" I told them.

"That would be more reassuring if his hackles weren't raised," Caleb commented.

"And if he wasn't growling at us," Jamie added, yanking his knife out of a support beam.

"You just tried to stab him!"

"Well excuse the hell out of me!" Jamie said, livid. "It's not like the rest of us can tell the difference! One huge hairy beast looks much like—"

Caleb gripped his shoulder. "Don't go there."

I belatedly realized that my feet were wet. There was maybe an inch of water in the hall, enough to slosh against the sides when I moved. "What's going on?"

"This place is flooding, as I told you," Jamie snapped. "We have to get out of here."

Cyrus bounded away and we followed. Water was inching its way down the tunnel as we neared the warded wall again. The floor must have been slanted, because the farther we went, the deeper it got. It was halfway up my shins by the time we reached the end.

Caleb threw a sound shield around us. "Careful. Some of them are still in the outer room."

I hadn't needed the warning. Someone had a light and it lit them up through the thin skin of the ward, like silhouettes in front of a bonfire. I cautiously stuck my face through the faux clay and got a shock.

The remaining Weres—and shit, there were a lot—were standing on the far side of the cave, near the door. The ward was still coughing and sputtering, hiccoughing floodwater into the cave every time it flickered out. When it flicked back on, the waterfall coming through the gap was chopped off like a neck on a guillotine. The level in the cave was rising fast, but for some reason, the Weres weren't leaving.

Then one of them was shoved forward by an older man with flowing silver hair and a goatee, a leather coat and dusty boots. Cyrus whined softly and I got the idea. Grayshadow.

The younger Were didn't look happy, but he cautiously approached the ward anyway, as if waiting for it to cut out again. It should have been permeable from this side, with no need to wait. But the water must have messed up the charm, because when he tried to jump through as I had, he missed.

Badly.

The ward flicked back on and sliced him in two lengthwise, killing him before he had a chance to scream. One half of his body tumbled back into the cave, the other fell into the river raging in the tunnel outside and was immediately swept away. Grayshadow made an expression of distaste, kicked the remains aside, and selected another guinea pig.

We watched as this one made it through—barely—and another took his place. This one wasn't so lucky. "He's trying to wear out the ward," Jamie muttered from behind me. "He's using them to sap its strength."

"Why are they doing this?" I demanded. "They don't owe him any loyalty! They're outcasts!"

"Not for long," Cyrus said, his voice tight. Jamie and Caleb did a double take. I guess they hadn't thought Weres could talk while in wolf form. Or maybe it was the deep, guttural sound of his wolf voice that startled them. "Grayshadow offered them a place in Arnou once he takes power."

"He's lying!"

"Of course, but they're desperate. It's the best chance,

maybe the only chance, most of them will ever have to regain Clan status. So don't expect them to disobey him— or to show us any mercy."

"Let's make sure we don't need any," Jamie said, pulling his huge sword.

"What is that?" I demanded. It was definitely not standard-issue.

"Claymore. I've noticed that knives don't work too well on these beasties," he told me. And then he charged, throwing himself through the warded stretch of wall, yelling at the top of his lungs.

The rest of us looked at one another, and then plowed through after him.

The reaction was a little different than I'd expected. The odds were heavily in our opponents' favor and Weres don't spook easily. But they were a gang, not trained troops, and they'd already been under enough stress. A screeching war mage brandishing a huge sword was the final straw.

The Weres started shoving toward the door, those in back pushing the rest in the direction of the ward's deadly bite. The ones in front panicked and started fighting back at the same time that we attacked from the rear. And things disintegrated from there.

A few of them either kept their heads or decided they'd have a better chance against us than the door. One ran at the wall, launched himself into the air and landed on four legs instead of two. And jumped straight at me.

I shoved my forearm sideways into his jaw and prayed the spelled leather would keep him from ripping my arm off while I stabbed him hard over and over in the side. He got claws into me anyway, under the shortened hem of my coat, before I could close a shield. I screamed—they hurt like *knives*—and snapped a shield in place.

We staggered together into the wall, my shield trapping his paw. He was unable to finish tearing me apart and unable to pull back, my spelled daggers following him like buzzing hornets. He smashed us into the wall repeatedly, trying to break free, as I struggled to get my gun up.

It was useless; I'd have to drop my shields to fire and

he'd gut me before I could pull the trigger. I concentrated on tightening my shields instead, drawing the power into a tight band around his wrist, slowly squeezing. A moment later his paw popped off in a gout of blood and my shields snapped shut around it.

The Were fell away, howling, and I found to my surprise that I was still in one piece. More or less. And then I was jumped by two more.

There was no more time to think after that. The fight grew too furious, and it was down to reflexes and training. It could have been five minutes or fifty before I looked up to see Jamie sever the neck of one Were, thrust his sword backward to impale a second, jerk it out and whirl to decapitate a third.

Caleb was fighting with his back to the wall a little way off, hard-pressed by two Weres at once. I reached for my potion belt to help him, only to find that it was empty. The pile of half-melted corpses bobbing in the water around me might explain that, but it was no help to Caleb. Then he proved he didn't need any, sending twin fireballs to engulf his opponents.

The bodies fell to the floor, splashing into the lake the cave was fast becoming. There were five more Weres standing, but Cyrus wasn't one of them. Neither was Grayshadow.

I clamped down on the panic rising in my throat, swallowing it back down like nausea. I had to shut down that line of thought before it could take hold. Before it could take me places I couldn't afford to go.

"Where—" I started.

"That way!" Jamie waved his huge sword at the entrance. "The cowardly bastard left a minute ago and your man took off after him."

Caleb nodded. "We can handle this. Go!"

11

THE water level outside the ward was higher than in the cave, coming up chest high on me. And the current was unbelievably fast. It swept me away before I got a single foot on the floor, pushing me down the pitch-black tunnel at a crazy pace.

I crashed through cobwebs, was tossed into unforgiving concrete, and then a pipe in the ceiling poured more water on me as I passed underneath. I surfaced, gasping and spluttering, only to be grabbed by the flow and thrown down a long stretch of tunnel that turned and slanted like a mine shaft. Cement blocks and rocks the size of bowling balls tumbled through the flood, pounding my shields over and over. Every time I started to stand up, the current knocked me down and I finally quit trying.

My waterlogged coat was threatening to drown me, so I shrugged out of it, then narrowly avoided being beheaded by another water pipe. I snagged it with one arm and stared around frantically for some sign of the others. Even with my owl tat, the tunnel was pitch dark, and all I could hear was the wind screaming like a banshee overhead. But I didn't think they'd gone out the way we'd come in. Weres are strong, but they don't have shields. And no one was battling that current without them.

A glance back the other way showed me I was right—two shapes, black on black, were thrashing in the water farther down the tunnel. It might have been my imagination, but I could hear Cyrus's breathing like the beat of my own heart, smell his sweat, see details I shouldn't have been able to pick out in the dark this far away. Which is how I noticed when a rainbow of colors streamed over his face—light from some outside source. And suddenly, they were gone.

I let go of the pipe and the water swept me after them, but not before throwing me against the wall. My shields popped and my shoulder took the brunt, twisting violently. I screamed, but it didn't matter; even wolf ears couldn't hear me over the drain's ceaseless roar.

A sliver of light grew in front of me, the ceiling rolled back and I found myself in an open air channel. Steaming hot rain was sluicing down, daggering into the swirling current and threatening to send my head under. Ahead of me was another tunnel mouth, and curtains of cement rose on either side at least fourteen feet tall.

Even with the flood, that put them well over my head. But they were topped by sturdy metal safety rails. I threw a lasso, but it hit the side of the channel and bounced back, almost snaring me. I let it dissipate and tried again, just as I was sucked into the yawning mouth of the next tunnel. My spell caught on something but I couldn't see what; rain and waves of filthy runoff slapped me in the face, blinding me.

But the lasso held, holding me back from taking a wild ride beneath the Strip. I concentrated on shortening it, slowly pulling myself out of the tunnel's mouth and toward the wall. My reaching hand grazed something rough and I looked up to see a sheer expanse of wet concrete, with the top looking impossibly far away.

Lassos are not usually difficult to maintain, but then, they're not designed to be used for climbing a concrete mountain where one little slip can mean disaster. It was just as well my shields were gone; I couldn't have concentrated well enough to maintain two spells. But the result was that I got battered against the side of the channel as I slowly pulled myself up, my injured shoulder screaming every inch of the way. I shredded my palms hoisting myself over the top, but I made it.

I rolled through the bottom opening of the safety rails and lay flat in the muck and dead leaves, trying to listen past the sound of my heart slamming into my ribcage. What I heard was the same thing I saw—steaming hot rain pouring down like ark-building wouldn't have been a bad idea. After a moment, I staggered to my feet, swaying a little from sheer exhaustion. But there was no time to rest. Ahead, the Strip was backlit by garish plumes of dark clouds, like a Vegas showgirl in full regalia, and in front of that backdrop two dark shapes were engaged in a fight to the death.

The flickering taillights of passing cars cast bands of ruddy light over them, causing their shadows to sprawl monstrously behind them. But even in the dim light, it was obvious where Grayshadow got his name. He moved like gray smoke, faster than any Were I'd ever seen. Faster than Cyrus, who was very obviously losing.

Grayshadow hadn't bothered to change to his wolf form, a studied insult to his opponent. Despite being in what should have been the stronger, faster body, Cyrus had dripping wounds covering his torso, and his right leg was trailing, almost useless. It wasn't hard to see why. There were four jagged gashes in his thigh, each at least six inches long, a mess of crushed and mangled muscles and tendons awash with blood. The skin around the edges was white, crinkled like tissue paper.

It was a bad wound, almost to the bone. In a formal challenge, a wound like that would almost certainly mean death. But this wasn't a formal challenge and I had no compunction at all about cheating.

If only I had something left to cheat with.

My potions were gone, my guns empty, my magic reduced to little more than shields, assuming I could get them up again. I still had my knives, but I'd have to throw them the old-fashioned way and they'd probably do nothing more than make him mad. And hand to hand with a Were was just a messy method of suicide.

Before I could settle on anything, Grayshadow saw me. He gave me a brief contemptuous glance, and the world exploded in pain. My shields had snapped back into place, but they were weak and the assault was like nothing I'd ever experienced. It was as if lightning had struck the ground at my feet. The world went soundless for a moment, full of white light and savage, tearing pain.

And then it was gone, veering off with the fickleness of all wild magic with no proper spell to hold it in thrall. And the final piece of the puzzle slipped into place. "You're the mage," I said, gasping in surprise and pain.

Grayshadow paused, his face twisted in anger. He looked like he thought I should be dead. And I probably would have been, if I hadn't been storing up my magic for most of the day. But that reserve was mostly expended now, along with my remaining strength. My legs felt like jelly and I had to fold my arms to keep them from shaking.

He threw another volley at me, combining the brute force of wild magic with the speed of a Were. It was a deadly combination. The best I could do was to deflect it and send it crashing into the railing, melting a section larger than my body. Grayshadow scowled, watching metal drip down the side of the channel, while I struggled not to let my shields collapse completely.

"Wild magic is difficult to control," I told him, trying not to wheeze. My whole body was clamoring for rest, for oblivion, but I couldn't afford to look like it. "You've obviously been doing some studying."

"Do not presume to think you know me, human."

"Laurentia of Lobizon was my mother," I reminded him. "You are *human*."

Great. The only one who agreed with me was the bad guy.

"Pot, kettle. If you didn't have some human blood yourself, you wouldn't be a mage. Somewhere back in the family tree—"

"You know nothing about me!"

"I know you murder your own kind."

Rage paled his eyes to silver. "Better that than have them remain enslaved to the humans!"

"As opposed to what? Enslaved to the Fey?" It had been a stab in the dark, just something to keep him talking instead of tearing out Cyrus's throat. But I saw when it hit home. "That's how you developed your talents, isn't it? There are almost no Weres born with magical ability, and certainly none as strong as you."

"Because your people made the substance that would free us illegal! Your only advantage over us is your monopoly on magic. Break that, and Weres will rule instead of serve!"

I didn't try to point out that Weres in no way served the magical community, much less the Corps to whom they were much more likely to give orders than to take them. Because you don't argue with a madman. And unless I was very much mistaken, that's what I was dealing with here. His voice was husky with feverish vehemence, his eyes were bloodshot and his hands shook.

"What substance?" Cyrus demanded, shifting Grayshadow's attention back to where I least wanted it to be.

"Fey wine," I said, scowling at him. "It brings out all sorts of latent talents."

"It also drives people mad," Cyrus pointed out, glaring right back. He must have guessed how close to bottoming out I was, or maybe he was picking up on my thoughts as I'd done his. *Damn it, Lia! Get out of here!*

The words rang in my head as loudly as if he'd spoken them. *How the hell did you do that?* I demanded, but got only a scowl in return.

"The weak-minded, perhaps," Grayshadow was saying, with the arrogance of all addicts. "It will weed out the feeble among us, enhance the power of the strong and make us invincible!"

"And subject you to the whims of your suppliers," I pointed out again, trying to calculate how long it would take Jamie and Caleb to find us. *Too long*, echoed in my mind. I wasn't sure if it was my thought or Cyrus's, but either way, it was likely correct.

"The Fey are weak. They fight amongst themselves too much to be anything else."

"And we don't?" Cyrus demanded, pulling those flat, silver eyes back to him.

"Once Sebastian and his human sympathies no longer divide us, that will cease to be a problem."

"Good plan," I said. "Unfortunately, there will be a dozen war mages here in a couple minutes to drag you off to face charges ranging from kidnapping to murder."

It was a lie, because I doubted Jamie and Caleb had the bars underground to call for backup, even if they'd managed to avoid getting their phones drowned. But there was no way for Grayshadow to know that. And if he got spooked enough, maybe he'd decide that a discredited war mage and an outcast who nobody would believe weren't worth the trouble.

"I answer to wolf law," Grayshadow told me haughtily, before glancing around like he expected my backup to come crawling out of a drainage ditch. Which, okay, fair enough.

"Wolf law takes a dim view of those who kill Clan."

"This one is *vargulf*," Grayshadow said, glancing scornfully at Cyrus. "No one cares what happens to him. Not even his own brother!"

"And White Sun? Last time I checked, he wasn't *vargulf*. And you had at least three other victims, two more of which were High Clan wolves!"

"None of which can be linked to me once you're dead!"

The final volley came fast and hard, my shields collapsed, and blood made a dark gash across the ground. I waited for pain and worse—and was still waiting when the smoke dissipated. I saw Grayshadow writhing on the ground, his coat half melted to his skin, one arm and shoulder a livid mass of black leather and red meat.

I glanced behind me, because no way had I done that, but there was no one. And then there was no time to worry about it, because Grayshadow stumbled back to his feet, snarling. I stared back at him, my hands hanging limp and nerveless at my sides, like they were attached with string. I was going to die, I thought blankly.

Then Grayshadow took off, clutching his ruined arm.

I watched him blankly for a second, until the pelting rain

hid him from view. And then my knees gave out and I hit the muddy concrete, stunned and dizzy. Cyrus was staring at me, looking equally bewildered as I crawled over to him. He didn't change back—he probably didn't have the energy—but it didn't matter. As soon as I laid my head against the silkiness of wolf fur, the hard ball of panic in my chest shrank until I could almost ignore it. I took the opportunity to breathe deeply for the first time that day.

Someone fumbled a hand over to grab mine, holding it so tightly that my fingers throbbed with both pulses. And I looked up into Cyrus's whiskey dark eyes. It seemed he'd had the strength to change, after all. "You okay?"

"Yeah, but I'm not sure why," I told him.

His nod of agreement was a ripple of shadow. "What the hell just happened?"

I felt something on my arm and looked down to see the dragon tat, frozen in place with a superior look on its tiny face. And something Caleb had said came back to me. "I think somebody decided to change sides."

"What?"

I held up my wrist. "It came off a dark mage, but it chose to help us out."

Cyrus looked at me strangely as he tried to heave himself to his feet. He slipped on his own blood and went down to one knee. "Lia. Wards don't think."

"Depends on the ward," I said, and stunned him.

A few minutes later, Jamie's head poked over the side of the channel, red-gray curls plastered to his skull. Caleb followed him out, both looking like hell but still standing. Jamie limped over and looked from the numb stick in my hand to Cyrus's slumped form. "Isn't that your boyfriend?"

"Yeah."

He frowned. "He won't be out long. That isn't strong enough to incapacitate a Were, even an injured one."

I dragged myself to my feet, stiff and soaked. "So take him in."

"On what charge?"

"Suspicion of . . . something."

"Suspicion of something? I don't think that's on the books."

"Just give him to Michaelson to process once the docs get through. It'll take at least a couple hours."

"And what are you going to do in the meantime?"

"Something stupid."

TWO huge Weres in wolf form guarded the almost invisible path that served as an entrance to the meeting place of the Clan Council. One of them moved to intercept me, changing fluidly from Were to human without so much as missing a step. His ebony skin gleamed in the light of a torch that had been wedged into a crack in the wall behind him. A lantern would have been a more practical choice, or nothing at all since I was the only one here without decent night vision. I assumed it was for ambiance.

It did add to the overall mystery of the place, not that it needed it. A sheer rock face rose five or six stories high, striated in uneven bands of cinnamon and gold. It wasn't raining here, and the black, clear sky with its pinprick stars and the sighing wind sliding over the cliff was beautiful and more than a little eerie.

The guard was doing his best to add to the effect. His skin melted into the night, leaving only the rippling muscles of his chest visible in the torchlight. His dark eyes gleamed, pricked with reflected flame. He might have been a creature out of legend, some mythical god of the desert.

And then he ruined it. He looked me over and one eyebrow went up. "Bad day?"

My clothes were streaked with mud, cobwebs and runoff, I smelled absolutely foul, and I had at least three pebbles in my boot courtesy of the hike here from my bike. I was in no mood to exchange banter with a naked guard. "Lia de Croissets, of Arnou."

"I know who you are." A slight smile crept over his face. "I thought you'd be taller."

If he'd treated my mother that way, she'd have ripped his face off. "Are you issuing a challenge?" I snapped.

His eyes widened fractionally. "No, I—"

"Then get the hell out of my way!"

I brushed past him and through the entrance, an oblong gash in the rock. The sides of the passage were inches from my fingertips, with no way out except straight ahead. It was the perfect place for an ambush should any unwanted visitors be stupid enough to try to enter. I hadn't asked Caleb and Jamie to back me up, because they'd have never made it past the guards. And Cyrus would have been killed on sight for daring to sully with his presence a place meant only for Clan.

Once Grayshadow passed into these walls, no one but another Clan member could touch him. So this was my fight. And, as exhausted as I was, I was glad of it. Some war mages specialized in the hunt, painstakingly piecing together clues, interviewing suspects, gathering evidence. I was a competent investigator, but I'd never pretended to enjoy it. I'd take a direct confrontation any day.

I just hoped I'd put the clues together right, or this was going to be a very short fight.

The passage twisted and curved, so I expected to hear the commotion before I saw it. But there was only the haunting sigh of the wind, a tendril of which reached down into the chasm to ruffle my hair. And then I was spilling out into open air and a wide expanse of hard-packed red sand.

The Clan Council met in a natural amphitheater, with jagged ledges of stone cascading down to a flat bottom. It was huge, maybe the size of a football field, and open to the

sky. The wispy glitter of the Milky Way arced directly overhead, bowed along the curved surface of the heavens. Were
elders stood on every side in ranked rows, torches flickering
here and there to highlight craggy faces and brilliant eyes.
Most were only a dark presence, a texture of shadow. I could
feel them waiting.

I wasn't sure for what.

And then I spied Grayshadow, striding across the sand,
heading for the dais on which the Council sat. Any Clan
member could attend a council meeting, but only the leaders
were supposed to speak. It looked like Grayshadow wasn't
feeling much like following the rules tonight. Luckily, neither was I.

I put on a burst of speed and caught him just as he reached
the dais. There was no time for subtlety—once issued, a
challenge couldn't be rescinded. Grayshadow was opening
his mouth to speak when I arrived, so I put my fist in it.

He didn't go down, but at least I had the pleasure of seeing him spit blood. Right before he lunged for me. It might
have been over right there, but the flat side of a spear caught
him in the chest, holding him back. It was in the hand of the
Speaker, the elder charged with voicing the decisions of the
Council. He also kept order when needed, as it often was.

The current Speaker was Night Wind of Maccon, a
grizzled powerhouse more than a century old and still built
like a Mack truck. His straight black hair, streaked with
silver, sharp dark eyes and strong, hawklike nose revealed
his mother's Native American ancestry. But I wasn't stupid
enough to think that our shared human blood would bias
him in my favor.

"Accalia of Arnou, why have you broken the sanctity of
Council?" he asked, in a voice loud enough to carry to every
corner of the vast space.

"To challenge," I said quickly, before Grayshadow could
cut me off. And before I could talk myself out of it.

"Whom would you challenge?"

I thought that was kind of obvious, considering I'd just
punched him in the mouth. But for once I bit my tongue.
"Grayshadow of Arnou."

As soon as the words were out, I almost felt relieved. The die was cast now, one way or the other. To back out of a formal challenge meant death.

"Until this moment, Grayshadow was presumed to be dead," the Speaker said, his sharp black eyes flicking between us.

"As he arranged. He killed a *vargulf* and mutilated the body to make certain it would be mistaken for his."

"This is ridiculous!" Grayshadow hissed. "She can't issue challenge. She is human!"

"The challenger speaks first, by Clan law," the Speaker informed him.

Grayshadow sucked in a breath. "You would put the claims of this creature before mine?"

"She is Arnou. It is her right."

"She isn't Arnou! She isn't anything! And even if you accept that ridiculous adoption, I am Third. I outrank her and I will speak!"

I rubbed my fingers together, trying to get rid of the tacky feel of Cyrus's blood drying between them. Some of it had settled into the lines of my palms and left a dark stripe underneath my nails. And suddenly I was so angry I could hardly see. "I am the daughter of Laurentia of Lobizon, wolf born, Clan reared. And an adopted daughter of Sebastian of Arnou. You do *not* outrank me!"

Grayshadow started for me again, but the Speaker's spear point was back against his chest. "She is allowed to speak."

I made it fast, but not because I feared another interruption. I was afraid I'd go for his throat and get killed before I ever found out if my theory was right. "There is no Hunter; there never was. Grayshadow killed four wolves— three High Clan and one *vargulf*—to pave the way to the *hardric's* position. With White Sun out of the way, he could challenge Sebastian and take it all. He killed the others as camouflage."

As short as the explanation had been, I'd had to raise my voice almost to a yell by the end of it. At the word *Hunter*, the stands had cascaded in one long ripple of fur and skin as hundreds of Weres rushed down the slope to the lower levels. None attempted to advance into the flat area, but they were as close as they could get. There was blood in the air, something no wolf could resist.

"She lies! The human lies!" Grayshadow was practically apoplectic. "I barely escaped alive from the clutches of the *vargulf* Cyrus, once of Arnou. He and this one conspired together to weaken the clans by killing our leading members! They care nothing for our ways, for our traditions! They think to use the war to destroy us, to dissipate our power and to allow the humans to enslave us!"

It wasn't a bad story, playing to all the hot buttons for the clans: raging xenophobia, distaste for the human war, and fear of those who possessed a magic they didn't understand. A rustling murmur came from the crowd, growing louder by the second, and I briefly wondered if I was about to be lynched. And then the Speaker's spear struck the ground with three heavy knocks that I swear I could feel through the soles of my boots.

"Challenge has been issued."

Grayshadow looked at him incredulously. "She is human! She has not accepted the Change! There is nothing in the tradition that defends it!"

"And nothing that prohibits. I say a second time, challenge has been issued against you, Grayshadow of Arnou. Do you accept?"

"This is outrageous! She and her human father killed four representatives of Lobizon! Her birth clan wants nothing to do with her! She is clearly—"

"For the third and last time. Challenge has been issued against you by a lawful member of the Clan. Do you accept?"

Grayshadow's mouth compressed into a sharp line, a wince of anger and contempt. But I wasn't worried. Clan law is remarkably simple in comparison to the human variety. If he wanted to clear his name, he had to fight me. To refuse would be an admission of guilt, and ringing us on all sides were members of the clans who had lost members to the Hunter. He'd never make it out of here alive.

Of course, if he accepted, I might not either.

He finally gave an abrupt nod, his eyes filled with not just pride but rage. It paled them out to silver, hardening a mouth shaped for smug, superior smiles and stiffening his walk to angry, snapping strides. I stood there, watching him move to the middle of the great space, unsure what happened now.

"Challenge has been issued," the Speaker intoned. "Challenge is accepted."

I started after Grayshadow, almost deafened by the renewed uproar of the crowd, only to be jerked back by an iron grip on my arm. I smelled the musky scent of woods and predation and looked up to see Sebastian. He was in human form, but his eyes were chartreuse and they didn't look happy.

"I asked you to find my brother, not to issue challenge!" he hissed, so low I could barely hear him over the crowd.

"I did find him. He's fine. Well, not fine," I amended. "But he'll live."

"Then your job is done!"

"Not yet." I tried to tug away, but got exactly nowhere. Sebastian might have been a column carved out of the surrounding rock.

"I'll take the challenge for you," he told me, his jaw tight.

"Like hell."

"Lia! Don't be a fool. I've seen Grayshadow fight! You can't win!"

"I guess we'll find out." The death grip on my arm didn't change. "Let me go, Sebastian."

"I'll repudiate you, dismiss you from the tribe! It will render your challenge meaningless."

I blinked. He looked utterly serious. "And that would help how? Then they'd kill me for being here."

"I will guarantee you safe passage." He started pulling me away, toward the sidelines.

"Then Lobizon will kill me tomorrow!" I dug in my heels, which did nothing but carve furrows out of the dirt. "Sebastian! He came here to challenge you! As soon as I leave—"

He rounded on me, furious. "I can fight my own battles!"

"Not this time. You're just going to have to trust me."

"I am not going to tell my brother I let his mate die!"

"Thanks for the vote of confidence."

"You don't understand. It would kill him! Our mother—" He stopped, a flash of pain cutting across those striking eyes. "She died in a contest much like this one."

"She was the woman you told me about," I realized. "The one who died defending her mate."

"Yes. And I can't watch that again!"

"You won't."

"You don't know Grayshadow like I do. He *will* kill you."

I looked over my shoulder, to where Grayshadow silently waited. Unlike me, he'd taken time to change clothes before approaching the Council. I could have picked him out as Arnou anywhere. It was in the shape of his long, dark cloak, cut from a template hundreds of years old that had been copied from one worn by their first clan leader. More obviously, it was in the peculiar mix of arrogance and elegance that no other clan quite managed, that calm conceit that said we are first because we are best.

My stomach clenched. "No," I told Sebastian. "He won't."

"You're afraid; I can see it on your face. Relinquish your challenge and let me get you out of here."

"Fear isn't a bad thing, if you use it right," I told him, and wrenched away.

The Council's servants had been busy lighting more torches, probably for the benefit of my lousy human eyesight. I wasn't sure if I was grateful or not. A circle of them now ringed Grayshadow in fire, shedding sepia light over the sand and gilding his face, deepening the crags, highlighting the lines and making him look like what he was—a warrior with a hell of a lot more experience than me. He seemed to think so, too, because he wasn't looking too worried.

"Tell me, human," he called before I'd even reached him. "Do you remember the story of Red Riding Hood?"

"Let me guess. You aren't the benevolent woodsman."

Grayshadow laughed. "He only exists in the modern version. Today, the foolish little girl is saved by the woodsman who kills the wicked wolf. But in the original French story, she was given false instructions by the wolf when she asked the way to her grandmother's house. She took his advice and ended up being eaten. And that was it. There was no woodsman and no grandmother, merely a well-fed wolf and a dead Red Riding Hood."

"Guess we're lucky it was only a fairy tale," I said, stepping inside the ring of torch light.

"But it reflected reality. The original story is from a harsher time, when my ancestors fought with yours for territory, for food—for survival. The writer understood: you were our enemy, and we were yours."

"Once, maybe. But we're allies now, in case you haven't—"

A clawed hand shot out and ripped through my shirt. I had shields up, or I'd have probably been bisected. As it was, talons like blades rattled across my ribs like a stick along a wrought iron fence.

Grayshadow rolled up his sleeve, exposing blistered flesh, while I fought to remain standing. "Now we're even."

I thought of the wolves he'd butchered, of the ruin he'd made of Cyrus, and my lip curled. "Not even close," I hissed, and pushed a section of my shields outward in a band that wrapped around his throat. Something hit me in the side, and I could hear the crunch of shattered bone. I bit my lip on a scream and held on, until a burst of raw power exploded against my ragged shields like a firestorm.

I staggered back and he tore away. My shields had to be almost gone, because this felt like a direct hit, with every cell in my body screaming that it was dying. The only thing keeping me vertical was the memory of countless training sessions, stretching on until I was so tired I could have wept, and my father's voice telling my mother "You underestimate her strength. Again, Accalia." He'd wanted to be sure that, if I joined the Corps, I was as prepared as he could make me. And no matter how much it hurt, it had been less impossible to do what was asked than to prove him wrong.

It still was.

The fire abruptly cut out and I staggered, gulping for air that wouldn't come. And when it finally did, it filled my lungs like ice water. I glanced around and realized that the last of my shields had dissipated along with the flames. Instead of protecting me, what remained of my magical ability was going haywire.

The desert floor, which hadn't seen a drop of water, was suddenly wet with an icy sludge. Cold bit at my face and hands as the moisture in the air began to crystallize. The water around my feet solidified as ice crawled across the sand, tracing delicate patterns in the muck. My feet went numb, my skin started to ache and there was frost in my hair and on my eyelashes. And still the temperature dropped, until I was gasping, trying to draw enough oxygen out of the thinning air.

Grayshadow was backing up from the approaching frost, uncertainty in his eyes. It couldn't hurt him—it was only ice. But he wasn't experienced enough with magic to know that.

"You'll never defeat me with wild magic," I taunted, as he hit a torch and jumped in a very undignified way. "You have power but no precision. Any war mage worth his salt could tear you apart."

"Feel free to try," he growled, whirling back at me.

So I threw a lasso around his feet and jerked. He hit the ground on his back and went sliding on the ice, an expression of almost comic surprise on his face. His feet were held immobile by the spell, and his arms were thrashing about in a vain attempt to stop himself. It didn't work, and he crashed into the torches on the other side of the ring, obliterating them.

The abrupt movement tore something in my wounded shoulder, and the pain was blinding. I gasped and had to fight not to let it turn into a cough, abruptly aware of a liquid, unpleasant sensation in my lungs. Wetness was spreading across my lacerated stomach, warm at first but chilling fast against my skin. I was running out of time.

"You know," I rasped, as Grayshadow threw off the spell

and stumbled back to his feet. "I've often wondered how that story would have turned out, had Red been a mage."

"You're not the only one with tricks, human!" he snarled, and four flashes of gold spilled into his palm.

I barely had time to recognize them as the missing wolf wards before they sank into his skin and changed, showing their true colors. They were beautiful; easily the best wards I'd ever seen, crystal clear and glowing with power. One was a rich dark brown with white streaks, another a beautiful russet and a third a blinding white, like the sun at midday.

The last was smaller and dimmer than the others, a slightly bedraggled gray with a white streak on his nose. The *vargulf*, I realized, and a new rage burned in my stomach. It wasn't bad enough that Grayshadow had stolen his life just because he needed a doppelganger; he was now planning to use what remained of him to kill me.

Only it looked like the tats had other ideas.

As soon as they touched him, Grayshadow started trembling like a fever had gripped him. He tried to brush them off, but they'd already taken hold, becoming part of him. They sprang up his body, and wherever they went, great gashes opened up in his flesh. He clawed more furrows out of his skin, trying to tear them off, but they stayed one step ahead. He screamed beneath their careful savagery, because it couldn't be borne and had to be; because there was no bracing to meet it and no escape.

He crouched a few yards away from me, hissing. I knew what was coming before he snarled and sprang, but there was no time to get out of the way. The air around him flared and his body came *apart*, more violently than any change I'd ever seen. I braced myself, even knowing it was useless. My shields were gone, and no way could I stand against an assault like that. But instead of being struck by a four-hundred-pound wolf, a wave of blood and raw, red flesh hit me like a fist.

I swiped my arm across my face, smearing the gore but not caring, staring around wildly. I didn't see anyone and went into a crouch, expecting another attack. But it didn't come, and slowly the truth dawned. The wards made from the wolves Grayshadow butchered had been thorough in their revenge. The only thing they'd left of him was a spreading pattern of blood on the ice.

Okay, I thought dizzily. *Now we're even.*

13

"GET it off!"

"I'm afraid I can't do that," Caleb told me, trying to look sympathetic. He failed miserably.

"Then get me someone who damn well can!"

"I don't know why you're upset," he said, flicking a finger at the tiny beast currently roasting my elbow. "That's an expensive ward you've acquired."

"I haven't acquired it! I don't even know why it's working again! It cut out on me last night, just when I needed the damn thing, and now—"

"It's a talisman, Lia. It expended most of its store of magic energy and needed to recharge."

"That doesn't explain *why it won't leave!*"

"It appears that stunning it caused it to reset. It now believes you to be its owner. That's probably why it fought for you as long as its power lasted."

"If it thinks I'm its master, why won't it turn loose when I tell it to?"

He shrugged. "How would I know? It's your ward."

The door flew open and Hargrove bustled in with his usual air of having ten other places he needed to be. I really wished he'd find one of them. I so didn't feel up to this today.

Caleb, the coward, slipped out behind the boss's back as he picked up my chart. He let the silence drag out while he stared at it. "The good news is that the docs say the battle used up my excess magic," I told him, not able to take the suspense. "So, uh, no more flying staffs. Or anything."

"Sanjay is running a pool in the pharmacy," Hargrove said after a moment. "They're taking bets on which bones you'll break in a given week."

"Really? What's the pot?" He looked up, eyes narrowing. I should have remembered; the guy had no sense of humor. "Look, I know I disobeyed your orders," I began, fully prepared to grovel. But I didn't get the chance.

"Which orders would those be?"

"The ones about not leaving the base?"

"That was between you and the doctor. The only command I gave was for you to report if any of this had to do with the Corps. Did it?"

"Uh, no."

"That is what Sebastian Arnou said, when he called on me this morning. As I informed him, Were politics are of little concern to me. I have enough trouble keeping up with our own."

I blinked. "Um. Sir? It almost sounds like maybe I'm *not* being fired?"

Hargrove rubbed his eyes. "I knew your father when he was in the service," he said abruptly. "He was impetuous, headstrong and occasionally reckless. He was also the best commanding officer I ever had. It would be well for the Corps if you managed to survive long enough to emulate him."

"Yes, sir." I tried really hard to keep the silly grin trying to break out over my face under control. I couldn't believe I was getting off this easy.

"Oh, and by the way," Hargrove paused halfway out the door. "Mage Beckett has requested to be reassigned to combat duty."

I frowned. "Why would he do that? He was one of our best instructors."

"He said he needed the rest." Hargrove smiled, and it was vicious. "You'll be taking over his trainees as soon as you recover."

Cyrus limped in a few moments later, while I was still reeling from the shock. He'd brought flowers, which I took as a good sign. He usually forgets stuff like that, although oil changes on my Harley are done like clockwork.

"So I guess I'm forgiven?" I asked, as he leaned over for a kiss.

"It will be at least a week until that happens. This is merely an injury-related time-out in my being pissed off at you." He settled himself gingerly in a chair, his own injured leg stretched out in front of him.

"Come to think of it," I told him, "I don't know what I have to apologize for."

"How about knocking me unconscious? Again?"

"I didn't have a lot of time for a discussion."

"And to think I used to dislike arguing with my girl-friends. Of course, that was before I encountered your method of ending a conversation."

I sighed. "Fine. No more numb sticks." Caleb had taken mine anyway.

"And as long as we're on the subject, what about taking on Grayshadow on your own and almost giving me a stroke?" Cyrus's words were light, but his expression was anything but.

"To be fair, you didn't know about that until later."

"I had a front-row seat courtesy of our bond. And without knowing you planned to sic his own wards on him!"

"About that bond thing—"

Cyrus shook his head. "That's not going to work. For once, we're going to finish one argument before we start the next."

"Fine," I said, giving him a look. "Although it should be pretty obvious that I couldn't tell anyone my plans. Not even Sebastian. You know what wolf ears are, and Grayshadow was right there! He might have overheard."

"And if he hadn't used the wards?" Cyrus demanded. "If he'd assumed he could beat you on his own? What then?"

"He didn't know my tat had run out of juice," I pointed

out. "And it had already hurt him once. He had no way of knowing that wouldn't happen again."

"And you had no way of knowing if that would be enough to convince him! Or that you'd guessed right about what his wards would do. They could have fought with him!"

"I took a calculated risk."

"Based on *what*?"

"Jamie's knowledge of the maker, for one thing. Some of the surviving gang members were rounded up and questioned last night. They'd been trading Wilkinson Fey wine now and again in return for protection wards, so they thought nothing of taking him the wolf pelts. He initially refused to have anything to do with them, but after they knocked him around a little, he agreed to give them what they wanted: weapons. What they didn't know was that he'd ensured that those weapons would only work against them."

"But if the interrogation was last night, you didn't know any of that when you challenged!"

"No, but I knew that a guy who'd had his only child killed by a gang wasn't likely to bow to pressure from another one. And he had to know he'd be killed as soon as he did what they wanted. He'd seen the wolf pelts and therefore was in a position to identify the ones who had taken them. It was the same reason his daughter was killed six years ago. So if he was going to die anyway, I thought there was a good chance he'd like to take a few of the gang with him."

"A good chance?" Cyrus looked like he was swallowing something sour. "If you'd been wrong you'd be dead!"

"If it had to be me or Sebastian, better that it was me," I told him, struggling for calm. Arguing with Cyrus was usually fun, adding frisson to whatever we were doing. But not when he got on this subject.

"Sebastian knew the risks when he assumed his position—"

"As did I. I'm a war mage trained to do exactly this kind of thing."

"I think if other mages went around fighting duels to the death in front of the Council, I might have heard."

"Maybe not in front of the Council," I agreed, "but just

about everywhere else. And with the war on, it's likely to happen again. Particularly with my new job."

Cyrus looked up from glaring at the rug. "What new job?"

"Hargrove has stuck me with the worst group of trainees you've ever seen. They scare me. I may be in here for a while, considering I have zero incentive to get well."

"You love teaching."

"They blew up the gym, Cyrus! Within a day of arrival! And I'm supposed to have them combat ready in six months!"

"Sounds like they already are." He looked much cheerier suddenly. I didn't have the heart to tell him that, in the Corps, teaching was considered one of the more dangerous activities. "But at least you weren't fired. By the way, why weren't you fired?"

"The same reason Caleb and Jamie weren't. Hargrove prefers to keep us around to torture."

He grinned. "I thought Sedgewick was the problem."

"He was, until he decided to autopsy a certain off-limits corpse. Caleb dropped by with the news a few minutes ago. Sebastian noticed the difference when the body was delivered and made it sound like it was going to cause a major diplomatic incident. In reality we don't even know for certain who the Were was."

"That's a politician for you."

"So we did a trade. My little lapse for Sedgewick's."

"Sounds like things are looking up."

"Yeah. So about that bond—"

"I have some news, too," Cyrus said quickly. "I've talked Sebastian into putting together a group of *vargulfs* to act as informants and to keep an eye on the Were gangs that remain in Tartarus. Grayshadow was able to turn them because there's almost no way for outcasts to redeem themselves. If they end up being of service during the war, he'll get them clan status after the dust settles. It'll be a low-ranked clan, but it's a start."

"What about you? He could tell Arnou that you caught the Hunter. Allow you to redeem yourself and rejoin the Clan."

"And then who would coordinate the *vargulfs*? A Clan

wolf can't be seen talking to them, nor would they be likely to take orders from one."

"But you could go home, Cyrus."

He leaned over to kiss my neck. "I already am."

I smiled back and slipped a lasso around his shoulders. "So, about that bond—"

He tried to pull back, and found he couldn't. He started to look a little panicked.

"Lia—"

"Don't even try it. You've been yelling at me for the last twenty minutes—"

"That wasn't yelling."

"Berating, then. So it's my turn. How come Sebastian knew we were bonded and I didn't?"

Cyrus closed his eyes and sighed. "You were so insistent that you weren't Were. It was almost the first thing you ever said to me. I didn't think it could happen. You're only half-Were and there were none of the usual signs—until you left. I almost went crazy the first week; it was worse than leaving Arnou, ten times worse. And when I realized why . . ." His eyes opened, and there was genuine pain in them. "How could I tell you? I'm *vargulf*. I have nothing to offer you."

"You have you."

He gave a short, unamused laugh. "Yes, and I'm such a prize. You had to rescue me."

"You were the one who found out what was going on," I pointed out. "If you hadn't told me, I never would have figured it out in time. And as I recall, you'd already freed yourself by the time I got there."

"Lia," he paused, searching for words as Cyrus never did. "This isn't wounded male pride talking. You could have died yesterday; you almost did die. And I could do nothing to save you."

His eyes looked haunted, and it wasn't hard to guess that he was thinking about the other woman he'd failed to save. Sebastian had said they'd only been children when their mother was killed, but I knew Cyrus well enough to know he blamed himself for it. "You're right," I agreed, and his head shot up. "You couldn't have done anything. Grayshadow was both a Were and a mage, albeit an untrained one. Only someone who was also both could have beaten him."

"I should have found a way, should have figured it out—"

"Even if you had, he would never have feared you enough to use those damn wards. Not after having pulverized you for most of the day. It had to be a Were who possessed the same advantages he did to make him believe that he needed extra protection."

"A Were?" One eyebrow shot up. "You're actually admitting to being one of us?"

"After today, the facts are kind of hard to ignore," I admitted. "If I wasn't Were, I would never have found you in time or been able to get before the Council to fight the duel. But if I wasn't also a mage, I would have lost."

Cyrus gave a lopsided grin. "You're saying I'm mated to a mutt?"

"You tell me. I have quite a few questions about—"

Cyrus was suddenly on his feet, bad leg and all. "Damn, look at the time. Visiting hours are already over."

"I don't think that applies if you're also a patient—" I began, but the door closing after him cut me off.

I stared at it in disbelief for a moment, before falling back against the pillows with a thump. Men! I picked up my bedraggled flowers, which had gotten a little squashed somehow. They looked like he'd picked them himself, from Sedgewick's potion garden, judging by the contents. I grinned. *"You can't run forever, Cyrus."*

"I guess you'll just have to get well enough to catch me."

Now that was what I called incentive.

armor
of roses

A HUNTER KISS NOVELLA

MARJORIE M. LIU

1

ACCORDING to Mark Twain, in a notebook entry dated in 1897, time is *atomized*, broken into infinitesimal fragments in which moments that have been lived are forgotten and without value, while moments that have not yet been experienced do not exist and are of no importance. Only the present, the immediate, has significance; time is isolated, time is discrete. Even memories, hardwired into the brain to give dimension to the temporal, are fleeting.

Because we die. Because each life is a single conscious moment, burning.

Lost, in time.

THERE were no zombies at the party. I would have been happy to find some. If nothing else, the small talk would have been less insulting. Nor would I have been as tempted to shove an opera singer over the railing of the yacht.

"But my dear, you look so *cultured*," complained Madame Borega, loudly enough that heads turned to stare. "What do you mean you're from *Texas*?"

Her affront was palpable, her distress audible in the

faint tremor of her rich vibrato vowels. Texas, apparently, was apocalyptic. I might as well have told her that I was a killer—and that the two tiny demons hiding in my hair would be more than happy to set her face on fire.

Both of which were true. But she didn't need to know that.

A gentle hand touched my elbow. I looked up to find Grant beside me, leaning hard on his cane. His gaze was faintly amused, but darkly so, and he settled his attention on Madame Borega with a smile that held an edge.

"Wonderful performance last night," he said in his deep rumbling voice. "Your *Aida* was a joy."

Madame Borega lowered her gaze, smiling—but, before she could thank him, or demure, or tell Grant that he was a hot, hot former priest and she wanted to pull a *Thorn Birds* on his ass, he added, "But frankly, Suzanne, I was shocked to learn that you were using an enhancer."

The woman froze, staring at him. A deep crimson flush stained her décolletage and rose into her face, all that red visible beneath the heavy pale cake of her makeup. I thought she was embarrassed, but then her lips tightened and her eyes hardened, and it was like watching a skunk lift its tail.

"My voice," she said, "needs no *enhancement*."

"I'm sure it doesn't," Grant said, in the most conciliatory tone imaginable. "I just thought, perhaps, that you had been ill. Using a microphone is nothing to be ashamed of, which is what I told Roger Breckin over dinner."

Madame Borega's gasp was so violent, this time people did more than turn their heads. Conversations stopped. Drinks were put down. I held myself steady in the three-inch heels I had been wobbling in all night, and casually rubbed the back of my neck. A small hot tongue rasped across the back of my hand.

"You told Roger . . ." began the opera singer, touching her throat. "Oh, my God."

And with that, she fled—in fits and starts, stopping every few feet to stand on her toes to scan the crowd. Grant made a small humming sound, slid his large warm hand around my waist, and guided me in the opposite direction. His limp was more pronounced than usual. I kept my steps deliberately short, pretending it was the heels that were making me careful.

"I'm no opera expert," I said, twining my fingers through his, "but I think you just ruined that woman's night."

Grant was taller than me even while stooping over his cane; a ruggedly handsome man with brown hair brushing the broad shoulders of his tuxedo, dark eyes keen with grim humor. "Roger Breckin helps finance the Seattle Opera House. He's one of the richest men on the West Coast. He's also Susan Borega's benefactor, but his standards are exacting. One hint that her voice needs a microphone to fill the hall he paid for, and she would be ruined."

"Ah. But at dinner we were seated with a Watanabe and Anderson. No Breckin in sight."

"Funny how that works," Grant replied, and tightened his arm protectively. I bit back a smile, and glanced over the railing of the yacht. I meant only to look at the water, still unused to living close to the sea, but instead spied three demons being dragged through the cold dark ocean like body surfers, their claws lodged in the outer hull.

Zee, Raw, and Aaz. Steam rose from their small angular bodies, along with bubbles and frothing foam. Red eyes glinted like rubies shot with fire, and when they saw me observing, I was given three vigorous thumbs-up signs. My boys, rocking out. I had vague childhood memories of them watching *Flipper* on old hotel televisions—that, and *Muscle Beach Party* with Annette Funicello, who they still thought was hot. All they needed now was sand, shades, and some chocolate-covered surfboards to eat over a bonfire, and their fantasy would be complete.

I flicked my fingers at them in a subtle wave, and two small voices began humming inside my ear, long bodies coiled against my scalp with a subtle sinuous weight that still, after all these years, made me want to pat my head to reassure myself that no scales, tails, or snouts were sticking out of my hair.

I forced my hands to stay still, relying on faith and trust. No one else could see Dek and Mal. I might feel them, but the two demons hidden in my hair were only partially in this dimension, bodies resting here and elsewhere, lost in some mysterious realm that all my boys traveled like armored skipping stones.

My protectors. My friends. My family, bound to my blood until I died and passed them on to the daughter I would one day have. Just as they had been passed on to me.

Grant peered over the rail, choked down a quiet laugh, and then turned to scan the crowd. Watching auras. Reading every guest's darkest secrets with nothing but a glance. For a long time he had thought he suffered merely from synesthesia—a cognitive peculiarity allowing him to see sound as color—but he knew differently now.

"Maxine," he said, speaking my name softly, so no one would hear him. I had used an alias all evening, but I missed being myself, hearing my real name. "Thank you for coming with me tonight."

I gave him a wry look. "And let you face the hyenas alone?"

He smiled, but it was tense, and I could not help but notice how he was careful to take the weight off his bad leg. His grip on the cane was a little too tight. It had been a long night standing, or having to sit with his knee bent. Bone did not heal well when crushed, but Grant never took anything stronger than Ibuprofen—and for an old injury like his, that was nothing.

Better pain than the alternative, though. For both of us, control was paramount. I might be dangerous, but so was Grant. More so, maybe.

I followed his aimless gaze, taking in the after-dinner party. We were on a luxury yacht, cruising around Elliot Bay. The sun had been gone for hours, and I could see the glittering lights of downtown through the far windows, glimpsed around men and women who dazzled almost as brightly. This was not my kind of crowd. Not Grant's either, though he moved among them with an ease that I envied. I had always been an outsider, but for once my feelings of isolation had nothing to do with not being human. I simply was not human like *them*.

Seattle's elite. Software moguls, Boeing executives, famed novelists and musicians, sports stars and movie stars; old money, new money, more politicians than I could shake a stick at; as well as one former priest who was a celebrated philanthropist—and me. His date.

The last living Warden of a multidimensional prison that housed an army of demons waiting to break free and destroy the earth.

But tonight I was in a dress. First one I had worn in years. And since it had been a long time, I had decided to make a statement. Deep neck, no back, short as hell. Bright red. Long black hair loose, faintly curled. Good thing this was a night event, or else I would have had to make adjustments to the wardrobe, what little there was. No one but Grant and a handful of others ever saw my skin while the sun was up. Safer that way.

Few ever saw my right hand, either, but tonight was another rare exception. I glanced down at the smooth metal encasing several of my fingers, veins of silver threading across the back of my hand to a shining cuff molded perfectly to my wrist. Not quite a glove, but almost. Bound so close to my flesh and the curve of my bones and joints that sometimes it seemed the metal had *replaced* flesh.

The armor was magic, or something close. Bound to me for life. And though possessing this . . . thing . . . had proven useful in the past, the metal had a bad habit of growing. I usually wore a glove to hide it—wore gloves anyway, during the day—but this was a good night to test an old theory: that most folks would accept most anything strange as normal, because the alternative simply could not be imagined.

I had not been proven wrong. Magic had become nothing more dangerous than jewelry. This was Seattle, after all. If you didn't have some kind of piercing or body art, you practically couldn't get service at local coffee shops.

"Did you find any sponsors for the shelter?" I asked, as a leggy blonde strolled by on the arm of a giant whose face I recognized in a vague, sports star sort of way. A member of the Seattle Seahawks, maybe. He stared openly at my breasts, and then my face—but did not appear embarrassed until he glanced sideways and found Grant frowning at him.

"Several," Grant said, still watching the football player. "Not much hard cash offered, just goods and services, which is all I was really after. I'll probably have to sell one of the Hong Kong apartments, but it's near the Peak. Even in this market I shouldn't have trouble finding some tycoon willing to lay down thirteen million."

"Right," I said dryly. "Small change."

"Whatever it takes." Grant gave me a grim smile. "I doubt my father expected that his money and property would be used like this when he left it to me."

"You make it sound as though he would have found it dirty. There's nothing shameful in keeping a homeless shelter afloat, or helping people."

"I know," he said quietly, still watching the crowd. "But I don't like the attention any more than you do."

True enough. Grant did not need donations to keep the shelter going, but there was little wrong with getting things for free, or involving the private and public sector in charitable works. Unfortunately, that meant events like this, where his looks, history, wealth—and how he was spending it— had made him a minor celebrity.

That was also why, over the past eight months of our relationship, I had declined attending other black-tie events that Grant had been invited to. Cowardice, excused as self-preservation. I was afraid of people asking too many questions. I was unused to attention. Not accustomed to being noticed, most certainly not for being on the arm of a man.

A man, I had been told, who had never once in five years brought a date to these events. Which, given what I knew about Grant, was not much of a surprise.

But it did make me stand out.

And that, as my mother had always said, was a good way to get dead, and fast.

THE dinner cruise docked an hour later. Every bone in my feet felt broken, and my soles burned. I hobbled down the gangplank, fighting to maintain my dignity. Grant was having his own difficulties.

"A long hot bath," I muttered.

"Long hot night after that?" he replied, grimacing as the gangplank bounced under the weight of so many people. His cane slipped on the red carpet that had been laid upon the thick metal rails.

I grabbed his hand. "You're getting ahead of yourself, buster. We haven't even made it off the damn boat yet."

He flashed me a pained grin. "Race you."

I groaned, and slung his arm over my shoulder, making it look as though I needed him to hold me. He sighed, and planted a rough kiss on top of my head.

Some of the guests had drivers waiting for them, but most had driven themselves and chosen the valet parking that the function organizers had provided. I was sensitive, though, about who got behind the wheel of my Mustang, and had left the car a block away in a short-term lot. I was kicking myself for that now, but it couldn't be helped. I didn't want to risk questions about why there were so many shredded teddy bears in my backseat, along with bags of nails, fast-food cartons, knives, and a half-eaten aluminum baseball bat—teeth marks plain.

So we walked, we limped, we hobbled down the sidewalk; and we were not alone. It was a crowded Saturday night. People everywhere, young and old.

And demons. My demons. My little boys.

Red eyes glinted in the shadows, watching us from cracks beneath closed doors and in the spokes of hubcaps. Above my head I heard whispers, and the rasp of claws against stone; and another kind of hum in the air that was partially from the throats of the demons in my hair, but mostly the city: engines rumbling low and warm, and the thrum of hot electricity running through the veins of the buildings around whose roots we walked. I heard laughter, glass breaking, a throb of music from the open door of a bar; a groan from an alley and the long liquid rush of urine hitting concrete; and a small dog, barking furiously from an apartment above our heads.

I saw no zombies in the crowd. Zombies, who were not the living dead, but humans possessed by parasitic demons who had managed for millennia to slip through cracks in the prison veil. The parasites could take over a weak mind, and turn a human host into little more than a puppet, a means of creating pain and misery: dark energy that was more than food.

We reached the parking lot, a parcel of concrete stuck between two office towers and bordered by a low wall covered with thick ivy and splashes of graffiti. Claws rasped, and I glanced to my right as Zee tumbled from the shadows beneath a scarred Pontiac.

He was only as tall as my knee, mostly humanoid, and preferred to stand with his shoulders hunched, the tips of his black claws dragging against stone and leaving narrow grooves. His small face was angular as the point of a knife, each thick strand of his hair razor sharp. A series of spikes rode down the length of his spine. His skin was the color of coal mixed with mercury, and I knew from experience that it was indestructible. Nothing could kill Zee or his brothers.

But the party in the ocean was over. His red eyes were solemn. I straightened with concern, as did Grant. Dek and Mal, who had begun to poke their heads from my hair, went very still.

"Maxine," he rasped. "Got company."

Grant glanced ahead, to his left where the Mustang was parked in the maze of cars, and narrowed his gaze. "One person. His aura is weak."

Weak. Which was another word for dying. I gave him a quick look, then slid out from under his arm, kicked off my heels, and flew across the concrete on light, silent feet. Raw appeared from under a car, bounding ahead of me to sweep broken glass out of my way. He was a blur of darkness beneath the strained cold fluorescent streetlight, and thankfully, no one else was around to see him.

The same could not be said for the man bleeding to death in front of my car.

He was on the ground, propped against the bumper with his cheek resting on chrome. Old man, maybe in his seventies—mostly bald, with a ring of feathery hair around the back of his head that was white as snow. Hands large and grizzled as leather meat hooks clutched his stomach, blood seeping through his fingers.

A lot of blood. He was sitting in a puddle of it, and even in the bad light I could see that his dark slacks were as glistening and soaked as the white dress shirt that stretched crimson across his soft torso.

His closed eyes snapped open when I was less than three feet away. A brilliant blazing gaze, sharp with pain—but even sharper with intelligence. He looked at me with such intensity, I stopped in my tracks, swaying.

"Finally," he whispered, his English heavily accented, though I could not place the origin.

I heard the rushed click of a cane behind me, but it was a dim sound compared to the roaring in my ears. "Sir. We're going to help you."

I snapped my fingers. Moments later a wad of gauze padding was flung at me from the shadows beneath a car. The old man did not seem to notice, which was what I had hoped for—though I could not account for the way he looked at me, with hungry recognition, as though I was someone he had not seen in years.

I picked up the gauze, and held out my hands. "Don't be afraid."

He grimaced. "Never. You look . . . the same."

I froze, and then forced myself to move again, stepping close, walking barefoot in his blood. It was shockingly warm, and squelched beneath my toes.

He had not been shot. Stabbed, multiple times in the same spot. Defensive wounds covered his arms, and there was a gash along his throat that I had not seen earlier.

I reached for him. "Sir, move your hand. I have something to put on your wound."

The old man shifted, but it was to reach into his pocket. I did not pay attention to what he removed, but crouched close, pressing the gauze against his wound and pushing down. He groaned, panting for air. Trembling so violently his teeth chattered. Pink foam flecked his lips.

I glanced over my shoulder. "Grant."

"I called nine-one-one," he muttered, drawing near. "Five minutes, they said."

We did not have five minutes. I glanced down at my right hand, at the armor glinting along my fingers, and tightened my jaw. I could do this. I could move us through space to a hospital. I could even take us back in time, though that posed a whole other range of risks.

But I never got the chance. The old man grabbed my hand, and squeezed with surprising strength—staring into my eyes with that same unnerving intensity. "You have to end it. We thought . . . it was over, but we were wrong. We were *wrong* . . . and she tried . . . to warn us."

I stared, but the old man was not delirious. There was too much clarity in his eyes, a profound need that was hard and cold, even terrifying. His desperation was the only thing keeping him alive—but that was fading, too.

"Maxine Kiss," he whispered, chilling me to the bone. "I have a . . . message . . . from Jean."

I knew only one Jean. My grandmother.

Heat roared through me. He pushed something into my blood-soaked hand. A flat plastic card, and a flap of leather.

"Finish what she started." He breathed brokenly, but I was too numb to ask him what he meant. The old man's eyes fluttered shut.

"Maxine," Grant murmured, bent over his cane, his fingers brushing my shoulder. "He's almost gone. I can see it."

Even I could see that. My eyes burned from seeing it. I heard sirens in the distance, and Zee crept close on all fours, peering at the dying old man with peculiar familiarity. Raw and Aaz were close behind him, twins in every way except for a dash of silver on Raw's chin. Dek and Mal uncoiled from my hair, making small sounds of distress.

"Ernie," Zee rasped, but the old man did not open his eyes. All his intensity, his desperation, had bled out of him. His breathing slowed. His muscles relaxed.

I watched him die.

Grant's hand tightened on my shoulder. I sat very still, hardly able to breathe—afraid to breathe—a small part of me crushed with inexplicable grief. I did not know this man, but I felt like I should have. I should have.

Zee sighed, running his claw through the old man's spreading blood. He placed the tip on his tongue, tasting, and glanced over his shoulder at the others, shaking his head. I would have to ask, but not yet. I could hardly swallow around the lump in my throat, and there was an ambulance coming; and with them, the police.

I tore my gaze from the old man, and glanced down at what he had given me. The plastic card was a hotel key, and I held it up over my shoulder. Grant took the key without a word, and slid it quickly into his pocket.

The other item was far less mundane. It was leather, and covered in an intricately inked design that resembled roses. But it was not normal leather. At least, not from anything that had moved on four legs.

I was holding a flap of human skin.

2

NO escape. The old man named Ernie was dead in front of my Mustang, but even if his body hadn't been blocking the car, it would not have felt right to simply leave him. He had been murdered. Murdered, while looking for me. And those two things, I feared, were related.

The police arrived with the ambulance. We stood aside as the EMTs checked the old man's vital signs and came to the obvious conclusion. And then we stepped aside even more as the police cordoned off the area and took us back to their vehicle for questioning.

Before they were done, a black sedan rolled up. Two familiar men got out. They took one look at us, whispered to each other, and then walked to the dead old man. Hovered, crouched, poked and prodded with latex gloves on their hands. I tried not to watch them. Or think about the hotel key and leather burning a hole in Grant's pocket. Red eyes blinked lazily from the shadows, and two hot tongues rasped the back of my neck.

When Detectives Suwani and McCowan were done with their cursory examination, they held three plastic bags, which they passed off to one of the uniforms waiting on the sidelines. Then, with careful deliberation, they walked over to where we were waiting.

Suwani was a slender black man, not quite as tall as me, but lean, with a sinewy strength that started at his hands and wrists, and no doubt reflected the rest of his trim body. McCowan, on the other hand, had already lost most of his neck behind his sagging chin, and the rest of him was built like the love child of a dump truck and an elephant. Big, lumbering—kind of cute, kind of soft, kind of bullheaded— kind of this, kind of that, which I suspected was just a mask, given that his eyes were anything but dull or dithering.

Suwani gave me a sharp once-over, but only McCowan stared at the low neck of my dress, his gaze traveling down my legs and then up again—barely reaching my face. Grant cleared his throat. "Gentlemen. I wish we could have met again under better circumstances."

I wished we had not met again at all, but those were the breaks. Suwani nodded, and looked at me. "Did you know the victim?"

"No," I said. "We were coming back from a party, and found him in front of my car."

"You have a bad habit of collecting corpses," McCowan replied. "Last time we met there was a dead man who had your name in his pocket. And now another corpse just happens to be found beside your car. You sure you didn't know him? Or that he didn't know *you*?"

Grant frowned, and this time when he spoke there was a faint melody in his voice, soft and filled with a thread of that old familiar power. He could do things with his voice. Change people. He could reach inside the heart of a soul and make something new. I could not imagine a more dangerous ability—nor a man whom I trusted more to wield it.

Grant was the last of the Lightbringers, just as I was the last of the Wardens, and the two of us should never have met. But we had, and now I was the only person who could keep him alive while he used his gift. We were bound together. Our hearts shared the same steady rhythm. Even now, I felt his pulse riding mine, soft and warm as a coil of sunlight.

"What did you learn from his body?" Grant asked,

his voice sliding through me with a shiver. I could not be affected by his power—nor the boys—but I felt the ripple nonetheless. Zee said it tickled. I had told the little demon that it made me uneasy.

Suwani blinked. McCowan swayed ever so slightly. But then their gazes cleared, and the black detective coughed into his hand. "He had a gun in his possession. Recently fired. Shots were reported near here less than an hour ago. We were called out to investigate, which is why we arrived so quickly."

"He killed someone?"

"We don't know that," Suwani said, and then frowned, as though he wasn't quite certain why he was talking so much. "But there was a body, a young man. Heavy drug user. His arms were so eaten up with needle tracks he had started injecting into his leg."

"Anything else?" Grant held his gaze, but this time it was McCowan who stirred.

"The old fellow's name was Ernie Bernstein," said the burly man, rubbing his brow as though he had a headache. "Israeli passport in his suit jacket, along with a thousand dollars cash. Nothing else on him except for that gun."

Nothing except a hotel key, and a piece of human skin.

And a message from my grandmother, dead now for more than thirty years.

THE distinction between human and animal skin was subtle, especially when aged and treated. Human skin was softer than animal, fine and supple, even more so than lamb; and thin, with a delicacy that belied its inherent strength. Most people would have been unable to tell the difference. That I could was not something that made me proud, but I had seen human skin before, dried and preserved for horrific reasons. It was not something I would ever forget. And it was on my mind now as Grant and I climbed the steps to his apartment: the entire top floor of the former furniture factory that housed his homeless shelter.

The detectives had driven us home to the co-op. My car

was part of evidence. Luckily, there were three little demons in my life who were capable of playing housekeeper when they wanted to, and when I had opened up that door—slowly—there were no knives to be found on those vintage leather seats; no chewed-up baseball bats, rusty nails, decapitated teddy bears, or issues of *Playboy*. Sixty seconds of good hard work. All they had left behind was a decorative square pillow that had *not* been there before, and that had I LOVE THE POLICE embroidered on it in big red letters.

My boys. Such comedians.

I carried my high heels in one hand, and held Grant's with the other as he made his way slowly up the stairs. His jaw was tight, but not entirely with pain. It had been a hard night. Zee paced through the shadows ahead of us, while Dek and Mal—now that I was in a safe place—uncoiled from my neck and slithered down my arm to join Raw and Aaz in the shadows.

"How long will you be gone?" Grant asked, when we were safe inside the apartment and its spacious golden comfort: oak floors, exposed brick, dark windows that filled the entire length of the southern wall—almost as many bookshelves built into the other. A grand piano stood in one corner, in addition to a cherry red motorcycle that Grant would never be able to ride again; and my mother's trunk, pushed against the wall alongside the workstation where he carved all his flutes. His gold Muramatsu was the only exception, and lay gleaming upon the dining table.

Zee and the others were suddenly nowhere to be seen. I headed directly to the bedroom, shedding my dress as I walked. Grant's sharp intake of breath cut through my heart, and I tossed the slip of red silk at his face. I was wearing a lace thong and nothing else: a far cry from the cotton granny panties that usually covered my ass.

"Not long." I glanced over my shoulder, watching as he crumpled the dress against his chest and made a slow inspection of my nether regions. "And if I find any answers, I'll come here first before I make any mission to mayhem."

"Hmm." Grant limped after me, a bit more spring in his step. He dropped the dress and began unbuttoning his shirt, exposing his strong throat. The bow tie already hung loose beneath his collar. I turned to face him, backing into the bedroom, slowly enough that he caught up with me before I was hardly through the door. His gaze was dark with something deeper, more raw, than hunger, and I placed my hand against his chest, over his heart. I trembled, or maybe that was him. Both of us like kids.

He covered my hand, and we stood unmoving. Just being with each other. As always when I was naked with Grant, he felt huge, permanent as a mountain, radiating heat as though lava burned beneath his skin. Immovable, resolute. I loved that feeling. I loved *him*.

Grant brushed my cheek with the back of his fingers, his touch impossibly gentle, and then did the same to my breast. I held still, savoring the ache that spread through me; taking pleasure in the fact that we were here now, together, when everything in our lives said we should not be.

"Be careful," he said quietly.

I kissed his throat. "You have ten minutes to show me how careful you want me to be."

THE name of the hotel written on the plastic key was Hotel Vintage Park. A quick Internet search had revealed that it was a boutique establishment located in downtown. I took Grant's Jeep and drove fast, listening to the *Strictly Ballroom* soundtrack version of Cyndi Lauper's "Time After Time."

Raw and Aaz sat in the passenger seat, legs dangling while they clutched teddy bear heads against their chests, white wispy stuffing trailing into their laps. Zee perched on my thigh, peering over the wheel at the road ahead of us. Dek and Mal, coiled around my shoulders, were busy singing a countermelody to the music on the CD player.

"So," I said. "Who was Ernie?"

"Munchkin," Zee rasped, placing his hands over mine to help me steer. "Little boy."

Not so little now. Not so alive. "My grandmother knew him when he was a child?"

"War child," replied the demon, leaning back against my chest to peer up at me with large red eyes. "Big bad war."

World War Two. My grandmother had been in Hiroshima when the Americans dropped the bomb. Luckily for her, the blast had occurred during the day, while the boys slept on her skin. They had protected her until she could get free of the danger zone—just as they had protected me under similarly lethal circumstances. If I died, the boys would die—or so the family legend went. Ten thousand years of women, a single bloodline that Zee and his brothers had survived upon—and one that they had no intention of giving up.

"I doubt Ernie was in Japan when my grandmother knew him," I said. "Germany? Israel?"

He picked at his sharp teeth with a long black claw. "China."

I frowned. "How and why?"

"War," he said again, simply, as though I should understand everything from that one word. Which I did not. Ernie Bernstein, I had guessed, was probably Jewish. And a Jewish child in China during World War Two did not add up. Not yet, anyway.

It was well into the middle of the night when I arrived, and the roads were almost empty as I drove up Spring Street past the angular glass behemoth that was the Seattle Public Library. At the Fifth Street intersection I saw the awning of the hotel on my left, next to the Tulio restaurant. No left turn. I had to circle two blocks before I found myself directly in front of the hotel, and parked across the street.

I sat staring at the front doors, thinking hard, and then patted everyone's head. Their skin could slice through solid rock, but only if they wanted it to. I had free rein to touch them—as did Grant and several others.

I braided my hair and tucked it under the collar of my navy sweatshirt, oversized and borrowed from Grant. Grabbed a blond wig from a canvas tote bag on the floor and slid it over my head. It was an expensive piece of work, with real hair instead of the coarse synthetic stuff, but I hadn't been especially careful with the thing, so it looked as though I had just rolled out of bed. I slapped a baseball cap on top, wrapped a pink scarf around my throat to partially obscure my chin, and then slid on a pair of heavy-framed glasses—lenses thick enough to blur my eyes, though they were nothing prescriptive. I stuffed chewing gum in my mouth, too, just to make my cheeks look puffier. Slid on a pair of pink knit gloves to hide the armor on my hand.

As disguises went, it was pretty awful, but if Ernie had used a credit card to stay here, then the police would track down his room sooner or later. Best not to be too obvious with my appearance. The boys could disable security cameras—out on the street and inside the hotel—but not eyewitnesses.

The front doors were locked, but I used the key card to get in and strode across the lobby with my shoulders slightly hunched, head ducked, a harried expression on my face. Apologetic, even. A young woman dressed in an ill-fitting brown suit manned the front desk, and gave me a questioning look as I approached.

I held up the room key. "Sorry to bother you, but my grandfather is visiting and forgot his medication in his room. He gave me his key, but I can't remember if he's in 304 or 403."

The woman smiled faintly, which eased the shadows under her eyes. "His name?"

"Ernie Bernstein."

"Oh!" she exclaimed, smile deepening as her short nails tapped the keyboard. "I like him. But it's not either of those numbers. He's in 610."

"Thank you so much," I said, and began to turn away. She stopped me, though, and dashed into a small room on her right. She was gone just for a moment, and when she returned there was a slender FedEx envelope in her hand, which she slid across the counter to me.

"This arrived for Ernie. And . . . could you tell him hi for me?" A pretty flush stained her cheeks, maybe because I was staring at her. "There was a . . . guest who was rude to me last night, just when Ernie was checking in, and he . . . you know, took up for me. I appreciated that."

I smiled, throat aching. "Yes. He's a . . . good man. He'll be glad to hear from you."

She beamed, which took years off her already young face,

and made her look twelve years old; a kid who needed a hug and pigtails. Made me hurt for her, that Ernie was dead—made me hurt for Ernie, too, who seemed to have been a decent man.

I took the elevator up to the sixth floor, and found the hall quiet and still. The door to his room opened as I approached. Aaz peered out, giving me a toothy grin. A DO NOT DISTURB sign hung on the brass knob.

There was nothing extraordinary about the room I entered, except that it was nicely decorated with cherry accents and a king-sized bed dressed in pale sunset-orange canopies. Covers rumpled, unmade. Curtains closed, all the lamps turned on, though the light felt stifled, strangled; like most hotel rooms. I had never been in one that felt truly well lit.

A briefcase lay on the desk. Behind me, the boys were prowling. Sniffing the floor and sheets, peering into the bathroom. I glanced over my shoulder and found Raw eating a bar of soap. I cleared my throat and he shrugged, also taking a bite out of the chrome dish it had been sitting in. He gave the rest to Aaz, who swallowed the metal without chewing, and licked his lips with a sigh.

"Maxine," Zee rasped, poking at the contents of a small carry-on suitcase. He dragged out a stuffed black sock, which he sliced open with one claw. Several wads of cash tumbled out, each one as thick as my wrist. Nothing but one-hundred-dollar bills.

It was a tremendous amount of money. After some thought, I scooped up the rolled wads and tossed them into the canvas tote bag I had brought with me. I did not need the cash, but it was Ernie's and if he had family somewhere, then they deserved to have the money sent back to them.

"You must know what this is about," I said to Zee.

The spines of the little demon's hair flexed, and he glanced at Raw and Aaz, now sprawled on the bed, rubbing their round little tummies. "Old hunt. Old work from our old mother."

Old mother. My grandmother. I gave them all a hard look, and focused on the briefcase. It was an antique but well-made, and the locks were crafted from solid brass. Dek slithered from my hair, humming to himself, his snakelike body coiled around my upper arm while his small furred head tilted in careful scrutiny. He touched his long black tongue to the lock, and it began sizzling from the acid in his saliva.

I had the briefcase open in moments, and found files inside. I flipped through them, noting yellowed pieces of paper covered in handwritten notes, along with typed documents: telegrams, letters, lists of numbers and codes that made no sense. In a large manila envelope I found black-and-white photographs. One caught my eye, and sent my heart scattering into a hard ache.

It was of my grandmother, a night shot. I knew because her arms were bare, and there were no tattoos on her skin. She was wearing a *chi pao*, a slender silk dress with a high collar and slit up her thigh that exposed a long trim leg. Her hair was down, her face very young. She looked just like me, but no older than eighteen. Zee and the others crowded close to stare at the photo, and made small choking sounds.

A little boy stood under her arm with a big grin on his face. He was skinny, with badly cut dark hair, and held a soccer ball under his bony arm. He might have been ten years old. No dates had been written on the photo, no identifying information, but it had to be Ernie. I recognized his eyes.

Another photograph caught my eye. It was my grandmother again, but just her face; less than a portrait, and more like someone's attempt to be artful. I saw the edge of an alley behind her, blurred laundry hanging from lines. A day shot. She wore a high collar and sweat beaded her brow. She was so young. Painfully new, but with the beginning of that hard edge in her eyes that I knew so well. Because it was in my eyes.

There were bumps in the image, and I turned it over. Found a message typewritten into the yellowing paper. Started reading, and my knees buckled. I sat down hard, missed the edge of the bed, and landed awkwardly on the floor. I hardly noticed.

Maxine, I read, in that small classic typeset. *If you get this, save Ernie. Save them all, if you can. I can't do any more here. She's*

But the sentence went unfinished. *She's* . . . and nothing. *She's dead,* I thought, *She's alive, she's a demon, she's—*

Spots of light flickered in my vision. I blinked hard, and reached out to grab Zee by the scruff of his neck. I felt dizzy. The wig was suddenly too hot. Sweat trickled down my back.

"My name," I hissed. "This note is addressed to me *by name*. Just like *Ernie* knew my name."

Zee quivered. I released him and stood awkwardly, knees still weak. After a few short steadying breaths, I threw the entire contents of the briefcase into the tote bag, including a box of bullets, and the unopened container of a new disposable cell phone.

On my way out, I stopped at the front desk again. "Quick question. My grandfather wants to make sure he's paid up for the next day or two. Did he use cash or a credit card?"

The young woman did not need to check the computer. She tilted her head, thinking. "Cash. He said he was old-fashioned that way. I think he paid for the entire week, so he doesn't need to worry."

I nodded, and left at a quick trot. The police would not track Ernie Bernstein to this hotel for a while yet, and if he had been as careful as I thought, then perhaps not at all. The man had not wanted to be discovered; in fact, he'd been paranoid about it if he had eschewed the use of a credit card. Or maybe he really was old-fashioned.

But somehow I didn't think so. Ernie had known he was being hunted. And the hunter had caught up.

Now it was time for me to do the same.

3

"SHANGHAI was a refuge for Jews during World War Two," Grant said, over an early breakfast. "It was the only place in the world that didn't require a visa, so thousands of Jewish refugees went there to escape the Nazis."

Long night. Almost dawn. I could feel it in my bones as I chewed on a piece of bacon, eyes burning with weariness— or so I kept telling myself. "But the Japanese occupied the city, and they were allied with Hitler."

"Allied, maybe, but they basically left the Jews alone. Forced them to live in a particular neighborhood, required passes to move around the city . . . a hard life, but compared to what was going on in Europe, it was nothing."

I finished the bacon, rubbed my hands on a napkin, and leaned over to stare at the files spread on the table between us. I still felt shaken by the message on the back of the photo. I should have been used to strange things by now, but my tolerance for the bizarre, apparently, was not that strong when it involved my family.

Raw and Aaz were on the floor by the television, watching an old Yogi Bear episode while fishing into a box of razor blades, eating them like potato chips. Zee had a laptop in front of him, delicately tapping the keys with his claws while his little brow wrinkled into a frown. My credit card and a copy of the *New York Times* were beside him, open to the financial section. Dek and Mal coiled over his shoulder, peering at the screen, occasionally whispering in his ear. Grant followed my gaze. "Stock broker now?"

I grunted, sipping coffee. "I'm not sure I want to know."

Grant picked up the picture of my grandmother. He had said very little about the message, but the line between his eyes had not yet smoothed away. "Remarkable resemblance. Have you spoken with Jack yet?"

"All the women in my family look the same." I reached for the FedEx envelope, already torn open. "And no. He's disappeared again."

Jack Meddle. My grandfather. A respected archaeologist and intellectual, who on the surface seemed like nothing more than a cheerful, dapper, eccentric old man who lived above an art gallery in downtown Seattle. But he was even less human than Grant or me—though I was no longer certain if humanity could be judged so simply.

There was very little in the FedEx envelope—which I had ripped into as soon as I left the hotel and gotten into the car. Contents minimal—just a handwritten letter, read for the first time in the dark, and now here, again, at the kitchen table.

E.

I hope this reaches you in time. Be careful. Don't do anything stupid. And don't get your hopes up. She's not Jean. She won't understand what we went through together. How could she? How could anyone? I don't care what Jean told you. That was more than sixty years ago. Grandmothers are not their granddaughters, and the dead don't speak for the living.

Nor do the living ever listen.

Best,
Winnie

As before, the words had a hypnotic effect. I could not stop staring at them. One, in particular.

Jean.

Strange, seeing my grandmother's name written in someone else's hand.

Almost as strange as seeing *my* name typewritten on the back of her photograph.

I reluctantly gave the letter to Grant. While he read, I twisted in my chair to look at Zee. "I want the story. I want to know what happened. These children who knew my grandmother. Why?"

Raw and Aaz stopped chewing razor blades. Zee sighed. "Double eyes, double life. Old mother worked undercover."

"Undercover," I echoed. "*Undercover?* Are you saying she was a . . . a spy?"

Dek made a tittering sound. Zee held his little hand like a gun and blew on his finger. "Kiss. *Jean* Kiss."

I slumped in my chair, drumming my fingers on the table. "For which country?"

Mal began humming the melody of "America the Beautiful." Grant coughed, but it sounded suspiciously like laughter. I tried giving him a dirty look, but it was difficult.

My grandmother, the spy. Of course.

"So she was in China during World War Two," I said, chewing over the idea. "Hiding out with Jewish refugees in Shanghai while spying on the Japanese?"

Grant stared at the letter in his hands. "It would have been easy for her to do. Twelve thousand Jews, plus a million Chinese, crammed into a neighborhood that was approximately one square mile in size? Good place to get lost."

"But what does that have to do with what's happening now? Ernie said *they* were wrong, that my grandmother tried to warn them about something. And that now it was time to finish what she started." I looked at Zee, frowning as the little demon's shoulders twitched. "Sounds like she did more than just spy."

"More," Zee rasped, sharing a long look with the others. But that was all, and he would not meet my gaze, no matter how close I leaned—even when I slipped out of the chair and crawled toward him, on all fours. I pushed down the screen of his laptop. It was almost dawn. I could feel it in my bones. Zee stared at my hand, chewing his bottom lip with sharp teeth.

Grant set down the letter. "I don't like this."

"Winnie, and the other people she refers to . . . all of them could be in danger. If nothing else, they'll know what's going on. Since the *boys* aren't feeling particularly *talkative*." Again, I tried to catch Zee's attention, but no luck. He simply sat, staring at my hand, his gaze finally ticking sideways, thoughtfully, to take in Raw and Aaz. Both of whom were sitting very still, watching us worriedly. Little comfort—but not much of a surprise. I had never been able to rely on the boys for complete answers. Just riddles.

I sat back on my heels. "There's a P.O. box listed for the return address on the FedEx envelope. The 10019 zip code is in New York City, an area just south of Central Park. Zee was able to lift a scent off the letter. I sent the boys on a hunt to see if they could narrow down the location of Winifred Cohen." I looked at Grant. "And they did. She's alive."

He slouched in his chair, fingering the letter. "You want to go there."

"I have to."

"How? Driving cross-country?" Grant narrowed his eyes. "I know that look on your face."

I hesitated, and held up my right hand, staring at the fragments of armor encasing my fingers and wrist. "I could be there in seconds."

"Not worth the risk, Maxine. You don't know what you're doing with that thing. You could end up in New York City before there even *was* a New York City, and what then?"

"Exploring America before it went European holds some appeal to me," I replied dryly. "How's that for a vacation?"

Grant shook his head, jaw tight with concern. I understood. I knew better than to try to time travel. I watched television. Folks who messed with that shit usually ended up destroying the world. I already had enough on my plate, thank you very much.

But she addressed the note to you by name, whispered a bleak voice inside my head. *Your name.*

I gritted my teeth. He said, "You'll have to fly. And I'm coming with you."

"I know," I said, staring at my hands, the armor—suddenly feeling like Zee, unable to look anyone in the eye. When Grant did not reply, I forced myself to meet his gaze—and found him staring. "You thought I was going to argue?"

"You usually do," he said gruffly. "Lone warrior. Venturing into the wilderness, beating your chest about how you don't want anyone else to get hurt."

I thumped my chest. "I don't want anyone else to get hurt."

"It sounds sexier when you're naked."

I wanted to thwack him in the head. "Is it too much to confess that I just don't want to be apart from you?"

His jaw tightened. "No."

"Good." I looked away from him, unable to handle the intensity of his gaze. Too many years spent alone, too many expectations to overcome that I would always *be* alone. And here, this man, who rocked me with emotions I was still unaccustomed to feeling. What I felt for him defied words.

My skin tightened. I glanced at the window, and found the overcast sky not much lighter. But the sun was moments away from cresting the horizon, somewhere beyond the clouds. Dawn.

Zee stepped over the laptop, dragging Dek and Mal by their tails. Watching me carefully, Raw and Aaz dropped their razor blades, and clambered close—all of them crawling into my lap, wrapping their long sharp arms around me in tight, fierce hugs. I felt tension in their small bodies, hesitation—too much left unresolved in their silence. They knew it, I knew it. Nothing to be done about it now. I kissed their heads anyway, thinking of my mother and grandmother, and listened to the symphony of purrs that rolled through my body like thunder.

"Sleep tight," I whispered.

I felt the sun rise. In the blink of an eye, the little demons

disappeared into my flesh, coating me with smoke and fire—
five pairs of red eyes, glinting across my body. Every inch
of me, from between my toes to the middle of my neck and
scalp, now covered in tattoos: my boys, tingling beneath my
clothes as they settled restlessly into dreams.

My face was the exception, but the boys could shift
positions in an instant if danger arose, making me entirely
invulnerable. Nothing could kill me while they slept on my
skin. Not a bullet, not fire, not a nuclear bomb. If I were
held under water, the boys would breathe for me. If I was
thrown into a pit and locked up without food or drink, the
boys would nourish me from their own strength.

But only while the sun was in the sky. At night I turned
vulnerable, mortal.

The armor on my hand had also changed its appearance.
With the boys away from my skin, the metal had been simple,
unadorned, bright as polished silver. Now, like a chameleon,
it had dulled to match the coal black shadows on my flesh—
engravings of coiled delicate lines appearing mysteriously
to blend with scales and the sharp etched angles that were
bones and hair, and claws.

Like roses, I thought, staring at my armored hand; and
then glanced at the FedEx envelope where I had placed the
fragment of leathery human skin.

Grant followed my gaze. "This is going to be ugly."

"Always is," I said, and reached for the laptop to start
searching for flights.

THE problem with murderers was that they usually took you
by surprise. Not just with the act itself (though few ever
really expected to die suddenly, violently). It was the actual
perpetrator who could be a shock: familiarity, motive, lack
of motive, the very fact that this was a person no one would
expect to kill.

Murder was premeditated. Murder was planned. Murder
required a commitment—not just to kill, but to live with the
killing.

I had taken lives, demonic and human, but always in

self-defense, or in the defense of others. I had learned to sleep at night despite the death on my hands. I could look at myself in the mirror without flinching. Usually.

In the case of Ernie's murder, I assumed that someone had been hired to take him out; perhaps the kid found shot nearby, or someone else. The attack on Ernie had been deliberate and vicious. Knives were always vicious. Stabbing someone again and again took a level of resolve and intimacy that pulling a trigger didn't quite reach. To kill someone like that meant you were used to murder—extremely desperate—or you really hated the guts of the person you were attacking. Sometimes all three.

Ernie had covered his tracks, though. It would have taken resources to follow him. Or someone who knew him well. The mysterious Winnie had known where he would be. Chances were good someone else he trusted had been in the loop, too.

I thought about that a lot during the flight. It was six hours from Seattle to New York City. I had never been on a plane. Never *wanted* to be on a plane. I hated the idea, even though I knew, intellectually, that a domestic flight would not be dangerous. It was international travel that caused trouble—moving from night to day, and back again. The boys might wake up.

But by the time we landed at La Guardia, I was a mess. Air pressure, air sickness, bad air, no air. No zombies, though. I had been seeing less of them over the past few months. Most of the parasites had left Seattle—run from my presence—but ten minutes inside New York City, I wondered if something else was at work. No dark auras, anywhere. Not even a taste. Far cry from the last time I had been here.

It was a little after seven in the evening when the cab dropped us off in front of Winnie's apartment building. It was located on a quiet street filled with brownstone walkups, tilting trees, and the nearby glow of a small deli. Still daylight. I listened to the hum of air conditioners bolted outside windows, and the hush of quiet laughter from the couple at the intersection.

Winifred's apartment building, unlike its neighbors, was

taller than five stories, a cream-colored concrete block of windows with a green awning over the double-wide glass doors, and an elevator visible at the far end of the small lobby. Red geraniums framed the entrance, overflowing from massive clay pots.

I watched the street, listening to the rippling sensation on my skin as the boys shifted restlessly in their dreams. Not quite a warning, but close enough. I glanced at Grant, and found him also watching our surroundings; intense, a hint of gold in his brown eyes.

"Anything?"

"Nothing remarkable. But something doesn't feel right." He briefly nudged my shoulder. "Don't."

I frowned. "Stop reading me."

"I can take care of myself."

"Who said I was worried about you?"

Grant smiled grimly. I shook my head. Maybe I *had* been too hasty in agreeing that he should come along. I was getting soft. Something I had been telling myself for almost a year now.

I dialed in the apartment number that Zee had given me and hit the buzzer. I let it ring until it choked off, and then tried again. No one answered. A deeply tanned, gorgeous young man—dressed like he was ready for a jog—exited the elevator, and pushed open the glass doors. He gave Grant a lusty smile, and with a lingering backward glance, strode down the sidewalk.

I stuck my foot in the doorway before we could be locked out. "Dude. You were just totally undressed."

"Try not to be jealous," Grant replied dryly, limping past me into the building. "I can't help my unbridled sexual magnetism."

We rode the elevator to the tenth floor. Seemed like a nice enough place. Quiet, clean, modern. I was no expert on apartment buildings, though I had inherited a place uptown, along Central Park. No strong memories of it, except that it faced the southeast, had a view of the trees, and had been bought by my great-great-grandmother during the Depression. I doubted seriously that I would be stopping by for a visit, though part of me wondered if some of my mother's things would still be there, covered in dust after more than a decade of absence.

Winifred Cohen's door was near the elevator. I lingered for a moment, simply listening, but heard nothing from within but the faint caress of soft music: violins weeping to Mozart.

Grant knocked. I nudged him aside. Safer than standing in front of a door when you did not know what was on the other side. Might not be Winifred. Maybe Winifred wasn't Winifred. People were never who we thought them to be.

No one came to the door, though I sensed a presence inside that apartment; like a mouse hiding in a hole, whiskers quivering just enough for the big bad cat to hear.

I knocked again, and leaned close. "Winifred. My name is Maxine Kiss. I'm here because of Jean, my grandmother. And Ernie."

Nothing. I shared a long look with Grant, and reached into my back pocket for the lock picks I had brought with me. "Winifred. If you're in there, please say something. Or else I'm coming in."

The music kept playing softly. No footsteps. No whispers of movement. But I felt something. She was there—or someone else was. I hoped it was not the latter.

It took me only moments to open the main lock, but there was a deadbolt on the other side, and probably a chain. No good way of undoing those without kicking in the door, and that was too much attention to bring on ourselves. I was ready to suggest that we wait another hour—until the sun went down—when I finally heard a faint shuffling sound on the other side. I stepped away, as did Grant, leaning against the wall beside the door while I stared at the peephole.

The locks clicked. Five metallic rasps as bolts and chains were thrown back. Then, nothing. Grant gave me a long look, and I shrugged. If she—or whomever—wanted to play games, then fine.

I opened the door. Found shadows in a long hall. Nothing but darkness, and the soft mournful keen of violins shrouding the air. I held up my hand to Grant, motioning for him to wait, and walked inside. Zee, sleeping between my breasts, began tugging gently on my skin. I ignored him, listening hard, but all I could hear below the music was my own pulse and the near-silent scuff of my cowboy boots on the hardwood floor.

Until cool air moved against my cheek and someone reached from the darkness to stab me in the throat.

The blade snapped instantly. I smelled perfume, heard the harsh rasp of someone breathing, and turned toward the darkened closet door that now housed a small hunched figure that swayed so unsteadily that I reached out, and brushed my fingers against a wrinkled elbow. My skin tingled beneath my tattoos; or maybe that was the boys, reacting. I felt strange, touching her. Light-headed.

The old woman began to back away, and then stopped, staring down at the broken knife: better suited for steaks than throats, though she'd had good aim. It took strength to cut into the cartilage of a human neck, but not if you stabbed at the soft part. Which she had. *More knives*, I thought, peering into eyes so dark they were almost black.

"Winifred, I presume," I said quietly, as Grant entered the apartment and shut the door behind him, watching her warily.

"You really are her granddaughter," replied the old woman, staring up at me with no small amount of wonderment and unease—glancing briefly at Grant with an even more troubled gaze. She had an American accent, though her vowels were tinged with the faint coil of another place and time. A stout woman with long gray hair and a round stomach that pushed against her blue housedress.

"Some test." I took the remains of the steak knife from her hand. "Were you expecting someone else?"

Winifred Cohen gave me a profoundly bitter look. "I was expecting not to live out the night."

And with that, she turned and shuffled down the dark hall.

4

"YOU have to understand that we were children," said the old woman some time later, nursing a cup of hot tea in her hands. "We knew there was a war raging, but to some degree we were insulated from it. Jewish refugees in Shanghai were tolerated, even encouraged to be enterprising. The Japanese thought our industry would help support their troops. We had school and synagogue. We had music. We had each other. It was, for that time, as good a life as could be expected. Especially compared to what the Chinese suffered."

"My grandmother," I said, perched on the edge of a pale blue sofa. I had been offered tea, and turned it down—as had Grant. No time for pleasantries, just patience. More patience than I could spare.

Winifred gave me a long steady look. "You resemble her. Uncannily. Even if I had not. . . . tested you . . . your face would have convinced me."

"But you chose violence."

"Survival," she replied without remorse. "Hit first, ask questions later. I'm meant to die, and I'm not ready."

She said it with a dull hard tone in her voice, eyes dark and pitiless; but it was her blunt acceptance that chilled me.

Death was coming. She knew it. No whining, no bargaining or depression. Merely resolve.

I had so many questions. Grant took over with the most basic. "Who wants to hurt you?"

Winifred hesitated. "Ernie?"

"I'm sorry," I said, wishing I could lie and tell her that he was still alive, charming hotel clerks and enjoying the sights of Seattle with his bundles of cold hard cash.

Winifred closed her eyes, and suddenly all that hard strength seemed to melt out of her. She set down her tea, hand shaking so badly that dark liquid splashed over the rim into her saucer. "I told him not to go."

"Ms. Cohen," Grant said again, his voice rumbling and· persuasive. "Why did he die? Why do you fear for your own life?"

"Because we helped *her*," said Winifred softly, with more than bitterness; melancholy, maybe, a profound sadness that was bone deep and weary.

Images from those old photos flickered through my mind. *Save them all, if you can.* "My grandmother?"

Winifred shook her head. "No. Another woman. She was called the Black Cat because in the late thirties she had been a hostess in a nightclub of the same name. A white Russian among Koreans. All the women who worked in that place had a black cat tattooed here." Winifred patted her backside and gave me another long look. "By the time your grandmother met her, she had many more tattoos than that."

I was holding my breath, and released it slowly, painfully. I had been more afraid than I cared to admit of hearing that my grandmother had somehow contributed to this old woman's trouble, and Ernie's death.

I considered the human skin in my backpack. "She can't still be alive."

Winifred stiffened. "Of course not."

Grant studied her with a great deal of thoughtfulness. "What did you do for this . . . Black Cat . . . that would be worth your lives? Especially now, after all these years?"

Coldness returned to her eyes. She stood slowly from her chair. He politely began to rise with her, as did I, but she waved us back with a faint hiss of her breath and left the room with a slow shuffling gait, as though her bones ached. Grant and I stared at each other.

"What do you see?" I whispered.

"Fear," he murmured. "Guilt."

"She believes she's going to die."

"It's more than that," he began, and then shut his mouth as Winifred returned to the room. She held a linen parcel, folded into a tight square, which she tossed down on the table in front of me. I unfolded it quickly, inhaling scents of lavender and something older, meatier, like death; and found myself looking at another block of thin delicate leather, tattooed in a pattern that resembled roses.

Grant made a rough sound. I stared long and hard at the skin before turning my gaze on Winifred. She had fallen back into her chair, wrinkled hands resting in her lap; posture boneless, limp, her gaze so distant and empty, she might have been dead.

"This is human," I said, "but you knew that."

"All of us took a piece of that woman," she said quietly, as though speaking only to herself. "We were told to by your grandmother."

I sat back. Grant cleared his throat. "How many of you?"

"Just the four. Ernie, me, Lizbet, and Samuel."

"And where are the last two?"

"Dead," Winifred whispered. "They married, later, after their families came to the United States in '47. Lived in Florida for the past ten years. Police found them shot to death in their home more than a week ago."

"I'm sorry," I said, as gently as I could. "But what made you and Ernie think their murders had anything to do with the both of you?"

Winifred tore her gaze from the scrap of dried human skin. "Because their killer mailed Ernie and me the . . . mementos . . . that Samuel and Lizbet had kept in their home safe. A warning, you see. A promise."

Her wrinkled mouth tightened with bitterness. "And because Jean told us what would happen for playing with the devil."

* * *

SUNSET. I fled to the bathroom. Waved along in the right direction by an old woman whose eyes were haunted, knowing. When I walked away, I felt naked, like there was a target drawn on my back.

The bathroom was small and simply decorated in white tile and a white fuzzy rug on the gleaming floor. Sparkling clean, a faint scent of shampoo mixed with bleach. I shut the door just as I felt the sun slip beneath the horizon—so much a part of my senses that it was easy as breathing to know the time. Survival instinct.

I leaned on the sink, staring at myself in the mirror, counting down the seconds. Watching my eyes. Remembering countless evenings watching my mother's eyes, or trying to, at that exact moment of the shift. She had never shown pain. Just smiled and laughed, and acted like it was a game, the old hard game, which would be mine one day, after she died. She had not wanted me to be scared of that future, even though I should have been terrified. She had wanted to keep me innocent for as long as possible—and she had, best as she could. I hadn't realized then what a gift that was, but I understood now. I understood too well. And there was no repaying that kindness except to pass it on, one day.

The sun ticked down, swallowed into my body. Zee and the boys woke up.

I had tried once to explain the sensation to Grant, but there were only so many ways of describing what it felt like to be skinned alive with acid and knives, before a girl felt like a whiner.

It hurt. It would always hurt. From my toes to between my legs, to my fingernails and nipples and scalp, to the very top of my neck. No part of me unscathed, except for my face. My hands tightened around the rim of the sink. I closed my eyes, unable to look at myself.

The boys dissolved from my skin in a cloud of smoke and silver shadows, red lightning flickering through the ghosts of their bodies as they flowed from beneath my clothes and coalesced inside the bathroom. I smelled burnt hair and a whiff of something stiff and cold, as though a tunnel had been opened to some cavern miles deep below the earth, where the air was so pure that a person could grow drunk on just one breath.

My eyes were still closed. Muscles quivered and sweat rolled. Strong arms wrapped around my legs, while two long bodies coiled over my shoulders.

Zee whispered, "Maxine."

I forced a smile on my face and drew in a long quivering breath; several, before I found my voice. "Hey, bad boys."

Dek and Mal licked the backs of my ears. I patted their heads. Raw disappeared into the shadows behind the toilet and reappeared moments later with a giant bag full of M&Ms and a six-pack of beer. He handed those to Aaz, and then disappeared again—returning with a bucket of fried chicken, a nail gun, and a plastic bin full of dirty syringes, plastered in orange BIOHAZARD stickers.

I sat on the edge of the toilet, scratching behind Zee's pointed little ears as he grabbed a fistful of individually wrapped packages of M&Ms and shoved them, paper and all, into his mouth. Behind him, Raw had picked up the nail gun and was shooting studs down his brother's throat. Aaz giggled, swallowing each one. Dek, watching them, made a small sound of protest—and I opened a beer, which he fitted his entire mouth over and then knocked back with a sigh. Mal, who had disappeared from my shoulders, poked his head up from within the fried chicken bucket, too much like some crazed demonic gopher. He licked his chops and gave me a toothy grin.

I nudged the container of used syringes toward Raw. He cracked it open and began popping each one into his mouth like candy bars. Over the crunching sounds of plastic, chicken, paper, and aluminum, I said, "Tell me about the Black Cat."

"Bad news," Zee rasped, licking his claws. "Gave our old mother a hard run."

"And that's the reason three people associated with this woman have been murdered?"

Zee lowered his hand, sharing a long look with the others,

who stopped eating. "Price to pay. No good road from that hunt. Bleed for darkness and darkness gets a taste."

Winifred was going to wonder why her bathroom smelled like fried chicken and beer. "Why? Was she a demon?"

Zee sighed, resting his chin upon my knee. Hair spikes flexed, and his red eyes narrowed with memory as his claws gently tapped the tile floor. "Almost."

"Almost. What does that mean?"

"Means *almost*." Zee scrunched up his face. "Blood never lies, Maxine."

I gave him a long look, suspicions and theories rumbling through my head. But before I could ask, Dek lifted his head and froze. All the boys did, staring at the door.

I was up in moments, out of the bathroom, running down the hall. Grant and Winifred were still seated in the living room, talking softly, but they stopped when they saw me. Grant did not need to hear my warning. He braced himself on his cane and rose in one smooth movement, knuckles white around the carved oak handle.

"Winifred," he rumbled quietly, still staring into my eyes. "You need to come with us now."

The old woman paled. No arguments, though. She stood, swaying, and Grant steadied her with his free hand. I moved ahead of them, Dek and Mal settling heavily in my hair. Red eyes winked at me from the shadows of the long hall. I listened hard, heard nothing.

The door loomed. Grant and Winifred lingered behind me. I held out my hand, gesturing for them to wait as I crept forward. From the shadows of the closet, Zee whispered, "Clear."

And it was, when I opened the door. Nothing there.

We left the apartment without incident, and took the elevator down to the first floor. Winifred watched me the entire time, with such intensity my skin crawled. So many stories in her eyes, so much she knew that had not been spoken. I hated secrets. I hated the mysteries in the past that no one, even if they tried, would ever be able to explain. To understand something you had to live it—or live something so close that the empathy was secondhand. What this woman had gone through—the events chasing her now—was beyond me. But that didn't mean I wasn't going to try.

As the elevator doors opened I said, "You have ten seconds to tell me why you're being hunted. No riddles. I want answers."

"We were children," Winifred said tightly, still evading my question. "We didn't know what we were doing."

I noticed she clenched that tightly folded square of linen in her hands, a hint of human leather peeking out from beneath the edge of cloth. I stuck my foot in the elevator door, holding it open. "Right. Because taking *that* from a dead woman is *morally ambiguous*. Try another one, Ms. Cohen."

Winifred gave me a haunted look. "She wasn't dead when we took it."

And then, almost at a run, she rushed past me into the lobby. Grant began to follow, and stumbled. I grabbed his elbow, clinging tight, feeling as though he was holding me up just as much as I was holding him. I stared at the old woman's rounded shoulders and whispered, "What is this?"

"Something worth killing over," he replied, voice strained. "She wouldn't say much to me, but whatever happened when she was a child left a black stain in her aura. Almost like a . . . handprint. I saw something similar in Ernie, but I didn't think much of it at the time. He was dying. He might have shot someone. Any of that would cause a shadow."

"I don't believe in coincidences," I muttered, and let go of him to hurry after Winifred, who had stopped by the glass entrance and was looking back at us with those old dark eyes. We were alone. No one around to hear more confessions. I reached for the old woman, intending comfort, strength—something, anything, that would reassure her that it was safe to tell me the truth.

Before I could reach her, the glass in the door shattered. Winifred staggered into my arms, collapsing against me. I gasped, stunned, falling down with her—and my fingers touched wet heat. Came away red. She had been shot in the back.

A roar filled my ears, deafening and cold. Grant began talking into his cell phone. I hardly heard him. Winifred was still breathing. I slid out from under her, trying to keep my hand on her wound. Pressing down with all my strength.

Save them.

Blood seeped past my fingers. Winifred's breathing was rough, little more than a strangled hiss—but except for that and the quiet persistence of Grant's voice, silence seemed to press around us. Such terrible silence, as though what little sounds we were making meant nothing to the crush of empty air surrounding our bodies.

A strong hand covered mine. Grant whispered, "Go. Find who did this."

I shook my head. "Not safe for you."

His lips brushed my ear. "Justice, Maxine."

I tore my gaze from the blood spreading through Winifred's clothing and gave him a sharp look. Found nothing in his eyes but that old grim determination; and deeper yet, anger.

I stood, and his hands replaced mine, pressing down on the wound. My fingers snapped at Raw, who was peering at us from around the ruined remains of the door.

"Protect them," I snarled.

And then I was gone, kicking out the remains of the glass to run into the street, searching for a shooter.

It was a cool Sunday night in New York City, and while this particular street was quiet, I heard the growling hum of cars and people rumbling through the night. No screams, though. No fingers pointing. Just me, and windows across the street, a mixture of light and dark. I stared, searching for movement, anyone watching—but found nothing except for a handful of people strolling across the intersection toward me. No sign that any of them knew what had just happened. I heard their careless laughter.

I began walking in the opposite direction. Zee flitted through the shadows, appearing briefly in nooks between brownstone stairs and garbage cans; leaping from the branches of slender shade trees and then reappearing moments later in the darkness beneath parked cars. I kept waiting for him to say something, but all he did was give me brief, uneasy glances that made my stomach hurt.

"What," I finally asked," did you find?"

"Nothing," he rasped. "Gone."

"You can find the shooter. Don't play dumb."

Zee fell backward into the shadows. I kept walking, scanning the street. Trying to let my instincts do what my demons would not. But ten minutes later, I had no answers. Nothing. Nothing, anywhere. Winifred's attacker had escaped. I had known it the moment I stepped free of her apartment building.

Zee peered at me from beneath another parked car. I gave him a long hard look. He ducked his head, fading away. But not far. Close as my own skin, if anyone threatened me. The boys felt those things. My life was sacred. They would have known a gunman was close. They *had* known. But the threat had not been for me, or Grant—who they protected almost as carefully. And so they had let the bullet go.

But that failed to explain why they did not want the killer found.

Winifred was being loaded into an ambulance when I returned to the apartment building. A crowd had finally gathered. I was trying to push through them when my cell phone rang.

"Stay where you are," Grant said, as soon as I answered. I found him by the ambulance, staring at me.

I stayed. I lingered, watching like everyone else. Grant was helped into the ambulance with Winifred, and when they left, I walked away, rounded the corner, and headed toward Central Park. Headlights dashed through my vision, warm fetid scents blowing over me, briefly. It was easy to get lost, to feel lost, to lose my thoughts to bullets and demons, and question what the hell I was good for if I could not protect one old woman.

I'd been having that conversation a lot with myself over the past several months. People always seemed to get hurt around me. It was why I had been raised to be a nomad, to never linger in one spot for long; to avoid making ties, roots, relationships that mattered.

I was such a bad daughter.

I walked for a good twenty minutes until my phone rang again.

"We're at St. Luke's. Tenth and Fifty-ninth," Grant murmured, and in the background I heard voices chattering, shouts, metallic clangs. "Police coming to question me. Winifred's in surgery."

And then he hung up again.

I flagged down a cab and headed for the hospital. Took me another twenty minutes to reach the ER entrance, but I did not go inside. I circled the hospital until I found a small stone wall to sit on, and perched there in the shadows, watching cars and people. A homeless man slept on a slab of cardboard some ten feet away, and beyond him a young woman crouched with a cigarette in one hand and a bottle of Gatorade in the other. She was humming to herself. No one paid attention to me. I sent a text to Grant's phone. Five minutes later, I received a reply.

STAY AWAY. GOT IT COVERED.

Which was the best I could hope for, though it bothered me that I was not in there with him. Where there was one bullet, there would be another. The killer would want to make sure the deed had been done. Unfortunately, until the police left it was best I keep out of sight. I could not afford for my name—alias or otherwise—to show up on another report. If word got back to Suwani and McCowan, and I had to assume it would, more questions would follow. Grant's mojo wouldn't be able to save me forever, and I was unprepared to move on.

I'm not ready, Winifred had said.

There was a small garden behind the wall I perched on. I glanced over my shoulder at a pair of sharp red eyes. "You did that on purpose. You deliberately allowed that woman to be shot."

Zee gave me an inscrutable look. "Debts paid in full, Maxine."

"Winifred is still alive," I snapped. "The killer will try again. I need to know who is doing this."

Still, he hesitated—and something broke inside me. I turned, grabbing his shoulder. Shaking him, or trying to; he dug in his heels and wrapped his claws around my arm. Both of us, pushing against the other. Pretending to, anyway.

I knew his strength. He could crush my bones with the slightest pinch, or flay me in strips with one judicious swipe. But I was not afraid. I had never been afraid of Zee, or the others. We were family. But family could be a pain in the ass sometimes.

Dek and Mal poked free of my hair. Raw and Aaz crept close, eyes huge.

"I am sick," I whispered, "of never hearing the simple truth."

"Truths never simple," Zee rasped. "Only death, simple. Only birth, simple. Between, threads and hearts and lies, and we are not interpreters. We are not *you*."

His grip relaxed. So did mine, but we did not stop holding each other. Zee whispered, "Past and present always tangled. Too many mysteries." He touched his chest. "Only truth is yours. Only truth that matters. What *you* see matters. Not what we see. Not what we tell you."

I closed my eyes. "Zee. I need help."

"We help," he whispered, pressing his warm sharp cheek against my arm. "But no answers here. Never were. Just shadows. Memories."

"You could have told me that," I said, all my anger slipping into weariness. "So if not here, then where?"

Again, that odd hesitancy. "Got to travel, Maxine. Far away."

"You promise there will be answers?"

"Promise enough," he replied.

"Grant and Winifred need to be protected."

"Time will protect them." Zee grabbed my right hand. His words echoed in my head—*time, time, time*—and terrible instinct made my heart tighten with fear. I opened my mouth to protest, but it was too late. Raw and Aaz wrapped their arms around Zee, and the armor on my right hand, hidden beneath my glove, began to tingle and burn.

My muscles turned to liquid around my bones, and every soft organ in my body seemed to shrivel and lurch. Darkness swallowed me.

Always, darkness.

5

IT was hot when I started breathing again. A sick slick heat that plugged my nostrils with slugs of air so pungent that breathing was almost like drinking rotten wine; I could taste the individual notes of urine and feces, along with garlic and smoke.

I rolled over on my side, head pounding, and gagged into a puddle that smelled worse than what I had been breathing. The back of my head was wet with the stuff. My stomach heaved again, pain sparking behind my eyes. Small hands touched me.

"Where?" I rasped, coughing. I dug my fist into concrete, pushing hard. Arms hooked around mine, tugging me up on my knees.

But those arms did not belong to a demon.

I froze, turning my head slowly to gaze at the small pale face pressed close to mine in the shadows. It was night, but my sight was good enough to see the dark glitter of concerned eyes.

I knew those eyes. And the recognition was so startling, so violent, my gut seized up as though punched. I bent over again, aching.

Ernie. Ernie Bernstein.

"Come on," said the boy, with an unnerving amount of compassion and maturity. "Hurry."

He grunted as he helped me stand, and when I touched his shoulder I felt only bone. He was gaunt, little more than a stick figure beneath the oversized button-up and shorts hanging on his frame. He grabbed my hand, grip tight and sweaty. I had no choice but to follow. Dazed, riding the moment. Dreaming, I thought. My life was nothing but a twisting dream.

He hauled me down a narrow concrete lane that curled like the gut of a snake; a suffocating space crowded with laundry lines, and open doors where men hunched in boneless exhaustion with their eyes closed. Faint lights burned behind them, revealing glimpses of movement; skirts and bare arms, and glass glinting, fleeting as ghosts. I heard pots banging, babies wailing; shouts, followed by the low throaty grunts of sex; and as I pressed my palm against my aching head I saw red eyes in the shadows, steady as stone and fire.

I could make no sense of the maze that Ernie led me down, and finally blocked out everything but the need to stay on my feet and breathe. It was so hard to breathe the air, which was unrelenting in its heat. Sweat poured down my body. My jeans and turtleneck felt like a burning coffin against my skin.

A breeze finally cut against me. Faint, but the movement of air felt like a splash of cold water against my face. I tilted my head, inhaling, and moments later found myself discharged from the narrow alley. Expelled in a rush, like something hard and dirty that had passed for days through some sweaty bowel. I stood on a wide avenue where the buildings, at first glance, resembled some mask of European charm; but then Chinese men, nearly naked and glistening with sweat, ran past me with their heads down, hauling empty rickshaws behind them.

Thunder rolled in the distance; man-made or a storm, I could not tell. I glanced at Ernie, who still held my hand. He was staring at my clothes.

"Hey," I whispered, afraid of my own voice. Afraid of

him, this place, everything around me. I was not supposed to be here. No one, I thought, should have that power.

His head jerked up, but there was nothing startled or young in his gaze. His eyes were old, far too old.

"Your head," Ernie said. "He hit you."

"He," I echoed. My head ached. I was still touching it lightly. "No. I was . . . sick."

He did not believe me. Just a glint in his eye, a thinning of his mouth, but that little shift in his expression made me feel small and cut. Like I had violated some trust between us that I had never known existed. That never had.

"But you ran from him," Ernie said, his English heavily accented. German in origin, I thought. Or Polish.

I hesitated, needing to sit down—feeling exposed on the sidewalk, far too vulnerable. "Run?"

Ernie frowned impatiently. "You only dress like a man during the day. Did you steal his clothes because you were in a hurry?"

He thought I was Jean. My grandmother. I took a moment, unsure how to respond. "I'd rather not talk about it."

Disappointment, even hurt, flashed across his face, but he nodded stiffly and gestured down the street, which seemed filled with sluggish activity; a quietness to each slow movement that made the night feel deep and old. "I can't walk you home. I have to go. *Mutter* does not know I slipped out." He released my hand, and teetered backward, still studying me. "You seem different."

No shit. "How did you know where to find me?"

Finally, Ernie looked uncomfortable. "You always see the *baojia* unit leader on Thursdays. But he drinks," blurted out the boy, and then stared hard at his shoes, which had holes where his big toes should be. "He's mean when he drinks. We all know that."

I thought of the hotel clerk, smiling as she talked about old man Ernie. And here, the boy, still a champion of women. I felt a howl swell in my throat, but swallowing it down only made my eyes burn with tears.

Here's your chance, I thought. *Ask him about the Black Cat. Don't waste time.*

But when I opened my mouth, all I said was, "Go on home, Ernie. Thanks for helping me."

Nothing else to say. Nothing. He was just a kid, and I was the grown-up here. Whatever was happening now was bad news, and would get him killed in sixty years. If I could take care of it without getting him involved more than he already was, if I could do this without upsetting time more than it already would be—then I had to try. I had to keep him, and his friends, safe.

Which meant talking to—and finding—someone else.

Ernie nodded, but still lingered—like there was more he wanted to say. He rubbed his wrist as though it hurt.

"What is it?" I asked, as gently as I could. "Ernie, you can tell me."

He ducked his head, fingers going still around his wrist. I glimpsed a mark there, half-hidden beneath his thumb. Reached for him without thinking. He flinched, taking a step back—and shot me a haunted look that cut me to the core. I had seen those eyes before, on other kids, and it was a bad look. Kids were not supposed to grow up that fast.

No chance to say a word, though. He turned and ran down the street. I let him go, and then became aware of others watching me, both Chinese and European. Curious stares. Some calculating. I was a new face, and fresh meat.

I melted back into the dark lane we had emerged from. It was still and empty, unlike the road; and I needed a moment. I needed more than a moment.

"Zee." I breathed, sliding down the wall into a crouch. I tugged at my collar, and then stripped off my leather gloves. Armor glinted along my fingers and the wrist cuff had grown in size, embedded now in my lower forearm with quicksilver tendrils. I would be lost to this metal one day. If I lived that long.

Small clawed hands touched my knees, long fingers edged in flesh sharp and hard as obsidian. Zee whispered, "Maxine."

"Playing games with my life," I murmured, listening to bells clang, and distant shouts in Chinese. I heard the echoing report of guns, very distant; synchronized single-shot blasts that made me imagine an execution. I smelled shit, and realized it was coming from my hair.

"You want truth," Zee rasped. "Give you truth."

I gritted my teeth. "I suppose we're in Shanghai. When?"

"Four-and-four." He glanced over his shoulder as Raw and Aaz melted from the shadows, chattering at him in their native tongue—which I did not, and never would, understand. Zee stiffened, and then relaxed. I tapped his hand.

"We know," he said quietly, still watching his brothers. "We know we are here."

We. The *other* Zee and his brothers—who were in their right place, and right time. I was probably creating some kind of planet-wrecking paradox by having them in the same place, together, but hell if I knew what to do about it. The boys had brought me here. I had to assume they knew what they were doing in between the teddy bear decapitations and soft porn.

"I need clothes," I said. "I stand out too much."

Raw disappeared into the shadows, and emerged less than a minute later with a bundle of cotton that, when shook out, appeared to be a dark brown dress, loose and flowing. Simple cut, with long sleeves, mother of pearl buttons up the front, and a round collar. The hem came down to just below my knees. He also gave me a new matching pair of lambskin gloves.

I moved away from the road into a nearby doorway, dressing quickly. I tossed my jeans and turtleneck to Aaz for disposal, and then reluctantly put aside my cowboy boots for a pair of brown shoes that had a hard, flat, sensible heel. Raw slid my other shoes into a cloth satchel the color of mushy peas. Inside, I glimpsed knives, and tins of food.

I felt like a stranger to myself. I stood for a moment, sweating and weary, and tilted my face to the sky. No stars. Just clouds, bruised with the faint reflected light of the city.

China, I thought. I was in Shanghai. And it was World War Two.

I found my grandmother less than thirty minutes later, flirting with a drunk Nazi.

I had been floating until that moment, drifting in a daze through the soup of the hot night and suffering a dreamlike schizophrenia; lost in the shadowed kiss of a European-flavored city, only to be torn sideways into Asian byways: meandering lanes and alleys no wider than the span of my shoulders. I passed elderly Chinese women perched on low wooden stools, playing mahjong while bickering at naked, shrieking children who played in the stifling darkness among piles of trash that had been swept into rotten heaps wet with water trickling down the narrow gutters.

Most ignored my presence, but some of the children chased me with their hands outstretched, begging for money, trying to sink their small hands into my bag. Open sores covered their arms and legs. I could count their ribs. I gave them the tins of food.

Zee led me; in snatches, glimpses. Dek and Mal were silent in my hair. I did not see Raw and Aaz, but knew they were close. I was comforted by that, but it was a painful, uneasy consolation. I was lost in time. What I did here would ripple into the future. It was not my first journey into the past, but I had never been set loose, faced with the potential cost of being that butterfly flapping her wings—and causing a thunderstorm on the other side of the world.

Ernie's young face filled my mind. *Save him,* whispered a small voice, but I could no longer blame the letter on the back of that photo for such urgency. *You have to make sure he doesn't die in your arms. Not murdered. Not him.*

Not any of them.

I heard music in the night. A lonely saxophone playing a heartbreaking version of "Over the Rainbow." Zee glided through the shadows, little more than a glimpse of spiked hair and sharp joints. Dek licked the back of my ear. I patted his head as I stepped free of the residential alley and found myself staring at a party.

Just a glimpse, beyond an open gate built into a thick stone wall that followed the curve of the road. Barbed wire fencing rose almost five feet higher than the wall itself, ending on the right-hand side at a distinctive fluted turret that was as out of place as the German signs framing the gate. Young Chinese children squatted on the sidewalk, playing what looked like rock, paper, scissors with a pair of Jewish kids, a boy and girl. Carts rumbled down the road between us, hand-pulled by gaunt Chinese men—who gave wide berth to a car parked alongside the street; a black Peerless, top down, revealing quilted leather seats that looked soft as a glove. I knew cars. This one was old-fashioned for 1944, but lovingly cared for. An Asian man sat behind the wheel, dozing.

No one paid attention to me: lone woman lurking at the entrance of the alley. The streets were dark. No electricity to spare. No oil to waste in lamps.

I heard glasses clinking, and smelled food. Yeast scents, and something meatier. Even a hint of coffee. My stomach growled. Zum Weissen Röss'l was the name of the place, according to the largest of the signs hanging above the gate—written, too, above the arched entrance of the elegant white building that was at the far end of the courtyard. Round tables and wicker chairs dotted the swept stone ground, and the saxophone's mourning tones were pure and sweet. I could not see the musician.

Business was good. Tables were full. I saw waitresses circulating in traditional Bavarian outfits—white frilly aprons, with white puffy sleeves and collars, overlaid with a dark button-up smock and full skirts—tucked and nipped to accommodate starved frames. Muted laughter spilled into the night, glasses clinking. A surreal sight, and nothing I would have expected to find in the middle of occupied war-torn territory.

I glanced down at Zee, who was little more than a bulge in the shadows. Found him staring at the restaurant, utterly rapt. Breathless, even. I had never seen that look on his face, and it occurred to me, with some shame, that—sixty years in the past, or ten thousand—confronting a world that had been dead and gone was no easier on him and the boys than it was for me. Worse, perhaps. I had no memories of this place. I had nothing to latch my heart on to. Except for my grandmother. And, perhaps, young Ernie Bernstein.

I looked back at the courtyard. And just like that, saw her.

She was sauntering out of the white building, bearing a tray. Nothing but her arm was visible, and a loose arrangement of long black hair. I could not see her face. But I knew. I knew with absolute certainty that it was my grandmother.

I almost crossed the road. Aaz grabbed my hand, holding me back. I did not fight him. I could not. I watched my grandmother serve a table full of Nazis.

I had not noticed them until that moment, but in hindsight I could hardly believe I had been so blind. They were sitting in plain view of the open gate, red armbands glowing upon their brown uniforms, sharp black swastika lines standing in sharp relief against white spotlight circles. Blond men, drinking beer and spearing thick sausages on their forks. Two uniformed Asian soldiers sat with them, bayonets leaning against the table. Japanese, I thought. A night out for the men in charge.

I held my breath as my grandmother leaned close, setting down mugs and taking away empty plates. Aaz tightened his grip on my wrist. But in the end, I did not need to worry. No one touched her body. Not that she looked as though she would have minded. I felt like I was losing my mind.

The first and second time I had ever met my grandmother, she had been a chain-smoking, hard-eyed, dangerous woman. Gritty, leathery, with a masculine edge to her clothing and walk. A mother, to boot. No funny business. Not this young thing with a sweet face and ready smile. Not this girl who wore black heels and a frilly white apron, and glanced at Nazis with a come-hither glint that was so startlingly sexy I wanted to look away in embarrassment.

I stood there in the shadows, suffocating, suffering the heat again as if my skin would melt off my bones, or stuff my lungs with cotton. Looking at my grandmother was like checking out an inferno that I could not control. I was totally at a loss about how to make contact with her. Wondering if I should. Remembering that I already had, given the note addressed to me on the back of her photograph.

Just as my grandmother straightened to walk back into the restaurant, her stride faltered, head tilting ever so slightly—as though listening to a whisper in her ear, or just silence. Perhaps the same silence emanating now from Dek and Mal, who had stopped purring and were so still I wanted to look over my shoulder to make certain no one had a gun aimed at my back.

My grandmother turned slowly, a faint smile on her lips—though it was strained now, more clearly a mask. I did not move. I did not breathe. I was deep in shadows across the road—not close by any measure—but she found me instantly. She met my gaze.

Her eyes widened, and she fumbled the tray in her hands. The Nazi she had just served patted her ass with a deep chuckle. She hardly seemed to notice. Just flashed me another look, and then walked quickly into the restaurant.

I sagged against the wall, and waited.

It took more than an hour. I watched people. Listened to a city that was sixty years in my past, embroiled in a war sixty years dead, and found myself thinking that life here, besides certain obvious differences, was not so removed from life in my own time. The toys might be different, and the clothes, and the setting, but people never changed. Fear and hate never changed, nor did love. Or courage.

I saw all those things in the courtyard beyond the wall. Jews who sat at tables around the Nazis, forced to pretend there was nothing wrong. Men scooted their chairs so they blocked their wives from sight, and the laughter I had heard earlier grew quieter, and edgier, as the soldiers drank more deeply from their cups. Those who had been eating left quickly. Those who thought about eating stopped at the gate, took one glance inside, and kept going. Some of them tapped the playing children on their heads, and made sure they came along, as well.

Until almost no one was left. Just the Nazis and Japanese. And my grandmother, who served them. No other waitress came near. The mysterious saxophone player was replaced by a violinist who began playing Strauss. My knees ached, and I settled into a crouch with the boys gathered close. Wondering where the Zee from 1944 might be lingering. Close, no doubt. Close enough to touch.

When the Nazis left, they tossed paper money on the

table—but one of the men slipped something else to my grandmother; an object small and dark, like a twig. Her only reaction was to thank him with a pretty smile, blushing when he chucked her under the chin.

She stood politely to the side as they filed out, one after the other, into the street. The Peerless sputtered to life. I had almost forgotten it. The driver rolled ten feet forward to the gate, and then exited quickly to open doors. Within moments, they were gone.

So was my grandmother, when I looked for her again.

I was patient. Nothing better to do. All the time in the world. Raw pulled a cup of hot unsweetened tea from the shadows, and placed it in my hands, along with a warm sugar cookie that melted in my mouth. Tasted fresh from the oven. I almost asked where it was from.

I sensed movement on my right. Watched as the Jewish boy and girl who had been playing earlier outside the gate reappeared, kicking a ball between them. The girl was blond and slender, no older than ten or eleven, while the boy was likely the same age, and dark as Ernie. Not siblings. Nor had they returned to the restaurant gate just for the hell of it, though they were pretending hard that wasn't the case. It was late, I thought. Probably almost midnight.

My grandmother left the restaurant at a brisk walk, dressed in a simple brown skirt and white blouse, short-sleeved and tucked in. Her heels clicked. No smile on her face. Nothing pleasant at all about the look in her eyes. She resembled, finally, the woman I remembered; but that did not comfort me as much as it should have.

The kids peered around the gate. My grandmother faltered when she saw them, glancing briefly over their heads at me. A warning in her gaze. I knew how to take a hint. I stayed put, melting even deeper into the shadows.

"Samuel," she said to the boy, and then rested her hand very gently on the girl's head. "Lizbet. Curfew will begin soon. You both should not be here."

I straightened. I knew those names.

Samuel pulled a slip of paper from his pocket and held it out to my grandmother. She took it from him, and then caught his wrist as he pulled away. He began to protest—she muttered a sharp word that sounded distinctly German— and the boy stilled. She dragged him near, holding up his arm to stare at his inner wrist.

I was too far away to see what she was looking at, but I recognized her anger. "This is recent."

The boy remained silent. Lizbet whispered, "It happened this afternoon. *She* said he was getting old enough to be a real man. *Her* man."

My grandmother made a small disgusted sound, and released Samuel. "You have to stop going to her."

"*Nein,*" he muttered sullenly, rubbing his wrist. "We need her connections. Our families need her."

"I can get you money, things to trade—"

"You cannot keep our families safe, *Fraulein,*" interrupted Lizbet softly, and grabbed Samuel's hand, tugging him away. "Her reach is too long."

My grandmother shook her head, swearing softly, and took several quick steps after them. She grabbed the girl's hand and pushed something into it. I had a feeling it was the same object the Nazi had given her. Money, maybe. Something valuable, if the stunned look on Lizbet's face was any indication. She swallowed hard, clutched the object to her chest, and gave my grandmother a fierce, grateful nod.

The children ran. The woman watched them, clutching her skirts. And then, slowly, tilted her head to study me.

She looked so young. Maybe eighteen was too old. It was hard to tell, but one thing was certain: the boys had abandoned her mother early, and left a teenager to fend for herself. No doubt my great-grandmother had been murdered in front of her daughter, just as my mother had been murdered in front of me. That was how it worked. Once you lost the protection of the boys, death always came knocking.

My grandmother finally walked toward me. Red eyes glinted from her hair. My own Dek and Mal also uncoiled from around my neck. Her pace faltered when she saw them.

And then she took a deep breath, and kept coming until she was so close I could smell the fried sausages on her body, and the beer, and the cigarette smoke.

I smelled like somebody's piss. Not that I cared, right then. My grandmother had died four years before my birth. Every time I met her it felt wrong and heartbreaking, and unspeakably profound.

"What are you?" she finally whispered. I had no ready answer, even though I had spent the past hour trying to imagine what I would say.

I was still holding my cup of tea. Zee pushed up against my leg, and the shadows rippled around us. Raw and Aaz appeared, but they were not alone. Another Raw, another Aaz, gathered close behind them. And Zee. *Her* Zee.

The boys stared at their counterparts, gazes solemn, knowing. As though this had happened before. As though they knew it would happen again.

Dread sparked. Time had become fluid in my hands. Perhaps there was a very good reason that Zee kept secrets from me. Because he *did* know things that I should not—because there was no safe warning for what had brought me here. Not without possibly changing some distant outcome that he knew would come to pass.

Terrified me. Gnawed at my gut. Surely the future was not set in stone. There had to be more than fate. More than the bleak certainty that what I did now was leading to some inevitable destiny that I could not change.

"I'm from the future," I said, figuring my grandmother could handle the truth; not having anything better to tell her. "Far, distant future."

Her eyes narrowed. "Bullshit."

Well, at least *that* was familiar. "You think the boys would just be standing here if I was lying?"

Her lips tightened with displeasure—also familiar, and startling. I had seen that expression on my mother's face. Made me wonder if it was something else I shared with them. Little bits and pieces of us, bleeding true in our veins from across decades and centuries.

Blood never lies, Zee had said.

But there was something else that bothered me. We'd had this conversation before. In my past, in her future. I had met my grandmother the first time I ever time-traveled. She had been in her thirties, and my mother had already been born. Fourteen years old.

But that had been the first time for my grandmother, too. She had never met me before then, I was certain of it. No one could be that good of an actress, and my grandmother would not have bothered trying to hide the truth. All of us were poor liars—if such a thing could be inherited.

Here we were, though. Standing side by side. Almost twins, except for the expressions in our eyes. I was glad that much was different. Something of me that was mine, and mine alone.

But it made no sense that she would not remember this encounter later in her life. No sense at all.

"Assuming you're telling the truth—" she began, but my patience had finally worn too thin.

I made a sharp gesture. "I'm here for Ernie. For Winifred, Samuel, and Lizbet. I'm here because you asked me to finish something, to save them, and now they're almost all dead. In my time, dead."

My grandmother flinched. "How?"

"A woman named the Black Cat." I watched carefully for her reaction. "Seems to come right down to her, though I don't know why or how."

But I thought my grandmother might. She closed her eyes, rocking back on her heels. Then, without a word, turned and walked away. Demons slipped into the shadows. I gave Raw my teacup.

And I followed.

6

WE did not talk. Not even when *her* Raw appeared from the shadows with a cream-colored silk scarf, which she passed to me. I wrapped it around my head, with special care to hide my face. Best if no one saw us together. It would be hard to explain where her twin had been all this time. Maybe the boys could find me eyeglasses or a wig— though that sounded stifling.

No one else was out. I remembered my grandmother reminding the children about a curfew, but except for a distant scuff of boots, and low drunken laughter, I saw no soldiers, no one at all positioned to enforce that rule. I felt the oppression, though—worse than the heat. There had been life in the streets earlier, but now it was just ghosts and a hush that was as heavy and suffocating as a plastic bag pulled tight over the mouth of the city. Life, choked out.

And hiding. Quivering. I thought of Winifred Cohen, and her presence behind that closed locked door. Like a mouse. Same now, but deeper. The fear and weariness of the people hiding behind the walls of their homes had bled into the air. Each breath made my skin prickle. My sweat felt like the product of poison, or fever.

We walked only five minutes before we reached a long street lined entirely with row houses. My brief impression was of large arched windows and gray brick; laundry lines sagging with holey shirts and underwear; and one light burning from a first-floor window. Every other was dark.

We entered a place of oppressive silence and climbed a set of rickety wooden stairs to the third floor, where my grandmother unlocked the last door at the back of the landing. Hot, stifling air rolled over us when we entered. I smelled mildew, so strong I choked, and tried to breathe through my mouth. We were in one small room with wooden floorboards, cracked walls. Not much furniture. Just a long, lumpy sofa, two battered chairs painted red, and in the far corner by the window—which opened out onto a glassed-in private balcony—a white porcelain sink that had been bolted into the wall, rusted piping trailing free from the bottom like a naked spine. A tin bucket sat on the floor, with washrags hanging over the edge, and a hose coiled from the faucet.

"Don't drink the water," said my grandmother suddenly.

I unwrapped the scarf, pushing sweat-soaked hair away from my face. "Don't touch the food, either?"

"Be careful," she replied testily. "Better if you only eat what the boys bring you. There's not much food here anyway, but what's available is usually spoilt rotten."

"No one at your restaurant seemed to notice. Especially the Nazis."

Her mouth tightened. "Locals usually only order drinks, but the Japs allow in special shipments of fresh fixings to keep the Krauts happy. They're the only ones who can afford those meals. We get a couple of them every week, crossing the creek to Little Vienna because it reminds them of home."

The disdain in her voice was biting, even hateful. I marveled at her acting skills in front of those men. "Your American accent doesn't bother anyone?"

Her dark eyes glittered. And then she spoke a stream of what was probably invective—and that sounded perfectly, flawlessly German.

I raised my brow. "I see."

"I doubt that," she muttered. "If you are from the future, then how does this war end?"

"Well. And that's all I'm going to say about it."

She gave me a cold look. "I don't like this. I don't even know if I should believe it."

"You're a spy," I said, matching her tone. "You should be used to a lot of things you don't like or believe."

She stared. And for one moment stopped being my grandmother, becoming simply, Jean: a young woman alone, with her whole life ahead of her. Dangerous, maybe—but vulnerable, too. Flinching, as Dek and Mal freed themselves from my hair, slithering down my arms.

Her gaze hardened again, though. I would have been worried for myself if I had been anyone else.

"Be careful where you say that," she said, her voice deathly quiet.

I tilted my head. "You use those children to help you?"

Her hand balled into a fist. Before she could reach me, both Zees tumbled from the sofa, standing in her way. She stopped. I did not move a muscle. Still as stone, radiating calm. Maybe I was as good an actress as she.

Around us, shadows moved, glinting with sparks of red. Aaz appeared—mine, I thought, though I could not say why. He carried two plates filled with a delicate shrimp salad. Raw swung a basket of rolls and butter.

My grandmother and I stared at the food, and then each other.

"Don't think this is any less bizarre for me," I said quietly.

She looked away, and reached up as if to rub the back of her neck. Except her hand was still balled into a fist. She uncurled her fingers, one by one, so stiffly I almost rubbed my hand in sympathy.

"Well," she said in a low voice, and took the proffered plate of salad. "Come on."

I did not move. "My name is Maxine."

Again she flinched, swearing softly to herself, and then sat down hard on the sofa. Dust particles flew into the air around her, and I backed up a step, trying not to sneeze, watching her through watering eyes. Her head remained ducked, shoulders bowed, toes turned inward toward each other. Like a kid.

I hesitated, took my own meal from Aaz, and perched gingerly in one of the red chairs. Raw placed the basket of rolls on the floor between us.

My grandmother picked at her shrimp. Seemed like a crime to eat so well with people starving around us, but I forced myself to take a bite. Tasted good, but not enough to distract me from watching the play of emotions across her face. Anger, still; and grief.

"Hey," I said softly.

"Maxine was my mother's name," she whispered, and shoved a forkful of salad into her mouth.

I had to call her Jean. Grandmother was out of the question. She had not asked how many generations removed we were, and I did not want to tell her. Less I talked the better.

"I was almost eight when we left the States," Jean said, over an entire apple pie, still warm and placed on the spare chair, which we had dragged close. Each of us held a spoon, taking turns digging directly into the tin. The crust was buttery and flaky, the apples full of cinnamon. Guilt and odd circumstances aside, it had become a lovely meal.

"It was after the market crash. I don't know why we left. But we landed in France, traveled through Germany, and then took a winding path through Yugoslavia, Greece, down into Turkey. Finally ended up in Iraq. I was thirteen by then. My mother had never been to China, but she made friends with people who had family there. Sephardic Jews, big-business types. By then, there were rumbles coming out of Germany. My mother remembered the first war, and wanted us far away from it. She thought China would be that place."

Jean stabbed the pie a little harder than necessary. "I've been here ever since. Got tied up when the Japs did their number on Pearl Harbor, and then the damn Krauts had to get involved because of that fool Hitler. Someone needed to play cloak-and-dagger on this side of the Pacific. Better me than anyone else."

Her mother could not have been dead that long. "So you pretend to be Jewish."

She shrugged. "Dark coloring is all the same over here. Makes you one way, even if you're not."

"You can't be fooling the people in this neighborhood."

"Only the *baojia* stick their noses in business that doesn't belong to them. Jewish tattletales, hired by the Japs. Some of them are stand-up, though. Especially if you pay them."

"You missed an appointment with one tonight."

Jean went silent, studying me again. I debated telling her about meeting Ernie, but she spoke before I could say a word—her tone cautious, careful. "His idea. He told me the Krauts were coming in for dinner at the White Horse. He thought if I waited on them, I might hear something."

"Did you?"

"Not enough. As far as Hilter is concerned, most of the hard action is in Europe. Won't waste good intel on the officers out here. But you never know. Little bits help."

"And the kids? I saw Samuel pass you a note." And Ernie seemed to have made himself her unofficial protector.

"They also help," Jean said quietly. "They're in a . . . unique position."

"With this . . . Black Cat. Who tattoos young boys and calls them her . . . men."

Jean said nothing. I leaned back, staring at the ceiling, which was covered in black patches of mold. It was still hot, but maybe I was getting used to it. I could breathe more easily. I heard gunshots again, in the distance. Jean looked at the window, drumming her spoon on the edge of the pie pan.

"Black Cat," she said quietly. "Russian whore. But she's got her hooks in the local underground spy network. Happened right after Richard Sorge got checked out in '41. He was a piece of work. Left behind a hole that needed filling, and the whore was in the right place. She had been one of his favorites, and knew some of his contacts. Except she's no patriot. Not for Russia, not for anyone except herself."

"Have you met her?"

"No." Jean hesitated. "She's dangerous."

"And you're not?" My tone was sharper than I intended; for a moment, I sounded like my mother.

Spots of color touched her cheeks. "You don't understand what's at risk."

"I understand she uses children to do her dirty work. I guess you all do, to some degree." I ignored the flicker of guilt and outrage that flared in her eyes. "What was on that boy's wrist?"

She sat back, jaw tight, glancing from me to Zee, all the boys sitting quietly in the shadows of the room, watching us, and each other. All of them, so quiet. So solemn.

"I don't like this arrangement," she finally said, ignoring my question. "I tell you everything, you tell me nothing."

I stood, dropping my spoon into the pie pan. "I'll find out what I need on my own, then. Wearing your face should count for something, I think."

She swore softly. "It was a tattoo. Of a rose. She brands all her . . . *men* . . . with them."

"Samuel doesn't look a day over eleven."

Jean said nothing. She did not need to. I looked down at my gloved hands. "I need to meet this woman."

"And do what? Kill her?"

"Whatever it takes." My voice sounded tough, decisive. It was a good act. Good enough to fool my grandmother, who, in this place, this time, was almost ten years my junior. I was the old guard here. It gave me new respect for my mother. And for Jean, for accepting my presence as well as she had. If my own descendant showed up one day to boss me around, I think I might suffer an aneurysm.

Jean stood, utterly grim-faced. "There are circumstances—"

A crashing sound interrupted her. It was from downstairs, like a door getting kicked in. Shouts followed: a frail male voice protesting in German, swallowed by louder, guttural Japanese tones. A woman screamed. I ran for the door.

Jean got there first, blocking me. Below us, more shouts, and the crunch and crash of furniture being broken. The woman's voice broke into a piercing wail. I could still hear the man speaking in German, but in ragged fits and gasps. The floor beneath my feet vibrated. I smelled smoke.

She grabbed my arm. "You intervene, you'll make it worse."

"Really," I muttered, trying to shrug her off. "You sure about that?"

"You'll make it worse for *them*," she clarified. "And for me. I can't afford to be noticed. Not like that, and not now."

I leveled my gaze. "Trust me. You can take it."

Her fingers tightened around my arm—a crushing grip. Behind me, at the door, someone knocked, but it was so faint it sounded like the scuff of a cat's paw. Jean and I froze, and then we heard it again, followed by a whisper. I could not understand the words, but I knew the voice.

Ernie.

Jean let go before I could shove her away. Raw and Aaz were already clearing the evidence of our dinner, shoving plates beneath the couch, and silverware down their throats.

"You can't let him see you," Jean hissed, blocking me as I reached for the doorknob.

"Too late," I muttered—and knocked her aside. I opened the door, saw a pale gaunt face, and in seconds dragged the kid inside—with the door shut and locked behind him. Cutting off, as I did, a rolling barrage of shouts that continued to rise through the floor in muted waves.

Ernie was dressed in limp pajamas, his chest bare. Ribs jutted, and his collarbone was so pronounced it could have doubled as a hanger. Sweat trickled down his skin. He stood, blinking at me with huge terrified eyes—as disconcerting as the violent tremors shaking his body. He snatched at his wrist, and then hugged himself convulsively, gulping down the beginnings of a tremendous, wracking sob.

I knelt, keenly aware of Jean standing in the shadows behind him. He had not yet seen her. I placed my hands lightly on his bony shoulders, and he surprised me by throwing his arms around my neck.

"I ran," he whispered.

I looked over his shoulder at Jean, who was tight-lipped, pale. She pointed at the floor, and mouthed, *"His home."*

I closed my eyes, and drew him closer. He smelled like mildew and sweat. "You did the right thing."

"*Mutter* told me." Ernie drew in a wheezing breath and began coughing. Below, the soldiers screamed in Japanese, and the answering replies in German were broken with sobs. The boy instantly slapped his hand over his mouth, cutting off both a cough and gasp, and took a broken step back to the door.

Or tried to. I refused to let go, and stood—sweeping the boy into my arms, carrying him to the couch. He weighed nothing for a kid his age. Just bone, gangly limbs, and clammy skin. He tried to protest. I ignored him, and sat down with him in my lap.

"Cover your ears if you need to," I whispered harshly, looking across the room at Jean. "But you're not going anywhere until those soldiers are gone."

He did not cover his ears, but instead buried his face against my throat, holding on with all his strength. I could feel his heart pounding. Mine, too. I remembered the feel of his old-man blood on my hands, the rattle of his last breath. His eyes, searching mine, for that one last time.

Behind Ernie, well out of his sight, Zee and the boys uncoiled from the shadows like deadly blooming roses, unfurling claws and wild razor hair. But their gazes were soft as they stared at the boy. As were the gazes of their counterparts, clinging close to Jean. I met her gaze and held it. Wishing I could read her mind.

She stood rigid, pale. Below, wood cracked. More shouts. A muffled scream. Ernie flinched. So did my grandmother. I was past that. What I was feeling did not allow room for flinches. Just violence.

But it finally got quiet. Boots tramped on the stairs outside, and then faded.

Ernie stirred, and when he did, demons scattered silently into the shadows. Jean had nowhere to go, and I watched something shift in her eyes—resolve, maybe. She moved from the darkened doorway. Standing in plain sight.

She nodded at me, and I let Ernie sit up. He rubbed his eyes—turned his head, just so—and froze.

Jean did not move. She stood with her feet braced, hands

loose at her sides—as though ready for a blow. Ernie was so still in my arms. And then, slowly, he tore his gaze from her to look at me.

I raised my brow. "Surprise."

He sucked in a deep breath and scrambled off my lap, nearly falling in his rush to get away. I did not reach for him, or move. Neither did Jean, but her gaze found mine for one brief moment. Tired, angry. Resolved.

"Ernie," she said gently. "Meet my sister."

"Sister," he whispered, backing up until he hit the wall. "You said you had no family."

"I had to. Maxine was doing . . . sensitive work."

"Still am," I told the boy. "That was me you helped earlier."

Jean gave me a sharp look. Ernie still seemed startled, but his shoulders relaxed, just a fraction. He mumbled, "Thought there was something different. In your eyes."

"You can't tell anyone," Jean said. "Not Samuel or Lizbet. Not even Winifred."

Ernie flashed her a defiant look. "You said you trusted us."

"Not a matter of trust." I pushed myself to the edge of the couch and leaned forward. "Safety. Anyone who knows about my presence would be at risk. Bad enough that I'm here at all."

Ernie was a brave kid. He held my gaze with the same unwavering intensity that I would see more than sixty years from now. "Someone looking for you?"

"Not yet." Jean stepped close. "But you'll need to be careful."

I finally stood from the couch. "I'd like to see your wrist, Ernie."

Jean stiffened. So did Ernie, but he grabbed his wrist, hugging it against his gaunt stomach. I walked to him. He tried to back away, but he had no place to go.

"I have to go home," he mumbled, ducking his gaze.

I held out my hand. Jean drew close and said, "Ernie. Samuel showed me his tattoo."

The boy gave her a hard, despairing look. "He promised he wouldn't."

Jean shook her head, and I felt her helplessness. "Not an easy thing to hide, short stuff."

He closed his eyes, banging his head lightly against the wall. "And did Lizbet and Winifred show you theirs?"

Jean blinked. "What?"

I knelt, and took hold of Ernie's wrist. My grip was gentle but firm, and I bit the inside of my cheek as I made him show me the tattoo.

It was familiar. I had seen it before, on a scrap of human skin. But this was smaller, singular; perhaps a rose, though the coiled lines felt more like the tangle of an unending knot, or a particularly distorted *ouroboros*. Reminded me of the engravings on the armor encasing my fingers and wrist—still hidden beneath my glove.

I tried to speak, but my voice croaked. I had to try again, more softly, almost whispering. "She did this to you?"

Ernie nodded, shivering. Jean knelt beside me, peering at the tattoo. "And Lizbet? Winifred? What was done to them?"

He hesitated, and touched a spot above his heart. "Right there. She did us all at the same time. And then made the same marks on her body."

I released the boy, rocking back on my heels. I stared at his feet. Bare, dirty toes digging into the floor. His breathing was loud, rasping. Like he was suffering from congestion in his chest.

It took all my control, but my voice finally sounded normal when I said, "It's gotten quiet downstairs."

He hesitated. Jean said, "Wait outside. I'll go with you in a minute to check on your parents."

I did not watch Ernie go. Nor did I stand until I heard the door shut behind him. I found Jean watching me.

"I wish you had never come here," she whispered.

"You afraid?" I asked coldly, softly, certain that Ernie had his ear pressed to the door.

Jean moved so close I could taste the sweet scent of apple pie on her breath. "There's a fine balance in this place. Upset that, and people will die."

"People *will* die." I pointed at the door. "You willing

to sacrifice Ernie and his friends? Because I promise you, kiddo, that's what you're doing."

"I've helped them all I can. I have to look at the bigger picture."

I forgot she was my grandmother. I grabbed the front of her dress and hauled her close, frustration and disappointment mingling with desperate, weary anger. "You listen to me, Jean Kiss. Every life matters."

She shoved back. "I'm just one person."

Oh, God. It was like listening to myself. "You're the most fucking dangerous woman in this world."

"I can't be killed," she rasped. "That's not the same as dangerous, and you know it."

I released her. She sagged backward against the wall, eyes glittering.

"I try," she whispered hollowly. "People think I whore for all the goods I get, but I don't care. I pass out food and items for people to trade. I get work passes for some, if they have no other way. Medicine, messages . . . when there's a need, *I do what I can*. Maybe where you come from life is different. Maybe you have the *luxury* of living in a world where people don't suffer. But this isn't it. I can't do everything. There are too many. There will *always* be too many."

I heard defiance in her voice, but mostly despair. Profound weariness. *Have mercy*, whispered a small voice in my mind. *Have mercy on your grandmother.*

Because she is right.

I drew in a slow, deep breath. And then, carefully, leaned against the door beside her. Red eyes glimmered from the shadows. I sensed a breathlessness in the boys; anticipation, even.

I almost asked about the Black Cat, but when I tried the words felt too heavy, too painful. I was a weak woman. I tapped my foot against the floor and said quietly, "The Japanese soldiers do this all the time?"

Jean closed her eyes, odd relief flickering briefly across her features. "More recently. Used to be that some of their best were stationed in Shanghai, but they've been sent into the Pacific to fight the Americans. All that's left are kids who hardly know how to hold a bayonet. But here they are, in a uniform, with power. Goes to some of their heads."

"What did they want?"

"Looking for American currency. Shortwave radios. Evidence of spying. That's their excuse, anyway, but I bet if you smelled their breath for liquor, it would set your nostrils on fire."

"It won't last," I whispered. "None of this."

Jean tilted her head, studying me. "How much longer?"

I hesitated. "A year or so."

But you won't be here when it ends, I almost told her. *And I don't want to think about how the experience will change you.*

Jean looked at the door and pushed herself away from the wall. "Stay here. I need to walk Ernie downstairs and make sure his parents are okay."

I almost told her to be careful. Instead, I went to the door, and watched her slip out of the apartment. Demons faded away with her. All of them, except the two Zees. They stepped free of the shadows and crouched in front of me, perfect twins, utterly inscrutable. I knelt, needing to look them in the eyes.

"Well," I said. "I hope you both know what you're doing."

"Doing life," said one Zee.

"Fitting pieces," added the other.

"Right," I muttered, wiping sweat off my brow. "But what if I make things worse? Or what if I don't do any good at all?" I looked at my Zee. "This has already happened before, for you. More than sixty years from now you'll remember what goes on in the next ten minutes, but for me, it hasn't occurred yet. But Ernie's still dead in the future we came from, so whatever I did here . . . it didn't work."

"Think too much," Zee rasped, tapping his forehead. "Just be."

"That's crap," I snapped. "Is the future set in stone, or isn't it?"

"Don't know." Zee held out his hands. "Nothing stays the same."

"Except when it does," said the other Zee.

I wanted to strangle them. Instead I curled my hands into fists and pushed them hard against the floor. I could hear faint voices below me, speaking German. No more Japanese. The soldiers had gone.

"Whatever caused her to send that message through Ernie hasn't happened yet. She doesn't even want to get involved. And," I added, tapping them both on the chests, "why is it her older self didn't—or won't—remember me? Care to explain *that*?"

Neither of them did, if their silence was any measure. I stripped off my right glove, holding up my armored quicksilver hand. My grandmother's Zee flinched when he saw it, and rasped a single unintelligible word. I ignored him.

"Am I supposed to help those children?" I asked my Zee. "Or is there another reason you sent me here?"

His eyes narrowed. "All kinds of help."

The other Zee's claws raked lightly across the floor. "Help *her*."

I stared. "Help my grandmother? In case you hadn't noticed, that's not the way it usually works. One dies, one goes on alone."

Which, I had to admit, was about as petty and selfish as anything I had ever said. Knee-jerk reaction. Of course I would help her. Of course. But for one brief moment—just a heartbeat that lasted a lifetime—I felt a prick of resentment. No one had come to help me after my mother had been murdered. No one.

Floorboards creaked outside the door. I slid my glove back on and stood. Jean slipped inside, a faint flush in her cheeks. She glanced from me to her Zee. "I need some clean cloth and antiseptic. Cans of sardines, too, and a couple flints. Hurry."

"Serious injuries?" I asked.

She shook her head and leaned back against the door, hugging herself. "But they blamed me. I could see it in their eyes. I think they were appalled that their son had gone to me for help."

"They don't know you spy."

"But they know I'm not one of them." Jean grimaced, bowing her head so deeply I thought she would be sick. "Does that ever get easier?"

"No."

Bitterness touched her mouth. "You ever wonder what we're doing with ourselves? You got *that* figured out in the future?"

I found myself shuffling close, heart so heavy my feet would hardly move. But I had to. I had to be near her. "You want to know what the point is."

"One woman responsible for the world," she breathed, her pain so palpable, so much *mine*, I could feel the burn of her tears in my own eyes.

"That's not the point," I whispered, wanting desperately to touch her. "Just the tagline."

"And?"

And, I was going to lose my dignity. I was going to lose myself in her grief, if I stayed here one moment longer. "The point is to do good. To do the things no one else can do *but* you. Because of who you are."

"A Hunter," she said.

"Jean Kiss. Hunter Kiss." I swallowed hard, filled with memories. My grandmother—her future self—had given me a similar lecture under the hot sun of the Mongolian steppes. I had been lost in time. Lost in every way. But she had been my anchor.

"You're not alone," I said.

Jean held my gaze. "And you, in your time?"

I smiled faintly. "It worked out."

Silence drew thin and piercing between us, until finally she whispered, "If you do this wrong, a lot of people will suffer. Not just those kids, but their families."

"That's why I need your help."

"A lot of people need help," she muttered, wiping her eyes as both Zees rolled from the shadows bearing small bags. "But the Black Cat is something else."

"You said it's complicated."

"She owns people. The right people. She specializes in compromising situations."

"And that matters during wartime?"

"Wars don't last forever. And some indiscretions are worse than others."

I studied her. "You're not telling me everything. Why did she tattoo those children?"

"All I've heard are rumors. No one wants to talk about her, not even the kids. And I've tried. She gets a hold on people. Not just with fear, but something deeper." Jean made a hooking motion with her finger, and slashed the air. "You stop owning yourself when you work for that woman. The tattoo is her way of cementing the bond. She's covered in them. Each one a life she controls."

"You knew this, and you let those kids near her?"

Jean gave me an angry look. "It's not like they asked for permission. And I wasn't their babysitter. It just happened. You do what you can to survive. I'm sure she made them an offer they couldn't refuse."

"Most predators do," I retorted.

Jean pushed away from the door and snatched up the bags that both Zees had left on the floor. The little demons watched her silently. She pointedly ignored them.

"With or without you," I said.

She did not answer me. Just fished into the cloth bag and pulled out a handful of thin metal rods no longer than my pinky.

"Flint," Jean said absently, as though she hadn't heard me. "More valuable than gold around here. Inflation has made cash almost worthless. People have to trade for goods. Canned food is always worth something. Just one of these flint rods, plus a couple tins of sardines will help the Bernsteins get back on their feet."

She began to leave, and hesitated, looking down at the floor, her hand on the knob, the wall—anywhere but at me. "Take a nap. We can't leave until dawn."

I did not ask where we would be going. "Thank you."

"Not yet," she said roughly, opening the door. "Not until everyone gets out of this alive."

She left. I stood for a long time, hearing her voice echo. Reading words inside my mind.

Save them.

I just wished I knew how.

AAZ brought me a blanket and pillow, which I tossed on the floor. I tried to sleep—and I suppose I did, fitfully—because I would close my eyes only to open them with odd visions haunting my brain: Grant, his large hand sinking warm through my breastbone to hold my heart; or old man Ernie, covered in rivulets of blood that wriggled like red worms upon his stained white shirt, coiling tight until they resembled the tangled outlines of roses. And in another dream, the last, I found myself a giant, colossal as a mountain, sitting naked and cross-legged upon a peninsula while watching the pinprick lights of a distant city glitter far below me like stars. If I breathed hard I would call down storms. If I wept, I would flood the plains. If I cracked my knuckles, earthquakes would rip through the mountains and collapse stone upon the city. I knew this. It made me afraid, and excited.

Frigid air caressed the back of my neck. I turned, ever so carefully, only to discover a pair of immense golden eyes floating within a sinuous trail of smoke. Blinking lazily at me. Smiling, even, but with cold and bitter humor. Lightning flashed within its body, burning with symbols: knots and coils, and tangled hearts.

We are both Gods, whispered the golden-eyed creature. *But they do not see us.*

Unless we make them, it added, moments later.

I woke up. Drenched in sweat. So nauseous I slid my hand over my mouth, fighting not to gag. My temples throbbed, and my neck was sore. Mildew seemed to crawl up my nostrils.

I forced myself to take deep breaths; listening, as I did, to gentle murmurs from the apartment below me. Jean sprawled on the couch. I could not tell if she was asleep, but red eyes glinted, and I heard the soft familiar crunch of jaws tearing through metal. Dek and Mal, coiled close to my head, began kneading my shoulders.

My dreams lingered, especially those golden eyes. Maybe it meant nothing. Maybe.

But my gut hurt. And when both Zees crept close, watching me carefully, there was something old and knowing in their gazes that only made me feel more ill.

I grabbed my Zee and dragged him close, pressing my mouth to his ear. "What are you hiding?"

His breath was hot as fire, but he said nothing and pulled away. Pulled me, too, and I rose carefully to my feet. Trying to be silent, though the floor creaked beneath me. Jean stirred, and glanced at me. Not a trace of sleep in her eyes.

"I need air," I said quietly. "I'll be back soon."

"Be careful of soldiers," she replied.

I was more careful of not making noise on the stairs. Soft steps, hugging the wall. Wooden splinters covered the second-story landing, but the largest had been swept into a neat pile. No more door, just a white sheet pinned in its place. I paused for a moment, thinking of young Ernie resting on the other side of that thin cloth. My hands felt warm for a moment with the memory of his old-man blood.

Hot outside, but there was a light breeze and no mildew scent. I stood on the stoop, inhaling as deeply as I could, again and again, until my nausea faded. Dek and Mal hummed against my ears: Kenny Loggins's "Danger Zone."

Several hours left before dawn. It was very dark outside. I listened carefully, but heard nothing except my heartbeat, and the faint scrape of claws as my boys rolled free of the shadows around my feet. I sat down on the steps, taking in the night. It was 1944, but this could have been a quiet street sixty years from now. Some things were not bound by time.

Like me.

"The Black Cat," I said to Zee, rubbing my knuckles as Raw and Aaz prowled around my ankles. "I need to know more about her. Like why she's so tough my grandmother won't take her out."

"Told you," Zee replied. "Connections."

"That's not enough when kids are getting hurt, and you and I know it."

The little demon leaned close, rubbing his cheek against my arm. "Different mothers, different hearts."

"Not that different." I ran my gloved fingers through the thick spines of his hair. "Just not confident. Not tested enough to be sure of how far she can push. I remember what that feels like. And you. . . . You came to her when she was still young. You left her alone in the world when she was just a kid."

"All kids. Every mother." Zee spat, and the acid in his saliva burned a hole in the stone steps. "No choice."

Bullshit, I wanted to say. *You could give us all more time.*

But that would be like telling thunder not to make sound, or water not to be wet. It just was.

Somewhere, distant, an engine chugged to life with a dull, throbbing roar. Made me flinch. I had not realized until then how silent the night was. "You're not going to tell me anything useful, are you? You never do."

"Safer not to," he muttered. "Safer to trust you."

And then he looked sharply at the door behind me, and snapped his claws at the others. Raw and Aaz fell backward into the shadows, while Zee leapt into the darkness between my legs and the stairs, slip-sliding from this world into another.

I heard a muffled cough. Found Ernie behind me, slight and pale as a ghost.

"Maxine, not Jean," I said.

"I know," he replied quietly. "I can tell you apart now."

I scooted sideways, and he sat down beside me. "My parents are finally asleep."

"Will they be okay?"

He shrugged. "They could be dead or sick. Anything else is okay."

Tough kid. But not tough enough to hide the quaver in his voice, or the way he twisted his fingers. I tore my gaze from him to watch the street. "They depend on you to help out with things."

"I don't mind working."

"How much does the Black Cat pay you?"

Ernie stiffened. "I don't want to talk about her."

"She's the reason I'm here."

"Then you should leave. She'll kill you." He began to stand. I caught his wrist. His tattoo was raised and warm beneath my hand—almost too warm, as though it were infected. Or burning with a life of its own.

"She can't hurt me," I told him, staring into his eyes. "But she can hurt you, your family. Which is why I need to be very careful in how I handle her."

He shook his head, despair creeping into his eyes. "You don't understand."

"I understand that she has connections, that she frightens you, but—"

"No!" He gasped, wrenching his hand away. "She'll make me betray you—and Jean. I won't have any choice."

I stood, looming over him. "If she threatens your family—"

He shook his head so violently that spittle flew from his mouth, and a low strained sound tore from his throat, guttural and hard. It was not the kind of sound any child should make—too desperate, too old, too wild. He began clawing at the tattoo on his wrist, nails raking so deeply he drew blood.

I grabbed his arms, holding him still. He would not look at me. I waited for him to say something. Anything.

"She asked me once about Jean," he finally mumbled.

"She asked all of us about her. Before she marked us. She asked if we knew a woman covered in tattoos. Tattoos that disappear at night. The others had no idea. But I . . . I've seen Jean when she didn't know it."

His voice was thick with shame. I wondered exactly what he had seen when spying on Jean, and quite honestly did not want to know. He was a twelve-year-old boy, though. I could take a wild guess.

"So you saw . . . her tattoos," I said carefully. "Anything else?"

Ernie's cheeks flushed bright red. "No. And I didn't say anything, not even when *she* asked." He rubbed his wrist. "If she asks again, I don't think I'll be able to hold back."

"You act like that mark gives her power over you."

"It does," he said simply.

I released him. He rubbed his arms, and pushed past me into the building. Head down, shoulders hunched. He never saw Jean standing in the shadows, watching him.

She waited until the floorboards creaked on the second-story landing, and then stepped outside to join me. Her hair was a mess, and there were circles under her eyes.

"How much did you hear?" I asked.

"Enough to know that I need to push some cotton into the keyhole of my door."

"Forget that. The Black Cat knows about our bloodline. She knows you're close. Which means she's not human . . . or very well informed."

Jean stared thoughtfully at her feet. Two tiny heads poked free of her hair, blinking lazily at me. Dek and Mal, who had been utterly still until that moment, returned the favor.

I said, "Were you already aware of this?"

"No," said Jean, but slowly, as if she was not entirely certain of her answer. "I had been feeling something, though. At the back of my head. Just . . . instinct."

"The boys never mentioned anything?"

"I never asked." She finally met my gaze. "My hands were full. I didn't want to know."

I stared, waiting to feel appalled, angry—but all that hit

me was a sense of deep, abiding sorrow. My grandmother was being truthful when she said that her hands were full. Overwhelmed, not sure what to do, whom to help, how far to extend herself. Fighting to survive—mentally, emotionally— in the same way that people here were trying to keep their bodies alive.

"How long has it been since your mother died?" I asked abruptly.

Jean stiffened. "What—"

"It's been five years for me," I interrupted. "Close to six. She was murdered on my birthday, shot to death in front of me. Right here." I touched my head. "Worst day of my life."

Jean backed away, and then stopped. "It's been seven years for me."

I don't know what I had been expecting to hear, but seven years was not it. Seemed like a lifetime. "You must have been a baby."

"Eleven." Jean's voice was strained, her eyes dark and empty in the shadows. "We were in the countryside, helping refugees. My mother had traded one war zone for another. I guess it was the times. But Zee . . . the boys . . . they didn't want us there. They thought it was too dangerous for me, with only my mother for protection during the day. I think . . . i think that's why they left her when they did. She wouldn't listen. She didn't . . . give them a choice. It was me or her."

They made the right choice, I almost said, thinking about my mother—who had done everything in her power to keep me out of harm's way. Taking me into a war zone would have been unthinkable to her.

I found Jean giving me a sharp look—as though she had read my mind and wanted to defend her mother—but the moment passed, and all the fight inside her seemed to shrivel up into a cold small shell. Jean rubbed her arms. "It was difficult. I was completely alone. No other foreigners for a thousand miles, and my Chinese wasn't good. There were so many times when I got into trouble." She stopped for a moment, her gaze turning inward, and then, very quietly said, "Men would try to hurt me, but the boys . . . The boys would make my skin burn, like fire."

Red eyes glinted from the shadows. Jean hugged herself—and then laughed quietly, bitterly. "For a long time, all I worried about was me. Some things don't change."

"You did fine," I said quietly.

Jean gave me an unpleasant smile. "Maybe. But I think it's time to do better."

WE changed clothes. Zee and the boys delivered the wardrobe. Jean was elegant in loose slacks, with a long-sleeved silk blouse tucked in and buttoned to the neck. A touch of red lipstick and several dabs of eye shadow made her look like a movie star. I, on the other hand, wore workman trousers, patched and stained with paint; and a loose white men's cotton shirt. No makeup. Just some dirt smeared lightly against my jaw. The boys also brought me horn-rimmed eyeglasses, the lenses nonprescriptive, but so thick the world was little more than a blur in front of me. I plaited my hair into two braids and tugged a canvas houndstooth billy cap over my head.

Jean frowned. "Someone should lock you up in the library you escaped from."

"I was going for hot and sexy," I replied dryly, "but I guess that'll do."

She grunted, and passed me a blue card, a folded sheaf of papers, and a round tin pin. "Put that on and never take it off. It identifies you as a Jew. The papers are from a woman who died here a month ago, but they'll do in case you're stopped. The blue card is the most important, though. It's a monthlong work pass. You'll need it to cross the bridge into the city."

"And our similarities?" I pointed at my face, and then hers.

Jean hesitated. "People see what they want. I doubt anyone will look too closely, but once we get close to the bridge, we'll split up and enter the checkpoint separately."

"How will your neighbors react to my presence?"

"Most people here are more concerned with how bad

their diarrhea is going to get, or with finding food, work. Are you fluent in any languages but English?"

"Just Spanish. I doubt that's going to be helpful here."

"So don't talk. And if the Japs ask you anything, pretend to have a German or Polish accent. Any accent. Act like you have trouble speaking English. Whatever happens, you're no longer American, or British, or any citizen of an Allied country. You're a stateless refugee like everyone else in this ghetto."

"I see some flaws in this plan."

"There *is* no plan. Just you, appearing in my life, when you shouldn't be here at all." Jean smoothed down her blouse, and I reached up to my shoulders where Dek and Mal were coiled, humming a Bryan Adams tune. I thought it might be "The Only Thing That Looks Good On Me Is You," and scratched under their chins.

Jean's frown deepened. "They sing for you?"

"Yours don't?"

She reached up to pat the little hyena heads poking free of her glossy black hair. "They mutter a lot to themselves."

They were still muttering—and mine were still singing—when the sun came up and their bodies dissolved into smoke. Jean and I watched each other as it happened, both of us silent, her expression as grave and uncomfortable as mine surely was. Given the peculiarities of the boys, and how they transferred themselves from mother to daughter, it stood to reason that no two Hunters of my bloodline had ever been in the same place at once, and certainly had never transitioned from night to day together. I felt naked.

I could not see her tattoos beneath her clothes, but mine were a new weight against my skin, rippling and electric; an organic, indestructible shell. Dreaming, breathing. I no longer felt the heat, except in my lungs and on my face. The boys absorbed my sweat. I flexed my hands, still encased in soft leather. I had not shown my grandmother the armor. Something in me was afraid to.

We left the apartment. No weapons. Too dangerous, Jean had said, in case we were stopped and searched. No sign of

Ernie on the second-floor landing, either, and it was quiet behind the white curtain. I wanted to poke my head in and ask after the boy—tell him to stay home today—but when I drew near, Jean grabbed my arm and pulled me away.

"He would have already left by now," she murmured.

Temperatures had risen with the sun. It was muggy outside, so humid that a haze filled the air, as hard to breathe as soup. I sucked as much into my lungs as I could, and it still was not enough. No one else seemed to have trouble. The street was already active; folks getting their day started before the heat became unbearable. I saw no zombies. Instead, boys clutching books raced down the street, some kicking balls to each other—nearly hitting an elderly Chinese man practicing *qigong* on the sidewalk alongside a European woman of a similar silvered age. A duet of violins played from an open window, music nearly lost beneath the chatter of Mandarin and German—voices buzzing around a shed where a slender Chinese man boiled nothing but water in giant cauldrons, ladling it into tin kettles and thermoses held by women and children. Money changed hands, and laughter sparked the air.

Buildings grew from each other like the trunks of bound trees—an organic growth, spurred by human pressure—bits and pieces added on, brick and scrap-yard patches that jutted into the sidewalk, replete with grass and delicate vines growing from tin roofs. Cook fires burned in the street. I saw a gaunt, brown-haired woman vomiting against a wall, the young fellow with her staring at her puke as though he was more sorry about the wasted food than her illness. Ahead of us, an older Chinese man pulling a cart stopped to ring a bell, and then stooped with a groan to pick up a wooden bucket that was shaped like a pumpkin—one of many that had been left at the side of the road. He emptied its contents into an enclosed stone container built into his cart. A terrible stench burned my nostrils. I made a small sound. Jean raised her brow. "Mr. Li handles the honey pot waste. He resells it to farmers for fertilizer."

She waved at him and he smiled—though he gave me a

disconcertingly sharp once-over. And then leveled that same piercing look at Jean. If she noticed—and I thought she must have—she showed nothing. Simply continued walking at a brisk pace that made my leg muscles burn. Few greeted her. Caution, perhaps, or disdain; or simply because they did not give a damn. But not, I thought, because she was unknown.

We split up at the checkpoint. A bored young Japanese soldier waved through Jews with little more than a glance at the passes, though I half-expected him to pull me aside. Instead, I watched him slap a baton against the shoulders of a Chinese man—and order a strip search, right there on the bridge in front of everyone.

The man did not fight or protest. He stood very still as his clothes were torn away and thrown into the river. When a baton prodded the crease of his buttocks, he did not flinch. Nor did he make one sound when that same baton smashed against his lower back, driving him to his knees.

The soldiers laughed, though one of them looked away, his smile forced. The checkpoint guard said a sharp word to the Chinese man, planting a boot on his back to hold him down when he tried to rise. I did not need to speak Japanese or Mandarin to know what he was ordering, and was unsurprised when the man on the ground began crawling across the bridge. I held my breath, hoping he would make it without a bullet in his ass. I finally understood, in that moment, the predicament my grandmother was in. She probably saw this, and worse, every day. Unable to lift a hand. Just as I was unable—unwilling—to step in. I had a job to do here. Like my grandmother had said, there was a bigger picture.

He made it, though. I was waved through several minutes later. Jean had gone ahead of me, and I saw her deep in the crowds of rickshaw pullers and hawkers. The naked Chinese man stood nearby, carefully not looking at her. Just as carefully not seeming to touch her as she passed near him to approach me. But I saw their hands brush, and he turned instantly to walk in the opposite direction; quickly, one hand pressed against the small of his back, but utterly shameless about his nudity.

"I assume he'll be able to buy new clothes?" I asked her quietly. "You gave him something to trade."

"Well, that would be a waste," she said. "I paid him for something else."

8

JEAN hailed a pedicab, and ordered the driver, in rough Mandarin, to take us to the former French Concession—a destination I learned about only after she translated. I had been there before, in the twenty-first century—quite unexpectedly, under terrible circumstances.

The appearance of the neighborhood was as I remembered, though I had to remind myself that I was from the future—and that it was mere luck and preservation that had left the French Concession, in my time, mostly intact after sixty years. Very little seemed different. There were still those quiet streets lined with old trees, and those glimpses of rooftops and windows visible over the glass-embedded tops of high walls. The air tasted cooler, cleaner. Not so many people out and about, and there were fine cars parked at the side of the road. Japanese soldiers patrolled in pairs, eyeing us suspiciously as we passed. But no one told us to stop.

We were let out at a leafy cobblestone intersection in front of a simple black gate that looked the same as every other that we had passed. But Jean stood for a long moment, staring at it as though the iron might burn her. "Are you certain you insist?"

"Tell me why I shouldn't," I said. "You have a reason."

"I'm no longer certain it's a sufficient one." Jean shot me a piercing look. "I do good here, whether you believe that or not. I help people. I may have to leave after this, and I don't . . . I don't know where I'll go. I don't belong anywhere."

I dared to graze her arm with the tips of my fingers. "If there's another way to remove those children from her control—"

"Even this might not be enough. The fact that she knows our bloodline exists . . ." Jean stopped, and studied the gate again, thoughtfully. "Ernie, Winifried . . . all of them. It sounds as though they lived long, full lives, regardless of what happened to them in this time and place. They died old. You and I both know that's a gift, even if it was cut short before their time."

It was a gift, yes, but a bitter one. I said nothing, though. Simply waited for Jean to make up her mind. I was not going to push this final step down her throat. Even if I had almost everything else.

I did not wait long. She raised her gloved fist and knocked hard on the dull iron gate. It opened so quickly, hardly before her hand was away, that I wondered whether we had been watched from the other side.

I hoped not. It was Ernie who faced us. Even Jean seemed startled to see him. He was dressed in new clothes—a starched, white short-sleeve shirt and black slacks. A uniform, maybe. It looked too large on his frame, the tattoo on his skin oversized for such bony wrists. A little tin pin was attached to his shirt above his heart. His expression was grave, which made him look like the old man he would become, instead of a little kid.

"You shouldn't be here," he said, giving me a piercing look as though I was somehow to blame. Which I was.

"I seem to have developed a nagging concern for your well-being," Jean replied. "You and the others. I've come to break your contracts."

"You can't. You'll only make it worse."

Jean laid a gentle hand on his shoulder. "Come on. Maybe you'll thank me for this one day."

Ernie backed away from the gate, one hand tapping spasmodically against his skinny thigh. Looking at us with desperate despair, as though his ragged heart was breaking in his eyes. He resembled a wild animal more than a child, or some kid raised by wolves and then tossed into human clothes—out of place, lost, and very alone.

But he was not alone. Behind him, standing in regular intervals throughout a carefully landscaped garden, were thick-necked white men—watching us, armed with rifles. All of them wore soldier uniforms, lightweight summer issue. They did not seem surprised to see us, or even alarmed, but their dead, flat gazes were profoundly cold. They reminded me of attack dogs—quiet, restrained, ready for that right, deadly moment. I wondered if they had tattoos on their wrists, as well.

I focused on Ernie. "Sometimes you have to believe in people, kid. Before you forget how."

He began to shake his head, but froze when Jean brushed her knuckles against his cheek. "If I asked you to walk through this gate and go home, would you?"

"I can't," he whispered, rubbing his wrist.

"Okay." Jean breathed. "Then listen. You and I never talked about the things you've had to do here. I'm sorry for that. I knew it was bad, and I never did a thing. But that's going to change. So chin up, short stuff. Your job is to stay out of the way."

Ernie looked so stricken. "She knows you're coming. That's why she had me come here to . . . welcome you."

I pushed past the boy, watching the guards—smiling so coldly at them that several stirred, hands tightening on their guns. "I know *I'm* ready to say hello."

Jean rolled her eyes. Ernie looked at me like I was crazy. But I winked at him, and his mouth twitched with a tentative, wary smile that warmed me to the bone.

He turned and led us down a gently curving path shadowed with palms and thick decorative grasses. The air smelled rich, with a mint undertone that clung to my nostrils.

The guards watched us, but did not follow. No need. There were a lot of them, and they stood in regular intervals within the garden and against the walls. I heard several speaking softly in Russian.

"Pogroms drove the Russian Jews into Shanghai, but revolution forced the rest," Jean told me under her breath, as though reading my mind. "Soldiers, mostly. The Japs recruited some for their police force, but the rest hired out as construction workers, or muscle."

French doors stood open in front of us, tucked beneath a stone arch built below a series of balconies and large windows. Rose vines clung to immense trellises. I heard a woman's throaty laughter. Ernie ducked his head, and led the way inside—but not before Zee twitched between my breasts. All the boys, stirring—and not just on me. Jean touched her stomach as though she was being kicked, and glanced at me warily.

It was crowded inside. Unexpectedly so. The chaos did not at first make sense. I saw old-fashioned movie cameras, and tall lights; men scribbling on notepads; a mix of Chinese and white women dressed in loose robes and heavy makeup, lounging in velvet armchairs while others dabbed sweat from their brow. I heard muffled shouts and gasps, and then brief silence; and I glimpsed beyond the milling crowd one long, naked tattooed leg.

Ernie pushed through. We followed. And it suddenly became quite clear to me what was going on.

Someone was making a porno.

A bed was the centerpiece, but all I could see were its round edges, draped in raw silk the color of butter. Again, a single tattooed leg stretched sinuously. I saw claws drawn into the flesh. Scales and veins of inked quicksilver. I glanced at Jean to see if she had noticed, and found her staring. All over my body, the boys twisted, roiling in their dreams. I knew I was looking at the Black Cat.

I saw the rest of the woman moments later, just beyond a break in the crowd. Most of her, anyway. A Chinese man knelt at the base of the bed; a giant, huge muscles straining in his back and arms as he drove himself forward into her writhing body with sharp, mechanical thrusts. He obscured her face, but I glimpsed tattooed arms, and the edge of a tattooed breast.

But not just tattoos. Flickering shadows surrounded every line and curve of her flesh. A dark, thunderous aura—one of the strongest I had ever seen.

The Black Cat was a zombie.

A photographer stood on top of the bed, taking pictures. Another crouched off to the side, doing similar work from a different, more intimate angle. Intense men, with jobs to do. Sweat rolled down their faces. Beyond them, leaning against the wall, I glimpsed three children.

I recognized Samuel and Lizbet immediately, but the other little girl with them did not immediately remind me of Winifred. The coloring was the same—dark hair, dark eyes—but there was a quality to her face that was distinctly different.

None of them was watching the sex. But not, I thought, because of embarrassment. Just boredom. As though they had seen the same scene played out so many times it meant nothing. Trays of empty glasses were at their feet, along with water pitchers and small bowls of diced watermelon. There to run errands, I guessed. Better than the alternative.

The crowd swallowed them. Ernie moved around several cameramen and disappeared. Less than a minute later a throaty, satin voice said, "I have business. Everyone, come back after lunch."

Men and women exchanged startled looks, but no one argued, not even a grumble. Without a word, they put down whatever they were holding—cameras, makeup, iced tea— and streamed past us to the door, exiting into the garden. The children followed, joined by Ernie. All of them, except him, stumbled when they saw Jean—staring at her with horror. Not a peep left their mouths, though. Too well trained.

The man having sex with the Black Cat was the last to go. He strode out naked, still erect and holding himself in his fist. Not caring who watched. And perhaps, in this place, no one did care. But that still left behind a handful of Russian bodyguards—and the Black Cat, lounging on silk sheets. Her aura pulsed with a dark fire that I had only ever seen in one other demonic parasite—the Queen of them all, Blood Mama.

This was not her. But the parasite was very old.

Unlike its host—an unconventionally beautiful woman. Her jaw was a little too thick, her nose a bit too pointed. She had a wide mouth and a crooked smile. But there was something in that smile, and something in those features— energy, personality, a crackle—cemented by the pure, raw aggression in her blue eyes.

Hard to know how much of that was from the demon— and how much was leaking through from the real woman, whoever she might have been.

"Now this is a sight," said the Black Cat softly. "Two Hunters, in one place. That just can't be right."

"Run, if you like," Jean said in a cold voice. "But don't pretend you're not frightened."

"I'm not," replied the zombie, stretching sinuously. Her body was all woman, covered in dimples and curves that not even her tattoos could obscure. But those tattoos . . . Those tattoos were something else. As the eye traveled, so did each tattoo—claws becoming roses, fangs lengthening into thorns. Petals and vines dripped with sweat, curving in an inked tangle across her breasts, up to the base of her throat. Even her fingers had been tattooed, but the art stopped around her pubic hair. A fact that I found strangely reassuring—but no less unnerving. I felt as though I was looking at a bad copy of myself, as though someone had tried to re-create from memory the body of a Hunter—but gotten it wrong in ways that were disjointed, dizzying. Her tattoos shimmered in my vision.

Something else, too. I could not name it, but I felt a burn on my tongue when I looked at her, as though tasting something bad in the air. And not just the parasite.

The Black Cat leaned on her elbow, fingers digging through her brown hair, and pursed her lips into a cold, assessing smile. There was nothing kind in her eyes, no amusement. Just business. Dangerous fucking business.

"You," she said, looking at Jean. "It's you I've felt all these months, creeping around my city. I knew you were close. I could smell you and the bastard Kings in the air. But you," she added, fixing her gaze on me. "You don't belong. And there's only one thing I can think of that would have the power to bring you here."

She looked pointedly at my gloved right hand. I did not want to guess how she knew about the armor, though I had some idea. It had been worn before by one of my predecessors. No doubt she had also skipped through time.

But all I said was, "You know how this is going to end."

"No," she said, smiling coldly. "But you do. Or else you wouldn't be here. Must be bad, I think. Bad for you."

Jean lunged. Men moved to intercept her, but I was right behind, grabbing the first thing within reach—a teacup—hurling it like a baseball at the nearest head. Glass shattered against a pale brow. I snatched apples, glasses of iced tea, throwing them with all my strength. It slowed down the men a little. I was surprised that none of them were using their guns—unless the Black Cat was worried about her host. Bullets ricocheting off our bodies.

The woman threw out her hand just before Jean reached her. "If you kill me, the children will never be free."

Jean hesitated. One of the men slammed into her, both going down in a heap. I was there in two steps, grabbing his ears and hauling backward with all my strength. He screamed, and then shouted in Russian. Large bodies loomed behind me.

"Stop," said the Black Cat suddenly, her voice so quiet I was certain the men would not hear her. But they did, and quit all movement—standing so perfectly still I wondered if they were human. Only their chests moved—faintly, quickly, in shallow breaths that made their nostrils flare.

I finished hauling the man off Jean. He fell on his knees, clutching at his ears. She hardly seemed to notice—staring only at the Black Cat. "What the hell do you mean they won't be free?"

"So naïve, little Hunter." The zombie smiled as she looked from Jean to me. "But *that* one . . . she'll understand."

"Cut the crap," I said. Or tried to. Because just at that moment, I saw a flash in the zombie's eyes, and it was not emotion, but actual light. Inhuman, golden light.

Jean gasped. I took a step closer, a cold hard knot forming in my gut. The Black Cat's smile widened, and the golden light in her eyes flared brighter, hotter. She seemed to swell in size, and gazed down upon my grandmother with a patronizing smile. "There were Gods once, little Hunter. Just so you know. They fought my kind and put us inside the prison. But not all. Those who were free left their spore in human flesh. Passed down and down and down. Until we have this." She trailed her hand across her tattooed hip. "Her name was Antonina before I found her. Known for being . . . odd in the head. Premonitions, dreams. Not afraid of spilling a little blood. She saw my true form, and welcomed me into her skin. Her extraordinarily *powerful* skin. She had no idea what she could do with her gifts until I stepped in."

"And the tattoos?" I asked.

"Charms," she replied, her aura thunderous, dancing with bolts of crimson light. "And irony. Because I care for you so."

I ignored that. "You use those marks to bind people to you. How?"

"How does a parasite feed on pain?" countered the Black Cat, gazing lovingly upon her tattooed arm. "How did those gods of old, our dear enemies, manipulate the flesh of humankind with nothing but a thought? How, dear Hunters, did they make *you*?"

She smiled. "A mystery, yes? But, truth. Here, truth. The tattoos are merely an anchor that I use to bind their spirits to mine." The Black Cat raked her nails across a petal etched into her stomach. One of the Russians standing behind me cried out in pain, clawing at his eyes. The Black Cat closed her eyes, shivering. Tasting his pain, no doubt. Like having straws stuck into her body, I thought. Every time the parasite hungered, it needed only to . . . poke herself.

"If you kill this body," she said breathlessly, digging her nails deeper into the petal, speaking over the Russian's cries as he dropped to his knees, "everyone I have marked will die, as well. Here, inside, in their hearts. Those children you care so much about will never live full lives. The world will be gray to them."

"Unless," she added, "they die first. But then, I don't suppose it would matter, anyhow."

"All we have to do is get rid of you," Jean said, though she sounded shaken.

The Black Cat gave her a disdainful look. "Forever? You'll never keep me away from this host. *And you can't kill me.*"

Jean snarled, staggering to her feet. This time, the guards used their guns.

9

THE boys raged in their dreams, surging over my skin to cover my face. Split second, less than a heartbeat. I glimpsed movement against Jean's cheeks, a shadow bursting—and then she was protected, as well. Both of us, wearing our demon masks.

None too soon. A bullet bounced off my forehead, the impact making me stagger. I heard other pings, and then a meaty thud, a low cry. One of the shooters bent over, clutching his stomach.

Hands grabbed my throat from behind, trying to choke me. I felt nothing, and slammed my elbow backward, sending it deep into a hard gut. Fingers loosened. I turned and drove my fist into the man's sternum. Heard a crack. He fell backward, screaming.

I looked for Jean, and found her already at the bed. Her torn blouse was gaping down the front. Somewhere she had found a knife—perhaps from the fallen men at her feet.

One of the few Russians left standing barreled toward her. I reached him first, taking us both into a heavy pile of camera equipment. Glass shattered. I found myself pinned by two hundred pounds of red-faced man. He grabbed my hair with fists the size of hams, trying to pound my skull into the floor. All I felt was a tickle. I let him work out his frustration, and was just about to use my demon-hardened nails to puncture his femoral artery when small arms reached around his neck, and hauled backward.

Or tried to. I spied a thatch of dark hair and determined eyes. Ernie.

The Russian let go of my head, reaching back. I surged upward, slamming my forehead into his jaw. I felt all the bone in the lower half of his face implode, and when I leaned away, the dent I left behind made his face resemble a crushed soda can. He swayed, staring dumbly at me, and then toppled sideways. Ernie did not let go quickly enough, and fell with him.

I reached for the kid. His eyes were squeezed shut, and he cried out when I tried to pry his arms loose. I whispered his name, trying to calm him, but when he looked at me, a shudder raced through him that was so violent I almost wished he had kept his eyes closed.

"Your face," he breathed.

"Pretend it's magic," I replied, and dragged the boy close—stuffing him into the small spot between the back of a chair and the wall.

"Stay there," I told him, and then, because he looked so scared, planted a rough kiss on his forehead. He tried to grab my hand when I turned away, but I ignored him, looking again for Jean.

She had been busy. Blood trickled from the Black Cat's mouth, and she lay pinned to the bed with a knife pressed into her throat. Jean straddled her, appearing every inch the lethal woman I remembered. Cold, hard, and mean as hell. But the Black Cat did not look frightened. She was laughing.

"Be quiet," Jean said through gritted teeth. I realized her hand was shaking, the knife dangerously close to slipping off the zombie's neck—a good or bad thing, I did not know.

"You understand now?" replied the Black Cat, arching sinuously beneath Jean. "You can't touch me."

I strode to the bed. "What the fuck is going on? Exorcise the bitch."

"I tried," Jean snapped, pressing the knife more tightly against the zombie's throat. "The boys . . . The boys didn't *do* anything."

The boys ate parasites. That was how it worked. We exorcised, while Zee and the others sucked the bastards in. Usually. I looked from the exposed tattoos on Jean's chest—red eyes glittering—and met the Black Cat's amused golden stare. "You cut a deal."

"*I* didn't," replied the demon inhabiting the woman, aura thundering silently around her head. "But it was made of blood, nonetheless, and binding. I cannot be killed by you. Or *them*."

I wanted to scream with frustration. This was not the first time I had been denied justice because of deals made between my ancestors and other demons. Promises that had to be honored, forever. Demons might be savage, but they always kept their word. As did the boys.

"And your host?" Jean raised the knife and plunged it into the zombie's shoulder. Somewhere, out in the yard, a woman screamed. My grandmother stilled for one horrified moment—and then quickly yanked out the knife. The Black Cat began laughing again.

"*Be quiet,*" Jean cried hoarsely. I stepped to the bed, and the Black Cat tore her gaze from my grandmother to look at me. Finally, something more than amusement flitted across her mouth, and that light burned again in her eyes: golden, tinged with red, something deeper that was older than the night.

The zombie murmured, "Hunter. Hunter of the Kiss. The old King's Kiss. What will you do with me now? Kill my magnificent host, and you will condemn those children. Kill my host, and I will find another, and another." She looked at Jean. "I will feed every man you ever helped to that Nazi Neumann, for his experiments; and send the women to the comfort houses to be whores for the Japanese. And I will take those sweet children you love," she added, in a whisper, "and take them, and take them, until they are nothing but rags on the screen."

Zee pulsed between my breasts. I drew in a deep breath,

fighting the tremor that started in my gut—rising up and up into my throat. A zombie was in front of me—nothing but a parasite—but there was demon in the blood of her host, and people's lives at stake. Jean made a small, frustrated sound—the tattoos on her face seeming to pulse in fury. A cruel smile touched the Black Cat's mouth. She was goading my grandmother. Pushing her. But all Jean did was quiver. That was all.

Because I took one look at her face, and I knew—*I knew.* She had never killed anyone. Zombie parasites, maybe, but those hardly counted. She had never, with her own two hands, taken a human life. Not even a host.

She could not do it now, either—and not simply because of the price that would be exacted on the children. I could see it in her eyes. I could feel it in my own gut. It was one thing to let the boys do the dirty work, but making the cut took a whole other kind of nerve. A nerve I didn't have, either. The only times I had taken human life was in the heat of battle, or by accident.

This was neither. This was cold blood.

I stripped off my glove, revealing the armor, and climbed on top of the bed. I showed the Black Cat my hand. She must have known it was there—she had intimated as much—and yet she still flinched when she saw it. Flinched, as though I had struck her. She stared at the dull metal and her smile slipped away. So did her contempt. Her aura shrank.

"You know this," I said quietly, and then pulled back one of my braids to reveal the side of my face. "And this."

I felt the boys shift position, revealing a patch of pale human skin—and the twisting scar that was just below my ear: a brand, a symbol of a birthright that I did not understand; only that it was power. The kind of power that terrified even the most dangerous of demons and their enemies. I was different from the others of my bloodline in more ways than one.

"No," whispered the zombie. "No, it can't be."

"Look closer," I snapped. "And tell me what you think it means."

Because I sure as hell had no clue.

The zombie, however, stared at me like I was going to open my jaws wide and swallow her whole. She bucked against Jean, her aura shrinking even more—hugging the host's skin so tightly it looked as though the demon was trying to hide. Jean gave me a startled look, but I ignored her, riding a dangerous edge; slipping past fury into something wild and hungry.

"Don't you fuck with us," I whispered, bending close, holding that zombie gaze, which was dark with terror. "Bargain or no bargain, I will make you pay. I will make you *scream*. You know I can. So you *will* let these people go. And you *will* leave this host and never return. And you will *forget* those threats you made."

The Black Cat closed her golden eyes, but when she opened them again they were brown and human. All the fight had gone out of her. Every ounce of defiance and arrogance. All that power, pissing away. I could taste it, and there was a quiet presence inside me that felt nothing but disdain for how quickly that demonic parasite had folded against nothing but armor and a scar.

She is ours, whispered that darkness inside of me. *All of them belong to us.*

Heat poured from the zombie, shimmering over her stolen skin. I grabbed Jean's shoulder, and hauled her away. The Black Cat remained on her back, chest heaving, her mockery of our tattoos suddenly resembling little more than a child's drawing. As if I were watching ink fade, only deeper: power, heartbeat, breath—breaking loose, leaving the zombie.

Those tattoos had been alive, I realized. Each one *a* life.

"I could have used them against you," whispered the Black Cat. "I could have spoken one word and forced those children to stand still while my men shot them. Or made them attack you. Or attack their own parents. They were mine, in every way."

I took the knife from my grandmother and dragged the tip, hard, across the stab wound in her shoulder, down her arm, across her ribs and stomach. I left behind a trail of blood. No one screamed outside. I looked over my shoulder and found Ernie staring from behind the sofa, eyes huge. Still rubbing his wrist.

"Where's his?" I asked roughly.

Her jaw tightened. "My breast."

I found the tattoo. It looked newer than the others. I sliced it open, a single shallow cut. Ernie did not make a sound, or show any discomfort whatsoever.

"Good," I said, also glancing at Jean, who was staring at the Black Cat as though she had never seen a zombie before. "Now get the fuck out."

That aura flared to life. The Black Cat said, softly, "This host is strong. And she *likes* my kind. If you don't kill her, someone else will take her skin. She will invite them."

"Then you better make sure your kind knows she's off limits," Jean whispered.

"How dare you," murmured the Black Cat, but there was no fire in her voice. Whatever the demon feared inside me had beaten her well and good.

"Go," I said. "You had your fun."

The zombie gave me a cold look. "I'll remember you. I'll warn the others. *And* my mother."

"Your mother," I said, startled.

"Blood Mama," she whispered.

"She's every parasite's mother. You're not special."

"Aren't I?" she said, finally smiling again.

Before I could say a word, that thunderous smoky aura gathered tight against the crown of the Black Cat's head, and slammed upward, away from its human body. In moments it was gone.

And all that was left was an unconscious woman covered in terrible tattoos, resting naked and limp on a large bed. I stared at her for one long moment, remembering what the parasite had said. There was demon blood in that woman. She had been given a taste of power. If she remembered her possession, if she continued hurting people . . .

Safer to kill her. Do it now.

But I never hurt hosts. Not enough to cripple or kill, anyway. A person had to have limits, and innocence was one of them. This woman, Antonina, had been possessed. She now had the chance to make a new life for herself. If she could. If society allowed her to. Folks, I had found, were usually made responsible for the crimes demons made them commit. Justice *was* blind.

I dragged Jean away. Grabbed Ernie on the way out, and then scooped up Samuel and Lizbet. Jean tossed away the knife in her hand, and swung the last little girl, Winifred, into her arms. No one stopped us. Maybe it was the tattoos on our faces, which disappeared by the time we reached the street. Or maybe it was the bodies left behind, clearly visible from the garden once the doors opened; the Black Cat in particular, sprawled on the bed.

Or, perhaps it was our eyes, which Ernie later told me looked like death.

Either way, we got out fast.

10

JEAN and I took the children home.

Samuel and Lizbet first, and then Winifred. She was a sweet kid, and had been playing in the garden while the fighting was going on. No urge to sneak a peek, which Samuel had succumbed to, especially after Ernie had gone back inside the studio. Ernie was quiet as we crossed the bridge to Hongkou, but Samuel kept sneaking glances at my face, and Jean's—as if he half-expected us to sprout tattoos all over again.

Winifred did not remind me of her older self. Not in the eyes, not in the face. But I guessed that was normal. I patted her on the head. Jean promised extra goods to trade, if they stopped by that night. Enough to make up for lost wages. But they were never to return to the Black Cat. Ever again.

"I promise to make sure they listen," Ernie said, later. It was just the two of us. Jean had gone out, thermos in hand, to buy hot water from the vendor down the street. I thought she needed air, and a walk—away from me. Enough time to get her head straightened out. I needed the time, too. Alone with Ernie.

"You can't tell anyone what you saw or heard today," I told him.

"Magic," he said solemnly, and with a trace of uneasiness. "You can do magic. Jean, too. It's how she gets us stuff, isn't it?"

"Jean cares," I said. "She was so afraid she would make it worse for you."

Ernie swallowed hard, shuffling his feet across the floor. He was still in his good clothes, which looked stark and impossibly new against the old sagging couch he was seated on. "Can . . . that woman . . . hurt us again?"

Part of me wanted to know how she had hurt him. Wondering if it would be good for him to talk about it. But I dashed that almost as soon as I thought it. No good.

But his question made me hesitate in other ways. Made me think about the future. How much I should say. If I told him to never look for a Maxine Kiss, then I would never be set on a course that would send me back in time. If I were never sent back in time, all of this would be different— maybe. And maybe, even now, I had done nothing to change the future. Maybe Ernie was still dead, sixty years from now. Him, Samuel, Lizbet—and Winifred.

Which bothered me. Something was still not right. Something big.

"I'm going to tell you some important things," I said to Ernie, holding his gaze—making certain he was listening. "It's going to sound crazy, but it's magic—just like you saw today. And it's the truth. Your life depends on it."

He swallowed hard, going pale. "Yes?"

I took a deep breath. And then gave him a date and time. A place. I told him about knives. I told him to be careful. I told him not to go out that night. Not to go at all. To write a letter to the person he was looking for. Just . . . to write a letter.

I did not tell him he might die. No one deserved to know the date of his or her death. Maybe that was a choice some would make, but it wasn't one that should be forced on a person. Ernie had a long life ahead of him. No need to dread the future.

Although, given the look in his eyes, I had a feeling he could hear between the lines.

"I'll be careful," he said, staring at me with that old-man gaze. "I'll remember."

I nodded, ducking my head to stare at my gloved hands—finding it hard to meet that gaze of his. A moment later he said, "You're telling me good-bye."

The apartment was very quiet, even though beyond its walls I heard voices in the street, and babies crying—metal being pounded in a loud, clanging rhythm. No match for the silence surrounding us, which muted those sounds, and dulled them. The air was hot. It was hard to breathe.

I looked at the boy. "Yes."

He nodded solemnly. "Will I see you again?"

"Maybe."

"Is Jean leaving, too?"

"Not yet."

He heard the "yet" and flinched. "But she will be."

"Even you," I said, as gently as I could. "Nothing lasts. Not this war, not this place. You'll find something better."

"But not magic," he whispered. "Not Jean. Not you."

I smiled. "You only met me last night."

He smiled back, but sadly. "I'll be watching for you. Everywhere I go. I promise."

"I'll be waiting for you to find me," I said quietly.

I heard a creak on the landing outside the door. Jean came in, holding her thermos. Still with that troubled glint in her eye.

Ernie excused himself, and left.

"SOMETHING'S not right," I said, sprawled on the couch. The seat was still warm where Ernie had been. The scent of mildew was getting to me again.

Jean sat on the chair, hunched over, running a wet rag over her face and the back of her neck. I thought about asking for one, too, but was afraid of disrupting my train of thought.

"I was told you skinned that woman," I said.

Jean stopped, and looked at me. "What?"

"The Black Cat. Skinned alive. You, or those kids, did

the deed. I held the proof in my hands. Human skin, with those same tattoos we saw on her body. I didn't imagine it."

Disgust made her grimace. "Why would I do that? And don't bring those kids into that kind of talk. That's horrible."

I slid my hands under my head, staring at the black mold on the ceiling. "I thought there must be a good reason. But it didn't happen. Why would Winifred lie about that? And where else would Ernie have gotten that piece of skin?"

Jean said nothing. I had a feeling she had hardly heard me. Finally, though, she muttered, "I made a mistake today. I didn't finish the job."

I heard the echo of those same words crossing old-man Ernie's lips, and suffered a chill. "Yes, you did."

"I knew I would have to kill her when we went there. Discovering that she was possessed made it easier . . . until I learned what kind of host she was. So I told myself, 'do it.' It was the only way to be certain that everyone was safe. The *only* way." She gave me a hard, stricken look. "It was one of the reasons I waited to engage her—long before you showed up. I could have used Zee or the others to assassinate her. I could have done it myself. Operations like that fall apart without a mind to guide them. Someone else would have stepped in, but it still would have been new territory. Old grudges gone. But I waited and waited, telling myself I needed her contacts, her information. And then, finally, when I had the chance—"

"Stop," I interrupted. "You did the right thing."

"No." Jean breathed, closing her eyes. "My mother—"

She stopped. I said, "My mother would have put a bullet in her head without blinking. If for nothing else than being the kind of bitch who rapes boys and films it to sell."

And my grandmother would have done the same, I thought. *You, kid, in fifteen years or less, will be that woman.*

And maybe so would I.

I stood, pacing, and then walked quickly to the door. I needed air. I needed to go back to my own time. Jean rose with me, and grabbed my arm. "There's more. You may not agree with it."

I waited, utterly silent. Her cheeks reddened, though her troubled gaze remained steady on mine. "I took precautions. That man at the bridge, the naked one. He works for Tai Li, chief of secret service for Chiang Kai-Shek."

I must have looked clueless, because she blew out her breath and added, "Tai Li is called the Himmler of China. I've worked with his people in the past, including that man. I told him that the Black Cat had discovered something big about the war that she was going to sell to the highest bidder. Information that would change everything. And that if they wanted it, they'd have to get to her first."

"You set her up."

Jean clenched her jaw. "That woman is probably having her fingernails pulled out as we speak."

I stared, stunned. "Jesus. And you were worried about not killing her?"

"I made these arrangements before I knew the woman had been possessed," she replied sharply. "Now, death would have been kinder. Demon blood or not."

I sagged against the wall, thinking about that. But less about torture and mercy than my own confusion. The future was still not adding up with the past.

Jean leaned on the wall beside me. "How old are you?"

"Twenty-seven," I said absently.

She seemed surprised. "You don't have a kid yet."

"Is that a problem?"

"My mother was sixteen when she had me. I keep waiting for Zee and the others to force the issue."

She looked so young. I hardly knew what to say. It was true, or so the family stories told, that if a Hunter waited too long to have a child, Zee and the boys would make certain the bloodline continued. One way or another. Lifelong celibacy was not an option, though I did not want to think about Zee condoning rape. I did not ever want to think about that.

"I don't . . ." I began, and then started again, more firmly. "I don't think you have to worry about that. You'll have a child in your own time, when you're ready. I'm proof of that."

"I want love," she said.

"You'll have love."

She gave me a sharp look. "Promise?"

I forced myself to meet her gaze. "Yes."

Yes, you'll have love, I thought. *And he'll love you. But you won't stay together. You won't grow old together. And neither of you will ever tell me why the hell not.*

I could not imagine that happening with me and Grant. I could not—I would not—let it happen.

Jean looked away. I cleared my throat. "Do you have recent photographs of yourself?"

"Some. Why?"

I shook my head, unsure what to say. "I came back to save those kids from something that happens more than sixty years from now, and I don't know if it worked. It all feels wrong. Winifred said—"

"Winifred?" Jean straightened, frowning. "You talked with Winifred?"

"Yes," I said slowly. "In the future. I told you that earlier."

She shook her head. "Winifred is mute. It's an actual deformity of her vocal cords, according to her family. She can't talk."

"Surgery?"

"I don't know. No one seems to think so."

She can't talk. I swayed, light-headed. Sixty years was a long time. A long, *long* time to find a cure.

But if she hadn't?

Then who the hell were we talking to?

"I gotta go," I breathed, pushing away from the wall.

Jean grabbed my arm. "Wait."

"I can't," I said, and flung my arms around her, squeezing so tightly she made a small grunt of protest. I had so much I wanted to say, but no time. It would take a lifetime. It would take more than I could spare, even though time was mine. The future was not going anywhere.

My clock, however, was running faster than the rest of the universe. I needed to see Grant and that old woman. Now.

I stripped off my glove, even as I stared into my grandmother's eyes. "Write me a letter. Warn me. Keep warning Ernie to be careful. Same with Samuel and Lizbet. And

Winifred. Make him promise to you, again, that he won't come find me. No matter what."

"I'll try," she said, and then her eyes went distant, and she began mouthing numbers. "That year you gave me. You'd be my—"

"Don't," I interrupted. "Just think of me as your friend."

Jean hesitated. "Will I ever see you again?"

It was the same question Ernie had asked me, but this time I smiled and snared my grandmother in my arms, holding her tight.

"You won't be able to get rid of me," I whispered.

And then I pushed away, my eyes burning with tears. I could not look at her—I could not—but I did anyway, at the last moment. Soaking in her impossibly young face, those glittering eyes that were already grieving. My grandmother. Jean Kiss.

"Be happy," I said to her, grabbing my right hand, thinking of Grant and the hospital.

And then she was gone—just like that—and the darkness took me.

11

THE journey felt shorter this time, or perhaps I was finally becoming accustomed to the weight of eternity collapsing around my body. When I finally saw light again, I was not sick. My head hurt only a little.

I was outside St. Luke's. It was night. The same homeless man I remembered from before was still asleep on the sidewalk, in the same position. The girl with the Gatorade was walking away. It had not been that long. Not long at all.

The boys ripped free of my body, driving me to my knees. I started running, though, before the transition was entirely complete—shedding demons from my skin in smoky waves that coalesced into hard, sharp flesh.

I found the emergency room, and within minutes was directed to a quiet area in recovery. Grant was there, perched on the edge of his chair—his head tilted toward the door as though listening for something. Maybe me. I skidded to a stop when I saw him. He looked so normal. All of this, normal, familiar. But in that moment all I could smell was mildew, and all I could feel was the heat, and I remembered the sounds of Shanghai at night and the Nazis with their laughter as they smiled at my grandmother.

"Maxine," Grant said, staring at me. "Your aura."

"Later," I said softly, staring past him at the old woman resting on the bed. Giving her a good long look that drew readily from fresh memories.

She seemed so ordinary. Such a sick, wounded, ordinary woman. Wrinkled, shriveled, with oxygen lines running directly into her nose, and heart monitors disappearing up her short sleeve to her chest. It was a miracle she still lived.

Or maybe not so much a miracle. I saw the truth. I saw it in a way that I never would have, had I not looked the Black Cat in the face. Despite the odds, despite her advanced age, this was not Winifred Cohen.

The woman lying in the bed in front of me was the Black Cat of Shanghai.

"This is not who we thought," I whispered.

"I know," Grant replied solemnly, rising with a wince from his chair. "Look at her arms."

I had not even paid attention, but I looked. Scar tissue covered her arms; rough, as though an electric sander had been taken to her skin. Or a knife. Something sharp that had cut and peeled.

"The doctors found those scars everywhere, as though she had been skinned alive," Grant said, his voice tight with disgust. "They asked me about it, but of course I knew nothing. It got me thinking, though. And then, the longer I was with her, and the more I studied her aura—"

"That dark patch you saw."

"Something . . . demonic. Buried so deeply, she might not even know it exists. There are many odd things about her aura. Fragments, just . . . floating. I'm not sure she knows who she is."

I did not care. The real Winifred Cohen was probably dead—and if so, this woman had killed her, or paid someone else do it. Set up the others, even as she took over the woman's life.

Should have finished the job. Should have finished. I felt my grandmother's consternation. I shared it, thinking of Ernie. I had not done enough. Not enough, by far.

I walked to the far side of the bed where the shadows

were thick, and tapped my foot on the ground. Zee rolled free, giving me an uneasy look.

"You knew," I said. "You must have. You pretended she was safe. Why the hell would you go to so much trouble?"

"Many reasons," he rasped, but a nurse chose that moment to approach the room, and he rolled back under the bed—leaving me fuming. The woman who entered took one look at my face—and then my ragged, ill-fitting clothing from 1944—and said sharply, "Is everything all right here?"

"Just fine," Grant soothed, a melody in his voice. "If you could give us a moment?"

The nurse shot him a piercing look that lasted for all of two seconds. She swayed, touching her head. Grant said something else to her, his voice little more than a buzz to my distracted mind. The woman nodded absently, dreamily, and backed out of the room. He shut the door behind her.

I said, "Can you wake her up?"

Grant limped close, studying my face, probably seeing all kinds of ugly emotions rising from my heart. But there was only compassion in his eyes. "You went somewhere. Back."

"Back," I agreed. "Can you do it?"

Grant hesitated, staring from me to the old woman. His eyes grew distant, thoughtful.

"She's aware of you," he said, limping to the side of the bed. "Even unconscious, a part of her is reaching toward you."

A chill raced over me. I watched the old Black Cat's slack face. Remembered her golden eyes, the vibrancy of her lush curves. That cruel zombie smile.

Antonina, I told myself. *Not the Black Cat.*

And yet, I could not separate the two. It was impossible.

Grant bent over, and placed his mouth close to the unconscious woman's ear. He sang to her, softly, but his voice rolled through me like the ghost of a summer storm, rich and heavy with thunder. I moved closer.

Her eyelids flickered. Her mouth moved, tongue darting over cracked lips. Grant motioned for me to grab a bottle of water from the nightstand, and I was ready when the old

woman drew in a long, rasping breath. I rested the mouth
of the bottle against her lips, and she instinctively tried to
drink. I was careful only to let her sip. She finally opened
her eyes, and met my gaze.

She recognized me immediately, but I could see now
that it went deeper than that. I should have noticed before—
realized *something* was wrong. The first time I had met this
woman, believing she was Winifred Cohen, she had known
things about me. I assumed, erroneously, that she had witnessed my grandmother in action. Only half right. Winifred
had seen little or nothing. But the zombie, on the other hand,
and her host . . .

"I know who you are," I said softly to the old woman,
when I was certain I had her full, conscious, attention.
"Antonina. Black Cat."

The faintest hint of a smile touched her mouth, sending
a chill through me. I wanted to back away, but held steady,
forcing myself to hold her gaze; golden-flecked, with shim-
mers that rose from the very human brown of her eyes. I
would never forget those eyes.

"Hunter," she whispered. "She was so taken with you."

"The demon who possessed you," I said.

She wet her lips. "My protector. I searched for her. For
years. I felt her close sometimes, as though she was watching me, but she never . . . came home. Not after that day.
You kept her from me. Both of you did."

I ignored that. "You've been up to your old tricks. Hurting people."

"Making right," replied the old Black Cat. "I forgot you
all, for a time. I forgot so much, but the Kuomingdang would
not believe that. They did many things to me, trying to make
me talk. All I could tell them were stories about Siberia. But
one day they pushed me too far. I killed those men. I didn't
know how. Just that they were dead. I got out, and forgot
them, too."

The Black Cat closed her eyes, sighing. "I had such
terrible dreams, Hunter. I wanted a new life. I wanted to be
someone else."

"You cut those tattoos off your body."

"Part of the bad dream." Her voice softened so much I could hardly hear her. "But I kept them. You don't . . . throw away pieces of yourself. Like trash."

Grant placed his hand on my shoulder. I straightened, fighting for my voice. "It was all a lie. You set Ernie up. You killed Samuel and Lizbet. Finally, you killed them. And you had yourself shot."

"Making right," she whispered again. "I dreamed of you, Hunter. All these years, dreaming of you. Feeling you, in my veins. And then one day I crossed paths with Winifred Cohen. I found her. I think I had been searching, all along. Quiet woman. But I could hear her." The Black Cat brushed fingers across her brow, but barely, as if the effort hurt and weakened her. Her hand fell limp into the covers, and her eyes drifted shut. "I . . . absorbed her. I made her tell me what she knew of the others. And your grandmother. I wanted to punish that woman. She loved those children.

"But it all became a dream again," she added, a moment later—sounding confused, and sad, and tired.

Grant drew me away. "Before, when we first met her, she truly believed she was Winifred Cohen. She believed everything she told us, right down to cutting the skin off a live woman. Which she did, apparently. Just to herself. Her immersion in that personality was flawless, even to me."

"And now?"

"It's like watching a quilt that has been cut into pieces. She's floating in and out. Part of her is reaching for the Winifred personality. Other parts are just . . . resting in what she was. She's crazy, Maxine. Well and truly scrambled. I think it's possible she ordered the hit on herself, believing she deserved it. That she was Winifred and needed to die."

I looked at the Black Cat. It had been only hours for me. Hours, since I had seen her as a young woman. And now she was shriveled, a shell, shot and maybe dying in a hospital bed. I had no idea what to do with a psychotic old woman who was part demon, who murdered, who believed herself to be both victim and predator. She had taken a fucking knife and cut the skin off her body. God only knew what else she had done in the past sixty years.

Dek and Mal were heavy in my hair. I looked for the others, and found them arrayed around the room, bathed in the fluorescent glow of the long bulb arranged in the wall panel above the Black Cat's head. Raw and Aaz ate popcorn as they stared at the old woman. Zee perched at the bottom of the bed, his claws bunched up in the covers surrounding her feet. Watching her solemnly.

Maybe she felt his attention. She opened her eyes, and stared right at him. Showed no fear. Just that faint smile, which shifted from sweet to cold, to cruel.

"Your highness," she rasped mockingly.

"Cat," whispered Zee. "Miserable Cat. Nothing left but threads."

Gold glinted again in her eyes, but stronger, brighter. Hot with fury. Grant stiffened, and in two strides I was back at the bed.

"You should have killed me then," she said, trying to sound threatening, though the effect was little more than an angry, bitter whine. "But you both were *too weak*."

I could have said something about mercy. I could have told her that she had been an innocent, and that the formerly possessed should be given a chance to start over. But I looked into those golden eyes, fading even now into dull human brown—glazing over with forgetfulness and confusion—and kept my mouth shut. Mercy, again. Mercy, me.

I snapped my fingers at the boys, and they fled into the shadows. All of them, except Zee. I said to Grant, "Can she harm anyone else?"

"She's dying," he said simply. "I can see it all around her. She's fading. I doubt she'll last the night."

I nodded stiffly, sick to my stomach. Sick to death. I was walking away, again, but I wasn't going to kill in cold blood. Not like this.

I met the old woman's gaze. "Good-bye."

"No," she murmured, brow crinkling with confusion. "Not yet. I didn't finish. I didn't finish with you. Wanted to punish . . . her grandchild. Punish *her*."

"You punished yourself," I replied, and left the hospital room.

* * *

GRANT and I went to my mother's apartment on Central Park. Everything was dusty. The white sheets that covered the furniture had turned gray. The windows were filthy. The air was cold and smelled faintly of mildew. But the electricity and water worked—paid for each month by one of the law firms that had overseen my mother's affairs since her murder.

In the closet I found clothes wrapped in plastic. I found a locked chest full of guns. A box crammed with cash and precious jewels. And in the kitchen cupboards, Spam. Along with two forks.

"I feel like royalty," Grant said.

I tried to smile. Around us, Raw and Aaz were tumbling along the hardwood floors, tossing Dek and Mal through the air like spears—making the serpentine demons squeal with delight. I looked for Zee. I walked through the apartment, thinking of the last time I had been here with my mother. Wondering if Jean had ever come back.

I felt Zee watching me before I saw him. I stood at the window, gazing out at Central Park. Waiting to hear what he had to say. Knowing part of it already.

"Old Cat dead," he finally rasped. "Took care of it."

I had thought he would. I searched myself for regret, and found none. "Did she suffer?"

Zee climbed onto the wide sill. "Not in sleep."

"And the one who shot her? Who killed Samuel and Lizbet? Ernie?"

An odd glint entered his eyes when I mentioned Ernie's name, but he shrugged and said, "Different men, different cities. Hired like thugs. Got the scent. Tomorrow, I cut them."

Cut them, kill them. I had time to think about that, and decide whether there should be another kind of justice. Human laws, human wheels. Evidence could be planted. Police tipped off.

I shot him a hard look. "And the rest of it? You could have warned me in time to save lives."

He dug his claws into wood beneath him. I noticed other

gouge marks, older and just as deep. "Old mother needed you. Needed you in order to . . . change. Be better. Stronger. Pivotal. No you around, she go on. Never look back. Black Cat get strong and stronger. Children die early. More children after that."

"She would have done something," I protested, though a small part of me wondered if that was true. "She would have fought to help those kids."

"No," Zee whispered, with utter certainty. "Would have been different. Colder, harder. No good mother. No heart. Seen it happen. Again, again." He rested a claw upon my hand. "You got heart. Heart from your mother, because your grandmother got heart. Because you shook up her heart. Shook her hard. Made her regret. Regret is sweet if it burns you right."

"So you're saying. . . . all this was to make me go back. To help my grandmother become a better person." I stared at him. "But she didn't even remember me. Later, the first time I met her. We were strangers."

Zee made a slashing motion across his brow. "Waited until lessons took, then cut you out. Better that way. No good remembering future. No good."

I wanted to argue with that, but stopped myself. If I had met my grandchild while hardly out of my teens, it would have messed me up. It would have been all I thought of. *No good remembering the future.* Because it stole from the present.

I wrapped my arm around his hard shoulders, and rested my chin on top of his head. I could hear Grant's cane clicking in the other room, coming closer.

"But we failed," I said softly, staring at the glittering city lights. "Those kids died."

Zee held up his clawed hand, splitting his long fingers like a Vulcan from *Star Trek*. "Live long and prosper."

I stifled a sharp cough of stunned, incredulous laughter. But mostly, I just wanted to weep. Grant peered into the room. "You okay?"

"No," I said. "There's been a lot of death."

"Lot more you're not telling me. If I checked your right hand, what would I see?"

I did not want to look. "More of your future cyborg woman."

"And the rest?"

"I couldn't save the people I was supposed to."

Grant leaned against the doorway, studying me. "You're talking about those kids whom Winifred knew, and who were . . . targeted. Samuel, Lizbet."

"Ernie," I whispered, aching.

Grant frowned. "You feel so much grief when you say his name. I can see it."

"He's dead," I blurted out, wondering why he should look so confused—and then remembered that Grant did not know. I had not told him yet, about going back in time. Seeing those . . . names . . . as children. Saving Ernie, at least for a moment. In this time, Ernie had been dead for days now, in my arms.

Unless he was not dead.

"Grant," I said slowly. "How did we get here? How were we warned to find Winifred?"

His frown deepened. "There was a letter, Maxine."

THE following week in Seattle, I picked Ernie Bernstein up from the airport. It was a rare day, sunny and warm, and I was the only person wearing jeans and a turtleneck. I did not feel the heat.

I saw him coming out of customs: a portly man, shorter than me, his hair silver and tufted. But his eyes were the same. I remembered those eyes.

He stopped when he saw me. Stood stock-still, staring. Drinking me in. I walked up to him, and smiled. Not bothering to hide the fine burn of tears in my eyes.

"I listened," he said hoarsely. "Even when Winifred called me out of the blue and said I needed to find you, and go in person. Even when she mailed me that scrap of skin and said the Black Cat was back. I waited, and did as you asked."

Time was a funny thing. I had assumed nothing could change, but it had. I could not explain the paradox that created. Only that moments counted. That it was possible—*it was possible,* against all odds—to make a difference.

"You did good," I said.

"I trusted magic," Ernie replied, with a tremulous smile. "But now I'm an old man, and you're still the same. I can only hope . . . I can only hope that Jean is doing just as well."

I hesitated. He saw the answer in my eyes, and bowed his head.

"Oh," he whispered, a little boy all over again, pained and grieving. "I never thanked you. Either of you. I regretted that, always. So I watched for you both. All these years, everywhere I went. I watched for your faces."

"I was hoping you would find me," I said.

He leaned in, and kissed me shyly on the cheek. "It was only a matter of time."

etched in silver

AN OTHERWORLD NOVELLA

YASMINE GALENORN

Without obsession, life is nothing.

—JOHN WATERS

If we can live without passion, maybe we'd know some kind of peace. But we would be hollow. Empty rooms, shuttered and dank. Without passion, we'd be truly dead.

—JOSS WHEDON (*BtVS*)

1

THE room was a shade darker than night as I pushed my way through the haze of pungent smoke, trying not to cough. The fragrance of stale wine and decaying lotus blossoms filled the air, cloying and overripe. Noise echoed through the dimly lit room, a cacophony of whispers and laughter, drunken singing and arguments from the gambling tables all rolling into one to give me a supremely bad headache. Yeah, the Collequia was jumping and so were my nerves. I'd had a very long, very bad day, and it wasn't over yet. Normally, I came here to hang out and play, but tonight was all business.

The hardcore opium eaters were out in full array. My nose twitched. Not only did they smell—think a week's unwashed sweat and grime—but they were looking for nookie. Check that. They were looking for money, and they'd earn it by giving a woman—or a man—anything she or he wanted. Considering their habits, they'd probably toss in a few extra gifts for free. Disease, lice, fleas . . . all lovely little bundles of joy that I wasn't interested in acquiring.

The pretty boys crowded around their tables in tight-knit groups, sucking on hookahs, gossiping, eyeing each new person who crossed the door. Oh yeah, they were hungry for money. Opium was a commodity, a pricey one, spurred on by our illustrious queen's habit, and she set the price point for distributors throughout the city. Selling sex was an easy way to score one more round.

Sometimes I wondered what drew me back to this club time and again, but to be fair, not everybody here was out for the drugs. I'd met a number of friends and lovers here.

I scanned the room, looking for any signs of my quarry. Roche, one of the Veiled Fae, was wanted for rape and murder. He also happened to be a member of the Guard Des'Estar. Or at least he'd *been* a member till he'd gone bad. Very bad.

When Lathe, my boss at the Y'Elestrial Intelligence Agency, had assigned the case to me I knew one thing: they didn't think that I had a chance in Hel's domain of catching him. They always gave me and my sisters the cases they couldn't solve. That way, they could blame us for ineptitude and save face. And we'd accrue another notch in a long string of botched jobs. *Camille D'Artigo at your service—on the fast track to nowhere.*

I meandered past a table for six, ignoring the bozos eyeing my boobs. Sawberry Fae, all of them—rough and crude. I couldn't blame them for looking, though. After all, I *was* dressed to attract. For one thing, Roche responded to curvy women, so I was playing it up to lure him out. For another, I'd been waiting for a chance to wear my new outfit. Tight, sheer magenta tunic, thin skirt with a slit all the way up my thigh, the barest hint of woven silver panties. I made quite an impression, all right.

So when men stared at my boobs, it was part of the game and I just laughed it off. But the sweaty hand reaching out to cop a feel on my butt crossed the line.

"That's one step too far, boy."

The man didn't budge, his fingers firmly fastened on my ass. "Hey girlie, give me a ride. I promise, I can do amazing tricks with my tongue."

"I said, back off. I don't offer pity fucks." I didn't pay for it either, and all the opium eaters were looking for was cash for another round.

"The pity would be if you *don't* fuck me." He snorted and squeezed.

Realizing I wasn't going to get out of this without making some sort of scene, I slid my leg through the slit in my skirt to show off the silver dagger strapped around my thigh. "Remove the fingers from my ass or I'll ram my stiletto through your crotch and you'll never use that cock of yours again. *Understand?*"

He scowled as his buddies laughed, but he let go.

I leaned on the table. "Listen, boys, some of you aren't half bad. Or you wouldn't be if your eyes weren't glazed over and your teeth were a couple of shades closer to white. Clean up your act and get a job."

Without warning, Mr. Butt-Grabber grabbed my wrist and twisted. Hard. "Bitch. When I want advice from a half-breed, I'll ask for it."

"What did you call me?" I couldn't reach my stiletto— he had my wrist, but he was standing, pressing against me, so I came down hard on his insole with my heel. He yelped and let go. I whipped out my dagger as he knocked over his chair. The dude was a good six-five and muscled, and it took everything I had to stand my ground. "Touch me again and you've touched your last woman."

"Filthy windwalker." He fumbled for his weapon, but his eyes were so glazed over from the opium that he couldn't get a good grip on the hilt. I knew the look, though, and it wasn't a safe one. Junkies were dangerous. "You should be grateful for any attention you get—"

"I suggest you apologize to the lady right now, unless you prefer to make an intimate acquaintance with my blade."

The voice came from behind the Sawberry. It was smooth and calm, like silk drawn across skin, and set up a vibration in the air that rolled through my senses like a wave. I slowly turned my head to see who was speaking.

The most gorgeous man I'd ever seen was standing there, serrated dagger out, the tip lightly pressed against Mr. Fingers's ribs. He wasn't even looking at the Sawberry, but instead, was staring at me—his gaze fastened on my face, not my breasts. His eyes were the coolest shade of blue I'd ever seen. Ice blue. Glacier blue. Blue like a frosty morning in autumn. They stood out against the onyx color of his skin, as did the shock of silver hair that flowed down his back, shining with cerulean highlights. His face, though . . . damn, he was *beautiful*. More handsome than any man had a right to be, with a refined nose that led narrowly down to thick, luscious lips.

My breath caught in my throat. *Touch me, kiss me, hold me, and help me get out of my head.*

The Sawberry glanced down at the blade, then at the man holding it and fear flickered in his eyes. He held up his hands. "No harm, no worry," he said, sitting back down. He swallowed his anger and added softly, "I'm sorry, miss. I won't bother you again."

Taken aback by the sudden turnaround, I looked back for the man who had cowed the giant but he'd vanished. Blinking, wondering if I'd imagined the entire incident, I hurried over to the counter.

"Petre bothering you?" Jahn, the bartender, wiped the polished wood in front of me. "He's harmless enough, though when he's hurting for another fix, I wouldn't lay odds on his behavior. I cut them off around dawn. They haven't paid their tab from last week yet, so they're probably ready for more."

"I almost had to cut him, but that man . . . Something about him scared the dude and he stopped right in his tracks. Apologized, too."

"What man?" Jahn reached for the brandy bottle. I shook my head.

"No brandy tonight." I looked around the bar, but didn't see the man who'd come to my aid. "I dunno, I don't see him now. He just . . . appeared from out of nowhere." I glanced back at the bottle he was holding. "I'm in the mood for something different. Something a little more . . . exotic."

Jahn let out a grin. "The day you're *not* in the mood for something kinky is the day I close this place down. What's the matter, Camille? Rough day?"

"Rough week." I shrugged, scooping up a handful of the torado nuts and popping the salty treats into my mouth.

Lately, my life had been a long string of one bad day after another. My job sucked. I sucked at my job. My father was on my case again about how I was running the house. Hell, I was a Moon witch, member of the Coterie of the Moon Mother, *and* I worked for the YIA. Between work and Coterie meetings and running with the Hunt, I barely had time to sneeze, let alone help the housekeeper keep things tidy at home. Not only that, but I was worried about my sister Menolly and the new job the agency had assigned to her. It was dangerous—too dangerous, and I had the uneasy feeling they were setting her up for a big fall.

"What happened?" Jahn tossed the bar rag over his shoulder and rummaged through the bottles on the shelves behind the counter. He held up a clear bottle, filled with a chocolate brown liqueur. "Here, try this. Straight from the Nebelvuori Mountains."

"Dwarven? Won't that be a little raw?"

He grinned. "Dwarves may be crude in the bedroom and at the dinner table, but they like their liquor, so the drink should be smooth and rich."

I actually laughed for the first time in days. "Set me up, babe," I said, resting my elbows on the counter as I glanced around the bar. Still no sign of Roche. He was *supposed* to be here. My supervisor had practically guaranteed it. And I had a tight deadline. Find the perv before he struck again.

He shook his head as he filled a small cognac glass. "You use the oddest expressions, Camille. But they fit you somehow."

"I have my mother to thank for that. She was human, you know, and she kept some ties over Earthside." And I missed her more than I could ever say. It had been years since she died, but her loss still left a gaping hole in our family that no one could fill, no matter how hard they tried.

"I remember her. She was a lovely woman, with gracious manners. So, you ever think you'll go Earthside when the portals are finally open to travelers?" Jahn pushed the glass my way and rested his elbows on the counter. His eyes were warm. He was one of the few friends I could count on who really gave a damn about my sisters and me.

I snorted. "Are you kidding? Hell, I have a hard enough time coping with one world, let alone two." But I lingered over the thought. Maybe it wouldn't be such a bad idea. Seeing my mother's homeworld might help me understand why she'd been the way she'd been. I had a while to think about it, though. The project would take a number of years to complete.

Jahn motioned for me to drink up. I tossed a coin on the counter and inhaled the aroma whirling up from the glass. One long whiff filled my nose with the fragrance of harvest time, and moss and trees and stone circles.

"You sure the dwarves made this?"

"I know. I was surprised, too," he said. "I gather they've discovered some new process or something for distilling the brew. Nobody's talking secrets, though. Taste it. I think you'll be in for a surprise."

I brought the crystal to my lips and took a sip. The flavors of warm honey and cinnamon raced down my throat, and then—an aftertaste of galangal and oats and . . . *kirmeth*? A potent flower bud, kirmeth produced a stiff kick when added to alcohol.

Coughing, I wiped my eyes, trying not to smear the kohl. "Whoa . . . this is a damned sight better than anything I've had lately. Pour me another, please."

He filled another glass and shoved it my way. "What's got you so wound up? You've been coming in here all tight and tense this whole week. You act like you're hunting for something, and I know you haven't found what you're looking for."

He reached out and took one of my hands in his. His skin was rough and his face was scarred. I wondered what battles he'd seen in his younger days.

"Sweetie, it's no wonder the men are scared shitless of you. They want you, don't get me wrong, but that glint in your eyes promises you'll take down the next man who even looks at you wrong."

I slugged the rest of my drink and pushed back the glass, toying with the second drink. As much as I wished I could tell him, I was under wraps. Agents of the YIA were sworn to secrecy, except to one another. Even though Jahn had been a friend of the family since before I was born, I couldn't confide in him. So I lied.

"Family stuff. Father's on a tear about the gardens again. Mother loved them. But I don't have the time to keep them up like she did, and I really don't have her green thumb. I can grow herbs—some, for my magic. But I'd rather talk to them than tend them."

"Green thumb?" He looked perplexed.

"Mother was able to grow things . . . like an herbalist. Anyway, so he's pissed about that. And I'm worried about Menolly." I stopped, frowning. *And here we come to another problem, folks—my sister and the YIA's unrelenting use of her in dangerous cases, thanks to her innate abilities to sneak into places and climb walls and so forth.*

"What's she done now?" Jahn knew all about Menolly's propensity for getting into trouble.

"It isn't what she's done, it's what . . . Oh, it's confidential. Let's just say I don't trust the mission she's been assigned to. I have a really bad feeling about this one, Jahn, but there's nothing I can do. We can't refuse our assignments."

I shifted on the bar stool, my body aching. It had been weeks since I'd had sex, at least with anybody other than my own hand. Or even a decent date. The last guy bailed on me when he found out I was half-human. Damned bigots.

Jahn noticed. He leaned closer and whispered, "I thought that's what was wrong with you. I'll take you home, darlin'. I'd jump your bones in a second if you'd let me."

That smarted. Not the fact that Jahn looked at me that way. I was flattered, actually, because he was a worldly, seasoned traveler who had finally settled down after a volatile career on a fishing boat up in the tumultuous Wyvern Ocean.

No, what smarted was that here I was, young, unattached, pretty—or so I was told, reasonably intelligent, hardworking, and willing . . . and nobody had looked my way in over three months. Well, nobody that I was interested in.

Race didn't matter. I'd dated a dwarf a few years back, a giant, even an elf, but lately it felt like I'd been classified as untouchable.

I stared at the bartender, mulling over his offer. Roche wasn't around and I might as well give up the hunt for the night. A fling with Jahn might be just what I needed. He was rugged and I had no doubt he knew how to use his hands—and everything else, as well. But he'd been after me for years and there was something a little creepy about sleeping with my father's friend. And Father would be livid. You just don't fuck old friends' daughters.

He leaned on the polished mahogany counter next to my drink. "You'll walk away more than satisfied."

Slowly, I reached out to run my fingers lightly over the top of his hand. "I'm incredibly flattered . . . I know you see beautiful women in here day after day. But I don't—"

"Stop. Just think about it for a moment," Jahn said, slowly pulling his hand away. "I'll make you come like you've never come before."

He turned to another customer as I sat there, playing with my drink. I was so tense, so in need of release, but something just didn't feel right about accepting Jahn's proposal.

"I don't think I can do it," I whispered, staring at my glass.

"You can do anything you set your mind to." That voice—Mr. Silk on Satin. Once again, something in his tone made me tremble.

I darted a glance to my right. Sure enough, it was the beautiful man again. "And who are you, to be interrupting my thoughts? And my fights?"

He arched an eyebrow and motioned to Jahn, who had just returned. The bartender's expression clouded over.

"Sonyun Brandy. Warmed over a slow flame, please." As the man tossed a handful of coins on the bar, he added, "And another drink for the lady."

I was about to protest, but another glimpse of those baby blues shut me up.

"I take it you're alone tonight?" he asked, turning back to me.

And then, I saw it—the sparkle of fire, the hint of magic. The man bled charm like a bee tree oozed honey.

He wasn't a wizard, nor a witch nor a mage. A sorcerer? No, I'd sense the magic. Nor did he look like royalty. Sometimes the nobles of the Court slummed in the nightclubs, picking up lovers to use and abuse. I couldn't figure out what game he was playing, but he intrigued me. I decided to accept his challenge. I'd learned to bluff from the best.

As Jahn let out an irritated grunt and moved off to warm up the man's brandy, I suddenly remembered his offer. Shit, I was being rude, and to a sweet guy, at that. But ignoring the man sitting next to me would be as hard as ignoring the pressure between my thighs.

I shifted on the bar stool. "Am I alone? That depends on who's asking. And you haven't answered my question yet."

The man smirked. "No, I haven't. Consider it a lesson in patience, which you obviously need, the way you're fidgeting in your seat."

Blushing, I slammed down my drink and stood. I leaned close and whispered, "You might like to play with pussycats, but you're not getting near mine. Not unless you can give me a damned good reason."

As I started for the door he reached out and lightly placed two fingers on my arm, not holding me, just ever-so-slightly touching. A ripple raced through my body. I grabbed for the counter, steadying myself as he swung in behind me and rested a hand on my side—tracing the curve of my waist with the lightest of pressure.

"Leaving so soon, beautiful?" he whispered, leaning close to my ear. "I was just starting to enjoy myself. I don't often meet women who can hold their own. I hope you aren't offended that I interfered in your tête-à-tête back there. I have no doubt you would have taken that idiot down alone, but I can't stand louts. They offend my senses."

The breath from his lips washed over my neck and I pressed my thighs together. I'd met plenty of gorgeous Fae over the years—hell, I was half-Fae myself and knew how to use glamour, but this was more than glamour. This was like being swept out to sea by a riptide of hunger. I wanted to strip naked and throw him down on the counter.

"Camille? Can I speak to you? *Alone*." Jahn set a snifter of brandy on the counter. "Here's your brandy. Why don't you let the lady go?"

Without missing a beat, the dark man said, "Mind your business, barkeep. She's a grown woman. She'll tell me if she wants me to leave her alone."

I didn't move.

"Camille, *please*, I need to talk to you." Jahn gave me a strained look and I reluctantly broke away. In a fog, I followed him to the end of the counter.

"That's the man who helped me out. Do you know him?"

"Oh, lovely." Jahn narrowed his eyes. "Not by name, but he's a Svartan. Surely you know what that means, girl."

I frowned, thinking for a moment, then understanding broke through. A *Svartan* . . . one of the *Charming* Fae, as cunning in nature as they are sexual. As predatory as they are suave.

"I didn't realize . . ." I glanced back at the man, who raised his snifter in salute, then took a long, slow sip.

Jahn let out a little groan. "Girl, promise me you aren't going to sleep with him. Please? Even if you don't sleep with me, for the love of the gods, do *not* get mixed up with the likes of him."

I listened to what he was saying. I really did. But the entire time, my gaze was fastened on the Svartan. After a moment, I let out a little sigh. Roche wasn't here and he wasn't going to come. Not tonight. Another wild-goose chase. Another black mark against my name.

"I think I'd better go home for the night," I said, feeling defeated. "Thank you, Jahn, for everything."

As I gathered my purse and turned to go, I realized that I couldn't just leave it at that. Feeling Jahn's disapproving stare follow me, I walked back to the Svartan and deliberately laid one hand on his arm.

He glanced down at my hand, then up to meet my eyes. "Yes?"

"Camille te Maria. I'm in here a lot. Next time—and I

trust there *will* be a next time—ask before you intervene."
I sauntered toward the curtains cordoning off the exit, then
paused in midstep to call over my shoulder. "Remember,
stranger. You still owe me your name."

As I swept out the door, I could feel him watching me.
But I didn't look back.

WHAT do you know about the Svartans?" I asked my father
that evening after dinner.

Sephreh ob Tanu jerked his head up from where he was
polishing his dress sword, his brow lined, a worried look in
his eyes. They reflected the violet of my own, and his hair
was the same color as mine—raven black and woven in a
shoulder-length braid. I took after him. My sister Delilah
took after our mother—golden-haired and tanned, and
Menolly . . . well, no one knew where her burnished copper
locks came from.

"What have you gone and done now?" He sounded posi-
tively overjoyed. *Not.*

I shrugged. Father was cagey. I'd have to walk softly
because I could already sense the storm brewing in his voice.

"I saw one in the club tonight." With a little luck, Jahn
wouldn't breathe a word to Father about my interaction
with Tall, Dark, and Dangerous. He'd keep his mouth shut
because he'd be too afraid I'd mention his offer, and we both
knew my father well enough to know just how *that* would
go over. Old friends don't fuck other friends' daughters. At
least not without permission.

With a look that said *I know you're up to something but
I don't know what,* Father shook his head. "Leave the man
alone. They're all a bunch of perverts. You know the city of
Svartalfheim rests in the Subterranean Realms."

"I've heard rumors about the entire city migrating back
to Otherworld."

"*Wonderful.* That's just what we need. If they do, I'll guarantee they'll bring a host of demons swarming with them."

"The demons can't get through the portals," I said.
"They're barred."

"So they say, but I'm not too sure about that." He grunted, then after a moment, cleared his throat. "Your sister Delilah needs to start dressing like a lady, at least for your aunt Olanda's visit. Take her shopping. Get her out of trousers and tunics, please." He gave me the once-over. "You're fine. Menolly, too. But . . ."

"Delilah's a tomboy and you know it," I said, laughing. "Those dresses will last a couple of days and then you'll never see them again. But yeah, I'll add that to my to-do list."

Father put down his sword and leaned back in his chair, crossing his right leg across his left. He was a handsome man, looking barely older than the three of us. Full-blooded Fae, he would age far slower than we until we drank the nectar of life. But that wouldn't be for some time yet. We were forbidden to touch it for now.

It was easy to see why Mother had followed him home from Earthside. She'd fallen for him before he ever kissed her, before he told her he loved her, and they'd been devoted to each other, right until the end.

"Camille, I've been meaning to talk to you about something." Sephreh looked uncomfortable. "Your mother provided for you over Earthside. You have means there, should you ever need it. But here . . . I've put aside what I can for the three of you, but it isn't much."

I frowned. "What do you mean? You're not sick, are you?" I slid down to his feet and rested my head against his knee, stabbed by a sudden fear. We couldn't lose both of them.

He shook his head and patted my hair. "No, I haven't taken ill. I'm talking about the fact that, by your age, girls normally start thinking about marriage and everything that comes with it—security, a title, convenience . . . I'm just not sure . . ."

"How well we'll fare in that department?" As I spoke, he grimaced and I knew what was bugging him. "You're afraid no one will marry us because we're half-breeds?"

He jumped up, grabbed my shoulders, and lifted me to my feet. Tipping my chin up, he stared at me, his eyes flashing. *"Never call yourself that.* Never, *ever* demean yourself. You are half-human. *Your mother* was human and she was the most wonderful woman in the world. In either world. You will not be ashamed of your heritage. I'm not ashamed of you or your sisters. *I'm* proud of the three of you, and I know you do your best to make *me* proud. Do you understand?"

Shaken, I nodded. "I'm sorry. I didn't mean . . . what I meant was—if someone can't handle our lineage, then they can go fuck themselves. None of us will ever marry a bigot. Besides, *I'm* never getting married. I like my freedom too much." I grinned, trying to take the edge off his worry.

Father searched my eyes. After a moment, he laughed and kissed the top of my head. "You take after me, girl," he said, returning to polishing his silver sword. "You prefer sex to breathing. Sometimes I wish you'd taken after your mother like Delilah. I think she'll have an easier road to walk than you will. As for Menolly, it's anybody's guess."

I was about to ask if he ever thought of remarrying but stopped myself. There were some places still too painful to tread.

THE next day, Menolly, Delilah, and I headed out for work together. Delilah was a few years younger than I, and her waist-length hair was pulled back in a ponytail. Tall—six foot one—she was so athletic she put me to shame. A real tomboy, she was in and out of trees like I was in and out of the shops. She was also a werecat and had a yowl that could wake the dead, especially during the nights leading up to the full moon.

Menolly, on the other hand, barely grazed my nose. Petite with a cloud of coppery curls that traced halfway down her back, she was the perfect acrobat. Well, almost perfect. We all had problems thanks to our half-human heritage.

My magic fritzed out at the most unexpected of times, and sometimes backfired in painful and embarrassing ways. Menolly could balance on her toes on a tightwire, but one short circuit and she'd go tumbling down the front steps. And Delilah shifted into tabby cat form, but she couldn't always control when she made the transformation.

We weren't the best employees the Y'Elestrial Intelligence Agency had, but they couldn't say we weren't loyal, or enthusiastic. Our father was a captain in the Guard Des'Estar. We'd joined the YIA to make him proud.

The YIA headquarters were in the palace. A monolithic tribute to overkill, the palace made me cringe. The architecture was beautiful, but thanks to the tastes of our queen, the whole effect came off as tacky.

Minarets jutted into the sky, their spires flying the flags of Y'Elestrial and Queen Lethesanar. Five flights of steps led up to the massive doors guarded by men strong enough to squash a goblin's head with their bare hands. Paired with wizards, they kept an eye out for magical intruders.

We stopped at the doors to show our credentials, then hurried through the doors toward the wing reserved for the agency. Clerks and scribes scurried every which way, their arms filled with paperwork and scrolls and books. Every now and then another agent would rush by, waving on the fly. We crowded into the briefing room to pick up our notes and assignments for the day.

Menolly grimaced as she was handed a single sheet of paper. "I knew it. Damn it, I wish they'd get off their butts and give me some help." She glanced around, making sure nobody was within earshot.

"Why bother whispering?" I snorted. "We're being eavesdropped on anyway. There are plenty of spies around and I have no doubt our supervisors can hear everything we say. Today's whine is tomorrow's whipping stick." I glanced at my own assignment sheet. "Fuck."

"What's wrong?" Delilah asked.

"My supervisor wants to see me. Again." I crumpled the paper.

Menolly shook her head. "Better that than my day. They've got me scheduled to sneak directly into the heart of the Elwing Blood Clan's nest. I've been putting it off, hoping they'll give me some backup. The damned job's just too dangerous to tackle alone. I think I can wrangle another couple weeks of research but after that . . . I'll have to either cave or quit."

"Maybe they think you're the best choice for the job," Delilah said, ever the optimist.

"Don't bet on it," I muttered. "I get the feeling they're deliberately trying to trip us up. You know, force us to screw up so badly they can fire us. That way, we couldn't lodge a complaint."

"You really think they're trying to get rid of us?" Delilah asked.

I shrugged. "Maybe. I do know that the assignment they've given me sucks. I'm supposed to find Roche, and all their leads are bogus. If I don't find him soon, they'll chalk up another failure on my record and absolve themselves of the problem."

"You think they might be looking the other way since he's a member of the Guard? Mother used to call it the good ol' boy system." Menolly was even more cynical than I was.

"I have no idea," I said, stopping as we turned down the hall leading toward the Special Investigations Unit. "Look—what's that?"

An unused wing of the unit was in the process of being furnished, and the movers were carrying in desks and chairs and an interesting supply of magical instruments. The placard on the wall next to the main office door read OIA.

"What the hell is the OIA?" I asked.

"I dunno," Menolly said, brushing her hair back behind her ears. "All I know is that I didn't get enough to eat at breakfast and as soon as we leave here, I'm heading down to the Naori Clipper to snag myself a bowl of chowder and a loaf of bread."

I came to my stop and blew a kiss to my sisters. "Be good. I'll see you for dinner. If you get home before I do, tell Cook to start roasting the chickens." They waved as I opened the door and slipped inside Lathe's office.

My supervisor was younger than me, and he was on a continual tear because I refused to fuck him. Even though he was cute, work and sex just weren't a great combo, and besides that, I'd heard about his peculiar habits. I enjoyed kink but I didn't enjoy pain and humiliation. Apparently, he was adept at both. So I danced around his advances and he kept giving me shit jobs. One of these days, I'd take it over his head, but that would cause a firestorm I just didn't feel like weathering at this point.

"What the hell's going on?" I said, marching into his office. He was leaning back in his chair, his feet propped on the walnut desk. His clothing was meticulous, as usual. He narrowed his eyes and slowly lowered his feet, motioning for me to sit opposite him.

"You find Roche yet?" He was mocking me. He knew I hadn't, and he knew that I wouldn't be able to without some legitimate help.

"Roche still has friends in the Guard Des'Estar, friends who wouldn't mind helping him even with the crimes he's committed. For all I know, you're in on this sham of an investigation." I squinted, wondering how far I could push his buttons before he freaked. Not that I really cared, but I didn't want to disappoint Father by getting myself fired.

Lathe sauntered around the desk, closing the door to the hall. He stood behind my chair and I felt a hand on my shoulder, his fingers gently massaging beneath the straps of my bustier.

"Life could be so much simpler if you'd just learn to compromise," he whispered, nuzzling my neck. I tried to shake him away but he held my shoulders tightly, squeezing so hard it hurt. "You could go a long ways in the agency, and I'd be a good ally to have."

"Uh-huh . . . tell me another one. And my heritage isn't going to make *any* difference, as long as I fuck your brains out, right?"

"Little girl, you've got a lot to learn," he said, kissing my ear. "I won't approve any transfer, promotion, or anything unless you learn to cooperate. And by cooperate, I mean *suck my cock*. Got it?"

I stared at the floor, cheeks flaming. I loved sex, but this was force coercion. I refused to be pushed. And regardless, I didn't mix business and pleasure. Father raised us to take pride in our work and do our best. He didn't raise us to whore ourselves for a promotion.

Shaking off Lathe's hand, I stood and slowly turned to face him.

"I have an idea." I slowly jabbed him in the chest with one finger. "Why don't *you* go buy a whore down in the Dives? I'm sure you can find someone willing to let you fuck her up the ass or beat her black and blue if you pay her enough. *But it's not going to be me.*"

"You've just sealed your fate, lovely," he said, his eyes flashing. For a moment I thought he was going to fire me, or strike me down—he was an accomplished mage—but instead he returned to his seat.

"Either you find Roche in a week, or I'll make an example of you in front of the whole agency. You'll be so embarrassed you won't be able to hold your head up in public after I'm done with you."

I planted my hands on his desk. "I'll find Roche, all right. But make no mistake—I'm not doing it because I'm afraid of you. I'll drag him in because he's a pervert and a murderer." And then, because I was my mother's daughter as well as my father's, I added, "So take your short, scrawny dick and get it the fuck out of my face."

As I slammed out of his door, I knew I'd just made one of the worst enemies of my life.

AS I headed out of the building, I made my way toward the Collequia. I needed help, and I knew where to get it. Jahn could scare up anyone a girl needed, including spies, wizards, and seers. Until now, I'd been avoiding asking for outside help because of the agency's privacy policies, but fuck it. Lathe had pushed me too far.

Jahn was behind the bar, dividing packets of opium and kysa—the poor man's version of the drug. He glanced up as I entered.

"You're early, girl. Something wrong?"

"My prick of a boss is what's wrong. You have anything

to eat back there?" It was too early for a drink, and my stomach was rumbling.

"Nut bread and cheese okay?"

I nodded and he pulled out a wooden tray that held a loaf of nut bread and a round of cheese.

He tossed me a knife. "Help yourself. I was going to eat that for lunch but I'll pick up something else."

I sliced into the fragrant bread, inhaling deeply as the scent of hazelnuts rose in a wisp of steam. The cheese was soft as I sliced into it and spread it on the bread. As I took a bite, the sweetness of the nut meal drizzled down my throat.

"Good." I licked my fingers. "Who made this? Your wife?"

Jahn shook his head. "No, she's been living with her lover the past moon cycle. I don't know when—or if—she's coming back. I think she prefers dandies. He's a tailor. I ever tell you that?"

A tailor? I couldn't see any woman leaving Jahn for a tailor, but then again, tailors knew how to use their hands so maybe she'd been missing out on something from the club owner's calloused hands.

"I can give you the recipe if you like," he added.

"Cook will appreciate that," I said, licking my fingers. "I need your help."

He glanced up, pushing the drugs aside. "What's going on?"

"I need to find somebody. And I need to find him as soon as possible. He's dangerous. He was a member of the Guard till he got kicked out, and rumor has it he's been hanging out here." I hesitated, then added, "My job's on the line. If I don't find this creep, my boss will humiliate me unless I fuck him to shut him up. And *that* would be a far worse punishment."

Jahn grunted and gave me a nod. "What's the guy's name and what did he do?"

"Roche. Roche ob Vanu. He was a member of the Des'Estar until he murdered his wife, his brother, and a few other innocents along the way. He's gone on a rampage. Raped five women so far, and murdered four of them. We know it's him because his magical signature is all over the case." I frowned, then added, "Do you have a bowl of water?"

"Yeah, hold on." Jahn slipped into a back room and returned with a silver bowl.

I glanced around the bar. At this time of morning, it was almost empty. I pulled the bowl to me and slowly breathed on the water. The energy of the Moon Mother coiled within me as I coaxed it awake, wending its way up my spine. A river of molten silver, it spread through the cells of my body, circling the spiraling tattoo on my shoulder blade. I slowly exhaled and a sparkling mist covered the water in the bowl, settling over the top of it like a thick fog on the lake.

Jahn gave a little gasp, but said nothing.

I glanced up at him, then back at the bowl and lowered my hand toward the mist, whispering softly. "Mist of the mountain, mist of the moon, show me the face of the one whom I seek. Moon Mother, grant me the power."

And then, the mist parted, rolling to the sides of the bowl, and there—in the water, was the face of the man I was hunting. Roche. He looked harsh, with a jagged scar over one eye that gave him a roguish look.

"Now show us his true face," I whispered, and waved my hand again. And the face in the water shifted, taking on a cruel, vindictive leer as his inner nature rose to the surface.

Jahn took a quick step back. "He's been in here, all right. I know that face, but I had no idea he was a member of the Guard Des'Estar. He's a bad one."

"When was the last time you saw him?"

"Three nights ago. He paid for a whore—the youngest we have, but she wasn't young enough for him and I had to stop him from beating her." Jahn grimaced, a look of distaste on his face. "I won't hire women who are under the age of consent."

"You're a good man, Jahn. And you haven't seen him since?"

"No, but that doesn't mean he hasn't been back. I spend most of my time behind the bar, not waiting tables, you know." He stared at the face still lingering in the water. "Next time I see him, I'll get word to you as soon as I can. You say he's a murderer?"

"Rape, murder, torture. A lot of things you don't want to know about," I said. "I wish I could cast a spell of Finding, but my magic doesn't always work right. I'm sure you've heard about that."

"Yes, darlin', I've heard," Jahn said. He stopped suddenly, staring at the door. I heard it open as someone came in. "Damn it, what's *he* doing back here?"

I knew who it was. Without even seeing his face, his energy swirled in ahead of him like a whirlwind. The golden man. The man with jet skin and silver hair. The Svartan. And then, without a sound, he was standing next to me, staring at the scrying bowl. He looked from it, to me, then back to it.

"Hunting?" he asked, his voice lazy.

I slowly turned my head to lock his gaze. "What business is it of yours?"

"I've seen your prey. Last night, as it so happens." He slid onto the bar stool and casually snagged a handful of nuts from the bowl on the counter.

"Where?" I clenched my fists on the counter. "What price do you want for the information?"

Jahn put his hand on mine. "Darlin', don't go doing business with his kind—"

"Excuse me, barkeep, but perhaps you'll answer a question." The Svartan's voice was smooth.

"What is it?" Jahn glared at him.

"If you disapprove so much of me, why do you continue to accept my money?" The Svartan gave him a faint smile, both derisive and yet challenging.

Jahn's eyes were cold but he turned away. "Camille, use your head. I know you've got one. You're too smart for the likes of him."

The Svartan slowly swiveled to face me. "I don't need your money. But if you would accompany me to luncheon, I'd consider that acceptable payment."

My father would have a fit, but I wanted the information and this man could tell me what I needed to know. And I *wanted* to know more about him. He was hot, he fascinated me, and we had some odd connection—I could feel it there, hanging between us, though I had no idea just how or why it had formed.

I swung off my bar stool and smoothed my skirt. "I don't accept dinner invitations from nameless strangers."

He smiled then, a smile to melt the coldest of ice statues. His teeth gleamed, sparkling white. "The name is Trillian."

As he offered me his arm, I slowly placed my hand on his elbow and he escorted me out of the bar. Deep inside, I could feel a whisper saying I'd just sealed my fate.

THE afternoon sun beat down, the dusky scent of summer wafting through the streets. Y'Elestrial was beautiful. Buildings of marble and stone stretched along the neatly patterned streets. Carts clattered past us, horses' hooves clicking delicately as they trotted along the cobblestones. Flocks of pedestrians milled through the thoroughfares, hurrying on their way to wherever they had to go.

We turned down the road leading to the central market where the vendors opened at sunrise and closed after sunset. Most lived in their stalls, spending their money on brandy and wine, sleeping off one drunken stupor after another under the canopies and awnings. Unlike regular shopkeepers, they were vagabonds—their wagons their only homes.

Bees droned their way past, lazily hunting through the flower arrangements that were for sale. The cadence of the vendors hawking their wares and of haggling customers filled the street with a cacophony of noise . . . an argument over the price of starflowers at one stall, quibbling over a bone pipe at another, women bargaining for fresh meat at the butchers' kiosks. The collision of voices and sounds sent a bustling energy through the air.

The vast market was four blocks long. Eventually we

came to the end and exited onto a smaller side street. Trillian pointed toward a low building with a sign that read THE STEAK AND ALE.

As I pushed through the door, the aroma of sizzling beef caught me short. My stomach rumbled and I let out a grateful, "Oh, that smells good."

Trillian returned my smile, winking slyly. "You're hungry." It wasn't a question.

I nodded. "I didn't get a chance to eat breakfast this morning. I was running late, and the nut bread Jahn gave me only took the edge off my hunger."

He led me over to a private booth and we slid into the upholstered seats on either side of the table, illuminated by a honeycombed candle, its wax fragrant and inviting. Trillian didn't speak until the serving girl approached. She blushed when she saw him. I realized he must have that effect on a lot of women.

"We have good beef today," she said. "And rosemary potatoes, fresh bread, and strawberry jam. Will that do?"

Trillian glanced at me.

I nodded. "I'd like a glass of water, please."

"Would you prefer wine?" he asked. I shook my head and the girl moved off to place our order.

"All right," I said after a moment. "I'm having lunch with you. Tell me what you know of Roche."

He gazed at me for a moment, not speaking, then softly said, "And so swiftly she veers to the contract."

"It's just . . . I need to know about him," I said, suddenly feeling rude. He'd been nothing but a gentleman so far. Since I was using him to get to Roche, the least I could do was extend a hand in peace. "I'm sorry. This is so very important. I have to catch this man."

Trillian rested his elbows on the table, leaning toward me. "I assume you work for the YIA. You don't have the look, but I recognize the harried expression. Don't worry—" he said, fending off my protest. "I'm not asking you to answer, just speculating."

I let out a long sigh. "You speculate right. And my neck

is on the line if I don't bring in this guy. My boss is doing everything he can to prevent me from succeeding." Suddenly, I didn't care anymore. I didn't care who heard me, or whether it cost me my job. I was tired of fighting, tired of being the scapegoat.

Trillian cocked his head to the side and slid his hands across the table, gently taking hold of mine. The feel of his skin against mine sparked like oil on flame. My nipples pressed against the lace of my bustier, the material suddenly feeling harsh and arousing. The spark traced a fuse that led down through my stomach to settle between my thighs.

His fingers, so dark against mine, were like coffee on cream, soft and velvety smooth. He slowly turned my palm face-up and rubbed the tip of one index finger against the cup of my hand, tracing the lines that creased my flesh. Every touch unsettled me. I clenched my thighs together, trying to hide my arousal, but I couldn't pull away. I didn't want to.

"Your supervisor seeks to fail you because you are *de'estial*?" Again, the silken voice.

I raised my eyes to meet his. He'd used the Sidhe term for a phrase that meant "walker of two paths," but I knew he was talking about my heritage. But usually, the word *de'estial* was given as an honor, not used when referring to a half-breed like myself. I searched his face, but there was no hint of repulsion, no sign that he looked down on me because of my human heritage.

Slowly, I nodded. "That, and he wants to sleep with me, and I won't comply."

Trillian pursed his lips, but a ripple of laughter broke free. "I can understand why he would want you," he said. "But a real man never forces a woman, even when he has the opportunity. *Even when he has the power to enslave her against his will.*" He stood and leaned over the table, his face mere inches from mine. "There is no pleasure in a hollow victory, is there?"

Mesmerized, I shook my head. All of Jahn's warnings were screaming at me, along with my father's worries, but

I swept them aside. Svartan he might be, but I could sense when people lied to me. And Trillian wasn't lying. Maybe he was prettying up his words, but outright deceit? No, I'd bet my paycheck that he meant what he said.

I realized I was clutching his hands now, holding them tight. Another glance into his eyes told me he was aware of my hunger. I slowly let go, forcing myself to sit back in the booth as I tried to catch my breath.

The serving girl brought our meals and Trillian paid her.

"Eat. I'm starving." He handed me the bread. I tore off a chunk and then pushed the rest across the table. "So you are looking for this man Roche. You work for the YIA. He's a fugitive?"

Grateful for the change in subject, I nodded. "Yes, he's sadistic, a rapist and murderer. My job is to catch him, but none of the leads panned out. I can only hope this perv stumbles across my path. That is, unless I can come up with some clues on my own. Ones I know aren't fabricated."

"Perv?" Trillian looked confused.

"Pervert. Twisted—in a bad way. It's an Earthside term. My mother was human." I stopped buttering the piece of bread I was holding.

"Was, as in she's dead?"

"She died when my sisters and I were young. She fell off a horse and broke her neck. I miss her."

Surprised, I felt tears well up. Every now and then, the memory of her death hit me in just the wrong way, but I was usually alone and locked in my room when it happened. Delilah and Menolly counted on me to be the strong one. I'd taken over when Mother died, and now I was mistress of the household. It was my duty to remain the anchor and support.

I tried to swallow my sadness, but one tear broke free and traced its way down my cheek. I started to look away, but his hand was suddenly cupping my chin and his eyes were surprisingly gentle as he once again leaned across the table and gently kissed the tear away. He didn't try to kiss me on the mouth, but settled back into his seat.

"Some hurts can never be mended," he said. "No matter how much time passes. They tattoo themselves on our souls."

I wasn't sure what to say, so merely bit into my food. The beef was rich and juicy, the potatoes a savory burst of flavor in my mouth.

"As I told you back in the bar, last night I saw the man you are seeking. He was in the marketplace, at the gambler's tent." Trillian took a sip of his water, then buttered another piece of bread. "He was involved in a game of q'aresh. He'll be back there tonight."

"What makes you think so?" I asked.

"He lost a great deal of money and became extremely vocal. He wanted a young girl that the marketer was offering as part of the wager. Your quarry appears to be on the obsessive side. The dealer told him to return when he could afford a rematch. Roche said he'd return this evening. I'm guessing he'll show up to see if the girl's still there." Trillian pushed aside his plate. "So tonight, we'll go see if we can catch ourselves a murderer."

I stared at him. "*We'll go?* Why would you want to go with me? This could be dangerous, and you have nothing to gain."

Trillian slid out of the booth and held out his hand. "I'll go with you because you need help. I'll go with you because I detest men who refuse to acknowledge the value of women. I'll help you because men who rape children and get their rocks off on hurting innocent women deserve to die."

As I listened to that velvet voice, the arrogance and sardonic façade fell away and I saw the man behind the mask. Beneath his jaded exterior, Trillian was a man who loved women. Who didn't count them by their heritage or status. He was dangerous and cruel, but only to those who gave him a reason to fight.

I placed my hands on his shoulders, feeling the well-toned biceps that were hidden beneath the meticulous tunic.

Trillian waited, his luminous blue eyes gazing down into

my own dark ones. The invitation was there—unspoken, but there.

As I raised up on the tips of my toes, pressing my lips against his, he wrapped his arms around me and I surrendered myself to his embrace.

3

HIS caress enveloped me with the most glorious glow I'd ever felt, and his lips were soft, like golden taffy. He gently parted my lips with his tongue and all thoughts as to why this might not be a good idea fled.

As he tightened his embrace, I could feel the outline of him pressing through his trousers, hard and eager, but he didn't push, didn't grind against me like some men would have.

After a moment, I needed to catch my breath. As if reading my mind, he loosened his pressure on my lips. I quickly gulped air before once again, his mouth was on mine, his tongue playing lightly over mine. His touch navigated a serpentine path up my spine as he pressed his hand to my lower back. Then, slowly, he began to withdraw, easing his hands off me, pulling back inch by inch.

I caught a ragged breath and stared at him. What the hell? I'd never felt such an intense kiss. Out of my mind with lust, I wanted his hands on my naked body, his fingers to slide over my breasts, along my stomach, to whisper their secrets between my thighs. The thought of him inside me electrified my body, and every muscle began to ache, I wanted him so much.

He held up one hand. "Before this goes any further, let me warn you. If you sleep with me, you may find it hard to walk away. I'm one of the Charming Fae. Our bodies are saturated with sexual magic, and very few are immune to the effect. Make no mistake, if you fuck me, this will be more than a casual bedding."

I didn't know what to say. I'd heard the rumors but they'd seemed exaggerated. Now, I wasn't so sure.

As he stepped back, part of me ripped away with him. "Don't answer. I can wait, and I refuse to hurry your decision. Go do what you need to do, and tonight, when the sun sets, meet me at the front entrance of the Marketplace. We'll find your prey and take him down."

He leaned in for another kiss, then stopped. When I moved toward him, he shook his head. "Not yet. Think it over, and then think it over again. The choice is yours. I want you, make no mistake about it. But you're the one who has to extend the offer." And then he turned and quickly slipped out the door.

I caught up with Delilah and Menolly a few hours before dinner. Mother kept an anniversary clock from over Earthside on the mantel and though our time-telling system was different, we had learned both and used them interchangeably.

We strolled down the street toward Lake Y'Leveshan, which was located at the southeastern end of the city. Midwinter and midsummer holidays were spent around the lake. Huge, it stretched so far, the other side was a distant blur. Boats dotted the surface, their crews angling for fish to sell in the markets.

The shoreline was surrounded by lush vegetation. Long-bladed grass, knee high, grew thick around the lake, and the clearing was dappled with copses of maple and weeping willow, birch and rowan and wild camaz trees. The buzzing of gnats and bumblebees filled the air, along with the ever-present birdsong. A lazy spell held sway around the docks.

Delilah swung herself into the lower branches of a nearby

oak tree. She dangled her legs over the edge and brushed away a strand of hair that had escaped her ponytail. "I love afternoons like this. I just hope the agency doesn't find out we're slacking."

"Who gives a damn?" I asked. "I don't care anymore. They're squeezing us by the balls. If they fire me, I'll just say good riddance. But listen, I think I'm actually on the heels of Roche."

I wanted to tell them about Trillian, but somehow I didn't think the news would go over big. Especially if Father found out. Maybe it was best to let it rest until I knew just how far this relationship was going to go.

Menolly stretched out in the grass and propped herself up on her elbows. Her shift was loose and filmy, and her hair cascaded down her back. Nobody knew where her red had come from, but the copper curls gleamed in the sun as she closed her eyes against the warmth of the light.

"I love days like today," she said, sucking in a long, slow breath of summer. "It feels like the sun is sinking into my bones." With a sigh, she added, "HQ wants me to scout the outskirts of the cave. I think I can hold them off for another few days or so—perhaps two weeks. But eventually, I'll either have to finish the mission or quit. I wish I didn't feel so bound to the damned job."

"You're really are going to have to make up your mind pretty soon about what to do," I said. "As for me, tonight I'm going to check out a clue to Roche's whereabouts."

"You want company?" Menolly asked. "I'd be glad to go with you."

"Me too," Delilah added. "I could use a night on the town."

I scrambled onto a flat boulder and crossed my legs, trying to think of a way to say no without making them suspicious. "Maybe . . . but don't you have class tonight, Menolly?"

She grunted. Menolly attended a twice-weekly intensive workshop for acrobats and gymnasts in the agency to keep in shape. "Yeah. Thanks for reminding me."

"And somebody better be home to eat dinner with Father. You know how he gets about family meals." I glanced over at Delilah. She rolled her eyes but nodded. "I'll be okay, don't worry. Jahn's helping me." A little white lie, though technically Jahn *had* helped me. Or at least he'd tried to.

Menolly darted a quick glance my way. "Jahn? Don't tell me you're taking up with that lecher? He's been after you since you first hit womanhood."

I grinned at her. "Better not let Father hear you talk about Jahn that way. He thinks the man can do no wrong, and frankly, there are far worse businesses than being a night-club and brothel owner. At least he treats the women under his roof with care and compassion. But you're right. He's been after me for a long time. He's not my type, though. He's sweet, but . . . no . . ." Jahn paled in comparison to Trillian.

Delilah swung out of the tree, landing next to me. She kept her distance from the lake. Like a typical cat, my sister didn't like water at all. When she was little, it had taken all of our mother's threats of taking away her toys and pets to get her to bathe. She still viewed bath time as punishment rather than pleasure.

She gazed over the water as the wind rustled the grass across the lea. "Do you think we'll still be doing this in ten years? Will we all still be single, working for the agency, living with Father?" She sounded almost wistful.

"I don't know," Menolly said, pushing herself to her feet. "I think I'm ready for change. Something different, you know? I feel like we're marking time. Maybe I'll marry Keris. Have children."

She'd been dating our neighbor for several months and things were heating up. He was Fae, but he didn't care about her half-human blood or that she also loved women. They'd recently started talking in terms of the future.

As I slid off the rock to stand beside them, something in the wind sent a shiver racing down my back. I closed my eyes, listening to the energy. A low rumble of static ran through the astral as a dark cloud rolled across my inner vision, reeking with the scent of fresh blood and flame and fear. As I stiffened, the echo of a shriek—long and drawn-out as if from far in the distance—washed over me. I staggered under the wave of malevolence and fell to my knees, forcing my eyes open.

"What? What's wrong?" Menolly knelt beside me.

I glanced at her, then up at Delilah. All of the joy had drained out of the day, and the sun seemed harsh instead of nurturing. I shook my head. Though I didn't understand it, the premonition had left me shaken and afraid.

Sometimes my magic went awry, and sometimes my foresight was blurred. But this . . . This energy had crossed my grave. And I knew in my heart that—perhaps not today, perhaps not tomorrow—but that in the near future something was going to happen. Something we weren't ready for, and wouldn't welcome. Change was in the air, all right.

THE market was a lot more risky at night when the thieves and muggers came out of the woodwork. Underage whores worked the crowds—runaways and orphans who were too afraid to brave the countryside where they might be able to hunt and forage for their food.

Pickpockets slid through the throngs, looking for easy marks. Vampires occasionally roamed the streets, looking to put the bite on someone. The vamps were the most dangerous. Most of the bloodsuckers lost their consciences after a while, falling to their inner predator. Our father hated vamps—he'd witnessed his cousin being killed by one and barely escaped with his own life. The bloody memory stayed with him.

I stood at the front entrance to the Marketplace, scanning the faces, looking for Trillian. I'd dressed to impress, a black sparkling bustier over a spidersilk skirt the color of a peacock's feathers. A pair of leather gloves covered my hands, in black, up to the elbows. I'd worn a pair of my mother's shoes—odd, high-heeled sandals made from leather with spiked heels and delicate straps. She'd had the same size feet as I did, and I'd claimed her shoe collection, since none of her clothes would fit me. I had also tucked her wedding dress away in my closet, secure in a wooden trunk filled with moth-repelling sachets. I was saving it for when Menolly got married—she'd fit in it no problem.

Now, I cautiously maneuvered over the cobblestones, sticking close to the entrance, hoping the Svartan wouldn't stand me up. But just as I was about ready to leave, there he was, dressed in black tunic and trousers, a silhouette gliding through the street, silver hair bound in a braid, a smile on his face.

Trillian reached out his hands and I took them, my heart jumping a beat. I pressed in, kissed him deeply and he returned the fire with his own.

"You came," he said. "I wasn't sure if you would."

"I promised. Did you think I'd space out?" I gazed into his eyes and saw a flicker of confusion. "Idiom from my mother's world. You really *didn't* think I'd come, did you?" Could he be as nervous as I was?

"I didn't know. To be honest, I haven't been able to think of anything else today. The image of your face haunts me."

I smiled, feeling unaccountably happy. But all I said was, "Is Roche here?"

And then, he was all business again. Trillian tugged my hand, pulling me behind him. "Yes, he is. Follow me and be careful. Did you bring something to bind him with should we catch him?"

"Right here." I touched the shoulder pouch hanging from my right arm. Inside, I had several things that could stop Roche, short of a bodyguard or a mage. The agency didn't know I carried them, or they'd take them away. But my sisters and I had accumulated a trunk filled with goodies that bordered on illegal. We figured we needed the advantage, given our faulty powers.

In my bag, among other things, I'd tucked a pair of iron handcuffs, careful not to touch them with bare skin. Not only were they iron, but they were bespelled with confusion magic, guaranteed to knock any Fae on his butt.

Torture device? Yeah . . . the iron would burn his skin until he was locked up and they were removed. But considering Roche's crimes, I wasn't exactly feeling merciful. In fact, Delilah thought I was an ogre for using them, while Menolly just gave me a knowing look. But I was rapidly learning that the only way to win with the YIA was to play down and dirty.

I also had a bottle of pixie dust that I'd picked up at the

flea market. Guaranteed to turn anybody who breathed it into a klutz. And resting next to the handcuffs and the pixie dust was a scroll that I'd spent a lot of money on. The magic was deadly, and if I broke open the wax seal on the charm and inserted Roche's name into the spell as I read it, he'd never walk this world again.

Death magic was more common than anybody wanted to admit. I didn't like using it—there was something too familiar, too enticing about it, but with his track record I wasn't about to leave my ass uncovered. The best of circumstances would leave me holding the death charm for a different time, but it felt good to have a little insurance tucked away.

Trillian led me along a winding path through the maze of carts and awnings and tents and canopies. We passed by the stalls of dancing girls and whores, of junkies and beggars sleeping it off by the edge of the road. Trillian paid them no attention, but my gaze flickered to the faces as we passed.

My mother told us that humans envisioned a utopia when they thought of Faerie Land. Then again, most didn't really believe Y'Eírialiastar existed. But the truth would shock them. My father's people were all too susceptible to the same problems that plagued mortals. Poverty, addiction, violence . . . we had it all.

We passed a Sawberry Fae hawking doses of kysa for ten *pen* each. Opium went for ten times the price. He caught my gaze and winked. "Care for a trip, my dear? Make life more bearable? Only ten pen."

He reached out to grab my arm as I pushed past him.

Before I could react, Trillian had hold of the man's wrist, twisting it so that it was bent back in the wrong direction. "Touch her again and I'll cut it off."

The Sawberry winced. "All right, all right. You wouldn't want to sell her, would you? She'd fetch a—"

He didn't get a chance to finish because Trillian's arm was suddenly wrapped around his neck, a knife aimed at his jugular.

"Don't touch her, don't speak to her, don't even *think* about her. Are we clear?" A dangerous light flickered across the Svartan's face, and I realized that he was ready to cut the man's throat and he wasn't even sweating.

"Yes," the Sawberry croaked, rubbing his neck as Trillian released him. He averted his gaze from mine and scurried back to his tent.

Trillian slid the knife back into its sheath, which was hanging at his side and shrugged. "Come," he said, holding out his hand. "This isn't the safest place for women."

I took his hand and followed. The stars were emerging, brilliant and beautiful and shining. The Moon Mother watched over us and I felt her presence in the pit of my stomach. She was nearing full, and the closer we got, the more I craved a man's touch. Trillian's hand was hot against mine. I tried to keep my mind on our mission—on finding Roche—but it was hard with him touching me.

"There," he hissed. "Up ahead. See that tent? A gambler named Bes runs a den there. Roche is there. I checked earlier and he was deep into the game. What do you want to do? Will he recognize you?"

I'd been careful, but an alarm rang in the back of my head. If the YIA was setting me up to fail, maybe they had leaked info about me to the rumor mill. Maybe Roche knew I was on his tail.

"I don't know," I said after a moment. "I can't guarantee that he won't know who I am."

"Come with me," Trillian said, pulling me toward a nearby stall. The vendor was sitting beside a rack of scarves and drapes, drinking goblin brandy. The stench filtered up to my nose and set me to sneezing, it was so thick with peppercorns and keva root.

"Let me see . . . This will work," Trillian said, choosing a sheer ankle-length cloak. Filmy and the color of amethyst, it was hooded and would cloak my face while still allowing me to see through the silken material. He draped the cloth around my shoulders and I slid the hood up.

Trillian gently tucked my hair inside the hood, making sure my errant curls were hidden from view.

"So beautiful," he whispered, tracing my chin with his

fingertips, gently running his fingers over my mouth. I parted my lips and he slid his index finger inside. Closing my lips around his finger, I swirled my tongue against the flesh, gently running my teeth over his skin as I pulled away.

He caught a harsh breath. "Do you know how lucky you are that I am not like the majority of my kinsmen?"

"Do you realize how lucky you are that I'm not like my sisters?" I countered, wishing we were anywhere but here. I hesitated. Would it be so bad to forget about Roche? To pretend I didn't know he was here, to run off to an inn with Trillian and slide my naked body across his? But then my father's training kicked in and I let out a long sigh. "Roche shouldn't be able to recognize me now. Let's go before I lose my nerve."

Trillian laughed, then. "Camille, somehow I think that if you lose anything, it won't be your courage. Come, pretend you're with me and keep quiet until we find him. They don't like women in the dens but they'll allow them if they're with a man. We can get a feel for what's going on and go from there."

He paid the man and we headed back to Bes's den. Trillian motioned for me to hang back a few steps while he talked to the two guards at the entrance.

The vagabond gambling dens were usually owned by criminals. Gaming wasn't illegal, but the safer dens were found in buildings and guaranteed the gambler safe passage in and out of the game rooms unless they invited trouble. The vagabonds' dens were strictly enter-at-your-own-risk.

Suddenly chilled, I realized how grateful I was that Trillian was with me. I could fight down and dirty, but the dens were dangerous places, and without my sisters, I felt vulnerable. I shifted from one foot to the other, wanting to get this over with.

Trillian motioned for me to follow him inside. The tent was a two-room affair, with the main room taken up by the den. There were two low-rise tables, around which sat a dozen men—six at each table. I glanced over the crowd and there he was. *Roche*.

His eyes were glazed and he looked rough, his face covered with stubble, his hair unkempt, and his clothes filthy.

Worse yet, he was stinking up the place. I wondered how long it had been since he'd had a bath. A pile of coins sat in front of him and he toyed with them, rolling them over and over in his hand.

Trillian sauntered up to the table and spoke to the dealer, who nodded curtly and pointed to a chair. As he sat down, he motioned for me to stand behind him. As I slowly crossed the floor, my gaze demurely pointed at my feet, something felt off. Very off. As though hidden eyes were watching me.

I leaned over Trillian's shoulder to whisper to him but then stopped. Roche was still turning over the coins in his hand, but his gaze was firmly fastened on me. Catching my breath, I placed a hand on Trillian's shoulder, squeezing in the hope that he'd get my message that something was up.

"In or out?" the dealer asked him.

Trillian tossed a few coins on the table. "In."

Roche glanced down at the pile of coins in front of him and anted up, then added twenty pen more. The bets went round the table, with each player meeting or raising the bet. Roche held up the dice and pitched them on the table. Out of five dice, they landed a total of twenty-one pips. He frowned as the dealer jotted down the number. Round the table they went, each man taking his turn. By the time Trillian was up, Roche was still the leader. Trillian scooped up the dice and neatly tossed them. They rebounded off the bumper on the other side and came up four sixes and a three.

"Twenty-seven. You're the current leader. What's your pleasure? Let stand or bet for the second round?"

Trillian shook his head. "Stand."

Roche snorted. "That the best you can do, Svartan?" He tossed another three coins on the pot. "Reroll." The dice came his way and he shook them in his hand, blowing on them for luck, then tossed them.

The dealer grunted. "Twenty-three pips. Still under. Next?"

Roche slammed his hand on the table but said nothing as the other four players took their turns. Two walked out, their pockets clean. The other two bet again but neither one hit the mark and they both folded.

Trillian glanced at Roche. He could either match what had been added to the pot and toss again for the third and final round, or he could stand on his mark and see if Roche bested him.

"Stand," he said, giving Roche a faint grin that bordered on patronizing.

That's the way, I thought. *Push him over the edge.*

Roche took the bait. He motioned to the dealer. "Kysa." As he lit up the hookah the dealer offered him, he glanced at me again. "What would you think of a higher wager—just between us? I'm sure I can make it worth your while."

Trillian grunted. "What do you have in mind?"

"A night with your woman." Roche gave him a lopsided grin. "Can't see her face but from the walk, she's got it where it counts."

What the fuck? The look on his face was that of a mad dog's. I stiffened, then it occurred to me this was the perfect way to get alone with him. I forced myself to relax, wondering if Trillian would think of that little fact, too.

Giving no sign that the request had unnerved him, Trillian leaned back in his chair, glancing up at me. "What makes you think she's for rent?"

Roche's breath came heavy as he leaned across the table. "Every coin in my pocket against a night with her."

Trillian frowned. "Let me consider it while I have a drink." He motioned to me. "We'll be back. Have an account of how much you're willing to wager." He paused, not turning as we reached the door. "And don't even think about lightening the pile on the table. I know exactly how much is there. I'm not lenient with thieves," he added. He motioned to the boy who was running drinks for the players. "Tygerian brandy. Now."

The boy scurried off and within seconds was back with a shot of brandy. Trillian tossed him a coin and then motioned for me to follow him out of the den.

"This is the way for me to get to him," I said when we were out of earshot.

"It's dangerous. Did you see the glint in his eye? He's hunting, and he's after you." Trillian shook his head. "I don't like the idea of leaving you alone with him, even for a few moments. I'll follow you, of course, but I can't guarantee I'll be able to get in there in time to stop him."

"I need to take him down," I said. "At first, I just wanted to save my job, but after seeing the look in his eyes . . ." My words drifted off as I glanced back at the tent. "Too many people are dead because of him, including his own family. They need justice. If I don't do it, nobody else will."

Trillian leaned down and brushed my brow with a kiss. "And this is what I saw in you the other day in the bar. I may be a mercenary, but I've got a code of ethics. And you, Camille D'Artigo, exceed my standards."

I shivered. "I don't want to do this, but I've got to. You'll back me up?"

He nodded. "I promise you on my honor. I'll do everything in my power to prevent him from hurting you."

I patted my bag. "I've got an ace up my sleeve. Let's just hope I don't have to use it." Checking to make sure my stiletto was strapped to my thigh for easy access, I straightened my shoulders and drew the hood back over my head. "I'm ready. Let's go."

Trillian parted the flaps of the tent. "As you wish," he said, but his eyes told me he wasn't at all happy about the plan.

4

ROCHE jerked his head up as Trillian slid back into his chair. He looked hungry, like he hadn't eaten in a long time, but it wasn't food he was looking for.

Trillian glanced at the pile of coins, then nodded. Apparently everything was still there. "I accept your wager. Empty your purse and pockets. I want to see everything you have on you."

Roche tossed his purse on the table. He slowly reached into his pockets. I held my breath, but he brought his hands into sight again, filled with coins. Large denominations, at that. He dumped them on the table as Trillian motioned to the dealer. The man, a burly bald Fae who was part-goblin by the looks of him, opened the purse and up-ended it over the pile of coins. The bet had tripled. I wondered if Roche had a stash of money hidden somewhere. He surely wouldn't be stupid enough to wager everything on the chance of winning a night with me.

Trillian glanced at me and I gave him a slight nod. He picked up the dice and tossed them to Roche. "Winner takes all."

Roche sucked in a deep breath and let the dice fly.

Everybody who was in the tent was watching the game by now and leaned in to see what he would land.

The dealer carefully tallied the points. "Twenty-six pips."

Trillian picked up the dice and tensed. I knew he was going to skew the numbers. Whether by magic or sleight of hand, he'd lose. He casually bounced them across the table. They skidded across the surface to ricochet off one of the bumpers and land squarely beside the pile of coins. Two fours, a six, a three, and a five. Twenty-two pips.

"Twenty-two pips. You lose."

Roche triumphantly gathered up the coins. "She's mine for the night. You aren't going to try to back out on me, are you?"

Trillian shook his head. "No, but I claim the right to wait outside." He stared at Roche. "After all, you can't expect me to trust you."

A dark cloud swept across Roche's face, but after a moment, he shrugged. "Whatever you say, but no interference." His voice was ragged.

I shivered. Maybe this wasn't such a good idea after all. He could do a lot of damage in the time it would take Trillian to bust through the door. But then I thought of the women and children Roche had murdered. Lathe thought he could break me with this one. I'd show him just how freakin' strong I was and bust his balls, and in the process I'd take down a killer.

Trillian stepped outside and I followed. Roche followed me. He was fixated—I could feel his energy sliming around in my aura.

To calm my nerves, behind the cowl of my drape I kept my mind on the surprise he had coming. Maybe I should just use the death scroll the minute we were alone, but the Moon Mother's energy was working on me. The hunt wouldn't be nearly so much fun if I gave him an easy exit. No, if I could capture him alive, the families of the dead would have the right to request blood-vengeance. And they would be harsher than I could ever be.

Trillian put himself between Roche and me. "Your name, first? I won't let anybody touch her without a name."

Roche arched one eyebrow. "She must really be good," he said. "They call me Roche. Follow me."

We followed him through the maze of vendors until we came to Azyur Boulevard, where he turned left into a long, narrow street. The streets were lined with worn cobblestones and the buildings were old, two-story stone and mortar. He stopped in front of a seedy-looking dive. The sign read CALISTO'S.

"Second floor," he said, leading us in through the foyer. The innkeeper—a short, squat rawhead—was sitting behind a roughly hewn counter, his feet propped up on the wood, a bottle of booze in his hands. He cast a quick look our way, then went back to his drinking. We couldn't count on him for help. Rawheads were nastier than goblins, out for themselves and nobody else.

We headed up the narrow stairwell to the second floor. Roche stopped in front of a door that was scarred with the wounds of past intruders. A patch job covered a fist-sized hole.

He turned to Trillian. "As agreed, you stay out here."

Trillian shrugged. "Play by the rules and we won't have a problem."

Roche unlocked the door and ushered me into the dingy room. It stunk of stale food and the faint scent of urine. I glanced around. The bed was a single cot with a thin mattress and ratty spread. Movement caught my attention and I looked closer. Fleas. *Gross.*

In one corner were a table and chair, and a small stand with a water pitcher and a bowl sat near the bed. There was no sign of bath or private commode—whoever Calisto was, he was definitely a slumlord.

My courage wavered and I decided to take the quickest way out. No chance in hell was I letting Roche lay one hand on me. If that meant using the death scroll, then that's what it meant. I edged toward the table, gently setting my bag on the splintered surface. Roche was watching me, I could feel his eyes on my back.

"Take off your clothes," he said hoarsely.

It was now or never. I covered what I was doing with my

body as I fished around in the bag for the handcuffs. As I touched the iron, he grabbed my drape and yanked it off. I dropped the cuffs back in the bag and whirled around.

"Just as I thought. A Moon witch."

"Is that a problem?" I asked, keeping my voice even. He hadn't noticed what was in my bag yet. Score one for me, but I had to get them on him before he knew what I was up to.

Roche stepped forward, the soft fall of his boots against the floor echoing in the stuffy room. For a moment he didn't answer, and then, his voice taking on a nasty tone, he said, "Normally, I'd be thrilled. Fucking a Moon witch is like fucking an expensive whore, but considering you're with the YIA and out to capture me, I don't think I'm really all that happy to see you."

Crap. He knew who I was. I spun, grabbing the handcuffs as I scrambled to get out of his reach. The look on his face was all I needed to see. I'd been set up. Lathe had sold me out and I knew it.

Roche lunged at me, and I screamed as I swung the handcuffs toward him, hoping to contact his face with the iron. There was a sound at the door. Thank the gods, Trillian!

But before Trillian could break through, Roche muttered something under his breath and the world shifted as he grabbed my hand. I frantically grabbed for anything I could to steady myself, but the chair, the table, the floor all vanished and we were standing in the middle of a misty field.

Looking around, I realized that we were out on the astral. I recognized it from the nights I ran with the Hunt under the full moon. How the hell had Roche managed that?

He was standing right next to me, but he'd dropped my hand as we shifted over   the landing had been rough—and I took the opportunity to swing the cuffs as hard as I could, keeping hold of one loop while using the other like the ball on a spiked flail. It hit him square on the cheek and the iron sizzled against his skin. Roche screamed and clutched his face.

Swinging again, I hit the other cheek, then raced off. Though I'd burned and bruised him, the wounds weren't enough to stop him.

I made tracks, not caring which direction I headed in. I had to find some place to hide. The astral realm had its own flora and fauna, of a sort, and I spotted a stand of twisted trees up ahead. They weren't *real* trees, of course, not like the ones we had back home, but they'd do.

Racing through the mists that swirled around my ankles, I thought I might be able to reach the stand before Roche caught up to me. I had one thing in my favor: when I ran with the Hunt, I was used to being out on the astral and I could run like the wind here. I sped up, leaving him in a wash of roiling mist.

As I slipped into the shadow of the trees, my mind was racing. How the hell was I supposed to get out of here? I couldn't shift on my own unless the Hunt was summoning me or dropping me off. Come to think of it, where the hell had Roche learned to shift realms?

I softly darted among the ancient beings, watching their gnarled knots and burls form into faces. With a little luck they'd be friendly. With bad luck, they wouldn't and I'd be facing a whole new set of problems.

There was no clearly marked path through the thicket—at least not that I could see through the mists—but the trees were parted to either side like they were flanking a trail so I headed down the center, searching for a fork leading off to the side. Maybe I'd get lucky and see a big sign flashing HIDING PLACE—YOU'LL BE SAFE HERE.

Damn it, I hadn't counted on Roche being able to jump realms. This was a definite kink in my plans. *Maybe a deadly one.*

A noise in the distance caught my attention. I tried to pinpoint the origin and decided it was probably Roche, nearing the woods. He was swearing, or at least that's what I thought I heard.

Time to get out of sight. I glanced around at the thick undergrowth that surrounded the trees. The shrubs were just as menacing as the trees, but beggars can't be choosers. It was either hide, or wait for Roche to knock me off. I plunged into the undergrowth, pushing through the waist-high bushes, trying to avoid leaving a trail.

The bushes grew taller as I continued off-path, and I finally found myself in front of a stand of brambles that had grown like a dome over a rock. A narrow crawl space allowed me to slip beneath the tendrils and slide behind the boulder. Once I was in my hidey-hole, I arranged the thorn-studded suckers to cover the access.

Of course, what I'd do after he left was another thing. Probably just wander around, hoping to find somebody who could send me home.

I waited, wondering what Trillian was doing. If he was like a hundred men I'd met, he'd take off, chalking it up to fate. A little part of me dared to hope that he'd come after me, but I knew better than to count on it. The Svartans weren't exactly the most loyal group of races around, and even if he defied the odds, very few from Svartalfheim had easy access to the etheric realms.

The sound of footsteps caught my attention and I held my breath. The thorns poked at me. I tried to adjust my position, but realized that it wasn't *me* bumping into *them*. Apparently the bush had decided to test out just what kind of creature I was, and one of the fronds was prodding me in the arm with its thorny tip. I grimaced and tried to gently wave it away. No such luck.

As it tapped me again, I glanced around, ready to pull out my dagger and chop the damned thing off, when I saw eyes gleaming at me from the base of the tree. The face stared at me impassively, then slowly blinked. The bramble that had been poking at me moved to point toward a low tunnel through the thorn bushes. That hadn't been there before.

I glanced back at the tree and then sucked in a deep breath and dove for the tunnel. As I crawled through the mist, I heard a sound and darted a look over my shoulder. The brambles had closed again, cocooning me in a cave of thorns and leaves. I could barely see through the tangle of protection. As I settled myself, an odd little creature crossed through the place I'd just been crouching. A foul stench filled the air as it lifted its tail. *A lycon*—a friendly little mammal with a very strong defense. Mother had called them skunks.

Gagging, I forced myself to remain silent as the lycon

rambled on through the undergrowth. Thank the gods I'd been out of the line of fire. Just then, a noise caught my attention as someone entered the area. Roche. Damn it— he'd probably followed my scent. I peered through a tiny gap in the brambles and could just make him out. He turned this way, then that, as if he were looking for something. I heard him curse.

Bingo! The tree and bush were helping me. They'd called in the lycon, whose spray had masked my scent. It would be impossible for Roche to find me now. And if I was guessing right, the brambles would put up one hell of a fight if he tried to tear through them.

Feeling like I actually might have a chance to come out of this alive, I huddled, waiting. The only thing I had with me were the iron handcuffs, and those I held gingerly, even with the gloves on. No use taking chances.

After a few moments, Roche turned and forced his way back through the undergrowth. I waited, barely breathing, until the branches around me relaxed. As they opened up, I crawled out, stood up, and cautiously adjusted my clothing.

Turning back to the tree, I let out a long sigh. "I don't know if you can understand me," I whispered, "but thank you. You saved my life."

There was a soft murmur, as if the air currents were gliding through the knothole that formed the tree's mouth. I got the distinct impression it said, "You're welcome."

After what seemed like an eternity, I pushed through the undergrowth back to the trail, pleased that Roche was nowhere in sight.

"Fuck," I whispered. "Now what do I do? I have no idea how to get back home."

The mist stretched out for as far as I could see. I could barely remember which way I'd come, or how far. I'd been running so fast that I'd lost track of the distance I'd covered.

After a moment's debate, I straightened my shoulders and decided to continue on through the copse. As I picked up the pace, the trees were no longer silent. They whispered and shook in the astral currents. I closed my eyes and tuned in on what they were saying. I had the gift of talking to plants, even though I wasn't all that skilled at growing them, and so I listened.

At first the murmurs surrounded topics I'd expect most trees—even astral ones—to discuss. Sun and growth and the mist, which apparently provided the water they needed to blossom and thrive. Scattered references to the lycons and other creatures of the astral realm dotted the conversation. But then, a sinister tone crept into the leaf-whispers, and I paused, dropping into a trance in order to pick up what they were saying.

"He's forming an army . . ."

"Do you think he'll come into our world . . ."

"We should pay no heed—it is not our affair . . ."

"But flame and fire are, and even here they can wound us . . ."

Eventually, the talk about the mysterious stranger died away, but the fear that had accompanied their words remained behind. Something was on the move and I didn't want to know what. After a few minutes, the whispers took up again, this time about the passing of time.

How long I walked, I couldn't say. Time didn't run the same on the astral as it did over on the physical realm. But eventually I came to the end of the wood and found myself standing on the edge of a long chasm filled with mist and sparkling fog. A narrow rope bridge crossed the abyss, looking about as supportive as a leisure bra.

Sucking in a deep breath, I stepped onto the suspension bridge, pausing as it swung back and forth with my weight. Cautiously resting my hands on the railings, I slowly began to cross, taking care not to get my heels caught in the knot-holes of the wooden planks that made up the passage.

I was about halfway across when I saw a figure on the other side, dressed in a long gray cloak with hood. Roche? My heart pumped wildly until it clicked that it didn't match his body type. When I reached out to touch the energy, I discovered a woman's signature, with no sense of evil sur-rounding her. Curiosity, yes. Caution—definitely. But no deranged chaos like Roche.

Maybe she could tell me how to get back home. She waited silently as I steeled myself and hurried across the wildly swinging bridge, taking care not to look down. I didn't like heights. I didn't like them at all and this was about as freak-assed high as I'd ever been. Running with the Hunt didn't count.

I came to the end of the bridge and glanced back as I stepped off it. The bridge vanished into the mists. One moment it was there; the next, it disappeared.

"Holy hell!" I jumped away from the edge toward the woman. "Where did the damned thing go?"

She towered over me, even more than Delilah. And when she spoke, her voice was muffled, as if swathed in cotton.

"The bridge is mine and appears only when one who has need comes searching for me."

She brushed back her hood and I gazed into her eyes. She might be any age . . . young, mature . . . ancient. Hair streamed down her back, silver touched with violet highlights. I couldn't place her race. Neither mortal nor Fae, that much was for certain. Her eyes were pale silver ringed by a black halo, and her pupils the darkest jet I'd ever seen.

A wave of magic rolled off her that almost knocked me down. This was no witch or sorceress. No, she was magic incarnate. I stared at her for a moment. Was she a goddess? An Immortal?

"I'm afraid I don't know who you are. I wasn't searching for you—just . . . for anybody who could help me, I guess."

She circled me with a dispassionate gaze. "I am the Lady of the Mists and you have entered my realm."

The Lady of the Mists . . . cripes! I was facing an Elemental Lord. *Queen.* Whatever you called her, she was one of the true Immortals. And—like all of them—she existed outside the realm of mortal and Fae affairs. I immediately fell into a deep curtsy.

The Lady of the Mists gazed down at me, and I felt her hand touch the top of my head. "Stand, Moon witch. What are you doing in my realm? This is not your time of the month to run with the Hunt."

"I'm lost," I said. "I was dragged over to the astral by a

murderer whom I was hunting. He meant to kill me, but I managed to get away." I held up the iron handcuffs. "I tried to catch him, but he surprised me. I had no idea he could shift through the realms."

She glanced at the handcuffs and grimaced. "Iron? You carry iron?"

"I do what I need to in order to fulfill my duties. Can you help me?" I wondered if the Elemental Lords were affected by iron like the Fae. But she merely brushed them away.

"Help you how? To catch him, or to return to your world?"

By the way she said it, I had the feeling she could do either. But it was dangerous to ask for favors from the Immortals—far more dangerous than even the gods. The Elemental Lords were capricious. Death to them was simply a blink of an eye.

"Can you tell me how to get home?" I asked, not even wanting to request that much, but I didn't have much choice. Of course, I could wait here until the full moon, at which point the Hunt would sweep me up, but that seemed ridiculous and even worse—would allow Roche to escape.

She tilted my chin up and her hand felt like a gentle breeze kissing my skin. "I can help you," she said softly. "But you will be in my debt."

"What do you want in return? What can I possibly offer you?" I asked.

The Lady of the Mists smiled then, and my blood ran cold. Her smile was ruthless, not evil or malign, but as cold as snow, as frozen as glacial ice.

"In time I will send someone to you. Someone connected with the mist and fog. You may not realize it when you meet her, but eventually you will remember this pact. You will help her. You will do whatever is needed to help her redeem herself. Do you understand?"

I nodded, my teeth chattering. Her touch sent me reeling with the cold. "What happens if I say no?"

She laughed, her voice echoing through the fog that swirled around us, whirling pools of dancing mist. "Then, my dear, you will journey over the abyss again, this time without a bridge."

Realizing that I was backed into a corner, and feeling the hand of fate squeezing me tighter, I gave her my pledge.

"Close your eyes," she whispered.

I did, and the next thing I knew, I fell forward, losing my grip on the handcuffs. My eyes flew open and I found myself tumbling toward the floor as if I'd been shoved hard from behind. I scrambled for balance, but Trillian was there and he leapt forward, catching me in his arms. I was back in Roche's room.

"I thought I'd lost you," he whispered hoarsely, a terrified look on his face. And then he was kissing me, and in the heat of that kiss, I tumbled headfirst into the fire.

TRILLIAN lifted me off my feet as his lips fastened on to mine. I melted into the kiss, willing it to go on and on as I wrapped my legs around his waist. The fear of dying at Roche's hands, of being lost on the astral, of facing the Lady of the Mists, all rolled together into one big horny rush as he kissed me. I slid my hands up to his hair, my fingers coiling tightly around the long silken strands.

He pressed against my inner thighs, rigid and searching behind the front of his trousers. I shifted, rubbing against him, listening to his soft moan as he tightened his grip around my waist. His fingers sparkled with magic and every place he touched tingled, sending a trail of desire singing through my body.

"Do you think it's safe?" I eyed the bed, then the floor. The floor was a better choice. Fleas—not so much.

"Oh great gods, I want to say yes. I want you. But, no."

"Will Roche come back here?" I lowered my legs to the floor and stepped back, panting raggedly.

Trillian reluctantly let go of me. It was then that I noticed he had a friend with him. Another Svartan, only with a well-trimmed beard. Stouter than Trillian, the man was leaning against the door frame, grinning. Yeah, we'd put on a little show, all right. I could see the amusement in his eyes.

"Oh, he'll be back," Trillian said. "He left too many valuables here and he'll want to make sure I didn't steal them."

I swallowed my desire, trying to focus on the here and now. "Are you going to introduce me to your friend?"

Trillian rubbed his chin. "Right. I almost forgot. Sorry."

"I think I was just insulted," the man said.

"It wouldn't be the first time. Camille, this is Darynal, my blood-oath brother," Trillian said, laughing. "Darynal, meet Camille." He sobered. "I'm calling on our oath here. If this woman needs help, she may ask you for your assistance—in my name."

The smile faded from Darynal's face. He bowed to me. "Camille, consider me in your service. Whatever aid you need, I will do my best to provide. Whatever information you require, I will do my best to tell you."

Feeling like I'd just been made an honorary Svartan, I cleared my throat. I wanted nothing more than to forget about Roche and the astral and the Lady of the Mists, and go fuck Trillian's brains out. But I managed to gather my wits and get back to the problem at hand.

I curtsied back. "Thank you. I won't abuse the honor." Turning to Trillian, I asked, "What happened after Roche dragged me onto the astral?"

His eyes took on a dangerous glow. "When I heard the commotion, I broke into the room. Roche had vanished and you were nowhere in sight. I searched everywhere. In the room, outside the building . . . but I couldn't find you. I did, however, pick up on the fact that he'd kidnapped you into a different realm. So I sent a message back to my hotel asking Darynal to meet me here."

"You're just lucky I'm in the city this month. I don't usually trade here in Y'Elestrial," Darynal interjected.

Trillian gave him a short nod, then turned back to me. "I had no intention of leaving this area. If Roche came back without you and I managed to catch him, I would have taken a very dull knife and cut him over every inch of his body until he led me to you."

I swallowed. I thought *I* could be ruthless, but the look on Trillian's face was cruel enough to slice rock. He'd make one hell of a nasty enemy.

Darynal just laughed. "Trust him, he'd do it."

I filled them in on my adventures in astral-land, including my encounter with the copse of trees and how the brambles had hid me from Roche's sight and sense of smell. I *didn't* give them the rundown on meeting the Lady of the Mists. *That* little tea party I needed to think over for a while before I said anything to anyone. Of course, Trillian noticed the oversight.

"How did you get back here?" he asked.

"I found someone to help me," I said, sidestepping the issue. "Some astral spirit who was in a good mood. So did Roche show up?"

"You don't see any blood, do you?" Trillian shook his head. "No, but trust me. He'll be back later, when he thinks we've given up. He's not going to want to leave this behind." He hoisted a valise holding a number of magical scrolls, as well as several questionable objects. "I found it in the closet. Locked, but most locks can't hold me out for long."

"We need to keep watch so we can catch him when he shows up," I said. "But he can't know I'm back. If he thinks I'm still stuck over there on the astral, then he'll assume it's safe. And you'd better put in an appearance of leaving because ten to one, he's watching the building right now." I frowned, digging through the items. Spell scrolls, potions, a few charms—all stuff that I could happily make use of.

Grabbing my bag from where I'd left it on the chair, I upended the valise into it, swiping the scrolls along with everything else that he'd squirreled away. Then, I closed the trunk and set it back in place.

Glancing up, I said, "I lost my iron handcuffs along the way, but I can find another pair in the markets. The scrolls are magical. Roche probably bought a butt load of magic to help with his little hack-up-the-women art project."

I looked up to find Trillian and Darynal watching me. They were both grinning. "What? What did I do now?"

Trillian shook his head, laughing gently. "Oh, Camille,

you're truly a woman after my heart." When I gave him a quizzical look, he just smiled.

"Okay," I said. "How are we going to work this?"

Darynal shrugged. "I suggest that Trillian leave rather noticeably via the front door. You sneak out the back—if you're around, chances are Roche will be able to sense your energy signature. I'll stay here and hide."

"Sounds good to me," I said.

"Both of you get a move on, then. He doesn't know I'm with you since I didn't enter the building with you. I'll hide in the closet. If I can trip him up, I will." Darynal replaced the valise where it had been and opened the closet door, grimacing when he saw the cobwebs strung through the space. "Honestly, don't they have any maids around here?"

"We'll return after we've found disguises," Trillian said. "I wish we had cell phones over here."

I stared at him. "What the hell is a *cell phone*? My mother taught me about something called a telephone over Earthside. Any relation?"

Trillian nodded. "Yes. Cell phones are portable communication devices."

"Wait!" I stared at him. He'd spoken far too calmly for what he just said. "You've *been* Earthside, haven't you? You've used these *cell* phones before!"

He raised one eyebrow. "I'm not at liberty to discuss it."

"Just you wait," I said. "When we have more time, we're going to sit down and have a good, long talk."

Trillian grabbed me and gave me a quick kiss. "Not before we have a good, long fuck."

Once again, my libido kicked in as I flashed on the image of Trillian driving himself into me. I let out an involuntary moan. Darynal chuckled. I scowled at him.

"Wipe the smile off your face, beard boy." Turning back to Trillian, I added, "Disguises aren't enough. We'd better cloak our magical signatures, too. There's more to Roche than meets the eye." I paused. "Darynal, what about you? Won't Roche be able to sense you hiding in here?"

He shook his head and held up a silver pendant. "This will take care of that little problem."

I recognized the design. Sorcerers used the amulets to hide their activities.

"Hey," he added at my look. "I'm a damned good hunter, but what do you think gives me the edge on some of the elk and deer I go after?"

"So you don't play fair," I said, a faint grin on my face. I was beginning to get a feel for him, and I'd bet anything he and Trillian were one hell of a pair of troublemakers when they went out on the prowl together.

Darynal snorted. "I play to win. That's something you'd better remember about your opponents, Camille. Most of them aren't going to abide by the rule books. If you're smart, you won't either."

Trillian wrapped his arm around my waist. "I have a feeling she learned that lesson a long time ago. Come on, love. Let's get moving."

As Trillian and I left the building, Trillian loudly via the front door and me sneaking out the back, I checked out the surrounding area, paying close attention to any niches or cubbyholes in which Roche could hide. If he *was* waiting for us to leave so he could return, he wouldn't be standing out in plain sight. He might be a psychopath, but he wasn't stupid.

The alleys and walkways were shrouded in gloom. The sky was covered by thick clouds that obscured the moon, and the air smelled like warm summer lightning was on the way. I smiled, feeling the surge of energy that welled within me, calling to the forks of lightning that were biding their time, waiting for the storm to break.

Lightning and I had a special affinity—part of a Moon witch's powers included the ability to harness the lightning and other aerial weather. I wasn't so hot with rain, though I managed. Snow was far more difficult for me to get a handle on. But lightning and I? We had an understanding. Of course, every time I called down the jagged branches of fire, I was terrified they would backlash and fry me to a crisp.

"What if he comes back before we return? What if he gets away from Darynal?" I asked as Trillian and I joined up a block later, once we were out of the sight line of the building. I had the nasty feeling Roche was going to hunt me down and try to kill me, even if I walked away and left him alone.

"We'll track him. Darynal can follow any quarry he puts his mind to," Trillian said, guiding me by the arm as he looked over his shoulder.

"I didn't know they have game down in the Subterranean Realms," I said.

Trillian glanced at me. "Not *every* Svartan lives in the Sub-Realms. Darynal lives in Darkynwyrd."

Darkynwyrd was an ancient and deadly forest. I'd never been there, but the rumors were that it was filled with beasties and nasties that made Roche look like a saint. The forest was bordered on the south by Guilyoton, the goblin city. To the east stretched the Tygerian Mountains. West of the wood were several vast expanses of grassland, along with Willowyrd Glen. And to the north—Thistlewood Deep, another glen that was reputed to be even *more* magical and shadowy than Darkynwyrd.

I shuddered. "I've never been in the dark forest. The Corpse Talkers are supposed to make their home there, you know." Pausing, I glanced around. Still no sign of Roche, nor were we being followed. My senses were on overdrive and I was keyed in on any hint of energy that might be directed our way. "What about you? Where do you live? In the Subterranean Realms or in Y'Eírialiastar?"

Trillian shrugged. "I commute, you might say. I have a home back in Svartalfheim, but I also live here. To be precise, I have an apartment in Y'Elestrial. Fully furnished, complete with a servant to clean the rooms and my clothing. I don't have to worry about anything except my food. Sometimes I'll stay with Darynal if I'm over that direction."

I had to ask. "I know you're blood-oath brothers, but are you lovers?"

Trillian flashed me a soft smile. "No, we are not. I'm not attracted to men. I prefer the pleasures of women." He led me through the market to a building that was unremarkable except for the magic I could feel emanating from it. To the eye, it was nothing more than a series of apartments, but I knew there was more at work behind the weathered double doors.

"Follow me and don't speak until I tell you it's safe," he said.

We entered the lobby, which again was unremarkable. A few benches lined the walls and next to them stood generic potted plants. A bored-looking dwarf manned the counter. He didn't even blink as we walked past him toward the staircase. Trillian led me through a long hall, lit by eye catchers, to a staircase. We stopped at the first door on the second floor.

He knocked three times, then pressed his palm against a silver plate on the side of the door frame that was glowing with a soft red light. The light flickered to green, and the door opened.

I dutifully followed him inside. The room was huge—it must have taken up a good half of the second story. Filled with heavy wooden tables, ornate armchairs, and a fireplace flickering with a soft bluish flame that came from neither wood nor ember, the chamber emanated so much magical energy that it almost knocked me flat on my back. I quickly leaned against Trillian to steady myself. He slid his arm around my waist and led me to a settee, where I quickly sat down.

"Wait here and don't move." He took off toward the other end of the room. I followed orders—there were times when I was happily willful and disinclined to obey, but the energy here could strike like a snake, and I was just a guest. I wasn't about to cause any waves.

When Trillian returned, he was followed by an incredibly tall man. I couldn't place his race of Fae—or even if he *was* Fae. He certainly wasn't a giant, though he was nearly as tall as one. He reminded me of the inhabitants of Aladril, the City of Seers. They all had that same regal quality, gliding instead of walking, with serene and aloof expressions.

He motioned for Trillian to sit, then took his place in an armchair opposite us. I waited for Trillian to introduce us but after a moment, realized that wasn't going to happen. Instead, he ignored me and talked directly to the man without addressing him by name.

"We need a spell to cover our magical signatures, to hide ourselves from someone we're seeking. He knows who we are." Trillian held out a marker and the man slowly accepted it.

"You realize once you cash this in, my debt to you is paid?"

I jerked my head up. Debt? I managed to catch a better look at the marker. A blood-debt marker. So whoever these people were, they owed a blood debt to Trillian.

"Of course," Trillian said. "I'm a man of my word."

"But not," the stranger said, "necessarily a righteous man."

"Righteousness has nothing to do with morality," Trillian said calmly. I sensed this wasn't the first time they'd had this debate.

"But morality without righteousness is a hollow victory for honor." The stranger shook his head. "You cannot eliminate the power of belief, the power of the gods."

Trillian snorted. "The power of the gods often leads to ruin for anybody but the gods themselves. Righteousness applied to morality is a dangerous mix, and zealots usually end up killing anybody who disagrees with them. No, give me my ethics, and leave religion out of it."

The other man regarded him quietly, then smiled. "As always, you stand by your beliefs, regardless of how much I prod you. All right, you will have your help, but remember— the marker is forfeit and next time we meet, I won't have any restrictions on killing you."

"Done. But only for *you*. The rest of your brotherhood are not involved. This is *our* fight. We leave my people and your people out of it." Trillian glanced at me. "And our friends, family, and lovers."

"Agreed." He said the word so mildly that I barely caught it, but I could feel the mixture of respect and anger welling off the man. Whoever he was, he didn't like Trillian. I had the feeling Trillian had just cashed in his safety net.

"Wait here," the man said, and glided toward the other end of the room.

I pressed my fingers onto Trillian's arm, giving him a questioning look. He shook his head.

"Don't ask. Not here." After a pause, he gazed into my eyes and whispered, "Camille." Then, without another word, he slid his arm around my waist and grazed my lips with his. As we touched, like a jagged spike of lightning, a jolt of energy seared its way through my core. Before I had time to gasp, an orgasm ripped me apart. But the energy didn't stop there. It grew stronger, weaving a cord between us, knotting our auras together in an intricate pattern. I could feel the magic shift and dance, drawing me in, pulling me to him.

I clung to him, shaking. "What's happening?"

Trillian looked just as dizzy and confused as I. He tried to push me away but the draw between us was too strong.

"Lady Hel preserve us," he whispered, clinging to me, his lips on my hair, my forehead, my neck, covering my face with kisses.

Another wave washed through, turning me topsy-turvy. The cord between us was now visible, sparkling like a thick string of faerie lights. My fingers tingled under the sensation of his skin. I welcomed the pressure of his mouth as he played me like a skillfully tuned harp.

"We shouldn't be doing this here." Once again, I tried to break away but he held on, leaning me back against the seat, his eyes gleaming with a hunger so deep that I thought he might gobble me up.

His own voice was just as breathless as mine as he pressed himself between my legs, holding me down. "I don't know . . . I don't know . . . unless . . ."

"Unless what?" I managed to roll out from under him, but it took every ounce of self-control I had not to throw myself back into his arms.

He grabbed hold of my hands and held tight. "I'm one of the Charming Fae . . . There are legends that sometimes a Svartan will meet another Svartan with whom the mesh is so right that they spontaneously bond. *For good.* It's rare, but it does happen."

"But I'm not Svartan."

"Svartan or not, I think that's what's happening." Trillian lifted my chin and gazed into my eyes, a haunted look crossing his face. "When souls mate, nothing can undo the link."

I stared at him. He wasn't bullshitting. From the core of my gut, I knew that what he said was true.

"We haven't even had sex yet," was all I could say.

"I know. But think about what it's going to be like when we do," he murmured, then quickly straightened himself as the strange man reappeared.

The man ignored me as he handed Trillian two small medallions.

"Wear these. They will block your signatures from everyone. While you wear them, you will appear as dwarves. They will only last for a little while, so you'll have to work fast."

Trillian nodded, then stood. He inclined his head. "The blood-debt is paid. You are free. But next time we meet, before raising your sword, think back on our discussions. Perhaps you won't be so hasty to have my head. You killed my sister already. That's the only member of my family you're touching."

The man stared at him, conflicting emotions running across his face. After a moment, he said, "While I value our debates, know this, Svartan. If I had it to do over again, I'd kill her again. No woman refuses me. And next time we meet, I'll be coming for you. Don't ever darken the doors of this guild again, lest you find me here." He nodded to the door. "Once you walk out of this building, I owe you nothing."

Trillian shook his head, smiling grimly. "As you so wish," he said, and led me out of the room. As soon as we were in the hallway, he draped one of the medallions around his neck.

"Mother pus bucket," I said, staring at him, still dazed from our tryst. He looked like a dwarf, complete with long beard, short stature, and rugged appeal. He was still handsome—no spell could take away that gorgeous demeanor, but he was definitely a dwarf.

He blinked. "I assume you learned that from your mother?" he said as he draped the other medallion around my neck. "Well, you certainly look better as yourself, but this will do quite nicely."

I glanced down at my arms and legs. Yep, I looked like a dwarf, too. A dwarf with really big boobs. Of course, a lot of dwarven women were busty. I glanced back at the chamber. "Mind telling me what the Hel we're going to do about what happened back there?"

"Hush, leave it until we're outside. Leave *all* questions until we're outside." He led me down the stairs and out the front door. Then, quickly, he tugged on my hand and we raced back toward Calisto's. I prayed that we were right, and that Roche would be on his way up to his room. Trillian had just sacrificed a huge marker for this, and I didn't want to see him wasting his get-out-of-jail-free card.

6

NIGHT was sweeping away the dusk, leaving a solid layer of stars overhead. As we slid through the streets, Trillian kept hold of my hand. My mind was racing with thoughts of Roche, of finally catching him and skewering my boss when I told the YIA that he'd been in on the perv's escape.

But, overshadowing everything was the lingering tingle of my skin, the memory of what had happened between Trillian and me. *There are legends that sometimes a Svartan will meet another Svartan with whom the mesh is so right that they spontaneously bond.* For good. *It's rare, but it does happen.*

His words reverberated through me. What did this mean? But I already knew. Something—by fate or chance—had brought us together. I'd known since our first meeting. And now we were bound, whether for good or ill, I didn't know yet. My father was going to have a field day with this one.

"There," Trillian whispered. "Calisto's."

As we watched, a figure emerged from the gloom. He was the right size and shape and an alarm sounded that yes—it was him. I clutched Trillian's arm.

"It's Roche," I said. "I know that energy!"

We waited until he'd entered the building, then we slipped past the rawhead who had passed out, an empty bottle of booze on the counter. The stench of stale vomit filled the air.

As we tiptoed up the stairs, I steeled myself. Roche was up there. Roche, who liked to carve up women and children. Darynal's warning came back to me—Roche wouldn't play by the rules, so I wasn't going to either. Whatever it took, I was taking the dude down. Hard.

As we reached the top of the stairs, Roche had already disappeared into the room and we could hear the sounds of fighting from behind the scarred door.

"Come on! Darynal's in danger." Trillian slammed open the door and rushed into the room. I followed.

"Stop or I'll kill him!" Roche whirled, holding Darynal by the throat, a knife with a glinting razor's edge poised at his jugular. He stared at us for a moment, looking totally confused. "Who the fuck are you?"

Darynal was limp, but alive. I could tell he was doing his best to relax into the hold, a good way to fool your opponent. Only Roche wasn't the sanest peach in the pie, so what might work on a normal psycho wasn't necessarily going to do the trick for him.

First things first—get Darynal out of Roche's grasp. I whipped out my knife from the sheath circling my thigh. The leather strap looked like it was fastened around the illusionary trousers I was wearing.

Praying my voice had changed along with my looks, I said, "Give us all your money—jewels, whatever you got." Yep, my voice had deepened, thank the gods. If we played guards-and-bandits, we just might confuse him long enough to throw him off guard.

Trillian took my cue and pulled out his own knife, a dangerous-looking kris. "Whatever beef you got with this guy, we don't care. We'll go through him to get to you if you don't give us your money. *Now!*"

Roche frowned, but apparently the magic of our disguises was top-notch and he slowly lowered his knife and pushed Darynal to the ground. "You can take my pack over there." He nodded to the table.

"Empty your pockets on the bed," I said with a snarl, waving my blade toward his face. As he began spilling his pockets on the bed, I suddenly felt the energy shift. The camouflage was breaking. Shit, we just needed a few more moments. While Roche was focused on Trillian's blade, which was dancing around his midcenter, I dropped my knife and whipped out the death scroll from my bag.

I had barely unfurled it when the illusion broke. Roche bellowed and grabbed for what looked like an amulet around his neck. Trillian thrust with his blade, but Roche darted away from him. He caught hold of the pendant and stared at me, his eyes gleaming as he shouted something in sorcerers' tongue. A whirling orb of energy blasted out of the talisman.

A blink of an eye till impact. No time to leap out of the way. I steeled myself for the flames. But before I could stop him, Trillian pushed me to the side and took the blast right in the chest, shouting as the magical flame burned through his clothes.

"No!" I swung around to face Roche, bringing up the scroll. "Enough mayhem. Enough murder. *Enough! Mordente dezperantum, vulchinin, mordente la saul ayt Roche!*"

Time seemed to slow. My voice hung heavy in the air, the words trickling out like honey on a cold morning. Roche's eyes grew wide and he dropped the knife. His head fell back and his mouth opened, as a black smoke poured out of his throat. Above our heads, a swirling vortex opened and sucked the smoke into it. With one last solitary shriek, Roche tumbled forward as the vortex closed.

Ignoring Roche's body, I dropped to my knees beside Trillian. "Trillian, Trillian, are you okay?"

Darynal kicked Roche once, very hard, then joined me.

Trillian groaned, wincing with pain. There was a platter-size burn on his chest—the material had melted to him. "I've been better."

"We should get a doctor—" I glanced over at Darynal.

He shook his head. "I'm skilled at healing. I have to be, living out in the woods on my own. Let me look at it."

Within minutes, he'd stripped away the burnt clothing and

was smoothing the skin with his hands. A crackle of magic told me that his healing abilities weren't limited to herbs. The pulsing heat of Trillian's burn began to fade. After a few moments, it was bright pink, but the worst of the blisters were gone.

"How's the pain?" he asked Trillian.

Trillian closed his eyes, then shrugged. "Bearable. Much better. Thanks, *druneh*." He took Darynal's hand and slowly rose to his feet.

I hesitantly moved toward him. "You saved my life. You took the hit that was meant for me. Being half-human, it would have probably killed me."

He gazed into my eyes, then reached out and stroked my lips with one finger. "How could I not? After what's happened between us? We're linked—I don't know how or why, but it happened. I'm not sentimental, Camille. You'll find that out very quickly. But what's mine, I protect. *And you are mine.*"

Normally, I'd snap off a quick *fuck you* to any man who said that to me, but Trillian wasn't playing testosterone games; he wasn't being the macho he-man. He meant it, and it was true.

I slowly kissed his fingers, then bit them lightly. "And you are mine."

"You should get the body back to headquarters now." He motioned to Roche. "You bagged your killer. This should shut up your prick of a boss."

"Aren't you coming with me? You're the one who made it possible for me to catch Roche. Without you, I'd still be trying to figure out where he was." I wasn't the kind of woman who took credit for other peoples' work.

"No. I want no mention in this. You take him back, you tell them you managed to track him down, and you get that idiot off your back. Or I'll take care of your boss in my own manner." His eyes flashed dangerously and I realized he was more than willing to take out Lathe if I asked.

I nodded, slowly. I didn't like lying, but in the greater scheme of things, what mattered most was that Roche was out of commission. "Thanks," I said slowly. "I owe you one."

Trillian shook his head. "Camille," he said softly, "that's

another thing you'll learn about me. With you, I won't keep score." He held out his arms and I slid into them. Once again, he held my heart. And in that moment, I knew what I had to do. What *we* had to do.

LATHE stared at Roche's body. I'd hired a wagon to haul him back to the palace and then dragged him through the halls by the scruff of his collar, ignoring the trail of blood as his body bumped over the rough marble. I was determined that my boss wasn't going to take credit for the catch and I made sure that every agent, guard, and noble that I'd met on the way to Lathe's office knew that I'd taken Roche down and brought him in.

"You got him?" The look on Lathe's face was priceless as I dumped Roche at his feet.

"No thanks to the false leads you threw my way," I said. "But here he is. Sorry I couldn't bring him in alive. He might have confessed that you were trying to help him get away then. *But you listen to me, Lathe.* Every agent and guard between here and the palace steps knows I collared Roche, so don't you dare try to steal credit for this." I jabbed him sharply in the chest, hard enough to leave a mark. "You play by the up and up or so help me, I'll make sure you're exposed for the sicko you really are."

Lathe blinked, then reached out and grabbed my wrist. "Don't you threaten me, little girl. You won this round, but one of these days you're going to go too far. And then, you'll have to run straight to me. And my price for help just went through the roof."

I pulled away from him and backed toward the door. "You wanted Roche. I brought him in. Do I get my promotion or do I tell people what scum you are?"

Without missing a beat, Lathe turned back to his desk. "Oh, you'll get your promotion. You'll get a raise for this, and eventually, you'll get a *promotion*. But Camille, you're going to wish you'd played it my way. Trust me." And with the flick of a hand, he dismissed me.

* * *

THREE nights later, Trillian was waiting for me by the doors to the temple of Eleshinar, the Fae goddess of passion and love.

"Are you sure you want to go through with this?" he asked, glancing up at the temple.

"I'm sure." And I was. Sure of only one thing in the world: that this was the right thing for us to do.

"You didn't suggest this out of some sense of obligation, did you?" Once again, he cupped my chin and gazed into my eyes. His touch was like fire, and I wanted him, all of him. "I don't want you only because you feel guilty, or because you feel you owe me something. Especially like this."

I clung to him. "I'm so hungry for you that I ache. I want you inside me. I want your arms around me. But there's far more to it than that," I whispered. "Last night, I asked the Moon Mother what I should do. And she confirmed what I was thinking. *Eleshinar's Ritual.*"

"This ritual—it can't be undone." He gazed into my eyes, his own ice blue ones searching my face, looking for the truth of my heart. I opened myself up so that he could *see* . . . could see that I wanted this more than anything. That I *had* to go through with this.

"We're meant to be together. What happened . . . you know we forged a link. All we're doing is formalizing it."

"I know. I may not pray to the gods, but I have my own sense of destiny." Trillian shuddered. "I've never felt this way before. You are part of my future. And so . . . for better or worse, yes, we'll perform the ritual." He let out a long sigh. "What will your family say? Do they know where you are?"

"They think I'm at the Collequia, as usual." I laughed, suddenly happy and feeling like a bride on her wedding day. "Oh babe, trust me, you don't want to know what they'll think. You don't want to know."

There was nothing more to say. I took his hand and we walked through the temple doors.

* * *

THE altar was composed of a long, cushioned dais, surrounded by tables filled with lush baskets of fruit, loaves of bread, sweet chocolates, and pastries. Another table, near the dais, held inks of all colors, and several long, thin brushes. Near the altar stood a stone tub, embedded into the floor, steamed with swirling water as the scent of roses and jasmine and ylang ylang rose to perfume the air.

Nori, the priestess I'd spoken to that morning, slowly glided up.

She was beautiful, bare-breasted, and her skirt was a sheer drape of sea foam and silk. Golden armbands encircled her upper arms, and her hair was smoothed back in a long ponytail. But most arresting, a brilliant tattoo of green and gold curled its way across her forehead to wind down the sides of her face and neck, coiling farther still to encircle her breasts and spiral in to her nipples.

When she smiled at us, the room lit up and I stared at her, unable to tear my gaze away. She laughed, her voice a tinkle on the wind, and my heart lifted. Whatever magic the priestesses of desire wielded, it was infectious.

"You are certain of this?" she asked.

"I am." I expected to hear myself waver but my voice came out surprisingly strong, as if I wasn't the one speaking but instead, the Lady of the Moon herself.

Nori turned to Trillian. "And you? Are you so certain, as well?"

He nodded. "I am."

"Then we shall begin." She gestured toward the tub. "Disrobe and enter the ritual bath."

Suddenly shy, I began to remove my dress. I'd worn a simple shift, aware that the ritual would entail removing my clothing. It was much easier than fumbling with a bustier and buttons and ties. As I slipped the straps off my shoulders I glanced over at Trillian, all too aware that he was watching every move I made. As the shift fell away, grazing my nipples, I shivered in the cool air of the temple.

Trillian's look said everything. Desire, passion, hunger, longing . . . it was all there. After a moment, he slid off his tunic and trousers and stood there, five-foot-ten inches of gloriously toned muscle. He looked like a statue carved out of onyx, polished and smooth. As I lowered my gaze to his hips, his cock rose, erect, smooth and with just a drop of liquid on the tip of the head. I licked my lips, aching to slide up against him.

Nori walked between us. "I can see it," she said softly. "There is a cord that binds you already. This ritual will only be the confirmation of what you've already begun."

She motioned for us to get in the tub. I carefully lowered myself into the chest-high water, spreading my arms as the bubbling warmth surrounded me. Trillian joined me, but we didn't touch. We were forbidden to touch. *Yet.*

Inhaling the fragrant steam, I closed my eyes and let the stress of the week wash off me. I tried not to think about the coming months. My father would be furious, my sisters, too. But this was something that I knew would happen sooner or later, and the sooner, the better as far as I was concerned.

"Please, dip fully under the water," Nori's voice spiraled into my thoughts.

I held my breath and lowered myself under the water level, letting it immerse every part of me. Trillian did the same and when we came up for air, he gave me a glowing smile, all I needed to remove any lingering doubts.

We exited the bath and Nori handed us long bath sheets to wrap ourselves in. The air had grown warmer, though I couldn't see any fireplace around. She pointed toward the dais.

"Please, lie down on your backs."

I settled myself on the dais and she helped me adjust my soaking hair. Trillian joined me, and we lay there, not touching, inches apart, the lazy air currents playing over our bodies. I sucked in a deep breath. He was inches away and I could feel him there. I wanted to reach out, to touch, caress, but forced myself to lie still, the tension in my body driving me crazy.

Nori's voice was a rustle on the wind as she began a faint

chant. I gazed into her eyes as she leaned over me, adjusting my position. Her breasts hung heavy and full like my own. Her lips were thick and lush as she softly sang out her spell. Part of me wanted to reach up and caress her, too. But she was as far away from my grasp as the Moon Mother.

After a few moments she gently moved away. Trillian turned his head to look at me. "Are you sure?" he mouthed.

I bit my lip. "Yes. Are you having doubts?"

He shook his head. "Never. I feel like we've been together for years. I feel like I already know you, know your body."

And then Nori returned, a second priestess with her.

"Liliabett." The priestess introduced herself.

Between them, they carried the table with inks and brushes over to the dais. Nori held her hands over my chest and warmth rained down from her body. Liliabett did the same to Trillian. Living beacons of passion, they were desire incarnate.

After a moment, Nori said, "We're ready to begin. Camille Sepharial te Maria, do you undergo this ritual freely, of your own will, knowing that what will be done can never be undone?"

I licked my lips. "Yes. I do swear." My voice was a whisper on the wind.

"Trillian Leshon Zanzera, do you undergo this ritual freely, of your own will, knowing that what will be done can never be undone?" Liliabett's voice was the perfect counterpoint, as sultry and warm as Nori's was cool and melodic.

"I do, by my oath and honor." His voice spiraled up and then out as if he'd never said a word.

"Then we begin."

Nori narrowed her brow, focusing on me as she lifted a fine-tipped brush and dipped it into a silver paint pot. With a steady hand, she began to trace an outline on my forehead, a swirl of glyphs, fine-lined and delicately fashioned. I closed my eyes as she worked, line by line covering my face.

The tracing tickled, but I remained perfectly still as she worked her way down my neck, leaving a trail of runes that sang as they touched my skin. Magic, her art was, and magic was the paint.

Onto my shoulders, working in silence, she deftly covered me. And then to my chest, making me suck in a quick breath as desire rose fiercely. She stroked my nipples with the tip of the brush, then the curve of my breasts, the undercarriage and down to my torso.

I began to drift, the rhythmic kiss of the brush lulling me into an erotic haze. The bristles flickered over my stomach, then down to my thighs and across my mound. She gently nudged open my thighs and spread open my labia, painting runes along my pussy and onto my clitoris. I shuddered, trying to control the hunger that flared as she touched me.

And down my legs, along my knees, encircling my ankles, she went. By the time she finished, I saw that Trillian was as covered—and aroused—as I was. The paint dried quickly, and we gently flipped onto our stomachs. The priestesses worked their way down our backsides, covering every inch of us with the silver glyphs and symbols.

When they were finally done, they asked us to stand. I gazed down at myself—a vision of silver fire on pale skin. Trillian cleared his throat. He was silver on black, the contrast incredibly beautiful. Like spun metal shining against dark velvet.

"Follow us," Nori said, and the two women led us out of the main chamber and into a private room, in which there was a bed that sat atop a floor covered in runes. She held out a bottle as we knelt in front of her.

Liliabett reached for my hand and I offered it, palm up. She placed a silver goblet beneath my palm and with a curved blade, slashed an inch-long shallow gash across the pad. As I watched, blood spilled into the goblet. After a moment, she did the same with Trillian.

Nori poured the contents of the bottle into the goblet and a swirl of smoke rose, boiling over the rim. She held the goblet out to me.

"Take it."

As I held the glass, she began to sing a low song in a language I didn't understand. But her energy flared brightly. She was a shining jewel.

"Drink and bind yourself through your bodies, through your souls."

I lifted the goblet, then glanced at Trillian. This was it. There was no going back. Before I could think about it, I swallowed a mouthful of the potion and fire raced through my body, arching me back. I would have dropped the goblet, but Nori caught it and handed it to Trillian, who tipped it to his lips and finished what was left. He shivered, clutching his arms to his chest as the pain took hold.

Nori stepped back. "And now, one thing remains to seal your union. If you do not consummate your relationship now, you will forever be half-bound, weak and hating each other. You must finish the ritual."

She and Liliabett excused themselves from the room.

I turned to Trillian, barely able to stand, the spasms were so intense. But as I tried to sort through the pain, I realized what I was feeling was actually desire—aching, searing lust so strong that it was cramping my body.

Trillian lifted his head to look at me. Behind the veil of his sky blue eyes, I could see the primal god. *The lord of the forest, the lord of the rut, the lord of the horn.* He leapt to his feet and for a brief moment I was afraid, but then the cramps hit again and all I could think about was finding a way to ease the gnawing hunger.

Panting, I stumbled toward the bed and he followed, his gaze never leaving mine. As I danced to one side, he reached out and grasped my waist, his touch firm and demanding.

"I will have you," he whispered, his voice almost a grunt.

Shivering, confused by the flurry of pain, I pulled away and he followed, grabbing my wrist to whirl me around and back me up against the wall.

"Let me in, Camille. Let me in." His hands planted on either side of me, he leaned against me. My pulse fluttered as he lowered his lips to mine, and then we were bathed in a silver light as his tongue played over mine and he enfolded me in his arms.

We began to spin, around and around he twirled me as his chest pressed against my breasts. I gasped, trying to clear my head, then pulled him to the bed. He loomed over me, his lips seeking my breasts as his fingers danced their way onto my clit. As he stroked my fire, I cried out and grasped his shoulders.

"You're the golden man," I whispered. "You taste like honey, sweet and warm and rich and thoroughly fine."

"And you're my queen, and you taste like moonlight and starflowers and the echo of birds at sunset."

He lowered himself to the outer lips of my pussy, setting off a string of explosions. Firecrackers sizzled one after another along my body, and all I could think about was that Trillian was about to slide his gorgeous, smooth cock into me and how much I wanted every inch of him, in every possible way.

"Fuck me," I begged him. "Don't make me wait any longer, please fuck me. Hard. Take me hard and rough—I don't want gentle."

Trillian let out a guttural laugh and plunged, driving himself into my core.

Under a shower of sparks that ricocheted through my body, I moaned and shifted my hips as he picked up the pace, pumping gently at first, then grinding into me, each thrust sending me into a shockwave of pleasure.

As we rode the wave, I began to notice through the sex haze that my skin was hurting. I glanced at Trillian's shoulder and gasped. The silver markings had begun to writhe, they were boiling like a swarm of creatures across his body and I knew that my own runes were doing the same. But the friction of our heat pulled my attention back to him.

I clung to him as he thrust, deep and hard with that silken cock of his. His skin was warm against mine, a perfect fit and in some little corner of my mind, I realized that I'd never had it so good in bed, never felt the same sense of connection before.

Everybody else saw me as the rock, the anchor, or—in the case of men—just a good fuck to hook up with and leave behind. But Trillian's eyes gazed at my soul; he was staring down at me and he was seeing me. All of me—*both sides of my heritage*, and he didn't flinch, didn't look away.

As thought began to slip away, and I came to the edge,

the markings on my body began to burn. I let out a sharp cry as Trillian grunted, wincing.

"What's happening?" I flailed, unable to stop either the pain or the rush toward orgasm. Every rune had become a flaming brand and with every move, their flames grew brighter.

"The ritual—it's part of the ritual," Trillian gasped out. "Can't stop . . . would . . . kill us . . ."

Everything took on the color of violet fire as the magical silver on our bodies burrowed deep beneath the skin, hissing and tattooing themselves through muscle and skin. Goading me with as much pleasure as pain, they pushed me toward the edge, toward the final release.

And then I looked up at Trillian. But instead of seeing his face, I realized I was looking through his eyes at myself. The braid that had spontaneously bound us had melted into a thick cord of silver and flame and passion and lust. The beating of his heart synchronized with mine, and in that moment, I felt his spirit pass through me and back into himself. Then, in a cascade of silver fire, came release.

THE pain subsided as we lay there, exhausted. I shivered and Trillian drew the blankets up to cover us. He slid his arm around my shoulders and pulled me close. The markings had disappeared from the surface of our skin, but they were there, beneath muscle and bone, tattooed into our spirits, binding us forever.

"What next?" I asked. "Where will this lead? What's going to happen now?"

"I don't know," he whispered. "I only know that you belong to me. You are *mine*, Camille. Even if you share yourself with others, you'll always belong to *me*. I'm your *alpha*. I'm your mate."

As he spoke, an image flashed through my head. A dragon circled overhead as a fox watched from below. Quickly the images came, and just as quickly, they were gone. I blinked, wiping my eyes. I was tired and spent. But in my heart, I knew that they related to the future—to our future. Just like I knew that a shadow loomed, waiting for me to discover it. And Trillian would be there to help me weather the approaching storm.

But I left all of that unsaid. Instead, I kissed him back, savoring the taste of his lips on mine. "Yes, I belong to you. And you belong to me. You saved my life, you saved me from humiliation at my boss's hand. And I think . . . you saved me from myself."

"What do you mean?" His voice was low.

I let out a long sigh. "I don't know. But in time I think I'll understand. And for some reason, the idea of that knowledge makes me very much afraid."

"Hush," he said, tapping me on the nose. "Don't worry about what might happen. Live for today. There may be no tomorrow, so for now, enjoy what we have and revel in it. I know I'm going to."

Trillian sought my lips again, and in the silver fire of his kiss, I forgot about visions and shadows and the future. For now, there was only his touch and my touch, and the merging of souls and bodies.

human nature

EILEEN WILKS

Note: Readers who are following my Lupus series will want to know that the action in "Human Nature" falls at the same time as some of the events of Night Season. While Cynna and Cullen were off having adventures, Lily and Rule had their hands full, too.

1

THE blouse was silk, crimson, and new. The blood was crimson, too.

Lily looked down at her ruined blouse, grimaced, and slid out of her government-issue Ford. She ought to put on her jacket. It was too damned chilly for April, dammit, and the jacket would hide the blood and her shoulder holster. She tried to avoid alarming the neighbors, which both blood and gun were apt to do—but the blood was still damp.

Bad enough she'd ruined the blouse. She didn't want to ruin her jacket, too. It wasn't new, but it fit like a dream.

Good thing she didn't have far to go. Wonder of wonders, there had actually been a parking spot only two houses down from the pleasant two-story row house where she was staying while in Washington, D.C. . . . which had been way too long. She missed San Diego. She missed the heat. She missed her cat, her grandmother, her father. She even missed her sisters. And maybe, though she was sure it was a sign of imminent mental collapse, she actually missed her mother.

Lily could have parked around back. There was a single-car garage off the alley with room for a second vehicle behind the first if you left the garage door open and didn't mind having the rear of your car jut slightly into the alley. But then getting the other car out—Rule's Mercedes—would be a pain, and she had places to go in that car tonight.

It was her birthday. She intended to celebrate, dammit.

Lily stabbed her key into the lock, entered, and shut and locked the door behind her. Rule was at the back of the house. That was one of the cool things about the mate bond: she *knew* where he was. The direction, anyway, and in a rough sense the distance.

"Sorry I'm late," she called as she sped for the stairs. "I need to shower and change, but I'll hurry."

"They'll hold the reservation."

The man who'd spoken came out of the dining room that bridged the parlor with the kitchen. His black dress shirt was unbuttoned at the neck. His black dress slacks broke at just the right point on his black shoes. His hair stopped just short of black, being mink brown, thick, and a bit long for current fashion. He had a lean face, sharp-featured, with a sensuous mouth and eyes the same color as his hair. The dark slashes of his eyebrows mirrored the pitch of his cheekbones.

Dressing all in black made most men look like Goth wannabes. Not Rule. Maybe it was the excellent body beneath the civilized clothing that made it work. Maybe it was the sheer arrogance of the man. He looked good. He knew it. He would have looked good in tattered jeans, a doorman's uniform, or in nothing at all.

He knew that, too. Lily's heartbeat hitched and she paused without intending to, one hand on the banister, and just looked at him.

Mine.

It was a thought, an attitude, Rule wouldn't have approved. Tough. He *was* hers and sometimes she just had to revel in that. In him.

"This is supposed to be dinner, not a race," Rule said mildly as he walked toward her. "If you . . ." Those wonderful eyebrows drew down. "Is that your blood?"

The way she stood, with one foot on the stairs and her back mostly to him, he couldn't have seen it. Must have smelled it. "Damned gremlins," she muttered, and turned. "Yes, but it's a scratch, no more. I was careless."

His eyes were getting blacker. Too black.

"There's no one for you to kill," she said firmly. "The surviving imps have already been sent back."

"Imps?" His eyes returned to normal and his eyebrows lifted. "I hadn't heard of an outbreak."

"It wasn't a biggie. Probably be on tonight's news, but the gist is that a seventeen-year-old idiot in Arlington used a spell from some Internet site to summon a demon. He got a handful of imps instead."

The eyebrows went higher. "This spell was on the Internet?"

She sighed. "So not good news, is it? MCD tries. They have people watching for stuff like that, but they can't catch everything." It would be worse, of course, if any of the summoning spells actually worked. This one had been more effective than most, since it actually did summon something.

Damned imps. "Supposedly the major search engines will wipe out the cache they have for that site, but who knows how many idiots have already seen it? Listen, I need that shower. If you want to hear more—"

"You need to be tended. Imps' claws aren't poisonous, but they probably weren't clean, either."

She waved that aside. "The EMTs already cleaned up the wound. Scratch," she amended. "It's long but shallow, honest. I just want to wash off, forget about minor hellspawn, and go eat something fancy by candlelight."

"Hmm." He studied her face, but whatever he saw there seemed to reassure him. "There may be a present involved, also."

"Another one?" He'd already given her earrings— exquisitely handmade lilies made from citrine, topaz, garnets, and what she suspected were emeralds. And the way he'd given them to her . . . well. Rule was big on presentation.

She grinned and started up the stairs. "Even better."

He followed. "I thought the FBI used Wiccans to deal with imps."

"They do. We do," Lily corrected herself. Now and then she still spoke as if she weren't an FBI agent herself, though it had been almost six months since Ruben Brooks recruited her for his special Unit. Which just proved how weird minds could be, considering the intensive training she'd almost finished at Quantico.

Training that had been much interrupted. Major upheavals between the realms will do that. "But the teenage idiot did his summoning just as I was headed back from Quantico, which of course Ida knew, since she knows everything, so she sent me. There were a couple patrol officers on-scene, but they aren't trained for imps. Still, we were able to keep them contained until the coven arrived."

"You had help, then."

"Sure. Those two uniforms." She unbuttoned her blouse and pulled it off. "Trash. This is just trash now." She sighed. The shirt was the perfect shade of red for her, but even if she got the blood out, the silk was ripped.

He took the shirt from her. "Here, I'll get rid of it. You and two uniformed officers kept an imp outbreak contained?"

"It wasn't an outbreak," she said, heading for the bathroom. The row house had been built in the nineteen-teens, way before people routinely put in master baths, so there was a single bathroom on each floor. But the bathroom on this floor was the one thing she'd miss when she finally finished her training and went home . . . marble floor, granite-topped counter with vessel sinks, a glass-walled shower stall, and a huge tub.

No time for that tub now. She reached into the shower stall and turned on the hot water. "Five of the nasty little creatures don't constitute an outbreak—just a huge pain in the ass. Good thing Gan's idea about baiting them with blood worked."

She fell silent. Gan—a former demon who'd become a friend in the most unlikely way—was missing. So was Lily's boss. So were two even dearer friends, Cynna Weaver and Cullen Seabourne. They'd been kidnapped, along with a few others—like a special assistant to the president and a trigger-happy FBI agent Lily had worked with. Not just kidnapped, either, but snatched into another realm. There was no saying if or when they'd return.

Lily was not naturally an optimist. What cop was? But she was determined to believe they were okay. All of them. They were okay, and sooner or later they'd find a way to come home. She refused to consider other possibilities—at least for six months. That's the deal she'd made with herself. For six months she'd assume the best instead of the worst.

Rule took her shoulder, turned her to face him, and kissed her gently on the lips. "They'll be fine, Lily. Even your obnoxious orange friend."

She found a smile. "I think it's my turn to say that."

"Nope." He skimmed her lips with his again. "Mine. As often as I want it to be."

Somehow she and Rule had managed to trade off worry periods. When anxiety about their friends started to choke her, he was feeling steady. When he was hurting, she'd been able to summon enough confidence to reassure or distract him. The thing was, their missing friends mattered to her, but one of them—Cullen Seabourne—mattered hugely to Rule. They were lifelong friends, heart friends, the kind you'd risk your life for . . . but there was no risk Rule could take that would bring Cullen back.

So Lily smiled and agreed. "They'll be back, safe and sound. But worrying is my hobby, remember? Speaking of which . . . maybe you should call the restaurant, make sure they won't cancel our reservation?"

This time his kiss suggested he'd just as soon be even later, but he straightened without following through. "They'll hold our table. Knowing how unpredictable your job can be, I made it clear they were to hold it if we were late."

"Okay, then."

"I'm going to take this"—he wiggled the shirt he still held—"to the Dumpster outside. The smell . . . bothers me."

"Because of the blood? Or because it's my blood?"

He smiled. "Yes."

The shower felt good, if hasty. The EMT had applied a gauze bandage she was supposed to keep dry, so that was a pain, but at least she could lather up and rinse the rest of her.

She hadn't gotten anything nasty in her hair, thank goodness, so she could skip the wash and blow-dry bit.

When she got out and wrapped up in a towel warmed by the heated towel rack—she *loved* this bathroom—Rule was downstairs. She heard him talking, probably on the phone. Maybe he'd decided to make sure about the restaurant after all. She hummed quietly as she hurried from the bath to the master bedroom.

Lily liked things tidy. Her socks were rolled, her bras folded and lined up in a disciplined row, and her jackets all hung together in a color-coded closet. It took only a second to pull out the black silk dress she planned to wear, another second to retrieve hose and bra.

For some reason, her passion for order did not extend to panties. They did all land in the same drawer—but that drawer was a colorful mess. Lily had a lot of panties, in all sorts of colors, fabrics, and styles. Back in her desperately broke days, a new pair of panties had been the one treat she could almost always afford. She still shopped carefully, sensibly . . . except when it came to panties.

So maybe she shouldn't have noticed the new ones right away—they were jumbled up with the rest—but she did. First she tugged out a silky leopard print bikini. The midnight blue she didn't recognize turned out to be boy-cut hipsters. There were a couple more bikinis, one in multicolored polka dots, the other an eye-popping chartreuse. Then she spotted a scrap of raspberry lace.

A thong, she saw, pulling it out.

Her eyebrows shot up. Ordinarily she didn't like thongs. But why not? Just for tonight, why not? He'd gotten them for her, tucked them away here as the sneakiest of surprise presents. She'd give him a treat, too.

She had on her bra and the new thong when she felt Rule coming up the stairs. She didn't hear him, but then, she seldom did. He moved as quietly as if his alter ego were feline instead of lupine. She paused with the dress over her arm and turned toward the doorway, smiling with pleasure and a touch of mischief.

His expression wiped out both. It was that damned

closed-down, locked-up look she hated. Something was wrong. "What is it?"

"My father called," he said quietly. "A friend of mine is dead. No one you've met, I think. Steve Hilliard. He's . . . he was Nokolai."

"I'm so sorry." Instinctively she went to him, but something in his face kept her from doing more than touch his arm. "I'm so sorry, Rule."

He put his hand over hers. His face was tight, his eyes hooded. "There's more."

She nodded.

"Steve's throat was cut. The police have arrested another Nokolai, Jason Chance. They plan to charge Jason with the murder." Rule's jaw tightened. "It's an easy out for them. No need to look for a killer—just charge the nearest lupus with the crime and forget about it."

"I take it Steve wasn't killed while in wolf form." Or else the authorities wouldn't have any interest in the death. Killing a lupus was only illegal when he looked human. "You don't believe this Jason guy did it?"

"No. Neither does my father. I have to go home."

"Of course." And this was the downside of the mate bond—the sheer inconvenience. Rule couldn't go unless Lily did, too. The mate bond didn't allow them to be far apart. Not that they knew exactly what distance would trigger the dizziness, because it changed. Without warning, without any pattern she could spot, it changed. Damned whimsical bond.

"I'm sorry to drag you away. You're almost finished at Quantico."

She shrugged. Her training—necessary since she'd been a homicide cop, not an FBI agent, until recently—had been interrupted constantly ever since the Turning hit in December. With the uptick in ambient magic, the FBI Unit she belonged to, which dealt with magical crimes and crises, was stretched thin. "Another delay hardly matters, and I'm not working a case right now. I'll have to clear it with Croft, but he'll be cool with it. He understands my situation."

With Ruben gone, Martin Croft was running the Unit. He

was one of the few humans who were aware of the existence of the bond that, in rare cases, formed between a human woman and a lupus. Of course, according to the lupi, the bond didn't form—it was bestowed on them by their Lady. Who, in Lily's opinion, wasn't nearly as mythological as she ought to be.

"Steve was killed in Del Cielo—or at least his body was found within city limits, and the Del Cielo police claim jurisdiction."

She frowned. The town sounded familiar, but she couldn't remember why. "That's north of Nokolai Clanhome, right? In the mountains."

"Yes. It's the home of Robert Friar."

Her breath sucked in. "Shit. The rat bastard who's started that stupid Humans First organization."

"Prejudice in Del Cielo isn't confined to Robert Friar. I've had . . . encounters with the police there, and I'm not the only one. Lily, those cops aren't like you. They won't find Steve's killer, and Jason may well stand trial for a murder he did not commit. I need you to take over the investigation."

Unconsciously her hand tightened on his arm. "I can't. Rule, you know that. I don't have any authority over a regular homicide. Only if magic is involved. You said his throat was cut. If there's any suggestion this was a ritual murder, a sacrifice, then I could check it out, but—"

"No. I . . ." He inhaled sharply, pulled away, and paced a few steps before stopping. "I'm not explaining well. I think . . . From what my father said, it's possible a federal crime did occur."

Her throat ached. He was hurting. "The Unit doesn't handle hate crimes. Croft's not going to give me a green light to investigate one, but if that's what this was, there are other agencies that might be pulled in, both state and federal. I'll see what I can do." Which might not be all that much, she was afraid. Prosecutors weren't lining up to prosecute hate crimes against lupi.

"Not that." He waved it away with an abrupt gesture. "I'm talking about the law against the use or manufacture of gado."

"Gado?"

Impatiently he said, "It's what they used to use to keep us from Changing."

"I know that, but why do you think gado was involved?"

"The tattoo. Steve's killer decorated his throat before cutting it."

2

LILY was about forty thousand feet over Ohio when she closed her laptop and reached in her purse for the final gift Rule had given her: a new iPhone.

He'd been almost apologetic about it. A phone wasn't romantic—and besides, he'd bought one for himself, too. But he'd covered the romance base just fine with the earrings and the panties; this was one very cool new toy.

She glanced up the aisle, frowning slightly, as she took out the phone. Rule was headed for the lavatory. He'd undoubtedly go another time or two or three, and not because he had a bladder problem. All lupi experienced some degree of claustrophobia, but however much he preferred to pretend otherwise, Rule suffered from it more than most. Moving around in the plane helped, especially with a long flight.

The stress of being closed up in a flying steel cage would probably be worse than usual. Grief made everything harder to bear. Then, too, they were in economy this time. Rule normally paid for the additional space of first class, but first class was full on this flight and he hadn't wanted to wait for another one.

Lily was just guessing about his feelings, though. When she'd asked Rule, he'd told her he'd be fine.

He'd said that pleasantly enough. Ever since they woke up at an ungodly hour this morning to make their flight, he'd been unbearably, damnably pleasant. It made her want to shake him. If only he'd scowl or snap or weep . . .

Grimly she turned her attention to something she could control and touched Nettie Two Horse's name in her contact list.

She had a permit for using the phone. The FAA clung to the idea that cell phone usage on a plane was potentially dangerous, but immediately after the Turning it had granted Unit agents a blanket exemption to the rule. That had been handy for the agents who'd crisscrossed the country dealing with various emergencies, but the FAA hadn't done it to help them out. They'd wanted to stop the crashes.

Magic gives computers indigestion.

For about a week after the Turning, with magic still belching from nodes in unpredictable bursts, the tech in planes hadn't worked consistently. Only one large passenger plane had crashed in the United States, but there had been several smaller crashes and dozens of close calls. Even after the Turning, problems occurred. The nodes were still leaking, after all, even if they'd stopped burping. And they leaked at a higher rate than they used to, creating higher levels of ambient magic.

Ambient magic was free magic—magic that hadn't been absorbed by earth or water. In the past, the leakage from nodes had been small enough that almost all of it had been soaked up quickly. But after the realms shifted, nodes leaked more magic than earth and water could soak up. The ambient magic level was higher than it had been in a couple centuries . . . and still rising. Rising faster in some places than others.

Ruben Brooks, Lily's boss, had had a hunch shortly after the Turning. Since he was an off-the-scale precog with the president's ear, the FAA had listened. Brooks suspected that anyone with a Gift soaked up magic in a small way—not like dragons, of course, who were enormous magical sponges.

But enough to make a difference to delicate equipment—especially if they were trained.

Unit agents were almost all Gifted, almost all trained in one of the many magical disciplines. They now flew for free on every major airline . . . and were allowed to use their phones.

That was a perk that might not last much longer. The airlines no longer flew over the noisiest nodes, so incidents of computer malfunction were down, and silk casings on computerized equipment did offer some shielding. But the FAA was quietly investigating whether the flights that did experience a brief malfunction were those without any Gifted on board.

Quietly, because there was still a lot of distrust for the Gifted.

Lily was an exception in one way. She was Gifted, but not trained; her Gift was essentially untrainable. As a sensitive, she felt magic tactilely, but couldn't be affected by it. Or work it.

She didn't feel guilty about taking advantage of a privilege she might or might not be earning. She was using her phone to protect and serve, not to chat about personal matters . . . though there was an uncomfortable overlap between the professional and the personal in this case.

When Nettie answered, Lily began with the words she'd used too often, professionally. "Nettie, I'm calling about Steve Hilliard. I'm sorry for your loss."

"So am I." Nettie's voice was gruffer than usual. "Are you going to handle the case yourself?"

"I don't know yet. Are you up to a consult?"

Nettie Two-Horses—a ritually trained shaman as well as a Harvard-trained physician—was Nokolai, as Steve Hilliard had been. Nettie must have known Hilliard, might have played with him as a child. She was close to Rule's age, Lily thought, though the years looked different on her than they did on him.

Nettie was clan, but she was female. Female clan weren't lupus. They aged normally.

"If I can help, I want to. Training and disposition mean

I can't go kill the bastard who did it myself, but I want him caught."

"Good enough. You know that someone applied a tattoo to his neck?"

"I've talked to Isen. Yes, I know about that."

"Okay. My first question's about gado. I've read up about it some." Not the full, need-to-know classified document, but an abridged version. She could probably get more if she had to, but she'd have to jump through some hoops first. "I've got a rough idea of its effects and a partial ingredients list. Apparently gadolinium and wolfbane are two of the key ingredients. I'm having purchases of gadolinium checked, but wolfbane is not regulated. What can you tell me about it?"

"Actually, gado uses a solution of an organic gadolinium complex—Gadopentetate dimeglumine, or Gd-DTPA—rather than pure gadolinium. Presumably the agency that tracks gadolinium sales is aware of this."

"I'll check. Can you spell it for me?"

"I'd rather you didn't. The various agencies that take note of such things are unaware of how much I know about gado, and I'd prefer them to remain ignorant. I did considerable private research on the subject when the government was using gado on the lupi they caught."

"Right." Lily considered asking just how much Nettie knew about the manufacture of gado. Best not, she decided. Best if she didn't actually know.

"Wolfbane, of course, can't be tracked," Nettie said. "It's far too common."

Wolfbane, aka monkshood, devil's helmet, or aconite, was a member of the buttercup family scientifically known as aconitum. Lily was an amateur gardener, but she'd looked this particular plant up. "It's not native to the San Diego area, I think."

"Not that we know of. It generally prefers wetlands, but one species—Columbian monkshood—is found in many parts of California. Also, the flowers are pretty enough that some landscapers use it, despite the toxicity."

"It's a neurotoxin, right? And it interferes with a lupus's healing."

"It does. If you're wondering whether wolfbane could account for the tattoo—"

"I am. The government used gado to tattoo registered lupi, but what I read suggests wolfbane might work, too. I'm also wondering about the fatal wound. Would a lupus heal that before bleeding out without the application of some agent like wolfbane or gado?"

"There's no way to answer your second question. Lupi healing varies, and I don't know enough about the wound. What structures were involved? Was the trachea severed as well as the exterior jugular vein? What about the carotid artery?"

Lily grimaced. So far, everything she knew about the case came from Rule's father and a single newspaper article. The local police had to send the FBI requested material, but if they felt uncooperative, it could take an amazingly long time to process a request. "I don't know."

"Until you do, I can't discuss that meaningfully. As for your other question . . . hmm." She considered that a moment. "Are you talking about topical woflbane, or ingested?"

"Either. Both."

"Applied topically, both wolfbane and gado retard healing in a lupus, but the mechanism and the duration is very different. Wolfbane's effects are quite brief."

"Define brief."

"That would depend on the lupus and the dosage, but most lupi rid themselves of it in two to four minutes. Some, like Rule, are almost unaffected by topical bane."

"He's been given bane, then."

"Certainly. Most clans expose young lupi to it so they'll recognize the effects. Rule has unusually strong healing, so his system throws off topical wolfbane almost immediately. The ingested bane made him as miserable as any other lupus, though for a briefer time than some."

"So eating wolfbane works differently than rubbing it on?"

"Oh, yes. With ingested bane, the effects are stronger, more unpleasant, and last longer."

"An hour? A day?"

"More than an hour. Less than a day. The thing about wolfbane is that it distracts a lupus's healing. Their magic immediately tries to heal them of it—and since for some reason they can't rid themselves of it quickly, their systems often focus on it to the exclusion of other, more serious damage. Not in a predictable way, though."

"Because lupus healing varies."

"The effect varies even for the same lupus. One time a lupus might heal a wound almost normally soon after ingesting a dose. Another time, the same lupus may fail to heal even a trivial wound."

Lily was reminded of the mate bond. It, too, was unpredictable. "What about injecting it? Does that make a difference?"

"It can't be injected—not if you want to affect healing, that is. When wolfbane is altered, the effects change in myriad ways, and there is no key active ingredient that can be extracted. To retard healing, you have to use fresh leaves or flowers."

"Not the seeds or roots?"

"No. And no, I don't know why. Either of those will cause a form of bane sickness, but it's much briefer and doesn't seem to affect healing."

"Are the effects the same for all the aconite species?"

"As far as we know, though the severity of the symptoms varies."

Rule was moving down the aisle now. Lily tapped her pen on her notebook. "It sounds like there's no reason to assume Steve Hilliard was given gado. Wolfbane would have had the same effect as far as the tattoo goes."

"Well . . . yes. Though gado is much more effective. It blocks all of a lupus's magic, not just the healing, and the effect lasts much longer."

"But it's a hell of a lot harder to get hold of or to make."

"True."

"Thanks, Nettie. I'll keep you posted." Lily disconnected, her lips thin. The tapping picked up pace.

Damn him. He hadn't lied, no. He'd just led her to believe something that wasn't entirely true.

Rule had stopped a couple seats up and was signing an autograph for a young woman with tightly kinked orange hair. The stewardess hovered behind him, smiling in an infatuated way. "You're sure you don't mind?" she asked, handing him a scrap of paper.

Rule didn't. He seldom did. His fame—or notoriety—was part of his father's plan to integrate lupi with human society, and Rule had known he would be the public face for his people long before he met Lily. Before the Supreme Court's decision made it safe to announce his heritage to the world, in fact.

He made a gorgeous public face. His features were sharp and elegant in a way the camera loved, with dramatic eyebrows and cheekbones. His body wasn't bad, either, if you went for long, lean, and powerful with the innate grace of an athlete.

Which, from what Lily could see, 99.9 percent of heterosexual women did.

Lily couldn't see who sat beside the woman with the orange hair, but it was another female, judging by the muffled voice. Rule leaned across the first woman and patted the other one somewhere—her shoulder, probably.

He didn't look like a man sternly suppressing the beast inside—a wolf who did not like being trapped in a metal cage. He did have some tells, but they were too subtle for even her to spot them unless she was close.

"I don't suffer from motion sickness myself," he said, "but Lily usually travels with some candied ginger, just in case. Shall I ask her if she has some?"

Lily heard the woman's words clearly this time. "Lily? Who's she?"

Rule smiled. "My beloved."

He said that naturally, too. Just as if everyone talked that way.

Lily could imagine the woman's disappointed expression. She'd seen it often enough on other female faces. Even women who weren't making a serious play for Rule enjoyed thinking they might be able to have him, if they tried. Lupi were notoriously promiscuous.

Except for Rule. Not anymore, that is.

He signed one more autograph, then at last slid into the seat beside Lily with a faint sigh. She caught a faint whiff of the honey and citrus scent of his shampoo. He'd switched recently because she loved citrus scents.

He made it hard to stay mad, dammit.

"Why," he murmured, "do people troubled by motion sickness feel impelled to tell everyone about their symptoms?"

"Did she want the ginger?"

"No." He looked at her, his brows drawing together. "You're upset."

"What I am, is pissed. You manipulated me."

His eyebrows snapped down. "What are you talking about?"

"You led me to think gado was probably involved. Wolfbane is a lot more likely, but you never mentioned it. I wouldn't have cause to investigate the use of wolfbane, would I?"

"I'd just heard that one of my oldest friends was dead. Excuse me for not thinking things through."

"We've been up since four A.M. today. We've discussed the case, the circumstances under which I can investigate— the restrictions I'm under." Croft had told her to avoid calling on other FBI agents unless she could confirm that gado was involved. "You never mentioned the possibility it was wolfbane, not gado, that let someone tattoo Hilliard."

"Steve," he said coldly. "His name was Steve."

She breathed in slowly, choking back her own temper. He was on edge. Grief did that. So did the claustrophobia he didn't like to admit to.

She couldn't do much about his grief, but the other . . . Lily took his hand. That was the one thing that helped, other than moving around. The mate bond brought comfort when they touched—even when she was mad at him. "This matters, Rule," she said quietly. "If you tricked me into investigating, misusing my authority—"

"No. Maybe. God." His fingers tightened on hers. For a moment he sat in silence, no doubt putting a lid on his own temper—which, unlike hers, ran cold more often than hot. "I didn't intentionally misguide you. I didn't think it out like that, but unconsciously . . . I suppose I did. I needed you to investigate. It was reflex."

She'd been sure already, so why did it hurt to have him admit it? Lily swallowed. "Lousy reflex. Long-lasting one, too."

The tension she hadn't seen in him earlier was plain now—in his tight jaw, his grip on her hand, his continued silence.

And yet the comfort she'd meant for him reached her, too. That's how the mate bond worked. She couldn't touch him without responding—and the response wasn't always sexual.

It was need the mate bond both created and answered. Need, not trust. Trust was up to them. She'd thought they were further along that road than this. Far enough that his first reflex would not have been to mislead her, even unconsciously. Far enough that he wouldn't shut her out.

When he spoke, his words came slowly. "The human response to pain is complex—tears, anger, the urge to defend or attack or sleep or find distraction. A wolf's response is simpler. If a wolf is wounded, he withdraws—physically, if the wound is physical. Emotionally, if it's not. I have both sets of responses, but when the pain is acute, the wolf's response dominates."

"You're saying this need for privacy is connected to your misleading me."

"The initial impulse was unhealthy. Wrong. The need for privacy, as you put it, kept me from correcting it."

"So you need to lick your wounds in private. I can understand that." She did understand. Her biggest loss had occurred when she was nine. Her best friend had been raped and killed in front of her. She'd never been able to talk out the feelings the way everyone seemed to think she should. Not then, not now. "I'm not much on talky-talky stuff, either."

"It's more than being unable to talk about my feelings. It's distance I need. A distance that hurts you."

Well, yes, it did. But . . . "You've let me tend you when you were physically hurt. You've let Nettie tend you. You know the instinct to withdraw doesn't work when a wound needs attention."

Surprise was clear in his voice when he said, "You're right."

How could she not smile? "It happens."

"But I don't . . . I don't know how to do this differently."

"Maybe you could tell me about him. About Steve."

"We were age mates. He . . . that means more, perhaps, with clan children, especially those raised at Clanhome, since we so seldom have siblings close in age. We got in trouble together." He smiled slightly. His grip on her hand eased. "For several years, he was my partner in crime."

"What kind of crimes did you commit?"

He spoke of climbing a nearby peak, of an unsupervised trip into the city, of practical jokes that sometimes worked only too well. The first two didn't surprise her; the practical jokes did.

"He sounds like he had an unlupus-like disrespect for authority."

"That's Steve." He was easy now, his hand relaxed in hers. "Before First Change especially, but even after he became an adult, he enjoyed challenging the status quo."

"Why didn't I know him?" she asked softly. Hilliard had lived in a town that bordered Clanhome. If he'd been such a close friend, why hadn't she met him?

"We . . . weren't as close in recent years as we used to be." After a moment, he added sadly, "He never had children. He wanted them desperately, but he never had children."

That wasn't unusual for a lupus. The magic that flooded their systems inhibited fertility. This was their big secret, the reason for their disdain for marriage or fidelity, for anything that lessened their chances of finding the right woman at the right time. The one who would bear them a child. "How did he deal with his disappointment?"

"Disappointment. It's a mild word, isn't it? As adults . . ." He shifted uncomfortably. "Age mates don't always remain close, but Steve and I did for many years. Even after I was named Lu Nuncio, we were close. But when Toby was born, when I had a child and he didn't . . . his longing for a child distorted him. He couldn't settle. He couldn't bear to be with those who had a son or daughter, so more and more he associated with those younger than him."

"There was a distance between you, and you hated it."

"Yes." He sighed. "The one thing that mattered was denied him, so nothing mattered greatly. He didn't sink into despair, but he made unwise choices."

"Risky choices."

He nodded. "If he'd been human, you'd have called him an adrenaline junkie. He loved high-risk sports—rock climbing, parasailing, sky diving. His first love, though, was motorcycles. He always came back to that, to his love for speed."

"Those are pretty expensive hobbies. How did he pay for them?"

"He had a motorcycle shop—repairs mostly, though he also sold used bikes. He made a decent living with it. He paid off the loan he took out to open the shop years ago."

"Who inherits?"

Rule shot her a sharp look. "Am I talking to the cop now?"

"I don't separate out that part of me the way you do your wolf."

"Fair enough. I assume you're interested in what his will says, not his private arrangements with his Rho? His will leaves everything to Jason."

"What do you mean by private arrangements?"

"We traditionally bequeath the clan its *drei*."

"I thought the *drei* was like an income tax."

"It's more of a tithe, but it also means any percentage of our personal wealth given to the clan. With an estate, it can be anything from ten percent to one hundred percent."

"But that isn't mentioned in the will."

"Traditionally, no. For centuries we've been careful not to leave a trail to our Rho in public records, and wills are public documents. Most lupi leave their estates to a clan member—a family member, if possible. Someone who will follow their private wishes, which they register with their Rho. Steve left his estate to Jason, but Jason won't retain all of it. Half will go to Nokolai."

By Nokolai, he meant his father. A clan's Rho owned all the clan's common property. As far as human law was concerned, Isen Turner was a very wealthy man. "I thought Steve lived publicly as a lupus."

"He did." Rule smiled. "When I made my public bow as Nokolai heir, Steve announced himself, too. That was his way of saying he stood by me. We weren't as close as we'd once been, but he stood by me."

"If he was known to be lupus, why the secret arrangements with his Rho?"

"Habit. Tradition. A disinclination to mess with the paperwork involved."

"As far as the local police are concerned, then, Jason Chance inherits everything."

His lip curled with scorn. "We don't kill for money."

"The local cops won't accept that as a given, and lupi do kill for other reasons. You seem pretty sure Chance didn't do it. How do you know?"

Rule shrugged. "How do we know anything about anyone? This would be wildly out of character for him. Jason's a calm soul, a beta with little interest in status. He'd be moved to violence only if there was an immediate threat. But to be sure, I'll ask him."

He meant that. He would ask Chance if he'd killed Hilliard, and if Chance denied it, Rule would believe him. That wasn't some bullshit belief in Chance's honesty. Rule claimed that no clan member could successfully lie to his Lu Nuncio.

"Earlier," Rule said, "you took my hand even though you were angry with me."

"I was pissed at you, not Nokolai. Wouldn't be good for the clan if you freaked out on an airplane."

He smiled slowly. Fully. "What color are they?"

"They?"

He stroked his thumb along the skin between her thumb and finger. "I didn't watch you dress this morning. What color are they?"

Oh. She smiled. "Leopard."

3

MORGUES in California are as chilly as those in other parts of the country. Lily was glad for her jacket—the one she hadn't gotten blood on yesterday—as she studied the pale body of a man who looked about thirty.

Caucasian, brown and blond, weight maybe one-eighty carried on a five-foot ten-inch frame. Steve Hilliard had been built like a fullback, with streaky blond hair and the sort of face that gets called all-American . . . if you think of Americans in terms of an all-white, *Andy Griffith Show* cast.

He was clean-shaven, which was typical for a lupus; Rule's father was the only one she could think of offhand who wore a full beard. No visible scars. Also typical, since lupi heal without producing scar tissue . . . unless the injury comes from a demon's poisoned claws. But demons were— thank God—rare, especially the ones with poison. Rule was the only lupus with a scar.

A quick visual told Lily that Steve Hilliard had no obvious physical flaws. Aside from the large one in his throat, that is. And as long as you didn't consider tattoos a flaw.

He didn't have a lot of dried blood on him, either. And that was odd.

"Look just like us, don't they?" the morgue attendant said.

Lily glanced at him. Morton Wright was over forty, reed-thin, with geek glasses and acne scars—not exactly Steve Hilliard's twin. But she liked the sentiment. "Lupi, you mean? Yes, they do. Some people have a problem with that."

He shrugged. "In this job, you get philosophical. Used to be, some folks got churned up about skin color. Now they worry about people turning furry or whatever. But they're all dead by the time I get to know them. Way I see it, black or white, part-time furry or not, dead is dead."

Lily didn't think everyone had gotten over the skin color thing, but she let that pass. "They do call it the great equalizer. Was Hilliard cleaned up before you got him?"

"Hell, no." Wright was offended. "We may be a Podunk little town, but we've got professionals here. We don't clean up a body before the autopsy."

"Sorry. I needed to ask. Not much blood on him, is there?"

Wright switched back to agreeable. "Not what you'd expect, huh? Not from a wound like that. You open up a guy's jugular that way, you'd expect blood to go everywhere."

"Yeah, I would." She hadn't seen the police reports yet, didn't know anything about the site where the body was found except the general location—higher up in the mountains, according to the newspaper.

It should have been a county case, dammit. Lily knew some of the county law enforcement people. But Del Cielo had drawn its city boundaries with great optimism, and they included the neglected hiking trail where Hilliard's body had been found.

A body that would be taken to the county morgue tomorrow to await autopsy. Del Cielo didn't have the facilities for that; this morgue was in the basement of their small hospital. "I'm going to get a few pictures of that tattoo."

She'd fastened her phone to her jacket pocket earlier, so unclipped it now and bent to study the tattoos ringing Hilliard's neck. The design went all the way around, like a wide, lacy choker interrupted by the gaping wound across the front of his throat. The tattoo was intricate and nonpictorial—no images of flowers or daggers or whatever. No words or recognizable symbols.

Recognizable to her, anyway. Briefly, fiercely, she wished for Cynna, whose body was covered in tattoos rather like this one. Tattoos that were actually spells.

But Cynna was in another realm . . . alive, Lily reminded herself. Alive and doing okay, according to the optimism she'd promised herself for another three months. She raised her phone and took pictures of the tattoo from various angles, then had the attendant roll the body on its side so she could get the rest of the pattern, which went all the way around.

Finally she put her phone away. "I'll need to scrub before I do the rest."

Wright nodded amiably. "Sure. You explained about that. Sink's to your left."

Lily scrubbed thoroughly. The body hadn't been autopsied yet, and though it was unlikely the lab results would be useful—body fluids from those of the Blood tended to screw up lab results, even after death—she'd do this by the book. "Did you know Jason Chance?" she asked casually.

"Sure. The chief's wrong there," Wright said. "So were the *jefes*. Jason's a good guy. Shouldn't've fired him."

Jason Chance was the lupus the police had locked up pending formal charges. He was also a nurse. It was not the profession where Lily expected to find a part-time wolf, and it made her curious about him in a nonprofessional way.

She returned to the body. "Did Jason come see you when he visited Hilliard?"

"Naw. Not this time, anyway. Last time he was in town he did."

Lily nodded. Then she laid her bare fingertips on the edges of the wound.

Cold, flaccid skin. A few flakes of dried blood. Nothing else. She probed gently inside the wound. Still nothing.

One more place to check. She touched an intact part of the tattoo on the side of Hilliard's neck. The tingle of magic was faint—too faint for her to identify the type. But it was, by God, present. "Mr. Wright—"

"What the *hell* are you doing?" demanded a tenor voice that did not belong to the morgue attendant.

Lily straightened and turned. The man who'd just entered was fat and freckled with thick, gingery red hair. Very Auld Sod. He wore a khaki uniform and badge, a hip holster, and a scowl.

The voice went with the scowl. "Morton, you'd better have a good explanation for letting this—"

Lily interrupted coolly. "He does. Would you be Chief Daly?"

"I am. Who the hell are you?"

"Special Agent Lily Yu, FBI. I left several messages for you."

"And just what are you doing here, messing with evidence?"

Lily raised her eyebrows. "Obviously you don't respond to your messages. Do you not listen to them, either?"

He waved that away. "I got your goddamned message. You want to stick your nose into my murder case. That doesn't give you the right to go messing with the victim's body, messing up evidence. You don't even have goddamned gloves on."

"Which is why I scrubbed first. I'm a touch sensitive. I can't gather information with gloves on."

"You're *what*?"

"A sensitive," Wright said helpfully. "You know, one of those folks who can feel magic when they touch it. Like on that old show, *Touching Fire*—you remember it? With Michelle Pfeiffer and that guy—I can't remember his name, but he played in—"

"Jesus Christ, Morton, spare me. I know what a sensitive is. I don't know what Agent Yu here hopes to prove by feeling up a dead werewolf."

Oh, yeah. Working with this red-headed ape was going to be fun. "Since you've torn yourself away from your other duties to speak with me, Chief Daly, perhaps we could take this discussion somewhere less chilly."

"Not much to discuss. You're butting out."

"No. I'm not. I need to wash up." She didn't wait for a

response, heading back to the sink she'd used before. "I understand the body was found by a hiker."

"That's right. He was found within city limits, which makes this my case. Nothing to do with you."

She turned, drying her hands. "No? Where's the blood?"

"You think I don't know your type?" One thick finger jabbed in her general direction. "Publicity hound. Gets you plenty of attention, doesn't it, swooping in here and stirring things up, calling the press to feed them whatever crap you think will get you a headline."

"You don't know me, Chief. I have not and will not contact the press, and I sincerely hope no one else does, either. I need to see the reports you have on this case."

"Yeah, well, I need a vacation. Doesn't mean it'll happen."

"I have the authority to require your cooperation." She returned to her purse, extracted the little folder with her badge, and showed it to him.

Lily was with Unit 12 of the Magical Crimes Division of the FBI. Prior to the Turning, people knew about MCD, but the Unit had been a well-kept secret. Almost all its agents were Gifted, and the Gifted were not trusted. After the Turning, Congress flip-flopped, giving the Unit rather broad powers. Too broad, according to some. Lily was careful not to abuse her authority . . . however tempting it might be at times like this.

Daly pulled a small notebook out of his shirt pocket and wrote down her badge number. "I'll check this out."

"Of course." Lily slipped the badge back in her purse. "Why don't you call now? I'd like to see those reports as soon as possible."

"I said I'd check. Don't you try to throw your weight around."

Morton Wright chuckled. Both of them looked at him.

"Hey," he said, holding up both hands. "Don't shoot me. Just thought it was funny, that's all, Pete, you warning that bitty little thing not to throw her weight around. She doesn't have much of it to throw."

That brought a smile, however reluctant, to Daly's

freckled face. "Guess not. Listen, Yu . . . damn, that's awkward. Your name, I mean."

She smiled wryly. "I know. But it provides amusement for so many people—'Hey, Yu! This is me—is this Yu?'"

He snorted. "Bet you've heard 'em all. I guess I came down a little hard."

"Not a problem." At least she hoped it wouldn't be. They were connecting better now. "At the moment, Chief, I don't know if this is my case or not, but it could be. Magic was used on that tattoo."

"Well, shit, I guess it would have to be, wouldn't it? Can't tattoo a werewolf without magic to make it stick. But the slice to his throat wasn't magic."

"No, but if magic incapacitated him, or prevented that slice from healing—"

"Is that possible?" He frowned heavily, then glanced at his watch. "I'm supposed to meet with one of my detectives in ten minutes. Going to be late."

"I'll walk out with you. Mr. Wright—"

"Morton," he said amiably.

"Morton, it was good to meet you. I like your philosophy. Chief," she said as she headed with him toward the door, "what's your theory about the lack of blood on the body?"

"Don't have one, but I'll be asking my people to account for it. My people." He snorted again and shoved the door, which opened into a small anteroom almost as cheerless as the morgue itself—cement walls and floor, battered file cabinets, a single desk for Morton Wright. "Don't mean to make it sound like I've got dozens on this case. I don't have dozens in the whole damned department. I meant the Medical Examiner and the detective who's got the case. She's county, of course—the ME—not one of mine, but we've worked together a long time now. She's solid."

He'd sure mellowed. "That would be Alicia Chavez, and I agree—she's solid. She's got good people under her, too. Do you have an idea when Hilliard was killed?"

"Tuesday night, probably between eleven and three A.M. That's unofficial, but it fits with when Hilliard was last seen."

"Who saw him last?"

"Other than the killer, that would be Amos McPherson, over at the Stop-N-Shop. You know Dr. Chavez? I'm taking the stairs," he added, headed that way. There was an elevator, of course, for the gurneys that carried the bodies to the morgue. It was painfully slow, so she didn't blame him for avoiding it. "I spend too damned much time at my desk. Need to move when I get the chance. Doctor doesn't like my blood pressure."

"Stairs are fine." She started up them behind him. "I used to work homicide in San Diego, so I've worked with Dr. Chavez and her staff."

"So you weren't always a Fibbie."

"No, that's a fairly recent change."

"What did you call Dr. Chavez about?" By the time the chief reached the top of the stairs, he was breathing heavily

"I needed to let her know to check for gado."

He pushed the door open. "Gado?"

"It's a possibility. I told her she could send the samples to our lab. No need for the town or the county to cover that expense."

"That's . . ." He stiffened, his voice trailing off.

His bulk completely blocked her view. "What is it?"

He spun around, his face distorted by fury. "You—you—I knew I'd heard your name someplace! Trying to make out like you're so professional—well, that won't work now!"

His face was so red the freckles had disappeared. "Maybe you should calm down. That can't be good for your blood pressure."

She thought he'd explode. "You—"

Rule's voice, smooth as silk, came from the other side of the furious man. "Congratulations on that promotion, Pete. Lily's right. You want to watch your blood pressure. I'd recommend anger management therapy."

Daly pulled himself together, but the color stayed high in his face. He didn't say a word. His hands were fisted at his sides as he marched off down the short hall.

Rule watched him, a small smile on his mouth, his hands shoved casually in the pockets of his jacket. His eyes were snake-cold.

The hall they were in seemed to be part of the administrative section. Lily could hear voices from an open doorway at one end; three closed doors studded the hall in the direction Daly took. He marched to a door at that end, jerked it open, and let it slam behind him.

"Oh, geez," Lily muttered. "Why didn't you warn me the two of you had a history? I had him ready to cooperate. Then he saw you."

"I said that the cops here weren't trustworthy. You didn't ask how I knew." Rule was still watching the door Daly had used. Slowly his gaze shifted to her. "Five years ago, Pete Daly—he was a detective at the time—tried to beat Steve to death. A difficult task, considering how fast we heal, but he did his best."

Her eyes narrowed. "Well, he's a bastard, then, and a disgrace to the uniform, but what did you do to him? Because that isn't the way a man reacts to someone he despises. Despises would mean he won, and he didn't. He's scared shitless of you."

"Ah." Now Rule looked at her, and his smile turned genuine. "Very insightful. To answer your question, I did nothing to Pete. How could I? He was an officer of the law. I was newly and publicly revealed as a lupus. I did nothing to him . . . over and over and over."

She studied him a moment. He was truly relaxed now. Before he'd faked it, posing to look at ease in the presence of his enemy, announcing how little he considered Daly a threat.

Dominance games. He was good at them. "You stalked him," she announced.

His smile widened. "I do love your twisty mind. How did—" A door opened in the short hall and a middle-aged woman glanced at them as she emerged from the office. "Perhaps we should discuss this elsewhere," Rule murmured and took Lily's hand.

"Quit that." She pulled her hand free. "I can't wander around holding hands when I'm investigating. You ever see a cop holding hands on duty? Or an FBI agent," she remembered to add. The woman *click-clicked* her four-inch heels down the hall toward the door Daly had used. "Come on. Explain while we head to the car. You can start by telling me why you were here waiting for me. Or for Chief Daly?"

"That's simple enough. I spoke with Jason's former supervisor, as I told you I planned to do, but she's on shift and couldn't give me much time."

"That wasn't exactly what I asked. I suppose you heard Daly talking to me on the stairs and that gave you time to pose for him. What did you learn from Chance's former supervisor? Was he or she responsible for him getting fired?"

Rule opened the door, holding it for her. "No, and they remained friends afterward."

The hall opened onto the hospital lobby with a Pink Lady station, tiny gift shop, the main exit, and a couple elevators. "He was fired after coming out as a lupus, you said."

"Jason didn't announce it openly the way Steve did. He simply stopped hiding certain things, such as his visits to Clanhome, and let others draw their own conclusions. They did. He was fired."

"He found another job pretty quickly." He'd moved to San Diego for it, but Rule said he returned to Del Cielo sometimes to see Hilliard, who'd lived here. He'd been here on such a visit when Steve was killed.

"The nursing shortage," Rule said dryly, "is acute. His current employers don't want to know if their suspicions about him are true, and Jason doesn't speak of Clanhome at work."

"Don't ask, don't tell."

"Pretty much, yes."

"I always ask."

Rule's grin flashed. "I know."

"Like right now, I'm asking why you brought me to the elevator instead of the exit."

He pushed the third-floor button. "So you could speak with Jason's former supervisor, too. She's a lovely older woman named Lupe. I thought she might be able to alibi him, and that he, for chivalrous reasons, had failed to mention this to the police."

Lily quirked an eyebrow. "She's that kind of friend?"

"Unlike you, I don't always ask. But if their relationship did include intimacy, it would be very like Jason to protect her by concealing that."

The elevator door opened. Three people got out; Lily followed Rule on. He usually took elevators even though he hated them. More like because he hated them. They were so small. "You like Jason."

"I do."

"Since you didn't open your story with the alibi, I take it there isn't one."

"Unfortunately, no. He did stop by to see her, but he did so here at the hospital, while she was at work. Since it's believed Steve was killed at night . . . unless that has changed?"

"I did get that much confirmed by Daly," she said, irritated all over again. "Between eleven and three A.M., he said. Getting anything else is going to be like pulling teeth. I'll pull them, but it won't be fun. Why do I want to talk to Lupe? And what's her last name?"

"Lupe Valdez. You'll talk to her because she's Robert Friar's nearest neighbor."

"Robert Friar? The guy who started Humans First?"

"Yes. She tells me that Chief Daly is a member."

4

LUPE Valdez, the senior charge nurse in orthopedics, was around fifty and maybe twenty pounds overweight, with thin lips, an asymmetric nose, and a weak chin. Even in her shining youth, most people probably wouldn't have called her lovely.

But her hair was glorious—thick and black, worn long and pinned up. Her smile was warm, and she moved with the lightness of a dancer. To Rule, she undoubtedly was lovely.

Lily wondered if Lupe smelled lovely, too. Lupi were a lot more scent-oriented than humans. "Ms. Valdez, I appreciate your willingness to talk with me." She held out a hand.

"Lupe," the woman said, taking Lily's hand without hesitation and giving a brisk shake. "Call me Lupe. I'm glad if anything I can tell you helps Jason. You want some coffee?"

They were in the crowded alcove that served as a break room. Lily glanced at the coffeepot, thought it looked reasonably fresh, and decided to take a chance. "Sure. Thanks. Black, please."

While Lupe poured two cups, after making sure Rule didn't want any—he didn't, coffee snob that he was—Lily sat at a table slightly bigger than a handkerchief and took out her notebook and pen.

Lupe Valdez had a hint of an accent and more than a hint of a healing Gift. Lily would bet her patients recovered faster than the norm. If she'd managed to find training for her Gift, some of her patients recovered more fully than their doctors expected, too. If she'd found another sort of training, she could have tattooed that design around Steve Hilliard's neck.

Rule parked himself against the wall, leaning there with arms crossed. Lily waited until the other woman was sitting across from her to begin. "I understand you and Jason kept in touch after he left town."

Her smile was small and private. "You could say that. He always stopped by to see me when he visited Steve . . . sometimes here, sometimes at home."

"But not on the night he was killed."

"Unfortunately, no. He dropped by here that day, spoke with me awhile, but I didn't see him that night."

"For the record, I need to know where you were the night of Tuesday, April twenty-eighth."

"At home. My daughter was home, too, since it was a weeknight. Sarita has to be home by eight on weeknights."

"No other company?"

"No. Well, one of Sarita's friends was there until ten—Lori's got a license and her mother lets her use her car a lot. I'm divorced," she added. "I don't know if Rule told you or not, but I'm divorced, so it's just me and Sarita at home now that Annie is at college."

"Annie? Is she your other daughter?"

She nodded. "Her full name's Anna Maria after her grandmother, but she's gone by Annie since she started school. She's at UCLA. They're on a quarter system there instead of semesters, did you know? She doesn't get to come home till the end of the spring quarter. Not till June."

"You must miss her. How old is Sarita?"

"Sixteen. She'll take driver's ed this summer." She smiled wryly. "I'm not looking forward to that nearly as much as she is."

"I'll bet. Did you know Steve Hilliard?"

She shrugged. "Slightly. We'd met a few times. I knew he and Jason were tight."

"You knew they were both lupus."

"Yes. I knew about Jason before he . . . well, before most people did. And Steve was open about his nature." She glanced at Rule. "That is, he was after you made your big announcement. That's been, what—five years now?"

Rule smiled. "Six."

Lily jotted down the names and info Lupe had given her. "You and Jason are good friends." She kept her head down so she didn't seem to be watching Lupe, but she was. She saw the glance Lupe gave Rule before she answered.

"Good friends," she said firmly. "He introduced me to another friend. Maybe you know her. Nettie Two-Horses."

Lily looked up, smiling. "I do. Nettie's one of my favorite people. Did she help you with your Gift?"

Lupe jerked back, frowning.

"Maybe Rule didn't tell you. I'm Gifted, too. I'm a sensitive."

"Oh. No, he didn't. He didn't mention that."

"I kept it secret for years, but that's not working for me anymore. I don't use my Gift to out people, Lupe. You don't have to worry about that. Rule tells me you live close to Robert Friar."

Her upper lip lifted. "That *nacimiento póstumo*."

"I haven't heard that one before."

"It means afterbirth. It's from an old saying that I made up." When she smiled this time, a dimple winked mischievously in one cheek. "Do you have pets, Agent Yu?"

"Uh . . . yes." Though Dirty Harry probably saw things the other way around. "A tomcat. He's neutered now, but don't tell him."

"You may not be aware that after giving birth, many animal mothers will eat the afterbirth to keep the den clean. What I say about Robert Friar is that his poor mother was confused—she ate the baby and raised the afterbirth."

"You really don't like the man."

Lupe leaned forward suddenly and grabbed Lily's hand.

"He is evil. Evil. He killed Steve, I am sure of it. You will find the evidence and arrest him, and Jason will go free. You must."

Softly Lily asked, "Why are you sure Friar killed Steve Hilliard?"

"He hates lupi. Everyone knows he hates lupi and all the Gifted, anyone tainted by magic. That's his word, *tainted*."

"There must be more than that, for you to be so certain."

She snorted. Some of her intensity faded, but she didn't release Lily's hand. "You ask him. Ask Robert Friar about his daughter, Mariah."

"All right. What can you tell me about her?"

"She had a baby two months ago, a little boy. She claims he's Steve's son."

IT was late in the afternoon in late April, the sun was shining, and Lily was almost too warm in her lightweight jacket.

That was as it should be. Why did cold weather, snow, and ice get such great press when it sucked? Of course, not everyone was lucky enough to live in San Diego.

"Why so smug?" Rule asked.

"Did you know that the U.S. Weather Service calls San Diego's weather the most nearly perfect in the country?" To be fair she added, "Hawaii's supposed to be nice, too."

He laughed. "You're glad to be home."

"Yeah." Even for a little while, and even if she wasn't exactly home. Maybe Rule's condo was supposed to be home now, but it wasn't hers. She didn't pay for anything there except some of the groceries. Which reminded her . . . "The lease comes due on my apartment next month."

"Hmm."

She glanced at him. "You're not going to tell me how stupid it is for me to keep paying rent when we're living together and your place is so much bigger?"

"Why would I tell you what you already know? You'll keep the apartment if you feel a need. If not, you'll let it go."

She walked beside him for a few steps in silence. "If I weren't investigating, I'd hold your hand right now."

Promptly he took hers.

"Hey." But she didn't pull away. She told herself no one would notice—they were mostly blocked from view by the parked cars. "Mariah Friar's baby. He isn't Steve's son, is he?"

"No. It's not uncommon for a woman to claim one of us as the father. Sometimes they believe it to be true. Sometimes they hope for support, emotional or financial or both. Sometimes they want the notoriety."

"Hmm." She accepted Rule's word as both honest and accurate. He would know. Lupi never had to play who's-the-dad. When a lupus impregnated a woman, he was instantly aware of it.

Lily might not have believed that if she hadn't been almost present when it happened once. Cynna and Cullen had made love in the next room, not in front of her—and thank God for that—but there was no doubt in her mind that Cullen had known immediately that his seed had caught.

Any lupus blessed with a child notified his Rho ASAP. One as desperate for a child as Hilliard had been would have announced it to the entire clan. Certainly to his oldest friend. "So, how exactly did you stalk Chief Daly?"

"I don't know why I thought you might forget to ask about that."

"I don't, either."

He flashed her a grin. "Smart-ass. All right. For about a month, I made sure good old Pete saw a lot of me. Sometimes two or three times a day. We'd run into each other at the post office or Joe's Burgers—he likes the chili burger with extra jalapeños. Sometimes I'd skip a couple days. Doesn't do to be predictable."

"That's enough to make him mad, not to make him sweat. He started sweating when he saw you."

"Some of the places where I ran into him would have been unexpected."

"Such as?"

"Now and then I'd wait for him to come home after a long day's work—he's divorced, lives alone—have a little chat, and leave as soon as he fell asleep."

She stopped walking. "He fell asleep with you there? You

broke into the chief of police's house, and he went to sleep instead of arresting you?"

"It was an apartment, actually, and he wasn't the chief then. And I had a little charm Cullen made for me."

"A sleep charm."

"Worked beautifully, too. So did the other charm Cullen gave me."

"And that was?"

He smiled, but his eyes were hard. "A confusion charm. Poor Pete wasn't sure of anything. What time did he see me? What day? He had a couple patrollers keeping an eye on me by then, but they swore I'd never gone near his place on the night he thought I'd showed up."

"He didn't even know which night you were there? Surely he could work it out."

"He'd wake up with the last few days jumbled. He wasn't sure when anything happened."

"That's . . . chilling."

"He was the chief detective in a town that borders Clanhome. Steve wasn't the first lupus he'd picked up for trivial or manufactured reasons and beaten. We heal so conveniently well, you see, that there are never any marks later. He needed to know he'd pay a price for indulging his little hobby."

"Did he do that to you?" she demanded. "Did he beat you?"

Something flickered in his eyes, too brief for her to read it. "No. But those he did hurt were mine to protect."

She frowned as she started walking again. "I've never heard of a confusion charm. How hard is it to make?"

"The confusion charm is Cullen's own creation, and he called it fiendishly difficult. I doubt anyone else has one, at least in this realm, though I suppose it's possible Cullen traded one for something at some point."

"Hmm. He probably wouldn't trade the spell itself."

"He's possessive about that sort of thing," Rule agreed. "We've reached the car."

So they had. It was a plain white sedan that all but shouted "I am a government vehicle." One of the regular agents assigned to the San Diego office had brought it to her at the airport. Someone from Nokolai was bringing Rule his car, but she wasn't sure who or when.

Just as Lily clicked the lock, Rule's phone chimed. He pulled it out, frowned. "I missed a call. Reception's not great in the mountains, but I've got bars here."

"Could be a bit of magical interference." One of the things magic interfered with most easily was cell phones. "Is there a node nearby?"

"A small one, I think. I'd better return this one," Rule said. He did so while they both got into the car. Lily started the engine, thinking about what she knew about sleep charms.

They worked on demons, though not as well as they did on humans.

They had to be touching whoever they were used on.

They weren't hard to make—at least not for Cullen, but sorcerers were at least as rare as sensitives. Cullen was the only one she knew about. Sorcerers had an edge on other practitioners in that they could see the magic they worked with. According to Cullen, that was like the difference between an electrician who could see the wiring and one who couldn't, but had a good idea of where the wires were supposed be.

Something had persuaded Hilliard to hold still while he was tattooed. She wasn't ruling out the possibility he'd done so voluntarily, but considered that less likely than force or coercion. With force . . . lupi could be knocked out, and the evidence was hard to find afterward, given the way they healed. But it took a lot of force. A sleep charm would be easier.

Would it be more certain, too?

Lily was pulling out of the parking lot when Rule disconnected. "Do sleep charms work on lupi?" she asked.

"Yes. They don't trigger our healing, since sleep is a natural state, so the effect is the same on us as it is on humans. Lily, we need to go to the jail."

"We are. I want to talk with Chance. If sleep charms work on you, why aren't they used when you need surgery?"

"They work, but not that comprehensively. Cullen's charm won't keep a lupus asleep through surgery. We've tried. Theoretically, someone could make a stronger sleep charm than Cullen can, but—"

"But I won't tell him you said so." She smiled to show she meant it. Cullen would return and she'd have the chance to avoid mentioning that, theoretically, someone might be better at one of the magical arts than he. "Tattoo needles don't penetrate as far as a surgeon's scalpel. Maybe they wouldn't hurt enough to interfere with a sleep charm."

He shrugged. "Perhaps. A higher level of pain might break the charm. Cullen believes it's the sheer disruption of surgery. Our healing takes no notice of spells, but it pays keen attention to our being cut open."

"Nettie can put you in sleep deeply enough to last through surgery."

"Nettie is a healer, and a Gift is always more effective than a spell-wrought effect. Plus, that particular skill of hers depends as much on the spiritual as the magical."

Lily knew that, since Nettie had actually put *her* in sleep. It shouldn't have worked. Magic did not affect her.

But Nettie's version of it did. Lily chose not to think about that. She signaled for a turn. "Who was on the phone?"

"Hal Newman."

"The defense attorney. He's with, uh . . . Cone, Levy, Rayner and Newman." She'd seen Newman in action once, though thankfully not on a case of hers. He was far too good at what he did.

"That's right. My father uses their firm, and Hal is representing Jason. He's arranged bond. Jason will be released as soon as Hal presents the necessary papers to the jailer."

"That was fast."

"Hal's a good attorney. He's meeting us at the jail. I need to be the first one into Jason's cell."

"What?" She glanced at him as she slowed. They'd reached the city jail, which was part of the local cop shop. "You know I can't arrange that. They'll have a guard bring him out."

"Jason has been locked up for twenty-four hours. He is uncomfortable in small, enclosed spaces."

Uh-oh. She should have thought of that. "As uncomfortable as you are?"

"Somewhat more so."

5

HAL Newman's white hair, silver-rimmed glasses, and char-coal gray suit fit the image of a top-flight defense attorney. He was California-fit and probably had his plastic surgeon on speed dial, judging by the smooth skin and general lack of sagging. He had the handshake down, too—just firm enough, neither hasty nor lingering.

The distinct tingle of magic when their palms touched didn't go with the image. It went with someone who turned furry on occasion—and would never need a plastic surgeon.

Lily shot Rule a glance. He smiled blandly.

No wonder the clan used Newman. He *was* clan. "Mr. Newman," she said, "I understand you have some recommendations concerning Mr. Chance's release that Chief Daly is reluctant to allow."

The chief looked smug. "We follow procedure here."

They were in the chief's office—her, Rule, Newman, and the chief jailer, a morose fellow named Hawes. It was crowded. Daly was no neatnik, and he hadn't bothered to shift the piles of papers from the single visitor's chair to let any of them sit.

Lily gave Daly a nod. "It's usually best to do so. What are

your procedures for releasing a lupus after he's been incarcerated for over twenty-four hours?"

"We're supposed to treat them like everyone else now, so that's what we'll do. Follow the same procedure we would for anyone else."

"Under the law"—Newman had a deep, rolling baritone—"equal treatment does not necessarily mean identical treatment. Some classes of prisoners require different treatment. A wheelchair-bound prisoner, for example. Minors, obviously. And the courts have consistently ruled that visually impaired persons must be—"

"Stuff the legal mumbo-jumbo." Daly leaned back in his chair, convinced he had the upper hand. "Jason Chance isn't blind or in a wheelchair. He isn't a minor. He's an able-bodied adult and he can walk out of here just fine on his own two legs." He smirked. "Once he's on two legs again, that is."

And that was the problem. Under the law, Chance had to be treated as having all the rights and responsibilities of citizenship when he was shaped like a human. Unfortunately, Daly now had a wolf locked up. Shortly before his lawyer arrived, Jason Chance had succumbed to his instinctive response to his race's claustrophobia. He'd Changed.

If Daly weren't a turd, that wouldn't matter. Rule could tell Chance to Change back. Rule possessed the heir's portion of the clan's mantle; even beast-lost, Chance would obey his Lu Nuncio. But Daly refused to allow Rule into the cell, or even into the jail itself. He refused to allow Newman in, too—"can't take chances with a wild animal like that. He's vicious. Likely he'd savage you."

And when Newman insisted he was entitled to see his client, Daly had said, "Wolves don't have attorneys."

Legally, he was right.

"What," Rule asked in a low voice, "do you intend to do with Jason?"

"Why, not a thing. But that wolf, now, he can't stay here. That's obvious. This is a jail for humans. Don't worry—I wouldn't do anything inhumane." Blue eyes glittered with malice and pleasure. "He'll be tranq'ed before we move him. Got an expert coming with a dart gun."

Rule's voice dropped even lower. "Tranquilizers don't work on lupi."

Daly's eyes opened wide in mock surprise. "You sure? Because if he can't be sedated, we do have a problem. The way that beast is acting, well . . ." He shook his head. "Can't take chances, and that animal is dangerous. I've already had to move the other prisoners out of that cell block, which creates a hazard. Can't keep them stacked up three or four to a cell."

This time, Rule growled. The sound was eerily like a wolf's, not the weak imitation a human throat makes.

Lily put a hand on his arm. His muscles were rigid. But a quick glance told her his eyes were still brown, not black-swallowed. He was in control.

She took a few seconds to consider options. Was Daly crazy enough to think he could get away with shooting Chance in wolf form? Maybe he just intended Rule to think he would. Maybe he wanted Rule to jump him so he'd have an excuse to lock Rule up, too.

Or maybe he meant it. He might really have one of his people shoot Chance. It wasn't illegal to shoot a wolf—not if the animal could be considered a danger to others. Not even if it was only a part-time wolf, and killing him meant killing the human, too. Daly might believe he could get away with it—a beast-lost lupus *was* a danger, no doubt about that.

If he had been free he would be, that is. Which was the whole problem.

"All right," she said crisply. "You've made your position clear, Chief Daly. Officer Hawes, please escort me to your prisoner."

The jailer blinked. "Uh—don't have a prisoner now. He's a wolf, and a wolf isn't a prisoner."

Which meant that legally they could do all sorts of things to him. Things that would keep him panicked and furious, unable to reason, unable to understand that he was better off in his other form. They'd keep him beast-lost because Daly wanted him that way. "Then let me put it this way. You have a witness I need to see in one of your cells, and I don't care what form he's wearing. I require immediate access to that witness."

Daly remained complacent. "Sorry. Can't do it. That animal's crazy, and until we have him subdued—"

"Chief." She stepped up to his desk and looked down at him. "You can't stop me."

"I for damn sure can. This is *my* jail, under *my* authority, and I'm responsible for—"

"I've presented you with my badge. You've had time to confirm that I am, indeed, an agent of Unit Twelve of the Magical Crimes Division of the FBI. Under the Domestic Security and Magical Crimes Law as amended on January tenth of this year, *you cannot stop me*. If you continue to try, I will arrest you for impeding my investigation."

His mouth opened. Closed. Red arose in a vascular tide to suffuse his face. Finally he spoke in a voice all but strangled with fury. "You wouldn't dare."

There were all sorts of things she might have said or done to defuse the situation, ways she could show respect for his position while insisting on her own authority.

Lily didn't even try. She planted her hands on his desk and leaned forward until her face was a foot from his. His breath smelled like stale chili. The veins stood out in his neck and forehead, and his freckles were pale splotches in his red face.

Her lips curled up. Softly she said, "Try me."

Hatred burned in his eyes. "You'll regret this. You're going to regret this for a real long time."

The Del Cielo jail was larger than expected for a town this small, but the city rented spaces to the state—and given the state's overcrowded system, it had no trouble funding the operation of its jail this way.

The setup was pretty standard. Probably built in the fifties, Lily thought, with cinderblock walls and cement floors. There were two cell blocks, each opening off a small control center with three screens—one for the hall splitting each cell bock, apparently. The third was dark.

Lily had suspicions about that dark screen. "Got a problem with your cameras?" she asked as Daly jammed a key into the old-fashioned lock on a heavy steel door.

He didn't answer. Didn't even look at her.

The moment the door opened, she heard the growling. Daly stepped aside and gestured for her to precede him.

She didn't like that, didn't want the man at her back. He hated too much; she didn't know his limits. But neither could she afford to look weak. She walked through the door.

There were three cells plus a shower on one side, four cells on the other. And two officers with high-powered rifles trained on the occupant of the fourth cell.

Something too pure to be called anger sizzled through Lily. She felt as if her hair should have bristled. She felt as if she could growl, too.

The sonofabitch. The stinking sonofabitch had intended to do it. He'd meant to arrange Chance's death. The stage was all set.

Unconsciously she brushed the large shirt she'd donned in lieu of her jacket. Rule's shirt, imbued with his scent. How far would Daly's hatred take him? Lily walked slowly down the short hall, watching the men with the guns. They were nervous. Their eyes flicked to her. One said, "Chief—"

"Shut up, Mills," Daly said from behind her.

"Agent Yu, FBI," Lily said crisply. "Your chief isn't happy with me right now, or he would have introduced us. Stand down with your weapons."

The two men looked at their boss. "No," he said tersely. "You don't command my men, Agent."

"Idiot," she said just as crisply. Then she reached the cell.

The wolf was small, for a lupus—which meant he was only twenty or so pounds heavier than an average wolf. His teeth were whiter than usual for a canid—but then, he brushed them in his other form. They were also large and bared. He had a lovely coat, brindled gray, with the hackles raised fully. His ears were flat. A continuous growl issued from deep in his chest.

He was backed up against the far wall.

A beta, Rule had said. He'd fight if threatened. He felt extremely threatened at the moment, and who wouldn't? He was also a man, even if the man was buried deep at the moment. He knew what those rifles meant.

Lily moved close to the bars of the cell, positioning herself carefully.

"Agent Yu?" one of the officers said. "You're blocking my shot."

"That's the idea. If you shoot that wolf, I will arrest you."

"He's dangerous, ma'am."

"He wouldn't be, if he'd been handled correctly. I'm sorry to say that your chief is a bloody, bigoted fool. If he's given you orders to shoot if the wolf moves"—and he had, the craven bastard; she saw it in the way the officer's gaze flickered—"you will disregard those orders. Jason Chance is my witness, and I will not allow you to tamper with my witness."

The man was confused, uncertain. The other one was cut more from Daly's cloth. He sneered and shifted position, keeping his rifle trained.

She moved with him, blocking his shot—and took her phone out of the shirt pocket. "Perhaps I should mention that I'm on an open line right now, transmitting images to FBI headquarters in Washington. Smile for the camera." She held out her phone.

Daly took an involuntary step back. "That's a phone, not a web cam."

"That's right. It's my new iPhone. Cool, isn't it? Want to see?" She turned it so he could see the screen—which showed his two men with their rifles trained on the cell's bars.

The rest was anticlimax.

Daly left. His men stayed, but lowered their weapons. She sat on the floor and waited, carefully not looking at the wolf. Sure enough, after about five minutes he approached—still bristling, still growling, but with his ears pricked.

He wanted to know why she smelled like his Lu Nuncio. She told him, subvocalizing—which both kept the officers from hearing and let him know she was clan. No one outside the clans would think to do it.

He stopped growling.

She showed him the necklace she wore, the *toltoi* charm she'd been given to mark her status as Chosen.

He dropped to the floor, whining submissively.

"You're getting out," she assured him. "Rule's here. Your lawyer's here, and bail's been posted. But we need you two-legged. Can you Change back?"

Ten minutes later, Lily left the cell block with a young man who looked like every cliché of a California surfer dude—sun-streaked blond hair, athletic body, and a quick, white grin. He wore ragged jeans and a blue T-shirt with a stylized wave.

The clothes had been on the floor of his cell. And he probably wasn't as young as he looked.

6

BOBBIE'S Grill was Rule's suggestion. The food, he said, was nothing special, but it arrived quickly and the portions were generous. Speed and portion size mattered for the same reason they were eating supper so early: the Change burns calories, and a hungry wolf is an edgy wolf.

Besides, his stomach was on the same clock as hers, and hers said it was after eight. On the way there, Lily checked her official email and found that the request for the police reports on Hilliard's death was still pending. Big surprise.

She also saw that the photos she'd sent of the tattoo had been passed to Arjenie Fox, a young witch who worked in research. Arjenie was good. Lily sent her a quick note asking to be contacted as soon as she knew anything.

Once they arrived, Lily saw one more reason Rule had chosen Bobbie's. It had outdoor seating. At this hour, the majority of customers were rushing home from work and opting for take-out, so they had the patio to themselves. The low wall around the patch of cement didn't do much to reduce traffic noise or provide privacy, but the openness would be soothing to a claustrophobic lupus newly released from a cell.

Another plus: fish tacos. "Did you know they don't have fish tacos in D.C.?" she asked Jason as Rule put down the plastic trays with their order.

"You're kidding." He shook his head and reached for the salsa. "How could they not, a cosmopolitan place like that?"

"They've never even heard of fish tacos." Lily grabbed her tacos and began doctoring them with extra shredded cabbage, a generous dollop of salsa, and pickles. Rule had had to ask for the pickles; for some reason they weren't a universally approved accompaniment for fish tacos.

"Go figure." Jason said that around a healthy mouthful of tortilla and batter-fried fish. He swallowed. "That was so cool, what you did with the phone. I didn't know you could do that—make it work like a web cam."

"I don't think you can." Lily decided the tacos needed more salsa and spooned it on. "At least, I know I can't."

"It was a bluff?" Jason hooted and slapped his thigh. "Man, I'd like to be a fly on the wall when Daly realizes you bluffed him."

Rule frowned. "What are you talking about?"

"Daly had a pair of officers training rifles on Jason," she explained. "With orders to shoot if he moved. I had to persuade him he couldn't get away with it, and I was short on options."

Jason turned to Rule. "I wish you'd seen it. She's got guts. They were aimed for me, so she stepped up between me and their guns. Told 'em their chief was a bloody idiot." Jason grinned. "And when they didn't—"

Rule broke in, his voice flat. "You stepped in front of their rifles."

Uh-oh. Rule hadn't been thrilled about her going in there alone in the first place. "I needed to interfere with their line of fire."

"Dammit, Lily, Jason can heal most wounds! You promised me—"

"I promised I wouldn't get in the cell with Jason until he Changed back. I didn't." But Jason had never been the main threat. Lily's pleasure in the fish taco faded. She put it down and said quietly, "He's a bad cop, Rule. Daly's not just a bully with a badge. If he hasn't yet killed, using the badge to protect himself, he will."

He met her eyes. She saw the turbulence in him, the desire to go back and tear Daly apart. Maybe rip down the jail, too. After a moment he grimaced. "I suppose now you'll tell me it must have been a good decision, since you're still alive."

"He intended to kill Jason. I wasn't sure about that until I saw how he'd set the stage. I interfered with his plans, but he was damn near mad enough to go ahead anyway. So I bluffed."

Jason spoke—more subdued now, but with a stubborn set to his jaw. "She handled herself. Handled Daly, too. She told him her phone was transmitting images to FBI headquarters. He bought it. Hell, I did, too . . . well, not immediately, because I was beast-lost at the time." He flushed beneath his tan. "I'm sorry for that. I couldn't . . . I knew I shouldn't Change, but I felt so trapped, I—"

"It's all right, Jason." Rule managed a wry smile. "I understand the experience, believe me."

"You wouldn't have given in. You wouldn't have Changed."

"I'm Lu Nuncio. You aren't. Why would you expect yourself to behave as if you were?"

Jason's grin flickered. "Just as well I don't, isn't it?"

Rule's phone sang out the opening bars from Mozart's *Night Music*. That meant it was his father. Lily turned to Hal Newman while Rule answered. "Why haven't I seen you around Clanhome?"

"You have." Mischief lurked in eyes as blue as those of the other Newman. "We didn't actually meet, but I was visiting my son and granddaughter there the first time you came to Clanhome. You looked right at me. What a blow to my ego that you don't remember."

Lily frowned, calling up memories of a day that remained vivid, if somewhat jumbled. There'd been a lot going on. "A large, silvery gray wolf?"

"Beth likes to play horsie."

"Beth." She smiled. "That's my sister's name."

Jason perked up. "You have a sister?"

"Two. One older and married. One younger and . . ." She looked at Jason's tanned and appealing face and finished wryly, "probably interested in meeting you." Beth thought Lily took too many risks. Lily thought the same of Beth. Different risks.

Lily kept the conversation on lighter matters, ably abetted by Newman, who insisted she call him Hal. She had plenty of questions for Jason, but she'd let him eat first, get himself steadier. Rule didn't take part; he was filling his father in on the day's events. Lily had finished both of her tacos by the time he disconnected.

The last of their conversation had been particularly interesting, though Rule's portion had consisted of, "She would, yes" and "I don't think so" and "No, she won't."

"That was about me," Lily said.

He looked at her, his face unreadable. "In part."

Hal—who'd eaten his tacos with a knife and fork—shepherded an errant bit of fish back inside the tortilla as he spoke, a trace of apology in his voice. "I couldn't help overhearing. The Rho is offended by Chief Daly?"

He meant that he'd heard both sides of the conversation—though Lily suspected the "couldn't help" part was hooey. He must have been listening carefully in order to hear Isen.

Sometimes she really envied lupi their hearing.

Rule's answer had an oddly formal ring. "Irrevocably offended."

Jason and Hal both went still for a second. Then Hal smiled, said, "Good," and popped his last bite into his mouth.

Lily looked from one male face to the next. "What? What does that mean? Is he offended the way a Mafia don is just before he takes out a contract?"

"Of course not." Hal smiled at her. "If Chief Daly were clan, a statement of irrevocable offense would mean Challenge. That's not applicable with a human, obviously."

"Challenge to the death?"

"Well . . . yes, if the offense is irrevocable. With clan," he repeated. "Daly is unlikely to accept such a challenge, if Isen were foolish enough to offer one, isn't he?"

She didn't trust those twinkling blue eyes. She looked at Rule. "Hal asked you if the Rho was offended. Not Isen. The Rho."

He sighed. "You pick awkward moments to deepen your understanding of us. Yes, there is a difference. If a Rho declares irrevocable offense, it means the offense was to the clan and it cannot be cleared by apology or atonement. Nokolai's full resources will be bent toward removing Daly."

"From his job or his life?"

"Murder is an untidy way of dealing with the human world. The repercussions are too unpredictable. Isen means to ruin the man, and he has many resources to draw upon— some of which you might not consider entirely ethical, so I won't discuss them."

She studied him a moment. Unethical might mean bribes, blackmail, or a frame. "Daly's a bad cop. I want him out, but legally."

"Isen didn't tell me what he plans. He won't, and I won't speculate on them. He understands that your view is different on such matters and doesn't wish to offer you uncomfortable choices."

Offer her uncomfortable choices. Ha. That sounded just like Rule's father. Lily scowled, but let the subject drop . . . for now. She turned to Jason. "I'd like to make this official now, ask you some questions. You've got your lawyer here."

But it was Rule Jason glanced at, not Hal. Rule said, "Before you begin, Lily, I need to ask Jason something." He looked directly at the young man. "Did you kill Steve Hilliard?"

"No. Of course not."

Rule nodded and leaned back. "All right. Then I expect you to answer Lily's questions honestly and completely."

"Okay. Sure. Whatever I can do to help."

Lily took out her notebook and pen. She could have asked to record the interview, but she wanted him relaxed. She took him through the basics—his relationship to the deceased, whether he knew about Hilliard's will—he did— and where he'd been and what he'd done the night Steve Hilliard was killed.

Home alone, he told her.

"Jason," Rule said. Just that.

The two of them locked gazes for a bare second before Jason looked down. "Okay, I wasn't home and I wasn't alone, not until about three the next morning. But the lady I was with doesn't need to be dragged into this. She has nothing to do with it. She didn't even know Steve."

Hal sighed. Lily suspected Jason hadn't told his lawyer about his alibi, either. "I'll keep her out of this if I can," she said, "but I have to speak with her and confirm what you've told me."

He grimaced, flicked a glance at Rule, and looked at the table. "She's married. She'd be really upset if her husband found out. They don't have, uh, an open relationship."

Rule spoke quietly. "And if your seed had caught in her womb, who would have raised your child?"

"I know, I know . . . but she's so sad. I wanted to make her feel better about herself."

Lily managed not to sigh, but she wanted to. Lupi had no moral objections to adultery per se. Only to situations where it would be difficult to claim a child born from the union. "I can't guarantee her husband won't learn or guess about your affair, but I'll do what I can. Her name?"

He gave her the name, an address, a phone number, and the time and place of their assignation—which, if accurate, would certainly alibi him, since he said neither of them had slept. And since they'd met at a motel and he'd used his charge card, there would be a record of their stay.

Next she asked about the tattoo. As she'd thought, it hadn't been there when Jason last saw Steve around eight. Jason had never heard Steve express any interest in being tattooed, and was convinced he wouldn't have done it voluntarily. Tattoos, to a lupus, meant the old registration laws.

Then she asked about Mariah Friar and the baby she claimed was Steve's.

"Yeah, he knew about that. He was . . ." Jason glanced at Rule. "Well, you know Steve. It hurt him for her to claim that, but he was gentle with her. Told her the baby wasn't his. She didn't believe him. Didn't want to, I think. She loves the idea that she really poked a stick in her old man's eye, you know?"

"Is she estranged from her father?"

"Yeah, but . . . see, Mariah's always trying to get a reaction. She wants him to get mad. To react like she mattered. He won't react because—this is kind of creepy—he says his daughter died. That's how he puts it. Mariah Friar is alive, but his daughter is dead."

"You know Friar?"

"It's a small town. We've bumped a few times, but I avoid him whenever possible."

"You seem to know Mariah pretty well."

"Well . . . yeah."

Something in those guileless blue eyes made her ask, "How well?"

"Geez." He rubbed his short hair with one hand. "If I answer that honestly, you'll think I'm scum. But Mariah's like clan. She thinks of sex as comfort or friendship or just pleasure. She isn't hung up on fidelity."

Lily didn't say anything. Rule didn't either. Maybe he smelled disapproving, though, because Jason spoke earnestly to him. "She was pretty messed up back when you knew her. She's a lot more together now, or I wouldn't . . . but Steve really helped her. She feels good about herself these days."

Lily took them back to the subject. "You met Mariah through Steve?"

"More or less. There's this group, see. They're all pretty young, or most of them, and they see themselves as rebels. They want to, uh, champion our cause. Mariah's one of them."

"Is this group mostly female?"

"Well . . . yeah, but not all of them."

"Lupus groupies."

"Some of them, maybe." Jason looked uncomfortable, glancing again at Rule. "They're pretty tame compared to the ones you'd find in the city at a place like Club Hell. More witch wannabes than lupus groupies, really."

Rule spoke. "And one practicing witch."

"Adele doesn't like to be called a witch. Everyone thinks that means Wiccan, and she isn't."

"Adele?"

"Adele Blanco."

Lily looked at Rule. He hardly ever interjected himself into an interview. "You know her."

"Slightly. She's older than the others in her little group."

Interesting. Apparently Adele wasn't "a lovely older woman." Lily studied Rule's face, which gave away nothing. But that, too, was a giveaway. "You don't like her."

Rule shrugged. "We had a disagreement a few years ago."

"Rule checks in on us from time to time," Jason said. "A few years back, he decided too many of the younger lupi were hanging with Adele's group, that we were, uh, listening to her more than was good for the clan. Rule told us to stop gathering here, and Adele took it wrong. You don't like her?" Jason asked Rule, more curious than upset. "I didn't think you blamed her."

"*Blame* is the wrong word. I believe she enjoyed her influence over the younger people too much."

"I don't see it like that. Some of her ideas don't work out, but she helps, too. She organized that protest outside Friar's home. She teaches some of the group who have a bit of a Gift."

Lily asked, "What's her branch of spellcraft, if she isn't Wiccan?"

"She calls herself an eclectic. She draws from a lot of traditions."

"Any that involve tattoos, like the Msaidizi? The Dizzies," she added when it was obvious the Swahili word meant nothing to him.

"Oh. I don't think so. She isn't African-American."

"Not all of the Dizzies were."

"Yeah? Well, I don't think Adele was one of them. She doesn't have tattoos, except for a little one on her ankle, and that's pretty standard stuff—a rose. That's how the Dizzies worked, right? They tattooed their spells on their bodies."

"Pretty much." That's how Cynna worked, anyway,

though her tattoo process didn't involve needles. "What about charms? Does she make them?"

"Sure. Doesn't pretty much every magical practice include charms?"

"I don't know. Hers any good?"

Jason grimaced. "I guess. I mean, I know they work sometimes, but I can't help thinking . . ."

"What?"

"If Adele hadn't let Mariah talk her into making that fertility charm, maybe Mariah wouldn't be so damned certain that Steve fathered her baby."

7

BY the time they left Bobbie's, the sun had dropped behind the western mountains. It wasn't full dark, but the air was thick with dusk and very still. Already the temperature was dropping.

Del Cielo was a town of slants. Tucked into a niche in the crumpled rock of the mountains, the only level spots were man-made. The sidewalk she and Rule walked to get to her car was buckled as the earth beneath it slowly resumed its accustomed warp.

Jason had left with Hal Newman, who would take him to Clanhome. Until this was sorted out, Jason would live under the watchful eye of his Rho—who'd pledged Rule's apartment building as bond.

That had startled Lily. "But that building's got to be worth several million. That's not a reasonable bond for an LVN."

Hal had answered. "Lupi are seen as flight risks. Some judges won't grant bond at all, but fortunately we got Judge Soreli. She knows enough about us to understand that if Jason's Rho says to stay put, he will. She wanted to make sure Isen was motivated to keep Jason around."

Lily wasn't sure money was the same incentive for lupi it would be for others. Isen would hate to lose that much of Nokolai's capital, but would he surrender one of his clan to unjust imprisonment in order to hang on to a building, however valuable?

She'd glanced at Rule and decided not to ask.

When she and Rule reached her dusty white sedan, she stopped, cocked her head, and asked, "You know how to find Friar's place?" Robert Friar might be Del Cielo's most prosperous citizen, but he didn't actually live in the little town, though he'd been born here. He had a small ranch just north of it.

"Yes."

"Okay." She tossed him the keys. "You drive. I want to think."

When they were both inside, Rule started the car. "Am I a chauffeur, or will I be going inside when we reach Friar's home?"

"Inside, I think. He'd be within his rights to refuse to be interviewed with you present. If he does, I'll have to take it private. But I'd like to see how he reacts to you." She buckled up and got started on the thinking.

But her mind stuck on one point. Rule knew where Robert Friar lived. He knew a lot more about Del Cielo and its inhabitants than she'd realized. She decided she'd better clear this up so she didn't keep sticking on it. "Apparently you've been hanging out here off and on for years and know several of the players in our little skit."

He was silent as he pulled away from the curb and into what passed for traffic here. "I should have told you more on the plane. I didn't intend to withhold information. I . . . This sounds foolish."

"You get to be foolish sometimes." Right after hearing of a close friend's death, for example.

"On the plane, I wasn't considering what I should tell you because I wasn't really thinking, but also because . . . You're so present to me now, so much a part of my life, that sometimes I almost forget that you haven't always been with me." He grimaced. "Foolish, as I said."

Yeah. Also unbearably sweet. She didn't realize she'd reached for his hand until she felt it close around hers.

For about a block, neither of them spoke. Then he continued in a more normal voice, "I don't hang out here. I do, as Jason said, periodically check on the places the younger lupi like to hang out, and Del Cielo was popular with them for a few years."

"Why? I mean, the chief of police wants to hurt them, the founder of Humans First lives here, and . . . oh. You mean that's why. The thrill of danger. Defying authority."

"Young lupi don't precisely rebel, but they do need to test themselves. They're allowed, even encouraged, to do so. You don't learn much by avoiding all risk. Unfortunately, young lupi don't always have any more sense than young humans. Some of them became too involved in Adele Blanco's causes—and Adele was more interested in publicity than I liked."

"You want to control the clan's PR yourself."

"Of course. But also, Adele's ideas aren't always sensible. I disbanded the lupus portion of her clique after she decided it would be a great notion to infiltrate Humans First. She persuaded one of Mariah's friends, a human boy, to join the organization. At the time, he was sixteen."

"Shit. Sixteen? If he's a local, they would have found out pretty quickly he'd been hanging out with what they consider the wrong crowd. What happened?"

"Fortunately, Steve told me what was going on before anything went seriously wrong. I went to the boy and explained that the clan appreciated his courage, but I believed Adele had misjudged her opponent, and his input wouldn't be helpful. He agreed to drop the project."

"Before anyone beat him up, then."

"I suspect Friar is too canny to allow that. He knew who the boy was and had been feeding him misinformation. He seemed to be setting up a nice, public confrontation in which Adele's group would look foolish."

She retrieved her notebook. "What's this boy's name?"

He glanced at her, smiling. "Dotting your *i*'s?"

"I never know what I'm going to need to know."

"His full name is Keoni Akana. He's Hawaiian. He lived here for a year with a cousin of his mother's while his parents were in Uruguay—they work for some alphabet-soup scientific foundation. Something about insects—I don't recall what. He's back in the islands now attending college."

"That was clear, concise, and useful. Do that for me with Adele Blanco and Mariah Friar."

"Not Robert Friar?"

"Later, maybe. I read up on him on the plane, but the Bureau doesn't have files for the others."

"I . . . didn't realize the FBI had a file on Friar."

"Of course it does. He started a hate group."

Emotions slid through his face, quick and subtle, impossible to read in the gathering darkness. "I hadn't realized that a group formed to brand us as beasts would be classified as a hate group."

"Humans First wants to kick out or keep out everyone who isn't an officially designated human, not just lupi. But yeah, your people are the main focus. Of course we're watching them. Not very closely," she admitted. There was too much going on of greater urgency. "But we have a file on Friar and a few of the others in his group."

"That's oddly disconcerting."

"I guess you're more used to having the government persecute you." And the government's policies toward lupi were still a mixed bag, but they were trending toward fair these days. "Now, about Adele . . . ?"

"Yes. Well. Adele would be forty-four or -five now, I think. She was born in Sacramento to an English mother and Hispanic father, who divorced when she was in high school. She moved here with her father at that time, left for college after graduating from Del Cielo High, then returned without getting her degree when her father was paralyzed in an auto accident. He has since died."

Her eyebrows lifted. That was pretty complete. "Her mother?"

"Returned to England after the divorce. She helped Adele financially, I believe, when she was younger, but they aren't close."

"Speaking of finances, how does Adele get hers?"

"She owns a small store here—Practikal Magik, spelled with *k*'s instead of *c*'s—where she sells what Cullen considers crap."

That made her smile. "Define crap."

"In this case it's popular books on witchcraft, voodoo, and less well-known traditions, as well as astrology and numerology. She also sells crystals, cauldrons, herbs, and other spell ingredients. The quality of those ingredients, again according to Cullen, varies widely. He didn't think much of her, ah, professional qualities after checking out her shop, but he said she has an unusual Gift."

"What kind?"

"I'm trying to remember. Earth, I think."

"Guess I'll find out when I talk to her." Most Gifts were associated with an element, yet were talent-specific. For example, precognition was associated with Fire, but a precog had no special power over fires. Clairvoyants were associated with water, but didn't control the waves.

Now and then, though, a Gift was strongly rooted in one of the elements, yet didn't bring with it a specific magical talent. Like Cullen. He could call fire with a flick of his little finger, but his hunches weren't any more reliable than anyone else's.

But those with elemental Gifts sometimes became strong spell-casters, if they could find training. Lily drummed her fingers on her thigh.

They'd left the lights of Del Cielo behind about the same time the last of the light fled from the sky, and were winding along a narrow paved road. She couldn't see much to either side—hills, mostly, with some kind of scruffy growth. Ahead was more curvy road. Empty road, no headlights. The darkness was punctuated by lights from houses here and there along the road, but she didn't see any headlights.

It was unnatural. They were in California, for God's sake. There was supposed to be traffic. "What about Mariah?"

"Idealistic, damaged, emotional."

"Does she have a Gift?"

"I don't know. I don't think Cullen ever met her, and I wouldn't have any way of telling."

"She lives with her father?"

"No. She moved out when she was seventeen—or was kicked out. The story varies. She'd be twenty now. She dropped out of school and has worked a variety of jobs since, some of them probably intended to get her father's attention, much as Jason said. She was working as a pole dancer, for example, the last time I saw her. But my impressions are a couple years old. I don't know where she's working now."

"Boyfriends?" If Steve wasn't her baby's father, someone else was.

"In the plural, generally. Mariah is quite pretty, with a fragile air that many men find appealing."

"You don't."

"No." He shot her a grin as he slowed. She couldn't see anything to slow down for, but she trusted that he had a reason. "I prefer warriors."

A warrior? Was that how he thought of her? Lily decided she liked that. "Give me your take on Robert Friar."

"Lupe was right. He hates. But he hates with patience and intelligence. He's gregarious, but on his own terms—likes to entertain, but always with a goal in mind. He likes to stay in control, both of himself and others. And he likes to win."

"You've met him?"

"We've been at a few parties. Political bashes—state, not national."

"Has Cullen met him?"

"Not precisely met, no. If you want to know if Friar has a Gift, Cullen couldn't read him."

"What?" Her head jerked to look at him. "What does that mean?"

"Apparently Friar has some sort of natural shield. Cullen says that may indicate a blocked Gift of the psychic sort—telepathy, empathy, that sort of thing. There was something unusual about Friar's shield, something that puzzled Cullen. He wasn't able to explain what that was."

She frowned, considering. "I need to shake the man's hand. According to his file, his wife died eight years ago. He's never remarried. He likes women?"

"He likes them compliant and well-endowed, from what I've seen. I believe sex is his weakness."

"What do you mean? Shit. Hold on a minute."

Her phone was chiming. It was the ringtone she'd assigned to Martin Croft, who was running the Unit with Ruben gone. She tapped the screen to accept the call. "Yu here."

"Yes, I am. And you've got to stop answering your phone that way. It brings out the worst in me." Croft's voice was smooth, but the humor seemed strained. "Have you listened to the news this afternoon?"

"No. Kind of busy here." Ah, there it was—a small gravel road, well graded, snaking off to the left. Opposite it was a small house with the porch light on. Lupe Valdez's place, Lily thought, from what the woman had said at the end of that interview. Rule turned onto the gravel road. In the beam of his headlights, she could see that there was a gate across the road, but it had been left open.

Croft wanted an update on her investigation. She complied, wondering about the connection between the news and Hilliard's death. When she'd finished, Croft said, "So there is reason to suspect magic was involved, even if gado wasn't. That the tattoo was some kind of spell."

"That's what I'm thinking. I'm waiting to hear from Arjenie in research, see if the design is on record as being spell-based."

"We'll need that, since your personal ability doesn't give us admissible evidence. Be cautious in interviewing Friar. He'd like to take a bite out of us."

Then he told her why he'd called. It wasn't good news.

Rule spoke as soon as she'd disconnected. "Two days isn't much time."

"No." She drummed her fingers on her phone's case, unsurprised that he'd heard both sides of the conversation. He usually did.

Croft had told her that another Unit agent, a precog, had played a hunch that hadn't worked out. That happened; precognition was probably the least consistent Gift. Unfortunately, she'd climbed out on a limb backing her hunch, using her authority to override the local cops in a ham-handed way. As a result, the real culprit had fled the country; the man she'd arrested had had a heart attack in jail; and the press was after blood. Croft was preparing for some congressional critters to use the incident to try to cut back the Unit's authority.

So he'd given her two days for her investigation. Two days to find concrete evidence that magic was involved in Hilliard's death, making this a federal crime. With luck, Arjenie's research would provide that evidence.

But luck was a fickle bitch. Lily didn't like to count on it.

Rule eased the car to a stop. They hadn't quite reached their destination, but it lay directly ahead. Looked like Friar went for what Lily called millionaire rustic: two stories of wood and glass; an enormous, staggered veranda; three gables; and steeply pitched roof sections to slough off the snow that so seldom arrived. The exterior was professionally lit and landscaped. The gravel road made a wide curve in front of the house before heading to the back, where presumably there was a garage.

An elderly, mud-spattered Bronco was parked directly out front. It didn't look like a rich man's car, not even as an off-the-road toy. "Help usually parks out of sight. You think Friar has company?"

"Friar has a live-in housekeeper who parks in the five-bay garage out back. That isn't her car, or one of his. You still want me to come in? My presence in the investigation may give him ammunition."

She glanced at him. Sounded like he was keeping pretty careful track of Robert Friar. Maybe she should ask to see his file on the man.

But for now . . . did she play it safe, keep Rule in the car? Or give Friar something to bitch about, knowing he might bitch to the press? "Ammunition be damned." She slid her phone back in her pocket, clipping it so it wouldn't fall out. "You say he likes control. I want to rattle his cage, and since I'm short on ammo of my own, you'll have to do. Pull on up to the door and let's go have a chat with him."

The live-in housekeeper answered the door. She was fiftyish, stocky, with dark skin and a lovely Jamaican accent.

She led them to an enormous open living area, the sort people usually called a great room.

There were two men in the room. One was tall and thin, midthirties, with even features and sun-bleached hair trimmed close to his skull. His Wranglers and J. Crew shirt seemed to go with the Bronco out front. He looked vaguely familiar.

The other man was shorter, maybe five-ten. He looked husky but fit, Lily thought, especially for a fifty-five-year-old. His jeans were damned sure not Wranglers. His shirt was loose, white, probably a linen blend. No shoes. His hair was black and shaggy with white streaks, and his skin was so deeply tanned he looked Mexican. According to the file, he wasn't. Both his parents were deceased, but there was one brother, Shawn, who'd been in rehab a couple times. Shawn lived in San Francisco and worked for an IT firm.

Also according to that file, Friar had made his fortune in the dot-com bubble of the nineties and had sold his firm for nineteen million before the bubble burst. He'd kept busy since by playing in the commodities markets, raising horses, and getting involved in right-wing causes, especially those dealing with immigration. When the Supreme Court's ruling made lupi citizens, he'd dropped his other to-do's to devote himself to Humans First.

Friar stood near the flagstone-faced fireplace, a snifter in one hand, and dominated the huge room. He turned to face her, his eyes cutting quickly to Rule, then away. "Miss Yu. I was beginning to think you meant to neglect me."

"Special Agent Yu," she corrected him, moving forward. "Am I supposed to be surprised that Chief Daly called you?"

His eyebrows climbed. "My, you do jump to conclusions. Turner," he said, looking directly at Rule. "I'd offer you a drink, but I'd have to throw out the glass afterward, and I abhor waste."

"Speaking of jumping to conclusions," Rule said as he kept pace beside her. "I could only contaminate a glass if I were moved to accept your hospitality. I'm not."

Friar smiled. His eyes were dead cold. He lifted his snifter slightly in a salute.

Lily stopped a few feet from the two men. Before she could speak, Rule brushed her wrist lightly. "Ray," he said to the tall man in Wranglers, "I'm surprised to see you so far from Sacramento. Lily, I don't know if you've met. This is Ray Evans of the *Sacramento Star.* Ray, Special Agent Lily Yu."

The man nodded. "Special Agent."

"Mr. Evans." Shit, he was a reporter. A shark of a reporter, too. She'd seen his byline on some sensational stuff. He did his research, though, and he wasn't anyone's pet. He just went for the blood wherever he scented it.

What was Friar up to? "Don't you usually cover state government?"

"I cover politics," he corrected. He had a smooth, warm voice. "This . . ." He gestured at Rule, then Friar, then her—"shows all the signs of being very interesting, politically. I understand you're investigating the murder of a lupus, Agent Yu."

"I have no comment at this time."

"You might want to change your mind. Otherwise, I'll go to press with what Robert has told me. Oh, and Chief Daly had a few things to say, too." He shook his head, his eyebrows lifted ever so slightly. "I don't think that man likes you."

Lily's lips almost twitched. Evans was good. Get her smiling, get her relaxed, get her talking. "Tell you what. I'll give you a statement after I've interviewed Mr. Friar."

"Sure. But . . ." He glanced at the silver watch on his wrist—a pretty nice watch, too, for a guy who drove a ten-year-old car. "I should warn you that I don't have much time to get my story in. I can wait maybe thirty minutes."

"I don't structure an investigation around your deadlines." She looked at Friar. "I have a few questions for you, Mr. Friar. We need to step into another room."

"Actually, we don't." He picked up a thin folder from the end table nearby. "This statement should answer your questions. I've signed it, with two witnesses—Ray was kind enough to serve that function."

She glanced at the reporter. "And did you read what you were signing?"

He smiled. "I have a copy."

Friar's smile was thin and basted with gloat. "My lawyer assisted me in preparing the statement. He also witnessed my signature, as you'll see. If you have any questions after reading it, you may ask them with my lawyer present. Call my secretary for an appointment."

"Most people don't request a lawyer unless they have a guilty conscience." She took the folder from him, but couldn't manage to brush his fingers with hers. Was he avoiding contact on purpose? Her Gift wasn't widely known, but it wasn't a secret. Not anymore.

"I'm afraid I don't trust you." He sipped his brandy, meeting her eyes over the rim of the glass. His irises were as close to true black as human eyes get—in other words, not as black as Rule's eyes turned when he was fighting the Change. "You brought this Turner creature into my house. You allow him into your body. What is that, if not bestiality? You make him part of your investigation. That certainly looks like bias, evidence of the unnatural hold he has over you." He sipped again, smiling.

"Now, that wasn't nice." He didn't have enough wrinkles, she decided. A few around the eyes, but his skin was too taut. That much sun over the years made sags and wrinkles on Anglo skin. She bet he'd had work done. Rule hadn't mentioned vanity when he described Friar, but that's what she saw. "I have to ask myself why you're going out of your way to insult me."

"I'm being true to my beliefs, nothing more. I've cooperated by giving you that signed statement because I have a great reverence for the law, but that's all I'm giving you tonight. I'm asking you to leave now."

She could push it. She knew it, he knew it. But that's what he wanted. Maybe he was hoping that if he was rude enough, uncooperative enough, she'd haul him in. That would make a great headline. Short of that, Ray could get in some good lines about FBI harassment if she pushed too hard.

Of course, Friar also wanted her to back down, because then he'd won. Rule was right. The man liked to win. "I'll be in touch, Mr. Friar." She looked at Ray Evans. "For the record, I am investigating the possibility that magic was involved in the death of Steve Hilliard."

Then she met Rule's eyes, gave a nod, and started for the door with him beside her.

Evans used his long legs to keep up with them. "What makes you think there was magic involved? Wasn't his throat slashed?"

"That's all you're getting. Oh, one more thing, Mr. Friar." She paused, turning back to face him. "Does your daughter know you've sicced the press on her?"

She hadn't looked in the file. She didn't know for sure he'd thrown his daughter under the bus, so to speak. But her guess struck home. For the first time, emotion touched his face—a quick tightening around his eyes, his mouth.

"I have no daughter," he said.

8

THE next morning, Lily rushed through her shower, blew enough hot air at her hair to have it mostly dry, and left the bathroom wearing a skimpy hotel towel.

In the end, they hadn't gone to Rule's place. The hour's drive back and forth from San Diego didn't make sense—as she should have known from the first. They'd gotten a room at Del Cielo's only chain hotel, a Holiday Inn, where one of Rule's clan had brought his car. That gave Lily time to go over the police reports—which had finally been faxed to the Unit's main office in D.C., then forwarded to Lily via email.

Rule was already dressed. He sat at a small table by the window, his laptop open and humming. "Our friend Ray wrote an interesting article," he said. "Not the slant I expected, or the type of bias I imagine Friar was hoping for." Then he looked up from the screen. His eyes darkened. "Well," he said, standing, "that's a lovely sight."

"Forget it," she said briskly, heading for the entertainment unit, in whose drawers she'd stashed her underwear last night. Lily always unpacked. Suitcases were so untidy. "I need coffee. Do I smell coffee?"

"You do." He was right behind her now. "But I know an even better way to wake up."

She bent to open the drawer. "We had some first-class bestiality last night. That'll just have to hold you until . . . oh." Her voice went soft.

Three more pairs of new panties were jumbled up with those she'd packed. Hot pink lace. Chocolate brown satin. And pinstriped—teensy thin silver stripes on charcoal. She smiled as she pulled out the last one. "Just the thing for a professional woman."

His arms went around her from behind. "Happy birthday to me."

She turned her head, smiling. His face was so close . . . "Your birthday isn't until November."

"I'm celebrating early." He nibbled at her neck.

She sighed. "I'm afraid not. I don't have time, not with that deadline Croft handed me. I have to get dressed."

"I know."

"That's hard to do unless you let go."

"You're creative. I'm sure you'll think of . . . damn." He let go. "I ordered breakfast. That will be it."

She hadn't heard anything, but a second later someone knocked on the door. "Don't let them in," she warned, hurriedly stepping into the new panties. He flashed a grin over his shoulder as he unfastened the privacy lock. "But I wouldn't have to tip if . . . ah." He stood so that his body blocked the opening. "Ray. Not a good time."

"I'm here with a warning."

"I'm listening."

Lily scrambled into her clothes as Evans spoke. Apparently the hotel lobby was hip-deep in reporters—most notably the crews from two TV stations.

"That's quite a turnout," Rule said. "Slow news day?"

"Partly. Also, I wrote one hell of a good story, and the chief of police here is shooting off his mouth—talking about how Agent Yu is abusing her authority, how she's shacking up with you. His words, not mine. The TV folks are after a shot of the two of you leaving your hotel room together, or at least a shot of the two of you in the hotel."

"That's a compelling visual, from their point of view. I'll have to see if I can come up with an equally interesting one for the press conference I can see I'll be giving soon. Thanks for the tip."

"Can I come in? They're going to find the right person to bribe soon to get your room number. I'd rather not be talking here in the hall when they do."

"And how did you get my room number?" Rule asked.

"Sheer, unadulterated charm. Also a cousin with a friend who works here."

Lily answered as she stepped into her flats. "It's okay by me, with two conditions." She'd long ago opted for easy with her work clothes, and owned a lot of black pants, black tees, and jackets in various colors. Made getting dressed in the morning a snap, even before coffee. She grabbed a jacket from the closet with one hand—blue, as it turned out—and the damp towel from the floor with the other.

"And those would be . . . ?" Evans said.

Rule glanced over his shoulder at her and grinned as she tossed the towel into the bathroom and pulled the door closed. She was shrugging into her jacket as she moved to the door. "First, what's said is off the record unless we agree otherwise. Second, I get to shake your hand."

His hesitation was brief, but enough to confirm her guess. "Off the record works, and I have no objection to taking the hand of a lovely woman."

Rule moved aside, opening the door wider. Lily stepped up, holding out her hand. Evans took it.

Lily smiled as she released his hand. She did so enjoy being right. "In case you've ever wondered, your Gift isn't the only reason you appeal to people. I find you likeable, and your Gift doesn't work on me."

Another hesitation, then a small smile. "Good to know."

Rule glanced at her.

"Charisma Gift," she said, moving aside so Evans could enter. "Not scary strong, but enough to make him good at his job. People want to tell him things." She looked at the reporter again. "Rule is the only one I'll tell. Your Gift is your business. It won't go into my official report."

"That's even better to know." He came into the room, glancing around. "I smell coffee."

"And I haven't had any yet, but if there's any left after I get a cup, you're welcome to it." Lily went to the vanity area, where a small Mr. Coffee waited. "You're in luck. There's almost a full pot, and I think it's Rule's blend, not the hotel stuff." She poured two cups.

Evans accepted the mug, glancing at Rule. "You have your own blend?"

"Not one made just for me, no. But I usually travel with some I've ground myself. Organic, dark roast."

"He's picky. Works out well for me—I get great coffee." Lily at last got her first swallow of coffee. She kept her eyes on Evans. "You want to tell us why you're really here?"

"Obviously, to persuade you to say something on the record."

"I'm more persuadable if you level with me."

"Have you read my story?"

"I have," Rule said. "Which is why I didn't object to Lily's invitation. I'd say you're fair—more so than Friar may like—despite your own bias."

"What bias is that?"

"You want Congress to limit the authority granted Unit agents after the Turning. I'm wondering why."

"Backlash." Evans paused, sipped. "This is damned good coffee, by the way. It's already started, the murmurs against the Gifted. It'll get worse before it gets better. Congress overstepped when it granted such broad powers to a unit comprised of Gifted agents. If they acknowledge that now, before the backlash deepens, it will protect the Unit."

"Maybe," Lily said, "but you didn't answer my question."

Evans's eyebrows went up. "Not interested in politics, even when it's your Unit at stake?"

Rule answered before she could. "When Lily's on a case, she does the job. Right now you're only interesting because you may affect the case."

Evans pulled out a notebook. "Can I quote you?"

Rule looked at Lily. She shrugged. "On that one thing, yes. So what do you want, Evans? Unless you plan to persuade me to kick Daly's ass and make headlines for the good of all Gifted everywhere, I don't see why you're here."

"Humans First. That's the real story. I've been cultivating Friar for months, and it's working—he called me when he wanted a reporter to give you two a hard time. You've read that statement of his by now."

"Of course."

"He's alibied up, down, and sideways for the night Hilliard was killed. What he doesn't mention is that while he was at a party in San Diego with about a hundred other people, a couple of his lieutenants were here in Del Cielo. One of them lives in Texas, the other in northern California."

"You think they killed for him?"

"I think they're capable of it. The two men I'm speaking of are Armand Jones and Paul Chittenden. They stayed here that night, checked out the next day."

Now that was interesting. "Who's your source?"

"Uh-uh." He shook his head. "I'm not about to lose him or her as a source."

Fair enough. "I've got an address for Jones. Chittenden wasn't mentioned in my file."

"He's a recent promotion. Here." He pulled out his Black-Berry, scrolled around till he found the contact info, then jotted it in his notebook and handed her the sheet of paper.

There was a knock on the door. Rule moved to it, stood quietly, then said, "This time it really is breakfast. I smell sausage."

"I'll leave you to your meal," Evans said, taking a last swig of coffee before setting the mug down. "Just one more thing. I hear there will be a meeting of the local branch of Humans First tonight." He smiled slyly. "I may be parked near the entrance to Friar's place. Be interesting to see who attends."

"Is that so?" Lily smiled. Time for some payback—of both kinds. "You might want to keep an eye out for Chief Daly. I hear he's a member. Certainly explains why he's so worked up about my personal life, doesn't it?"

Evans's eyebrows went up. "That so? Who's your source?"

"Uh-uh," she said, and shook her head just as he had.

"And you didn't hear that from me. You can use it, but I get to be an anonymous source."

He grinned, gave Rule a lazy salute, and left.

"I like Ray," Rule said after tipping the waiter who'd unloaded their food, "but now I'm wondering if that's me, or his Gift."

"I liked him, too. Don't trust him, of course." She piled scrambled eggs on her plate. "Not that I think he lied, exactly. But he has an agenda. That may be just what he said, plus a good dose of ambition, but we don't know yet."

"True. What's on your agenda today?" Rule added the rest of the eggs to his plate, which already held half a dozen sausage patties. "I've a suggestion. Why don't we split up? I can have a little chat with the press, distract them from you."

"I'll take you up on that. I've got too many places to be today to waste time digging out from a press huddle." She ate absently, her mind turning over possibilities. "I need to see the place where the body was found, but at least I've seen the photos now, so that can wait a little longer. So . . . Mariah or Adele?" She tapped her fork against her plate. "Mariah first. Maybe I can catch her before the press batters her too badly."

Rule had finished his eggs while she wasn't paying attention. He poured more coffee from the carafe that had arrived with the food. "Surely you want to check out those two men Evans told you about. Jones and Chittenden."

"I'll do a run on them, sure, and will see if I can confirm what Evans said about them staying here. But they aren't my first priority."

"Why not?" he asked sharply.

"My first priority is determining whether I have jurisdiction, remember?"

"The tattoo proves magic was involved."

"The tattoo proves someone used magic to apply a tattoo. It suggests a lot more, but doesn't prove it. Not unless Arjenie can tell me those symbols translate as 'kill this guy.' "

"That can be sorted out later. Clearly Friar is behind this."

"No," she said slowly, "that isn't clear. Hate isn't enough. Hilliard lived here for years. Why kill him now?"

"There's a baby," Rule said tersely. "It isn't Steve's, but Friar doesn't know that. I don't imagine he's happy with having what he believes is a lupus grandson."

"I repeat, why now? The baby is four months old. I can come up with possible motives, like if Steve found something out Friar didn't want spread around. But that leaves some big holes in the fabric. What's the tattoo for? Friar might condone killing, but would he condone using magic? Would one of his lieutenants be Gifted?"

"You won't know until you check."

"True, but it doesn't feel right. Why did Steve meet with his killer in that out-of-the-way spot?"

He shoved his chair back. "He could have been tricked, lured there."

She tipped her head back to watch as he began pacing. He was tied tight all of a sudden. "Maybe. That's all I've got right now, lots of maybes. But if Steve knew something dangerous about Friar, wouldn't he have passed it on to his Rho right away, rather than jaunting off to this deserted spot for whatever reason?"

"I don't know. Yes, I suppose he would, if he understood it was important."

"And once the bad guy got him there, how did he immobilize Steve? If it was wolfbane, that means Steve was relaxed enough to eat or drink something the killer gave him. Surely he wouldn't be that comfortable with one of Friar's lieutenants."

"For God's sake, Lily, they could get around that. Those men are from out of town. Steve probably didn't know they were in Humans First." He waved a hand, brushing that off. "We can figure out how they tricked him later. You're getting hung up on minutiae."

Yesterday she'd wanted him to quit hiding behind all that damned pleasantness. Looked like her wish had come true. "That's how I build a case. Minutiae. Though I like to call it motive, means, and opportunity, and right now, they aren't adding up."

"What if he wasn't killed there? They could have killed him elsewhere and dumped the body where it wouldn't be found right away. It was their bad luck someone decided to hike that trail when he did."

"Look, I'm not crossing Friar or his men off the list, but we can't make the evidence fit what we want. We have to go where it points." She pushed her chair back and stood. "As for where he was killed, I know you haven't seen the crime scene photos—" She'd made sure of that. She'd shared the written reports with Rule, but he didn't need to see pictures of his friend's corpse—"but they support the idea that he was killed where his body was found."

"Where's the blood?" Rule demanded. "If his throat was slashed there, why wasn't the ground soaked in blood?"

She stared at him, her stomach clenching sickly. "I didn't tell you that. I didn't tell you there wasn't much blood at the scene."

Another impatient gesture. "I don't need to be shielded. I appreciate the sentiment, but I don't need to be shielded. I know what death looks like. I checked out the photos this morning before you were up, and there isn't enough blood."

"Shit. Shit. You can't do that. Those files are password-protected."

"I've lived with you for months now. Of course I've seen you enter your password. That's not the point. If there wasn't enough blood, why—"

"It's damn sure the point to me! Some of the documents behind that firewall are secret or top secret! Do you have any idea how much trouble I could be in if someone found out you had access to all that?"

"How could anyone find out?"

"And that makes it okay? Jesus." She scraped a hand through her hair. "Dammit, Rule, I trusted you!"

He looked cold. "That doesn't sound like trust to me. I didn't root around in all sorts of secret files, nor would I. I looked at the photos of my friend's body."

"You used my password. You did that without asking, without permission." She snatched her shoulder harness from the back of the chair. She'd left it off in her hurry to get dressed earlier. "I'm headed out now."

"You'd best give me a few minutes to distract the press."

"Sure. Fine." She buckled herself into the harness, not looking at him. He was locked into that cold face, cold voice bit. She hated that, but she'd stick to the program—and the program was her investigation, dammit. "How long do you need?"

"Fifteen minutes should do. I'm going to offer them an interview outside the police department. Good visual."

Daly would hate that. He might come trotting out and add to the reporters' enjoyment, too, by yelling at Rule. "All right." She slid her jacket back on and looked at him. "I'm not finished with this discussion."

"I am." He turned abruptly and left.

9

LILY got away from the hotel without drawing any press attention, but she still had an escort. A black-and-white. Daly, damn him, must have sent one of his people to follow her, because the asshole rode her rear the whole way.

At least he kept on going when she pulled up at a small, mud-colored duplex. It was the sort of neighborhood where a parked black-and-white would make people nervous. One side of the duplex was clean and tidy, with pots of cherry red impatiens on the three steps up to the stoop. The other side featured a collection of beer cans and newspapers.

Lily sniffed as she waited after knocking. Someone was enjoying some weed.

The door opened. "Yes?"

Mariah Friar both was and wasn't what Lily had been expecting. The sweet, scrubbed-clean face didn't seem to belong to a former pole dancer—or to the daughter of Robert Friar, for that matter. Her hair was bleached blond, short and spiky with lavender streaks, and she liked body adornments. In addition to the nose and eyebrow studs, Lily counted three earrings on one side, two on the other. She wore baggy jeans and a snug, long-sleeved purple tee. No shoes.

She was at least an inch shorter than Lily and maybe ten pounds underweight. Her eyes were a clear Dresden blue. They were also reddened and puffy.

Fragile, Rule had said. Yes, she had that look. "I'm Agent Yu," Lily said, holding out the folder with her badge. "Mariah Friar?"

"Yes." She smiled as if pleased that Lily had her name right. "Not that my father will admit it, not the last name, that is. Has he told you that my mother cheated on him, but he forgave her and raised me as his own until I turned on him?"

"There's something about that in his statement." Among other things, such as a reference to the legal action he was taking to try to force Mariah to stop using his surname.

"He doesn't believe that about Mom, but he wants other people to. You'd think I wouldn't want to claim that relationship, either, but we don't help ourselves by denying reality, do we?"

"May I speak with you inside?"

"Sure." She stepped back. "Little Stevie's asleep, but noises don't bother him. As long as we aren't too loud, he'll be fine."

Oh, Lord, she'd named the baby after Steve.

Lily stepped across the threshold into one of those shotgun living-dining areas common in small apartments, with the kitchen in an alcove off the dining area. Instead of a table, though, this dining area held a crib and chest of drawers.

There were plants in here, too—a luxuriant ivy on the chest of drawers and a thriving ficus next to the front window. In the living area, the couch and chair looked like they'd come from Goodwill, but their bland beigeness was nearly drowned in colorful pillows—yellow, pink, orange, green. The television was old, its screen dark. What sounded like harp music floated in from behind a barely open door that Lily guessed led to the bedroom.

Baby toys were scattered on a scuffed but scrupulously clean wooden floor. Also a baby. He lay on a pad of some sort where a coffee table might normally be found, a tiny huddle beneath a poofy quilt, with just a patch of dark hair and one teensy hand showing.

Lily stopped, looking at the tiny hand, the dark hair that was utterly unlike Steve Hilliard's streaky blond.

"I'd move him, but he always wakes if I pick him up, and he's comfortable there. Have a seat," she said, plopping down on one end of the couch and dislodging a bright green pillow in the process. "You'll have to excuse me. I've been crying about Steve. I miss him."

Lily opted for the other end of the couch, mainly because the armchair was piled with folded clothes. A plastic clothes basket sat next to it. Lily walked gingerly around the sleeping baby, moved a couple pillows, and sat, turning so she faced the young woman. "I'm sorry to intrude."

"You aren't." Unblinking blue eyes met Lily's. "This is so odd. Well." She held out a hand. "Let's get this out of the way first, okay? Then you can ask me questions."

Lily's eyebrows lifted, but she wouldn't turn down a chance to get information. She had to stretch to reach the young woman's hand.

Mariah's clasp was surprisingly firm. The magic coating her skin made Lily think of a sun-warmed pond, the kind with a silty bottom your toes squished into.

A distinctive magic. A familiar one. Lily's heart ached for the young woman on the other end of the couch. "Did Steve know about your Gift?"

"No. At least I don't think so. I don't speak of it, you see, not ever." Her smile was small and sad. "My father trained me well. He said it was for my own good, that people would hate me if they found out. I knew better, of course. He was harsh because he despised and feared me. He feared what people would think of him if they knew, too. You'd think I could set that training aside, knowing it was false, but . . ." She shrugged. "It was quite difficult to take your hand."

"You knew that I'm a sensitive. You wanted me to know you're an empath." Empathy was one of the most burdensome Gifts. The only one worse was telepathy—conventional wisdom had it that all telepaths were insane. But empaths who managed to function well in a world crowded with people were usually partly blocked. Mariah's Gift wasn't blocked at all.

"Yes. It's strange to have you know. It's even stranger to sit here with you and not have any idea what you're feeling, but I like it. You're . . . soothing to me. I didn't think you would be," she confessed. "I thought you might remind me of my father now that he's shielded, but it isn't the same at all."

"Your father wasn't always shielded?"

"Oh, no. I think he got someone to do that, to put a shield on him, because he was afraid of me. Adele says that isn't possible, that he must have done it himself somehow, but it was just suddenly there one day. Wouldn't it have to grow a little at a time if it came from him?"

"I don't know. How long ago was this?"

"Three years. No, almost four now. That's when I moved out. He didn't do it—didn't get the shield—to help me, but it did. Once he was shielded I didn't have to . . ." She faltered, running her fingertips nervously over the bead in her eyebrow. "Didn't have to do what he said anymore."

Lily didn't have to be an empath to hear the pain in that statement. "Why did you want me to know about your Gift?"

"I have something to ask you. But even before Steve—before he was killed, I wanted to meet you. Steve kept up with Rule, so when you and Rule got together, Steve talked about you being a sensitive. Plus I've read about you. You and Rule. I'm fascinated by . . . Your face looks funny. I can't tell what you're feeling, but I think I'm bothering you somehow."

"I'm a little uncomfortable with your curiosity."

Mariah nodded. "That's how Rule felt about me, too. Uncomfortable. Well, he also felt sad because I was a big mess back when we met, so he was very kind and careful, but he's got a strong sense of privacy, doesn't he? Maybe you do, too. I think on some level he sensed I could intrude on his privacy. I don't mean to, you know."

"I know," Lily said gently. "Did Steve not sense the possible intrusion? I'm told he cared about you, both before and after the baby was born."

For a moment, her face glowed. "Steve loved me."

"I guess you would know."

She grinned suddenly. "It's fun, trying to guess what you're feeling. I don't mean he was in love with me. He wasn't. I mean that he *loved* me. And no, Steve didn't have a big sense of privacy. A lot of lupi don't, which is why I like being around them. But Steve really cared about me. He liked me. He liked being with me, both for sex and just for company, and it didn't bother him if I was with other men sometimes. It truly didn't."

"I understand," Lily said carefully, "that sex is different for empaths."

Mariah giggled like the teenager she'd been only a year ago. "We're the easiest of easy lays. I've heard that isn't true for all empaths—some of them don't like to be touched at all, but maybe they've got a stronger Gift than I do or something. For me, well, if someone wants me and he isn't an asshole, and I can make him feel wonderful, and I know it would feel wonderful to me, too . . . because it does," she added frankly. "It feels fantastic, because I experience his feelings, too. So I get caught up in the moment real easy. But Steve didn't mind. Mostly if men don't mind it's because they don't care about you, but Steve did care." Sadness swept over her face. "He loved me."

"I'm sorry for your loss." And ready to admit that Rule was right. This fragile, oddly gallant young woman hadn't killed the man she loved. She truly wasn't capable of it. "You said earlier there was something you wanted to ask me."

"Oh. Oh, yes." She looked down, toying with the bead in her eyebrow. "Nothing I know because of my Gift is evidence, right?"

"No, it wouldn't be admissible. Nothing I learn from my Gift is admissible, either, though I'm allowed to consider it in the process of an investigation. Just as I could consider something you tell me, even if it couldn't be used in court."

Mariah nodded without looking up. "I guess I'm not sure enough to tell you about this . . . this thing that's bothering me. I could be wrong."

"People tell me things they're wrong about all the time. It's my job to sort that out."

"But it would affect someone else." She kept rubbing that little bead. "I need to think about it some more."

Lily tried another tack. "I've heard that empaths know when someone is lying."

"Hey, you're a good guesser." Mariah flashed her a smile and tucked one leg up on the couch. "I bet people lie to you all the time, too. You get where you sort of expect it. People do lie a lot." She shook her head. "That was confusing to me when I was little, especially when they didn't know they were lying. My father doesn't always know. He makes himself think something is true when it isn't, so when I was small I couldn't tell when he was lying."

"Can you tell now?"

"Well . . . not always. People say things they want to be true, or they say things they're afraid are true, but they don't know, so I pick up that fear or that wanting. When someone isn't sure if what they're saying is true, I can't tell, either. I just know they aren't sure. That's why I told everyone little Stevie is Steve's baby."

Lily blinked. "What?"

"That's what you're wondering, isn't it? Why did I lie? Or else, why did Steve lie? Because one of us has to be wrong, yet we stayed together. Or as much together as anyone is with a lupus," she added practically. "Except for you and Rule."

"You're saying that Steve wasn't sure?"

She nodded. "He said he was. He said he'd know if Stevie was his, but he wanted to be wrong. He wanted that badly, and that's what I 'heard' when he told me Stevie wasn't his—he wanted to be wrong. He wanted me to prove him wrong. And he could have been, couldn't he? I used the fertility charm with him, not with anyone else."

"Why did you use a fertility charm?"

"Because Steve wanted a baby so much, of course." She glanced down at the sleeping bundle on the floor, her face soft and shining. "Not that I don't want little Stevie for his own sweet self, because I do. But I guess I wouldn't have thought of having a baby right now if Steve hadn't wanted one so much."

"So you went to your friend Adele—"

"No! Oh, sorry." She flushed prettily. "I interrupted you. But I didn't go to Adele. She came to me and offered to make the charm. That way the baby would be a gift from both of us, you see. Because she loved Steve, too."

LILY spent a little longer trying to pry out the "thing that was bothering" Mariah, but she was a stubborn, slippery little waif. Had to be, no doubt, to survive her father. Lily did get names and contact info on several of the others in Adele's little group, and straight answers to some basic questions. Mariah had been home alone, except for her baby, the night Steve was killed. Her neighbor had been home, though. Maybe he could alibi her.

No, she didn't know any spells. Adele had offered to teach her some, but Mariah wasn't interested in that sort of thing. Did Adele know that Mariah had a Gift, then? Maybe. Mariah hadn't told her, but Adele might have guessed. They used to be really close.

Used to be, Lily thought grimly as she pulled up in front of a narrow store wedged between a Mexican restaurant and a hardware store. Had their closeness ended when Steve grew especially close to Mariah? Mariah had clammed up when Lily asked that . . . which pretty much answered the question.

Mariah's neighbor hadn't been able to alibi her. He didn't

say he'd been too high to know if he was home himself, much less his neighbor's status, but Lily would bet on it.

She got out of her car, shut the door, then stood there watching the patrol car roll slowly by. It was the same asshole. And that might not be fair, calling him an asshole, because it wasn't his fault his chief gave shitty orders, but she wasn't feeling especially fair.

Practikal Magik was located at the edge of Del Cielo's tiny downtown, and all the on-street parking was metered. Lily fed the meter a couple quarters on the theory that a touch of paranoia was helpful and she did not want the asshole ticketing her. Then she went to look in the window.

The display included an array of quartz crystals—clear, pink, and amethyst—several books, a scattering of polished stones, and a large silver-colored cauldron set on a low stool. She couldn't see inside the store—a gauzy curtain veiled the window behind the display.

She went to the door. Locked. No note, but it was nearly noon. Adele had probably gone for lunch somewhere. Lily had two numbers for her—one for the store, one for her mobile phone. No answer on either, so she started knocking on doors.

Adele wasn't eating at Casa Gomez next door, nor had anyone there seen her, but Lily learned that Adele usually parked her three-year-old Honda in back. A quick check showed that the vehicle was gone. According to the owner and chief cook at the little restaurant—Maria Esperenza Valenzuela Gomez—that wasn't unusual; Adele often took long lunches, shutting her store for a couple hours or more.

No, she didn't know where Adele liked to eat. Adele was one of those people who seem *simpática, comprendes?* A good listener, yes, with a nice smile, and always offering help or advice. But she says nothing of herself. And her help, it is always the help she wishes to give. Not always the help that is needed.

Yes, Adele was odd in her ways, but Mrs. Gomez didn't hold that against her. Did she not herself have a great-aunt who was a *curandera?* And not a Catholic at all, she added, crossing herself. But Tía Jimena was a good woman, and God understood her heart. But *Tía* did not talk to strangers about her craft, no, not ever. She lived in the same village in Mexico where she had always lived, and she would not speak with someone from outside, and so she had told Adele when Adele asked.

After that, Mrs. Gomez said with a shrug, Adele had not offered help and advice so much.

Wolfbane? Mrs. Gomez knew nothing about that. Tattoos? Oh, yes, Adele used to work at a tattoo parlor in the city. She knew this because her sister's son had gotten a tattoo there, a dragon of all things, and Felicia had been so upset, but she—Mrs. Gomez—had told her it was nothing, to forget it. It wasn't a gang mark, was it? Boys need to do foolish things, so thank the good Lord it was nothing more than a silly tattoo.

After the interview, Lily ate a couple of Mrs. Gomez's enchiladas, extra hot, at a tiny table while she jotted down notes. They were pretty good, though the "extra hot" should have come with an incineration warning. Then she checked her messages.

Rule had texted her at eleven. He was going to check out the crime scene. Lily looked up, chewing her lip. She wanted him to call, dammit, not text her a couple piddling lines. And that was just stupid. He usually texted instead of calling, especially about the little stuff, especially when she was on a case. He knew she kept her text alert on silent, so sending a text message didn't interrupt her.

What she really wanted was an apology. He was wrong, dammit. He shouldn't have used her password. He'd crossed a line, and he needed to know that.

But that had to wait until they were together. It couldn't be discussed over the phone, and damn sure couldn't be covered by a text. She checked her watch. Twelve twenty. Huh. Her inner Rule-compass, matched with the map she'd studied of the area, suggested he was still there. Either he hadn't gotten to the scene right away after texting her, or he'd found enough of interest to keep him sniffing around awhile.

Well, if he learned something significant—like, say, if he found Adele's scent all over—he'd call. Pissed or not, he'd call if it mattered.

There was a text from her sister—Beth had another boyfriend, and this one was hot—and one from Arjenie Fox: CALL ME.

She did. And then she called Croft and told him she was now officially investigating murder by magical means.

The lacy choker tattooed around Steve Hilliard's neck was a spell, all right. One that stopped his heart. That's why there wasn't much blood—his heart stopped pumping before his throat got cut.

"The slashed throat was intended to throw off the locals, keep us from being called in," Lily told Croft. "It could have worked. The chief here is a member of Humans First. He wouldn't look too hard, and if the body hadn't been found so quickly, there might not have been enough of him left for us to even know about the tattoo. I bet she was counting on that."

"She?" Croft said. "You've got a suspect already?"

"I do, but right now it's all motive and speculation." Hunch, she might have said, or instinct. Whatever she called it, she knew she was on the right track, but she didn't have proof. "She does fit the M.O. She's a spell-caster, an eclectic, so she could have learned that spell someplace."

"You'll need more than 'could have.'"

"I'll call you when I have it."

As soon as she disconnected, she called Rule—and was shuffled off immediately to voice mail. Damn. Probably the mountains were interfering with reception.

She left him a brief message, checked her notes, refused the refill on her Diet Coke Mrs. Gomez wanted to give her, and set off to plug the meter—the patrol car was still cruising by every so often. Then she headed for the gas station on the corner. She wanted badly to get into Practikal Magik and look for Adele's tattoo equipment, but she didn't have enough for a search warrant, not yet. So she'd go see the closest member of Adele's little group, one of the few males.

The pumps at the station were self-service, but there was a garage out back. That's where she found Mannie Bouchard, scowling up at a Suburban raised high by the hydraulic lift.

Early twenties, six feet even, weight maybe one-fifty, black and brown. His skin was dark enough to suggest that Mannie might be short for Manuel in spite of the French surname. Slim verging on skinny, but his arms were ropy with muscle. Ragged hair, grease-stained jeans, sleeves ripped out of his T-shirt. A tattoo on his right bicep, but she couldn't see what it was from here. "Mannie Bouchard?"

His head swung toward her, the scowl undisturbed—until someone flipped a switch and his thin face lit in a grin. "Hey! You're Lily Yu, aren't you?" He started toward her, pulling a rag from his back pocket to wipe his hands. "I'm Mannie, yeah." His voice dropped as he reached her. "And I'm *ospi* to Nokolai." He held out a hand.

Her eyebrows lifted. *Ospi* meant out-clan friend; used as he had, as introduction, it probably meant he was related to someone who was clan.

She shook his hand. No furry magic, but a small bump of a Finding Gift. "Your mom's Nokolai?"

"Yeah. Dora Bouchard. You know her?"

It took a second, but once Lily placed the name, she smiled. "Nice lady. There's no nonsense to her." Dora was the daughter of one of the Nokolai councilors, so was considered clan. Her children weren't. "Would you be the wild child she blames for her gray hair?"

"Sorry to say, but yeah. Though I'm getting my act together finally." He grimaced. "I should tell you I'm on probation."

"Oh?"

"Drove drunk, smashed up my car and someone's parked truck. Just lucky I didn't kill myself or anyone else. I've paid off the fine and damages. Got another month on probation." He repeated that quick, blinding grin. "Got another car, too, a sweet little '65 Mustang. Needed a new engine, so it's not original, but man, is she sweet. No way I'll take a chance on busting her up."

"Sounds like you're doing it right this time. Can you talk to me for a few minutes?"

"Sure. You want to go in my office?" He waved toward the front of the station and, she assumed, the tiny glassed-in cubby where she'd seen a chair, a counter, and a cash register.

As they headed that way he asked, "Is this about Steve? Man, that's some seriously bad shit."

"It is." She glanced at him. "I'm thinking that, being raised by clan, you'd be able to speak frankly of sexual matters."

"Well . . . yeah, I guess. Since you're clan, you'll understand."

"Tell me about your group. The one that included Steve, Adele, and Mariah."

He did. They had some really bad coffee in the glassed-in cubicle with him on a stool behind the counter, her in the single chair, and she learned that the group was loosely organized around a belief in sexual plurality and an interest in magical exploration. Adele was the leader in both realms. According to Mannie, Adele hadn't minded sharing Steve physically, but she got twisted up when Steve spent too much time with any of the other women.

Like when Steve took up with Mariah?

"Yeah. I mean, Adele really was cool with the sex part, she wasn't fooling about that, but Steve wanted more than a variety of bodies. Mariah was special to him, and Adele could see that. Shit, we all could. Adele still said the right things, but there was a strain, you know?"

Lily was pretty sure she did know. "You said you're more interested in the magical exploration bit. What kind of exploring did Adele do?"

The grin was just as white this time, but more sheepish. "I didn't mean that I was, like, immune to the sex. At first I liked that part, too, but after a while . . . I thought it would be more like clan."

"It wasn't?"

"First time I turned someone down, I saw the difference! Man." He shook his head. "Adele says some of the same stuff clan does, but she gets it wrong."

"How do you mean?"

"You know how the fundamental thing is that everyone owns their own sexuality? Everyone, all the time, no exceptions once you're adult. So if a guy is turned on by other guys, that's okay, or if you want to take a vow of chastity, that's cool, too. Hard to understand, maybe." A quick grin. "But okay. You don't get to think you know what's best for someone else, because it's *their* sexuality, right? And it's just as okay to say no as it is to say yes."

"Adele doesn't agree?"

"She says the thing is to be kind to each other—well, that's what Mom says, too, but she doesn't mean it the same way. Adele thinks the only kind, healthy answer is yes. If you turn someone down, there's something wrong with you." Another head shake. "I think it's a control thing with her. I tried to tell Steve that once, that she's using sex for control, but he didn't see it. But she never pulls that control shit with them. With the lupi, I mean. Not anymore."

"Not anymore?"

"I wasn't part of the group when Rule came in and pulled the plug a few years back, but I heard about it. He didn't try to tell the older lupi like Steve what to do, but he had a word with the young ones, and pfft! They were gone, just like that, and they didn't come back. Shook Adele up, I think." His smile was sly. "I know it pissed her off."

"If you aren't happy with Adele's sexual philosophy or her efforts to control the group, why stay with it?"

He sighed. "You read me, right? I've got a little bit of a Gift, nothing special. But that's what rocks me, studying magic. I like working on cars, too, but they're second. If I could make a living with spells . . . but, shit, even if there was a job like that, I don't have the power."

"Adele's willing to teach you."

"Yeah. Not many are, not when I'll never be a power-house, and I get that. The ones with big-ass Gifts need help getting them under control, and they can do more with what they're taught than I could."

"I've always thought desire has as much to do with where we end up as raw talent. Stubbornness counts, too. Did

Adele teach you any, ah, runic spells? The kind with patterns, drawings?"

He lit up. "No, those are more my thing. She's into charms and potions, but potions are really hard to get right—the results can be unpredictable, you know? And charms take power. Me, I get off on the drawn spells. Lots of spells have a drawn or written component, but putting one all in symbols, that's rare. I've been working on how to convert other kinds of spells to runic."

"Maybe she's asked you to convert a spell that way sometimes."

"Yeah, she has. I'm pretty good at it." He might have been trying to look modest. It looked more like delight. "She asked me to help her with one a couple weeks ago. Well, she didn't show me the whole spell, just part of it she was having trouble with. She said I wasn't ready for the whole thing, but I think she just likes being mysterious, making like she knows everything."

In that moment, Lily truly hated Adele Blanco. She didn't want Mannie to know what his teacher had done with his help . . . but she wasn't going to be able to prevent it. For that alone, Adele Blanco needed to go down.

She reminded herself that Mannie could be playing the *naïf* to deflect suspicion. And she did listen to herself—she just didn't believe it. "What was the deal with wolfbane?" she asked casually.

"You heard about that?" he asked, surprised—and immediately supplied his own answer. "I guess Steve told Rule. Well, it didn't work out. She and Steve were trying to find a way to use it for an anesthetic, but all she got was a kind of paralytic. It made Steve real drowsy and he couldn't move, but didn't really knock him out. From the way Steve described it . . ."

His voice trailed off as, at last, he caught on to her line of questioning. Horror dawned, quick as a punch to the gut. "You think . . . you think she. . . ."

"What did she do with the bane to make it a paralytic?"

"I don't know. I don't know. Something about drying it, combining it with other stuff. . . . God." He scrubbed a hand over his face. "This is awful. This is beyond awful. I can't get my head around it. I think . . . yeah, she made some kind of incense. She didn't talk about it, but Steve said—he talked about the smell of the smoke. It smelled like watermelon. He said he didn't know if he'd ever be able to eat watermelon again because when it was wearing off he got sick, and—and he—"

Mannie stopped, put his clenched fist on the counter, and tapped it over and over. His Adam's apple moved as he swallowed.

She put her hand over his fist. It was unprofessional as hell. She didn't care. He immediately unlocked his fist to clasp her hand. Hard. His eyes were blank, staring at something horrible.

"You didn't know," she said gently. "You couldn't have known."

"I should. I should have."

"Steve didn't. He was a lot older than you, and he was smart. If he didn't suspect she was capable of something like this, why would it even cross your mind?"

"It didn't. That's for damned sure. Excuse me." He shoved off the stool and tried to pace. There wasn't room for it. "I need to move. I need to hit someone. You'll get her, right?" He stopped, fixing her with a scowl that didn't hide the sheen in his eyes. "You'll get her."

"Count on it." She stood. "What did . . . shit. That's my car. That's my fucking car."

Steve turned to look at the white Ford sedan being towed behind a wrecker with ACE WRECKING on its door. "You must have pissed off Chief Daly. He pulls that sort of shit. You wouldn't believe how many tickets Steve got for jaywalking. Had his bike towed off twice, too, when he forgot to plug the meter."

"I plugged the damned meter. I don't have time for this. I don't have freaking time for this." She pulled out her phone. Rule had his car. He could come pick her up and . . . and he hadn't called her back, had he?

She checked the time. She'd left him a voice mail over an hour ago, and he still hadn't called. Automatically she checked her Rule-compass. As far as she could tell, he was exactly where he'd been last time she checked. Not that she was accurate enough to say he hadn't moved at all, not at this distance, but . . .

The phone's display told her she had a text message from him, sent right after she left the voicemail. She touched it.

Headed 4 clanhome. CU 2nite.

Fear slid through her, soft and slick as vomit. Rule never used texting abbreviations. He loathed them. And he wasn't headed for Clanhome.

He was in trouble. From Adele, from Friar, she didn't know which—but he was in trouble. And she had no car, no backup.

Or did she? She spun to face Mannie, thumbing through her contact list. "You have a car. A Mustang."

"Yeah, I told you . . . what's wrong?"

"I need it."

11

THE Mustang jolted over one last rut and rocked to a stop in the packed earth at the base of a craggy hill. "We're there," Lily said into her phone. "Putting you on speaker now." She did so and slipped the phone in her pocket, clipping it to be sure it stayed.

Steve's body hadn't actually been left on the hiking trail, but slightly off it, in a small cul-de-sac walled by rock and packed earth. There were two ways to reach that spot—the trail itself, which was used often enough that it had a parking area at its foot. And the route she'd be taking.

No one came this way, according to Mannie. It was a rugged scramble with no rewarding views. He knew about it because he coursed all over the hills gleaning flowers and roots and stuff.

So did Adele, but it seemed she hadn't come this way today. Her car wasn't here.

"Jason hasn't reached the parking area yet," she said, throwing open her door. "But he's close. We aren't waiting."

"Okay." Mannie climbed out of the passenger's side. "What about the others?"

She'd called out backup of the unofficial kind—Jason,

who was close. And Rule's brother Benedict, who was not. But he was in charge of security at Nokolai Clanhome, and he was good. Very, very good. He was bringing some of his people. "ETA forty to fifty minutes. We'll move in and I'll assess the situation. If it's stable, I'll wait until they're in place."

"If not?"

"Then I don't wait. You remember the signals?"

"You'll tap my shoulder if you're close enough. Otherwise you'll tap your head or face or whatever you think I'll see. One tap means stop, freeze, hold. Two taps means keep going or come closer. Three taps—get the hell out of there any way I can."

He answered easily enough, but he was taut. Jumpy. She was insane to bring him. "It's okay to be nervous, you know. I'd be worried if you weren't. Just remember your role—guide and consultant on the magic stuff, if needed. Not Rambo."

"No Rambo shit. Right. I'm cool with that. Did you ever notice how everyone but Rambo gets killed?"

"Yeah," she said dryly. "I have. Let's move."

This part she didn't like. Every instinct said she needed to get out in front. She had the badge, the gun, the training. She couldn't be affected by charms or whatever magical hoodoo Adele might pull.

But she didn't know the way. Mannie did. Instinct lost this round.

He led her around a boulder the size of a Buick standing on end. There was a path of sorts—at least, there was a route up among the tumbled rocks.

For maybe fifteen minutes they went up—almost straight up at times, scrambling over rock in all shapes and sizes, slithering up scree. Slipping a time or two, but not badly. Here the stone was granite, some loose, some fixed, earth's tawny bones poking through where the skin was thin. Many of the larger boulders bore a reddish residue from the aerial spraying used on a wildfire a few years back. Grass sprouted in the oddest places. So did pines, scrub oak, and thorny manzanita.

Lily's breath was labored by the time the ground leveled out some, and she'd scraped one palm. No snakes, though. If they made it the rest of the way without seeing a snake, she'd count herself lucky. They set out along a narrow vee between two steep, stony shoulders shrugged up by some distant geological upset. About ten paces in, Mannie stopped, looked at her, and pointed.

Smoke wisped up in a tattered tail, barely visible against the blue of the sky.

She nodded grimly. Smoke meant a campfire, which meant Adele Blanco, not Robert Friar, waited ahead. That's what she'd expected, but confirmation was good. Lily took out her phone. No bars.

No surprise. They'd thought they would lose coverage as they moved up among the rocky hills. She had to hope Jason spotted the smoke, too, and avoided getting a whiff of it. Lily tapped Mannie's shoulder twice.

They were close, dammit. She wanted to shove him aside and race to Rule—but that was stupid, and stupid got people killed. Mannie knew the path. She didn't. Lily set her jaw and kept following.

Problem was, while she could get her feet and hands to do what they were supposed to, she couldn't make her mind behave. And she couldn't make sense of this. Why had Adele taken Rule? Had she just wacked out and decided to kill everyone who'd ever pissed her off? Had Rule caught her doing something that revealed her guilt?

Maybe she was willing to kill just as a distraction. Lily had run up against killers cold-blooded enough for that— people who'd kill a second time just to throw the cops off the scent. She might have set up some cockamamie alibi. Or did she have some crazy notion of using Rule to bargain with?

But she hadn't tried to contact Lily. Hard to arrange a bargain if you don't let the other side know about it. No, she meant to kill him.

But she hadn't. Not yet.

Why not? If she had Rule paralyzed, he was helpless. There were so many ways to kill a helpless man—quicker, easier ways than tattooing a spell around his neck. But Adele hadn't gone for quick and easy. Lily knew that much, held on to that certainty. If Rule had been killed, the mate bond would have snapped. It hadn't.

How long did it take to ink a tattoo all the way around a man's neck?

Lily didn't know. She didn't have any goddamned idea, so all she could do was keep going forward and pray. And all she could manage for prayer was *oh, God, oh, God, oh, God . . .*

Mannie stopped. He looked at her and jerked his chin, indicating they went up again. This time "up" wasn't a scramble, but a vertical climb. Not for very far, thank God— after about ten feet they'd reach a ledge. That ledge wandered off to the right, leading to a crevice.

The crevice led to Rule. Lily's heartbeat picked up. She gave Mannie a nod, studied the rock face briefly, and reached for the first handhold.

This was where she took over the lead.

It wasn't a tricky climb. Hard work, but not tricky. The hand- and footholds were good. But it was impossible to make it completely silently. Every scuff of a foot, every loose pebble, sounded horribly loud. Her scraped hand stung as she hauled herself up on nearly two wide feet of blessedly level ground.

Hard to say who was more startled, her or the rattler she'd disturbed.

Lily took two hasty steps back. It didn't seem to calm the snake any. It was curled up except for the tail, which shook—and the head, which was lifted, testing the air with its tongue.

No time. She had no time—Mannie was coming up right behind her. Where was a stick when she needed it? There was nothing in sight, and she had no time.

Lily pulled off her jacket, lunged forward, and tossed the jacket over the snake just as Mannie's hand appeared on the ledge. Then she kicked it—jacket, snake and all.

The two separated in midair. Mannie froze with his arm on the ledge, his head swiveling to watch as the snake landed below. Then he scrambled up the rest of the way.

She barely waited for him to make it safely up before hurrying to the crevice. It was low and narrow. She got on her knees, twisted sideways, and started wiggling forward.

It was about a yard long, and taller at the other end. According to Mannie, she'd come out about seven feet up from the floor of the cul-de-sac. She stopped just before reaching the end and unholstered her weapon. Her heart pounded so hard she felt it in her ear canals, yet she was calm.

He was still alive. She'd made it in time.

Slowly she peered around the rocky lip of the crevice.

Ahead of her—rock. Below was more rock, this with some dirt atop it. And Rule. He lay on his back on a bright blue blanket, his eyes closed, his head a couple feet from a small camp stove. His hands were handcuffed in front of him. At his feet was an ordinary ice chest. And those were . . . rose petals? Someone had sprinkled rose petals on the blanket?

No one else in sight. The cul-de-sac was about ten feet by fifteen, with no visible hiding places.

She heard Mannie coming up behind her and reached up and tapped her head once: stop. Was this some kind of trap?

She eased farther out, craned her head. She couldn't see anyone, and no one shot at her. Always a good sign.

She twisted around and leaned closer to Mannie, barely visible in the deep shadows of the crevice. "Stay up here," she whispered. His head moved in what she hoped was a nod.

She straightened, sat, and swung her legs up to her chest—hard squeeze to get them fully twisted around in this tight space, but she made it, letting them dangle out the opening. She dropped, weapon out.

Nothing. No one fired, no one came running out of some previously unnoticed hidey-hole. Two quick steps took her to Rule. She knelt and put her hand on his neck—his clean-skinned neck. No tattoo.

His pulse was strong. She kept her weapon out, her eyes scanning the area. What the hell was going on?

The scuff of feet. A woman's voice, too low for her to catch the words. The sounds came from the opening to the cul-de-sac—a wide opening, not a narrow, slither-through-it crevice. From the trail beyond—and not very far down that trail.

With her empty hand she tapped her head once: *stay put*.

Question was, did she do the same, or try to ambush whoever was coming? She did not like leaving Rule stretched out, helpless and unaware—but logic said he'd be safest with his kidnapper caught, and the best way to catch her was by surprise.

Lily stood and started for the side of the cul-de-sac that would screen her from whoever was approaching. And stepped on a damned pebble. It slid under her, making her jerk to regain her balance—making her make noise, dammit to hell. She froze, listening.

The voice was silent. The footsteps had stopped.

Never mind stealth, then. Lily swung out around the rocky wall, weapon held out in both hands. "FBI! Freeze! Hands up!"

Two women, not one, looked back at her. One was Mariah Friar, her eyes huge in her pallid face. The other was taller, older, heavier, with dusky skin and dark brown hair in a wild froth of curls halfway down her back. She wore jeans and a snug, short-sleeved black sweater.

With one arm, she kept Mariah's arm pinned high behind her back. Her other hand kept her snub-nose Beretta jammed under Mariah's chin. Her eyes were tilted and smiling, as were her full lips. "Maybe you should freeze, too, FBI."

Now it made sense. Crazy sense, maybe, but Lily knew she should have figured it out the second she spotted those damned rose petals. Adele had watched too many episodes of *Murder She Wrote*. She thought she could stage a murder-suicide. Lily could read the script the woman had written: Mariah lured Rule here for sex. Rule, being lupus, accepted. Mariah—for what reason, Lily wondered?—killed him instead of fucking him, then shot herself.

No doubt Adele would have supplied some kind of motive, given time.

"You've got a problem, Adele. Your little plan to kill a

couple more people to distract me didn't work." Lily shook her head. "And your staging sucks. A romantic tryst on rocks? What were you thinking?"

The woman's eyes flashed, but her smile didn't budge. "You don't think it's a pretty setting? I'm crushed—or would be, but your presence here makes your opinion less important than it was. It seems we will have an even worse tragedy than I'd originally thought."

"How're you going to manage that, Adele? If you shoot Mariah, I shoot you. If you move that gun so you can shoot me, I shoot you. Seems like you wind up dead no matter what—unless you put that gun down."

"Oh, you're tough, aren't you? Not so tough you'll stand there and let me shoot poor little Mariah, though." She jammed the gun harder into that terribly vulnerable spot, her face twisting with hate. Mariah whimpered. "Shut up, Mariah. God, but I'm so sick of your whiny little feelings. All that sweet, sweet neediness of yours seducing Steve . . ."

Suddenly she laughed. "You want to know how to lie to an empath, FBI? All you have to do is mean it when you say it. She can only read what you're feeling right that moment, so if you keep the hate pushed down deep, she doesn't know."

"I knew." Mariah's' voice was thin and shaky, but clear. "I knew how jealous you were, but the friendship was real, too. You know it was."

"Shut up." She jerked Mariah's arm higher, making her cry out. "And you, FBI. Put the gun down. I've got nothing to lose. Might as well shoot this little friend of mine, eh?"

"You're lying," Lily said calmly. "You want to live. You shoot her and I shoot you. We're only ten feet apart. This close, I can go for a head shot, no problem."

For the first time, uncertainty flashed across the woman's face—only for a second, but that sublime, crazy confidence had faltered. "You ever killed someone, FBI? You think it's easy? Think you're up to it?"

Lily let the memories in, chilling her. Flattening her voice. "With a gun, you mean? I've only killed one human, but that was with my bare hands. With a gun, though, I've hunted demons. You'll be a lot easier to kill than they were."

Adele laughed again, but it was shaky. "What are you, crazy? You think I'm going to believe you've been demon hunting? Never mind. Never mind, damn you, keep your stupid gun. But stay there. Stay back." She took a careful step backward, her gaze never leaving Lily. "You stay back."

"Sure. Just one problem, Adele. There's a wolf behind you."

Her lip curled in contempt. "I'm supposed to turn around now, I take it. Fool. Rule isn't going to wake from that stupor for at least an hour, and when he does, he'll be too sick to Change."

"I said there's a wolf. I didn't say it was Rule."

Some fifteen feet down the path, Jason—tawny and huge, hackles raised and lips peeled back from really large teeth—growled.

Adele jerked. She yanked Mariah with her, half-turned—saw the wolf gathering his legs beneath him—and shoved Mariah at Lily.

Mariah cried out, stumbling. Jason leapt. A shot rang out. Another. Adele was running straight at Jason, firing. Lily was running, too, unable to get a clear shot.

The big wolf yelped and landed hard, but he thudded into Adele, knocking her down, too. She lost the gun and rolled, ending up flat on her back just as Lily skidded to a halt beside her, gun pointed right between her eyes. "Don't move."

Adele stared, her chest heaving—and all of a sudden flung her head back and screamed in rage, her hands digging into the dirt on either side of her.

The earth moved.

A small lift, first—but enough that Lily wobbled. A couple rocks slithered, fell. Then the ground danced—a horrid, rolling shudder as if rock had turned liquid to roll beneath them like the ocean. More rocks fell. She heard Mannie cry out. She fell to one knee, arms out, trying to balance on the shifting planet.

Adele howled with laughter, pushing up onto her hands

and knees. "Go! Go! Or I'll bring it all down! Rocks falling on your lover, your precious lover—rocks falling on all of us! Go!"

She was doing it. Adele was using her Gift to do the impossible—to call an earthquake.

Something hot and fierce swelled up in Lily so fast she didn't question, didn't think. She dropped her gun and threw herself on top of the laughing madwoman—wrapped her arms around her, holding tight, *reaching*—

Power, vast and raw, power like nothing she'd ever touched—power called from earth—power reverberating between woman and earth, call and answer, again and again, a shuddering cascade building out of control—

No! Lily squeezed her eyes shut, squeezed her arms tighter, squeezed with everything she was as if she could stretch herself around the woman and cut her off, *shut it down, close it off, you cannot reach this woman, she has no call, no power. NO.*

The earth stilled.

Dizziness swam through Lily, a vicious, sucking exhaustion. She pried her eyes open and shook her head, trying to clear it. What . . . ?

Adele lay motionless beneath her. Lily pushed up on one trembling arm, suddenly afraid she'd squeezed the woman to death or something. She'd done . . . something. She couldn't quite remember . . .

But Adele was quite alive—and staring up at her in horror. "What did you do to me?" she whispered. "What are you?"

Lily dragged in one shaky breath. Another. Several feet behind her, Jason was panting like he hurt. But panting meant he was alive.

From farther away she heard Mannie call, "Don't be mad, but when the rocks came down, so did I. Rule's okay, though. None of them hit him. I'm okay. Limping, but okay. Are you okay?"

She got one more good breath into her and called back, "I'm good. I don't know about Mariah. Jason's hit. Drag

Rule out of there, if you can." The earth had stopped moving, but there could be loose rocks. Aftershocks.

Then and only then did she look at Adele once more. "What am I?" She smiled a nasty, satisfied smile. "I'm the FBI bitch who's arresting you. You have the right to remain silent. Anything you say can and will be used against you in a court of law. You have . . ."

epilogue

IT was raining—a rare and splendid event here in San Diego, though it happened with annoying frequency in D.C. The window in Rule's bedroom—in *their* bedroom—faced the bed, and the drapes were open. Water blurred the glass. The smeared shimmer of city lights outside fit well with the washed-clean feel of Lily's body, as if all her edges were blurred, too. Her fingers tingled. Rule's hand sifted slowly through her hair.

The apartment was on the top floor, high enough that the loss of privacy was more symbolic than real; Lily was getting used to it. At the moment, curled into Rule's body, warm and drowsy with the aftermath of passion, it didn't bother her at all.

She stirred, unready for sleep. "This morning I notified the manager at my place that I'm not renewing my lease."

His hand stilled—then brushed the hair from her face so he could press a kiss on her temple. "Good."

"We have to talk about how we're going to split expenses here."

"Mmm. Do we have to talk about it now?"

She smiled. "I guess not. But I'll need to know how much your utilities run, and the——"

He propped up on one elbow, kissed her firmly, and said, "I'll print you out a spreadsheet in the morning."

"We're leaving in the morning."

"My printer's quick." He stayed propped up, looking out the window. His words had been light, but his eyes were heavy.

No wonder about why. Steve's memorial at Clanhome had been today. His body wouldn't be released for another couple weeks, so they would be making yet another cross-country flight then, for the burial. Lily wouldn't attend that, but Rule needed to.

After a moment he said, "I haven't been kind in my grief."

"Grief is seldom kind."

"No." Now he looked at her. "But I regret being an ass."

A smile flickered at the corners of her mouth. "You apologized already." When he woke from the bane stupor, and right after throwing up the first time, he'd apologized for using her password. He'd done it again when the dry heaves hit.

Wolfbane really did make lupi sick as dogs . . . though that was a phrase she'd refrained from using. So far.

"I felt guilty," he said quietly. "I'd allowed such distance to grow between me and Steve . . . he still mattered, but . . ." His words ran out, leaving his mouth tight with pain.

"Don't a lot of relationships have cycles? Neither of you had given up on the friendship. That's what counts. If Adele hadn't killed him, there's every chance you and Steve would have grown close again when the time was right." She flattened her hand on his chest. "She robbed both of you of the chance for that."

"She nearly robbed me of more. If you hadn't checked your messages, or if you hadn't understood right away something was wrong——"

"Let's not go there."

After the nausea passed, Rule had been keenly embarrassed by how easily Adele had tricked him. She'd called and asked him to meet her for a memorial ritual at the spot Steve was killed. Rule had planned to check out the spot anyway, plus he'd been fixated on Friar as the culprit. He'd agreed. When he arrived, Adele had tossed some herbs on the little camp stove. He'd lost the use of his body, and Adele had gained the use of his phone. She'd used it to send that text message, hoping to distract Lily so she could grab Mariah and set up the phony murder/suicide.

Rule smiled, but his eyes had that determined look. He wasn't finished. "In addition to guilt, I was afraid. I'd allowed myself to lose one dear friend in some ways even before he died. How did I know I could keep you—keep *us* . . . Hell. I don't know how to say it."

"Oh, because you have such trouble with long-term relationships, you mean? Like Cullen. It's terrible the way you've allowed that friendship to falter, and him so easy to get along with."

For a second she thought she'd said exactly the wrong thing, reminding him of a missing friend. Then he barked out a laugh and eased back against the pillows. "Easy to get along with. Yes, that's how I think of Cullen. Are you trying to say that all relationships don't follow the same path?"

"Also that I'm not Steve." She threaded her fingers through his. "I don't let go easily. Kind of like chewing gum. You'd have to keep scraping me off."

"There's a romantic image." He squeezed her hand, clearly amused. "I wanted it to be Robert Friar, you know. He seemed . . . a more worthy enemy."

"I know." She suspected Rule considered Steve's death at the hands of a jealous lover somehow undignified. But to Lily's way of thinking, death was like sex—it mattered, it had meaning, but it was not dignified. "You lupi aren't exempt from human nature, though. Part of your nature *is* human, and you're tangled up with humans."

"True." He sighed.

She glanced at him. His eyelids were drooping. She smiled and fell silent.

He'd been sleeping more than usual, but he said that was normal, even though nearly three days had passed. Apparently getting over bane sickness was like getting over the flu. Even after the bug had been defeated, the body wanted extra rest.

Of course, for Rule, extra rest meant getting seven or eight hours' sleep instead of five. Lily snuggled down into the covers more fully and closed her eyes . . . but her brain wasn't ready to shut down.

There were still some loose ends with the case that bothered her. What had Friar's lieutenants been doing in town? The timing was coincidence, had to be, but she'd like to know what he was planning. Sooner or later, that man was going to be trouble.

Then there was the weird way Adele had burned out her Gift. The woman had nary a hint of magic left. They were keeping Adele's role in the earthquake quiet—it had been a small quake, fortunately, and anomalous, which meant the seismologists were puzzled. Lily figured they could go right on being puzzled. She didn't want any other Gifted assholes hearing about it and deciding to give it a go, in the hope they could pull it off without burning out. And she didn't want the un-Gifted population to have one more reason to fear their Gifted brethren.

But it nagged at her that she couldn't remember exactly what had happened when . . .

Her phone buzzed. The same phone—it had survived being tossed off a short cliff with a snake with nary a scratch. The buzz meant it was Croft, so she sat up and reached for it on the bedside table, frowning. It was pretty late, D.C. time. "Yu here."

"Yes, I am," Croft said jubilantly. "And someone else is, too. Someone you want to talk to. Here."

Lily didn't talk much. She listened, she laughed, and if her eyes filled, that was okay. And of course she passed the phone to Rule, who'd heard it all anyway.

Who'd have thought it? Sometimes the optimists turn out to be right. "Here," she said, grinning fit to bust. "Cullen's back. Cynna's back. They're all back, they're fine, and Cullen wants to say hi."

From *New York Times* Bestselling Author

KAREN CHANCE

"Karen Chance takes her place along
with Laurell K. Hamilton, Charlaine Harris,
MaryJanice Davidson, and J. D. Robb."
—*SFRevu*

"Thrilling."
—*Romantic Times*

CURSE THE DAWN
MIDNIGHT'S DAUGHTER
EMBRACE THE NIGHT
CLAIMED BY SHADOW
TOUCH THE DARK

penguin.com

From *New York Times* Bestselling Author

MARJORIE M. LIU

DARKNESS CALLS

❧

Demon hunter Maxine Kiss wields her living tattoos to fight the darkness and the predators that threaten the earth. Now she's on a mission to rescue the man she loves—but her only chance to save him could end with her lost in her own darkness.

"Readers of early Laurell K. Hamilton
[and] Charlaine Harris...should try Liu now
and catch a rising star."

—*Publishers Weekly*

M499T0609

NEW FROM *NEW YORK TIMES*
BESTSELLING AUTHOR

Yasmine Galenorn

BONE
MAGIC

"Galenorn's kick-butt Fae ramp up the action in a wyrd world gone awry!"
—PATRICIA RICE

Another equinox is here and life's getting more tumultuous for the D'Artigo sisters. Smoky, the dragon of Camille's dreams, must choose between his family and her. Plus, the sisters can't locate the new demon general in town. And Camille is summoned to Otherworld, thinking she'll reunite with her long-lost soul mate, Trillian. But once there, she must undergo a drastic ritual that will forever change her and those she loves.

penguin.com

M551T0809